Dear Romance Reader:

This year Avon Books is celebrating the sixth anniversary of "The Avon Romance"—six years of historical romances of the highest quality by both new and established writers. Thanks to our terrific authors, our "ribbon books" are stronger and more exciting than ever before. And thanks to you, our loyal readers, our books continue to be a spectacular success!

"The Avon Romances" are just some of the fabulous novels in Avon Books' dazzling *Year of Romance*, bringing you month after month of top-notch romantic entertainment. How wonderful it is to escape for a few hours with romances by your favorite "leading ladies"—Shirlee Busbee, Karen Robards, and Johanna Lindsey. And how satisfying it is to discover in a new writer the talent that will make her a rising star.

Every month in 1988, Avon Books' *Year of Romance*, will be special because Avon Books believes that romance—the readers, the writers, and the books—deserves it!

Sweet Reading,

Susanne Jaffe
Editor-in-Chief

D1085869

Other Books in
THE AVON ROMANCE Series

Coming Soon

ROGUE'S LADY

VICTORIA THOMPSON

AVON BOOKS ◆ NEW YORK

AVON BOOKS
A division of
The Hearst Corporation
105 Madison Avenue
New York, New York 10016

First Avon Books Printing: December 1988

AVON TRADEMARK REG. U.S. PAT. OFF. AND IN OTHER COUNTRIES, MARCA REGISTRADA, HECHO EN U.S.A.

Printed in the U.S.A.

K-R 10 9 8 7 6 5 4 3 2 1

With love and thanks to
Jim, Lisa, and Ellen,
who put up with a lot
to make it all possible

Prologue

When young Joey burst in on the private poker game in the back room of the Last Chance Saloon, only the greyhound puppy that had been sleeping at the mayor's feet looked up. The mayor kept his gaze steadfastly on Chance Fitzwilliam, the only other player remaining in the game. Fitzwilliam, the proprietor of the Last Chance, kept his gaze fixed on the cards he held. The other four men seated at the table simply watched the fascinating byplay between the two adversaries.

Finally Chance smiled. "Well, Mayor, you've piqued my interest. I think it might be worth another hundred to see exactly what kind of hand has made you so damn reckless." With a flick of his wrist, he sent a chip clattering into the untidy heap already piled in the center of the table. "What have you got?"

Mayor "Dog" Kelley, so nicknamed because of his habit of taking at least one of his prize canines with him wherever he went, grinned confidently. "Two pair, threes and sevens." He spread the cards out so everyone at the table could marvel.

Chance made a clicking noise with his tongue. "Not enough to beat three lovely ladies, I'm afraid," he said, laying down his own hand.

Kelley groaned in good-natured despair while the other players chuckled their appreciation.

"Whose deal is it?" Chance inquired as he raked in the pot and began to sort his winnings into neat piles.

1

Joey was beginning to wonder if he could now state his business when Mr. Fitzwilliam glanced up at him. "What is it, Joey?"

"It's . . ." He paused, momentarily intimidated by the other players who had also turned to listen. The five men sitting with Mr. Fitzwilliam represented the leadership of the Dodge City Gang, the most powerful political group in town. In addition to the mayor, there was Marshal Wyatt Earp; Sheriff Bat Masterson; Nicholas Klaine, editor of the *Dodge City Times;* and attorney Michael Sutton.

"Yes?" Fitzwilliam prompted patiently.

Joey cleared his throat. "Mrs. Claster is outside looking for her husband again."

"Damn. Is he here?"

"Yes, sir. He's pretty far gone, too."

"Well, tell her you haven't seen him and send her back to her temperance friends," Fitzwilliam said with annoyance.

Joey's young face squinched in distress. "But Mr. Fitzwilliam, she's crying and—"

One of the other players murmured an oath.

"—and she's saying how he spent all their money and she don't have any food in the house and her kids are hungry—"

"Here," Fitzwilliam said, selecting a chip from his pile and tossing it to Joey, who caught it two-handed. "Cash this in. Give her the money and tell her to hide it from her husband or he'll spend it on drink, too. And tell her she shouldn't be hanging around saloons."

"Should I tell her he's here?"

"No, say you haven't seen him."

Joey nodded and hastened out. The mayor lifted his eyebrows and shifted the cigar in his mouth. "A hundred dollars, Chance? Looks like I'm not the only reckless one around here."

"I'd pay a thousand to avoid a confrontation with a hysterical woman," Fitzwilliam replied, and the other men at the table murmured their agreement.

But Kelley was looking for a little friendly revenge. "Shouldn't you have sent Claster on home?" he taunted. "Don't you think it's your Christian duty to protect the man from his own weakness?"

"I wouldn't be in business very long if I sent home every man whose wife didn't want him to drink. If she wants him home, let her keep him there herself." Fitzwilliam glanced expectantly at Masterson, who had been idly shuffling the cards but making no move to deal them.

"It's getting late," Masterson said. "I was thinking maybe we ought to call it a night. You've got all the luck, and my stomach is reminding me I haven't eaten since noon."

Fitzwilliam nodded. "As anxious as I am to clean you boys out completely, I guess I'd be willing to accompany you to Delmonico's instead. I've been meaning to try that new salmon dish their chef's been bragging about."

The men had begun to gather up their chips when Fitzwilliam remembered something. "I finally got that shipment of brandy I've been expecting. I'll bring a bottle along so we can sample it after we eat."

"And then we can go over to Summer's house and sample *her* new shipment," Masterson said. "I hear she's got a new girl who can . . ."

As he described the woman's unique talents, the other men groaned in disbelief.

"Maybe we should skip the meal and go right to Summer's," Kelly suggested.

"Not me," Fitzwilliam said. "I think I'll save the salmon for another time and get the chef to fix me some oysters. A *large* serving."

Raucous laughter followed him as he went into the small room he used as an office. Pulling a key from his vest pocket, he unlocked a corner cabinet and selected a squat bottle from the collection inside. After carefully relocking his private stock, he turned to go but then remembered he would need more cigars. Taking some from the humidor on his desk, he happened to notice the pile of letters lying there unopened.

He frowned, remembering how Summer Winters had cheerfully delivered them to him that afternoon. He had been so furious at her presumption and at her thinly veiled hints about how well she would look after him once they were married, he had forgotten to read his mail. Summer simply would not believe he had no intention of marrying a whore-turned-madam whose major interest in him was the Fitzwilliam family estate he had so reluctantly inherited.

His frown deepened when he noticed the return address on the top envelope. He picked it up, testing its weight. Yes, without question it was the quarterly report from his accountants in Chicago. Without even opening it he knew exactly what it would say. The carefully printed columns of figures would reveal yet another failure.

Despite all his efforts, despite his relentless dedication to squandering every cent of the income from his various holdings on the follies of factory improvements, higher wages, and increased safety measures, he would once again have turned a handsome profit. No matter how many times he disregarded the sage advice of his attorneys and bookkeepers, no matter how much power he gave his progressive factory managers, it was always the same. Like Midas, he was cursed: all his enterprises turned to gold he did not want.

And all the gold in the world couldn't bring the yellow-haired girl back to life.

"Coming, Chance?" Masterson asked from the doorway.

"Yes," he said, shaking off the memories with difficulty. He handed the brandy bottle to the sheriff for his inspection.

"Looks like good stuff."

Chance nodded, wondering if he should bring another bottle just in case he felt the need for more of its numbing effects than usual. Then he remembered the new girl at

Summer's. Maybe she could help him forget, at least for a while.

"Now tell me, Bat," he said as they made their way out of the Last Chance, "what's this new girl's name, and who was the lucky devil who lived to tell you about her?"

Chapter 1

In the normal course of her life, Elizabeth Livingston would never have entered a saloon. Since her father's death, however, her life had taken a different turn. Not only had circumstances conspired to bring her all the way from Philadelphia to infamous, lawless Dodge City, Kansas, but now she must enter a place where no lady should ever go. Elizabeth squared her shoulders, lifted the hem of her maroon traveling suit, and stepped through the swinging doors into the Last Chance Saloon.

Pausing just inside, she glanced around. Despite her limited experience, Elizabeth understood instinctively that this was no ordinary saloon. The papered walls, the beautiful—if somewhat lewd—paintings, and the gleaming mahogany bar with its shiny brass fixtures all told her she had entered Dodge City's finest.

"Can I do something for you, miss?" inquired one of the bartenders, rushing forward to intercept her. A burly man with long side whiskers, he was wearing a slightly soiled apron. From his expression Elizabeth guessed that the bartender was as unaccustomed to seeing ladies in such an establishment as she was to being there.

She smiled stiffly, hoping no one could tell how nervous she was. "Yes, I should like to see Mr. Fitzwilliam, please." Elizabeth's hands grew damp inside her gloves. She shifted her heavy carpetbag.

The bartender stared at her. "Mr. Fitzwilliam isn't here just now." He glanced around, making Elizabeth painfully

6

aware of their audience. In spite of the early afternoon hour, the large room was half-filled with customers. Men of all descriptions, some in range clothes, others in frock coats, paused at their various endeavors to look at her. All sound had ceased as men left poker hands untouched and neglected freshly poured drinks so they would not miss one word. Elizabeth pretended not to notice.

The bartender cleared his throat. "If you'll just tell me your name and where you live, miss, I'm sure Mr. Fitzwilliam would be more than happy to call on you."

Elizabeth watched his beefy hand come up in preparation for conducting her back out the door, and she lifted her chin stubbornly. "I do not live anywhere, sir. I have only just arrived in town. Do you, by chance, know where Mr. Fitzwilliam might be found?" she asked, proud to note her voice did not betray her mortification at making such a public spectacle of herself.

"I . . . I think so."

"If you will tell me, I shall be more than happy to call on him."

"Oh, no, you can't go *there.*"

This time, Elizabeth stared. No one, it seemed, wanted her to see her Cousin Chauncey today. Even the stationmaster had tried to deter her from going to find the cousin who had failed to meet her train, insisting Chauncey Fitzwilliam's place of business was no place for a lady. He had certainly been correct, Elizabeth had to admit. If Cousin Chauncey could now be found in a place even a bartender thought unsuitable, she had best not seek to meet him there.

She straightened her stiff smile. "Then would you be so good as to send word to him that his Cousin Elizabeth Livingston has arrived in town and is anxious to meet him? He is expecting me."

"Cousin?" the bartender repeated. The word seemed to reverberate through the large room as several dozen other men repeated it.

"Yes, *cousin,*" Elizabeth told the bartender. "I shall wait for him here."

"Here?" the bartender croaked.

"Well, I . . ." Elizabeth looked around uncertainly.

The bartender suggested she might be more comfortable waiting for Mr. Fitzwilliam in his rooms. A few moments later, Elizabeth found herself in her Cousin Chauncey's private living quarters located above the saloon. The bartender sent a young boy named Joey scurrying off to locate Mr. Fitzwilliam, and now all Elizabeth had to do was wait.

As she paced apprehensively around her cousin's small parlor, she hoped the wait would not be long. The room was sparely furnished with a few well-worn chairs and serviceable tables. A shade was drawn over the one window, and Elizabeth raised it before forcing herself to sit down in one of the chairs. On the table beside her she noticed a plate filled with cigar butts. Beside the plate lay the pieces of a broken collar button.

These purely masculine articles triggered a sharp sense of loss, reminding her of her father. He had been gone more than six months now, and although she had long since come to terms with her grief, she did not think she would ever stop missing him.

Of course, remembering what a stubborn, unreasonable man he had been helped some. It helped especially when she reminded herself it was entirely his fault she had had to come halfway across the country from her home in Philadelphia to the godforsaken town of Dodge City, Kansas.

Recalling what he had done to her in his will made her just as furious as she had been the first time the lawyer had explained the terms to her. Her father, convinced no woman could ever manage his vast fortune but would squander it on dresses and hair ribbons and the like, had put the money in trust for her. In spite of Elizabeth's efforts to convince her father she was a mature, responsible, intelligent person, he had never seen past the fact that she was a female, a species he considered incapable of rational thought. Once his mind was made up, Jacob Livingston had never let his opinions be swayed by mere facts.

Elizabeth indulged in a few minutes of righteous indignation until the sound of hurried footsteps on the outside stairway broke into her reverie. She first thought her cousin must finally have arrived, but whoever was coming was taking the stairs two at a time. Elderly Cousin Chauncey could not be so nimble. Somewhat alarmed, Elizabeth rose to her feet as the door burst open.

"Who are you?" a deep baritone voice demanded.

Elizabeth blinked in surprise at the man's rudeness. She had been correct. This man was not her cousin. He was too young by thirty years or more.

As he stepped into the room, she noticed he was tall and good-looking, or would be if he were not scowling so fiercely. His hair was jet black and tousled, as if he had not yet combed it after arising from bed. His clothing, too, was disheveled, as if he had dressed in a hurry, and his black, well-tailored suit coat was rumpled. Irrelevantly, Elizabeth noticed his shirt was collarless and buttoned crookedly, with one extra button sticking up at his throat.

The man came a step closer and looked her insolently up and down, effectively wiping all thoughts of his slovenly appearance from her mind.

"What kind of game are you playing, lady?"

Elizabeth stiffened. "I might ask you the same question, sir," she replied, trying to sound haughty instead of frightened. "How dare you come barging into my cousin's home and interrogate me?"

"What's all this business about you being my cousin?" he asked. His dark eyes narrowed.

Steeling herself from showing her trepidation, she looked him straight in the eye and willed herself not to flinch. "I assure you, sir, I am no relation to you whatsoever. I am waiting here for my cousin, Chauncey Fitzwilliam, to return home, and—"

"I'm Chance Fitzwilliam," he said, placing his hands belligerently on his hips.

Her mouth dropped open. "But you can't be," she said after a long moment of stunned silence.

"Well, I am."

Suddenly the room felt very close, and Elizabeth felt very tired. She sank into the chair in which she had been sitting. For a few moments everything inside her brain seemed to be spinning out of control, her thoughts racing by, blurred and confused. There was an answer to this riddle, she knew there was . . .

"That's it!" she cried, springing out of her chair and startling the man who had been watching her very carefully the whole time.

"What's it?"

"Were you, by any chance, named for your father?" she asked, unwilling to explain until she had checked her facts. "Are you Chauncey Fitzwilliam *junior?*"

"No," he told her, seeming to take perverse pleasure in her disappointment. "In point of fact, I am Chauncey Fitzwilliam *the fourth.*"

Elizabeth sagged with relief. "Then I'm right. Don't you see. It's your *father* I'm looking for."

His expression clearly showed he did not see at all.

"Oh, my," she said with a flustered laugh, laying a hand over her fluttering heart. "You must think me mad. I haven't even introduced myself. I am Elizabeth Livingston, and if you are my Cousin Chauncey's son, then you and I are cousins, too, although we're only third cousins, once removed, which hardly counts, I suppose, except in the strictest legal sense." Although aware she was rattling on, she was too relieved to care. This man was no threat to her. He was family.

But his dark eyebrows lifted skeptically, and she knew he did not believe a word she had said. "Does that make us kissing cousins?" he asked, again taking her in from head to toe.

Elizabeth frowned. Was he trying to frighten her or simply annoy her? Deciding she was far too sophisticated to be either, she lifted her chin haughtily. "I should like you to take me to your father now."

"That will be difficult," he said, his voice silky. "You see, he's been dead for over five years."

"But he can't be!" Elizabeth exclaimed.

"Well, I suppose we could dig him up if you like, just to be sure."

"He can't be dead," Elizabeth insisted again. "He sent me a telegram not two weeks ago."

Her tormentor tilted his head to one side, obviously impressed by this piece of information. "I don't suppose you have this telegram."

"But I do," she said, thankful beyond words her father's lawyer had insisted she keep every document, every piece of correspondence, and that she bring them with her. She was equally thankful she had decided to carry the carpetbag containing them with her from the station. Brushing past him, she retrieved her carpetbag and produced the telegram, handing it over with an indignant flourish.

Chance accepted the paper and gave her shapely figure one last, interested perusal. She certainly was a beauty, he decided, and a good actress in the bargain. Those huge emerald eyes were glittering with outrage and her magnificent breasts were actually heaving with fury. For one brief moment he allowed himself to wonder how her ebony hair would look spread out on a pillow instead of pinned up under that ridiculous bonnet. Yes, she was a beauty all right. With her looks and talent, she should be taking the theatrical world by storm instead of trying to hustle a man far too experienced to be hustled.

Without hiding his skepticism, he glanced down at the telegram she had given him. "What the . . . ?" he muttered in confusion, and then read the carefully printed words again. "Who sent you this?"

Elizabeth sighed. "I thought your father sent it to me. Since it's signed Chauncey Fitzwilliam, that leaves you."

He shook his head, experiencing his first doubt but reminding himself anyone could send a telegram.

"There was a letter, too," she remembered, going back to find it and then handing it to him.

He read the letter once and then again. Lifting his head, he studied her face, trying to find some hint of duplicity. He saw only sincere innocence. "None of this makes any sense," he muttered.

His expression was still grim, but Elizabeth saw with relief that he was starting to believe her.

"I have a feeling there are a whole lot of things I need to know," Chance concluded. "Perhaps you would be so good as to explain this to me, Miss—"

"Livingston," Elizabeth supplied. "But you may call me Cousin Elizabeth . . . *if* you really are Chauncey Fitzwilliam the fourth."

He frowned in irritation. "Please sit down, *Cousin Elizabeth,* and tell me the whole story."

She sat. He took the chair opposite hers and crossed his arms in a gesture she interpreted as a silent challenge. One she was only too happy to meet. "As I said," she began, "we are cousins. Our fathers knew each other well as boys and young men, but when your father emigrated to . . . Chicago, I believe?" He nodded. "They lost touch with each other. My father passed away about six months ago." She paused, half expecting some expression of sympathy, but she received none. "My father left me his entire estate in trust, and he named your father as trustee. No one knew where your father was, so we had to hire some Pinkertons—"

"Wait a minute," Chance interrupted. "Are you trying to tell me you father left your money in the hands of a man he hadn't seen in . . ." He groped in vain for a figure.

"Over thirty years," Elizabeth supplied. The thought still rankled.

"Good God! He must have been insane!" Chance said,

not consciously aware that somewhere along the line he had started to believe her wild tale.

"My father was completely sane," Elizabeth replied, responding to a compulsion to defend her unreasonable parent even though she had entertained the exact same thought herself. "He simply had some fixed ideas on certain subjects."

"Such as?"

"Such as," Elizabeth said reluctantly, "a woman's ability to manage her own affairs."

His dark eyes widened in surprise, then narrowed thoughtfully. They would be nice eyes, she noticed, if he ever smiled, but as yet he had not. "You strike me as an educated woman, Miss Livingston," he remarked.

"I attended Vassar."

Chance looked her over once again. Her dress was obviously expensive and most certainly the height of fashion, but it bore none of the extravagance of design so many women of the upper classes insisted upon. It was a sensible outfit, and the clear, green eyes meeting his gaze were sensible, too. She was young, certainly, and unreasonably pretty, but she didn't appear to need a keeper as many young ladies of her class might have. "I can't believe your father thought he had to leave you in the care of a man he hadn't seen in thirty years."

Elizabeth's face warmed as she relived her outrage over the situation. Her lawyer had been appalled by her initial reaction and had spent an hour calming her down, trying to convince her all was not lost. Perhaps her Cousin Chauncey was dead, he had argued. The court would then appoint a guardian more to her liking, or perhaps they would even permit her to take control of the estate herself in a few months when she turned twenty-one. But investigations had shown that was not to be.

Carefully schooling any trace of lingering anger out of her expression, Elizabeth explained. "In spite of the evidence to the contrary, my father believed all women were helpless, brainless creatures incapable of rational thought.

In his opinion, any man could manage better than any woman, and he believed blood ties to be the strongest. Your father was his closest relative, so naturally . . .'' She folded her small, gloved hands tightly over each other.

"So you sent the Pinkertons after my father," he said. "Didn't they find out he was dead, too?"

"They found out he had moved to Dodge City," she informed him, making a mental note to write a letter of complaint to Allan Pinkerton. "My attorney contacted him . . . *you*," she corrected, gratified at his disgruntled frown. "A letter came, the one you saw, insisting I come at once. Having no other choice if I wanted to see one penny of my inheritance, I arrived on the noon train."

Chance chose to overlook her bitter, if unspoken, accusation. Instead, he considered her story carefully. She was much too natural to be lying, so she must be telling the truth, as unbelievable as it seemed. He was surprised to discover he believed her without reservation. He usually made a habit of disbelieving women, considering his past experiences with them. "I hope you understand that I never sent or received either of the communications in question. I knew nothing about you until just a few minutes ago."

"But *someone* sent me those letters," she reminded him.

"It would seem you have been the victim of an elaborate practical joke, Miss Livingston."

"I fail to see any humor in the situation. I have had to travel halfway across the country to get here."

"Weren't you a little suspicious when Cousin Chauncey didn't meet your train?"

"But someone did meet my train."

"Who?" he asked with a frown. Perhaps this was the clue he was looking for.

"Two . . . women," she hedged, uncertain how to describe them. The stationmaster had called them "soiled doves."

"Do you know their names?" He straightened up and leaned forward.

"One was named Hattie, I think, or Hettie—something like that. The stationmaster said they worked at . . . at Miss Winters's house."

"Damn!" He lunged to his feet and began to pace the room. It was worse than he'd thought. "I should have known. Who else would have done a thing like this?"

Elizabeth knew it would be pointless to chasten him for using profanity in her presence. "Do you know who was responsible?" she asked, stopping him in his tracks.

"Just someone who thought it would be amusing to play a trick on me."

"Was it Miss Winters?"

"It doesn't matter." He dismissed Miss Winters with a wave of his hand. "I'll take care of her." And he would, too, in spades. "So Hettie and the other woman brought you here?"

"No," Elizabeth said, making a mental note that he was acquainted with this Hettie person. "They were distressed when they saw me, as if I was not the person they had expected. They hurried off and left me standing in the station. I asked the stationmaster where I might find you, and then I came here."

Chance considered this information for a moment but was unable to make sense of it. Well, he'd get the whole story out of Summer Winters, even if he had to drag it out of her. Right now he had more important things to think about. "I am, of course, sorry you had to come all this way for nothing. I'm sure you have no desire to stay in Dodge another minute." The last thing he wanted was the responsibility for a spoiled rich girl who had probably spent her entire life learning how to manipulate men to get her own way. Chance's days of being manipulated by spoiled rich women were long over. "I'll take you over to the hotel and get you a room, and tomorrow you can start back for . . . Philadelphia, was it?"

Elizabeth blinked at the sight of his smile. It was utterly charming, but it did not hide the fact that he was trying to get rid of her.

"Wait a minute," she cautioned, coming to her feet again. "There's still the matter of the trusteeship. I can't touch a penny of my estate without permission from my trustee, and if your father is dead, then . . ."

Her green eyes met his dark ones across the small room as the truth dawned on them.

"Oh, no!"

"It can't be!"

They spoke in unison. A cold knot of dread formed in Elizabeth's stomach. "My father's will names Chauncey Fitzwilliam as not only the trustee of his estate but also as my guardian. *You* are Chauncey Fitzwilliam."

"But I'm the *wrong* Chauncey Fitzwilliam." He did not sound nearly as assured as Elizabeth would have liked.

"What will we do?"

Chance was wondering the same thing, but he'd been in enough legal tangles to know there was usually a way out if you knew the right people. "We'll see a lawyer," he decided. "He'll get us out of this." Chance felt a small pang of disappointment at the obvious relief in her large green eyes, but he reminded himself he shared her eagerness to end their relationship as quickly as possible.

Chauncey explained that his lawyer's office was only a block away, at the end of the street. He escorted Elizabeth back down the outside stairs and onto the broad wooden sidewalk. Once again, she was startled by the sight of the infamous Front Street. Here the railroad tracks formed a dividing line separating the town into two very distinct halves. On the north side carrying firearms was illegal and the law was strictly enforced. Though several saloons like the Last Chance flourished here, the mood was orderly and a lady could move down the street unmolested.

On the other side of the tracks men wore their guns openly and the only women on the streets were trying to lure customers inside. Elizabeth avoided looking toward the railroad tracks and beyond. There was quite enough sin on this side of Front Street to hold her attention.

The Last Chance was not the only saloon doing a brisk

business at this early hour. Men wearing the broad-brimmed hats and high-heeled boots that clearly marked them as Texans came and went through the swinging doors of the half-dozen drinking establishments Elizabeth and her cousin passed. Others lounged on the benches lining the ten-foot-wide sidewalks and watched her progress down the street with unabashed admiration.

Several times Elizabeth felt certain one of these strangely dressed Texans was going to speak to her, but each time the man drew back after glancing at her companion. The fierce scowl that had intimidated her just moments ago was now protecting her. Elizabeth felt reassured. When her cousin took her elbow to conduct her around an inebriated gentleman, her reassurance warmed into a disturbing sense of awareness.

"The office is right over there," Cousin Chauncey said, pointing across the street.

To cover her sudden difficulty in breathing, Elizabeth pretended an interest in the large brick building they were passing. The sign said Wright, Beverley & Company, Dealers in Everything. From the display of merchandise she glimpsed through the open front doors, the claim appeared to be true.

Cousin Chauncey directed her across the street with a gentle nudge to her elbow. Elizabeth held herself stiff under his touch and was greatly relieved when he released her once they were safely on the opposite sidewalk.

Passing McCarty's Drug Store, an emporium as lavishly stocked as any in Philadelphia, they came to a narrow two-story building, the second floor of which was accessible by an outside stairway. As Cousin Chauncey conducted her into the downstairs office, she concluded that Lawyer Bates—the name painted on the sign outside—must also live above his place of business.

"Bill! Are you here?" Cousin Chauncey called, startling Elizabeth.

"Chance," a voice replied cheerfully from the rear of the building. "Come on in."

Cousin Chauncey indicated Elizabeth should precede him, and she made her way to the door of Lawyer Bates's inner office.

Lawyer Bates met them there. "What brings you—" He stopped in midsentence when he saw Elizabeth. He looked her up and down in a manner that was becoming annoyingly familiar.

His pleasant expression deteriorated rapidly into shock, and then fury. "You son of a . . . I won't do it, Chance," he declared. "I won't get you out of it. For once in your life, you're going to have to do the right thing."

Cousin Chauncey made a sound indicating profound irritation. "Shut up, Bill. You're making a fool of yourself."

Lawyer Bates glared at his friend, who glared right back. Bates was a pleasant-looking young man, approximately the same age as her cousin, whom she judged to be around thirty. He was almost as tall as Chauncey, too, and as fair as he was dark.

"Before you say another word," said Cousin Chauncey, "allow me to introduce my *cousin,* Elizabeth Livingston. She has only just arrived from Philadelphia. She has a legal problem about which she needs some advice."

It took a moment for Bill Bates to comprehend this information. When he did, he began to blush. "Oh, excuse me, Miss Livingston. For a moment there, I thought . . . But never mind what I thought. Very pleased to meet you. Welcome to our fair city. Please, have a seat."

He bustled around, pulling up a chair and dusting it off with his handkerchief. When she had seated herself, he stepped close to her cousin and whispered, "I'm sorry, Chance. Naturally, I thought . . . I mean, why else would you come in here with a woman?"

Chance continued to glare at him. "Let's get on with this, shall we?"

Elizabeth pretended not to hear, but her mind was busy replaying Lawyer Bates's earlier remarks. He'd thought her Cousin Chauncey had gotten her into the worst kind of trouble and had come to consult a lawyer about making a settlement on her. Elizabeth tried very hard not to blush.

"Well, now, Miss Livingston, what seems to be the problem?" Lawyer Bates asked, sitting behind his cluttered desk.

Briefly Elizabeth explained the terms of her father's will. "You see my concern, Mr. Bates. The will appoints my cousin, Chauncey Fitzwilliam, as my guardian and trustee, and *this* is my Cousin Chauncey."

Cousin Chauncey frowned, but she ignored him.

"I'm sure Cousin Chauncey is a gentleman of impeccable honesty and virtue," she continued, "and I know no evil of him whatever," she added, choosing to overlook for the moment that he owned a saloon. "However, his age and his unmarried status make him unsuitable as a guardian. I'm sure you can understand such an arrangement was never my father's intent, Mr. Bates."

"Not to mention the fact that I am totally unwilling to serve as *anyone's* guardian," Chauncey added.

Elizabeth nodded stiffly. "A perfectly understandable sentiment, Cousin Chauncey," she agreed, having decided he disliked being called "Cousin Chauncey." She had also decided it was rude of him to be so anxious to be rid of her.

"Show him the will," Chance said through gritted teeth.

Elizabeth retrieved it from her drawstring purse and handed it to Mr. Bates.

"If you knew how your Cousin Chaun—your cousin felt," Mr. Bates corrected, catching Chance's glower, "I'm curious as to why you made the trip here all the way from Philadelphia. Surely your lawyer there could have handled the matter."

Chance and Elizabeth exchanged glances. Elizabeth was not certain how to reply, not knowing exactly how much her cousin would want to reveal.

Chance shrugged. "Her lawyer wrote to me thinking I was my father, but somebody must have intercepted the letter and replied in my name, telling her to come at once, so she did.''

Mr. Bates looked flabbergasted. ''Who would've done a thing like that?''

''Cousin Chauncey believes it was a Miss Winters,'' Elizabeth said.

''Summer?'' Mr. Bates sounded both shocked and amused. ''Why would she go to so much trouble?'' he asked, but Elizabeth suspected he already knew.

Chance's expression was murderous. ''Will you read the will, please?'' he said, his voice dangerously low.

''Oh, yes.'' Bates grinned and unfolded the papers Elizabeth had handed him.

Elizabeth waited impatiently as the lawyer read, her cousin's restless pacing making her even more nervous. Finally, she said, ''Why don't you sit down, Cousin Chauncey?'' At her cousin's glower, she realized he didn't appreciate her testy command.

''Tell me, Cousin Elizabeth, have you by any chance made out your *own* will yet?'' he inquired pleasantly, placing one hand on the back of her chair and leaning over her.

Nonplussed, she leaned away from his overwhelming nearness. ''Why, no, I haven't,'' she managed to say.

''Perhaps you should, because if you call me Cousin Chauncey one more time, you will find yourself in need of one.''

Elizabeth gasped. How dare he be so unspeakably rude! She was, after all, just an innocent victim. ''I beg your pardon, *Cousin Chauncey,*'' she replied, letting him know she did not fear him or his threats.

He jerked back as if she'd slapped him, his finely molded lips whitening with the effort of controlling his temper. Then, as if suddenly remembering they had an audience, he turned to find Bill Bates studying them. ''Well?'' he snapped.

Lawyer Bates jumped. ''Oh, yes, well . . .'' He gave the papers one last cursory glance. ''The terms of the will are clear," he began, with what struck Elizabeth as too much smugness, "and, I'm afraid, irrevocable. The will states Chauncey Fitzwilliam is to be Miss Livingston's guardian, and since it does not specify *which* Chauncey Fitzwilliam and since you are the only one living—"

"Oh, no!" Elizabeth protested

"There must be something you can do," Chance insisted.

Lawyer Bates shook his head with feigned regret. "I'm sorry. You might take it to court, but such things can drag on for years."

Chauncey muttered something that sounded suspiciously like profanity. Elizabeth managed to ignore it.

Lawyer Bates continued to smile smugly. "I advise you to settle here for a while, Miss Livingston, until Chance has familiarized himself with the details of the trust. And, Chance, if you like, I can begin making arrangements for you to assume your guardianship."

Chauncey made a growling noise.

"Uh, Chance, maybe I'd better speak to you privately," Bates suggested, hastily rising from his seat. "If you'll excuse us, Miss Livingston?"

Elizabeth nodded as Mr. Bates hustled Chauncey into the outer office. She could not help but overhear their whispered conversation.

"Chance, get hold of yourself," Bates said as he shut the door behind them.

Chance, seeing his friend's obvious concern, made a concerted effort to do so.

"What in God's name is the matter with you? I've never seen you so . . . so *upset*," Bates said. "And what happened to you? You look like you dressed in the dark. Do you know your shirt is buttoned crookedly?"

Chance swore under his breath. Had he actually walked down a public street with her looking like this? "I was over at Summer's this afternoon," he explained, "when Joey came hammering on the door, hollering about how some lady had waltzed into the Last Chance claiming to be my sister or something and demanding to see me. Naturally, I was in rather a hurry to find out who she was."

Bill Bates bit back a smile. "Were you . . . visiting Summer?"

"Of course not." Chance glared at his friend. Bill knew he and Summer hadn't been involved for months.

"What makes you think Summer is the one who got Miss Livingston to come here?"

"Because she sent two of her girls to meet the train today." Chance's lips tightened again as he recalled Summer's part in the charade. "I don't have any idea what her reasons might be, but I intend to find out."

"What do you intend to do with . . ." He gestured toward Elizabeth.

Chance swore again. The day was deteriorating rapidly. "Damned if I know. I suppose I'll have to find her a place to stay first of all."

Bates slapped his shoulder sympathetically. "Don't worry. I'm sure she won't be much trouble. All you need to do is make sure she doesn't squander her fortune. From the bequests listed in the will, that would take some doing, so you'll have no problem there. And you only need to worry about her until she gets married. When she does, her husband will take over for you, and you'll be off the hook. From the looks of her, I'd be willing to bet she'll attract a husband before the summer is over. In fact, I just might be willing to take her off your hands myself."

For some reason, Chance did not find this offer comforting. "Be careful, Bill. Remember, she's my responsibility."

Bill's blond eyebrows lifted in surprise. "I promise to conduct myself like a perfect gentleman," he vowed, and before Chance could reply he added, "Why don't you go upstairs and straighten your shirt? You can borrow one of my collars."

Chance swore yet a third time at this reminder of his uncharacteristic dishabille and moved quickly toward the front door. "I'll be back in a minute," he called over his shoulder, aware that his words sounded like another warning.

When he reentered the office a few minutes later, he was startled to hear laughter coming from the back room. Female laughter. Very musical female laughter. Then he heard Bill say, "And after all that, he had the nerve to ask if I thought they'd hang him!"

Elizabeth laughed again. "What a perfectly dreadful man. Was he found guilty?"

"No, I got him acquitted, but he ran off and never paid my fee," Bates concluded. "Well, here's Chance."

Elizabeth turned to see Chance standing in the doorway. He looked quite imposing. His clothes had been straightened and he was wearing a collar and had combed his hair. Elizabeth would have thought him extremely handsome had he not been glowering so fiercely.

Chance was experiencing an unfamiliar emotion: outrage. Bates certainly hadn't wasted any time trying to take her off his hands. Then she turned and he saw the way her green eyes sparkled. But the moment she set those eyes on him, the sparkle and the smile disappeared. "I'm sorry to keep you waiting," he said.

"That's quite all right. Bill has been entertaining me," she replied.

"*Bill?*" Chance frowned in disapproval. Elizabeth Livingston did not look like the sort of young lady who would call a man she had met only moments ago by his first name.

"I was just explaining to Miss Elizabeth that we're much less formal out here in the West," Bill said, rising from behind his desk.

"I'll bet you were," Chance muttered.

"And she was reminding me how improper it would be for her to live alone without a chaperone."

"A chaperone?" Chance frowned again. From the way Bill was looking at the girl, Chance thought it odd he would be so enthusiastic about finding her a chaperone. His interest seemed far more likely to involve getting her off alone someplace. Suddenly, the idea of a chaperone seemed very appealing. Not that Chance cared what happened to her, of course, but she was his responsibility, after all.

"Yes, a chaperone," Bill said. "You'll have to find someone right away. I was thinking Reverend Folger might be able to suggest someone."

Chance almost groaned. "Not Folger. Definitely not Folger."

"Is something wrong with Reverend Folger?" Elizabeth asked, tired of being excluded from the conversation.

"Certainly not," Bill said.

"You're damn right there is," Chance contradicted. "The old hypocrite is trying to put me out of business."

Elizabeth considered this information a point in the good reverend's favor. "Is he succeeding?" she asked sweetly.

Chance glowered at her, but before he could speak Bill said, "Think about it, Chance. Folger is the most respectable man in town, and a preacher no less. Miss Livingston is obviously a gently bred young lady of impeccable reputation," he said, echoing Elizabeth's words. "You wouldn't want anything to happen to that reputation, would you?" He did not wait for a reply. "Her being your cousin is one black mark against her with the people whose opinion counts in this town. If we're to make certain she gets no more black marks, we have to put her under the protection of morally unimpeachable people, and Folger heads the list."

Chance understood Bill's argument and agreed with it, except for one detail. *"We?"* I fail to see how you became involved."

"Well, I . . . naturally, I . . ." Bill stammered, flushing. "Of course I'm concerned about Miss Elizabeth's welfare, as her attorney."

"As her attorney, you're fired," Chance said, scooping up the pages of the will from the desktop and tucking them into his inside coat pocket.

"Chance!" Bill exclaimed in disbelief.

"Cousin Chauncey!" Elizabeth cried in mortification.

"Come, *Cousin Elizabeth,* let's go see the preacher," Chance growled, taking her arm in a far from gentle grasp and hauling her to her feet.

"Really, this is the most outrageous—" Elizabeth began, but gave up when she realized a tirade would have no effect on her discourteous cousin. Beside, he was already pulling her out the door. "It was so very nice to meet you, Bill. I hope I will see you again."

"You most certainly will," Bill promised just before Chance slammed the door behind them.

"Take your hands off me," Elizabeth demanded, wrenching free once they were outside on the sidewalk. She was tempted to add "you cad," but thought better of it when she saw the murderous gleam in his eye. "Your behavior toward Bill was inexcusable." She kept her voice low so they would not draw attention from the people passing by.

"What about his behavior concerning you? Don't you know he was only trying to—" Chance broke off when he realized what he had been about to say.

"Trying to what?" she asked.

Chance gazed down into her green eyes. He couldn't seem to get enough of looking at them. She had the longest, blackest eyelashes he had ever seen, and she really did have a very lovely face, so fresh and innocent. Yes, that was it, innocent.

"Trying to what?" she repeated, stamping her foot in frustration.

"Nothing," he said, taking her elbow and turning her in the proper direction. She *was* innocent and Chance had every intention of keeping her that way while she was under his care, a time he fervently hoped would not be long in duration. "Let's go see the preacher," he repeated. "The church is just two blocks down. Reverend Folger lives right next door."

Elizabeth had to walk quickly to keep up with his longer strides, but after they turned down Bridge Avenue, he

seemed to notice her difficulty and slowed to accommodate her. She had a thousand questions she wanted to ask
him but decided a public street was not the proper place
to do so.

The preacher lived in a small frame house with a white
picket fence around it. Chance held the gate open for her.
As she moved in front of him, he noticed not for the first
time how very slender she was, with a waist so small he
could probably span it with his hands.

She was, he admitted grudgingly, an attractive girl. If
only he could shut her up for a few minutes, there was no
telling what interesting situations could develop.

Realizing Chance had not followed her, Elizabeth
paused halfway up the walk. When she looked back, he
was still holding the gate open and he had the oddest look
on his face. "Are you coming?" she asked, a little sharply.

As if awakening from a trance, he started slightly and
moved to follow her. Against her will, Elizabeth noted the
smooth, effortless way he moved. How could such an attractive man be so impossibly rude? she wondered vaguely.
Snapping out of her own reverie, she continued up the
walk and, without waiting for her cousin, knocked on the
door.

Reverend Folger stood a good six feet tall and had a
full head of silver hair which was brushed straight back
from his patrician face and flowed to his shoulders. He
looked exactly the way Elizabeth pictured God. She
couldn't help staring.

"What can I do for you, young lady?" he asked in a
voice so deep it might have come from inside a well.

Chance came up behind her. "We'd like to speak to
you, if you don't mind, Reverend."

Reverend Folger's stately head jerked up. "Chance Fitzwilliam," he said in surprise. His gaze flickered back and
forth between Chance and Elizabeth. "Come in, come
in." He stood aside for them to enter.

Elizabeth stepped far enough into the small entrance
hall so Chance could follow her.

"Reverend Folger, may I present my cousin, Miss Elizabeth Livingston? She has come all the way from Philadelphia. She arrived just this afternoon, and—"

"Mama! Come quick!" Reverend Folger called in his booming voice. "You won't believe who's come to get married!"

"Married!" Chance and Elizabeth repeated in unison, both horrified.

"We aren't . . ."

"We haven't . . ."

"Oh, no . . ."

"Certainly not . . ."

They stammered until a tiny lady with hair as white as Reverend Folger's appeared, smiling beatifically. Her smile faded when she heard the heated denials being made by her visitors.

After five minutes of explanations, the Folgers finally understood the relationship between Chance and Elizabeth, although they were both visibly disappointed to learn she was not his intended bride.

"I thought you were the answer to my prayers, Miss Livingston," Reverend Folger finally told her. By this time they were all seated in the parlor. "You see, I've been praying for this boy to see the error of his ways, and when I saw you I thought the Lord had sent you. There's nothing like a good woman to set a man's feet on the straight and narrow," he added, giving his tiny wife a look full of love and devotion.

Beside Elizabeth on the sofa, Chance shifted uneasily. "As her guardian, I have to make sure she's taken care of," he said in an attempt to change the subject. "Obviously, she can't live with me."

"Oh, my, no," said Mrs. Folger, sounding thoroughly shocked by such a suggestion.

"So she'll have to have her own place, but she'll need somebody to live with her, to serve as a chaperone. I thought perhaps you could suggest someone who would be suitable," Chance said.

Reverend Folger steepled his fingers in front of his chin and studied his guests for a long moment. "I'm surprised to find you so concerned about Miss Livingston's welfare, but it does my heart good to think there's a streak of decency in you somewhere, Chance." Elizabeth heard her cousin draw in a breath and could only guess at the difficulty he was having holding his temper. Before Chance could reply, however, the minister continued. "Let me think a minute. I'm sure we can find someone." He thought.

Finally, his wife said, "Barbara Jenks."

"Just what I was thinking, Mama," Reverend Folger agreed, nodding his silver head.

"Who is she?" Chance asked.

"She's a widow," Mrs. Folger told them. "She and her husband homesteaded a farm about ten miles out of town, but he died last winter of pneumonia. Barbara is working hard, but she'll never be able to get the crops in by herself, and she's bound to lose the farm. Then she'll be penniless. She's not a young woman and the Lord never blessed her with children. She's all alone in the world, but a finer woman God never made. She's been such a help to us in the temperance movement, too." Pretending not to notice Chance's frown of disapproval, she added, "Of course, she's awfully strong willed and . . . and outspoken."

Chance gave Elizabeth an amused glance. "They should make a fine pair, then," he remarked.

Elizabeth flashed him an angry look, then turned back to the preacher. "I would like to meet her first, before I make up my mind."

"Certainly," Reverend Folger said. "Why don't you both come to supper here tonight. I'll ride out to Barbara's farm in the buggy and bring her back. You can spend the evening together and see how you get along."

"Thank you, Reverend Folger," Elizabeth said, giving him a grateful smile. "You're very kind."

"I'm afraid I have other plans for this evening," Chance said, more irritated than he cared to admit by the sight of

Elizabeth's smile. She never smiled at him, and he, too, had certainly been kind to her.

"You mean you won't come to supper?" Mrs. Folger asked, disappointed. "Don't you want to approve the woman who will be chaperoning your ward?"

"If you vouch for her and Elizabeth likes her, that's good enough for me. Besides, I work in the evening, remember?" he reminded the minister's wife with satisfaction, making her blush.

"Well, I'll certainly be here," Elizabeth said to cover the awkward moment.

"I'll be glad to come and fetch you if you'll tell me where you're staying," Reverend Folger offered.

Elizabeth gave Chance an inquiring look. He had not mentioned where she would be staying until she could find a place of her own.

"I'm going to put her up at the Dodge House for the time being. She'll be safe enough there until your Mrs. Jenks takes over," Chance said, rising.

Elizabeth rose also and thanked the Folgers once more. When she and Chance were again outside and walking toward Front Street, Elizabeth could contain herself no longer. "Why couldn't you have accepted their supper invitation? It certainly wouldn't have done you any harm."

"Didn't I tell you the old windbag wants to put me out of business? And not just me, every other saloon owner in town, too. His wife is trying to organize a Women's Christian Temperance Union right here in Dodge, for God's sake!"

"A very noble ambition."

Chance ignored her. "What he forgets is what would happen to his precious town without the money Front Street and the Texans bring in. The only other customers for the stores around here are the sodbusters, and most of them are as poor as your Mrs. Jenks, widowed or not. If Folger shuts down Front Street, Dodge City will dry up and blow away like a tumbleweed."

Elizabeth pursed her lips as she considered his prediction. He was probably right, but she refrained from pointing out that such a prospect was far from frightful.

The Dodge House stood at the far end of Front Street, directly across from the train station. It was a large wooden structure, two stories tall with a balcony running across the front of the second story. Immediately adjacent to it was a billiard hall. Elizabeth pretended not to notice the way the cowboys gathered in front of the billiard hall gaped at her as she mounted the steps to the front door of the hotel. Inside, the situation was much the same, as everyone stopped what they were doing to look at her. She and Chance walked over to the registration desk.

"Deacon," Chance said to the dignified-looking man behind the desk, "this is Miss Livingston. She would like the best room you have."

The deacon looked first at Elizabeth and then back at Chance. His face turned a deep red. "You can't . . . I mean, this is a respectable place, Chance. I simply can't allow you to—"

Chance's lips tightened dangerously and he spoke in a very low, very chilling voice. "Miss Livingston is a respectable young lady, as you would know if you would take a look at her. She is my cousin and my ward, and I expect her to be treated with the utmost courtesy, which is why I brought her to your hotel."

Deacon Cox, co-owner of the Dodge House, cleared his throat. "Of course, Chance. I beg your pardon. And yours, too, Miss Livingston."

Elizabeth only hoped her face was not as red as it felt. Thus far today she had been mistaken for an impostor, Chance Fitzwilliam's cast-off mistress, his intended bride, and now his paramour. Perhaps she would be better off to miss the supper at Reverend Folger's and simply hide in her room until morning.

"Miss Livingston would like a quiet room with a lock on the door," Chance was saying. "And charge it to me."

"I can pay for my own accommodations," Elizabeth protested.

"Don't worry, I fully intend to let you reimburse me when your funds have been transferred. Meanwhile, I'll take care of everything."

"Do you . . . do you have any luggage, miss?" the deacon asked reluctantly.

Elizabeth's face heated up again. What must this look like to the casual observer? Chance Fitzwilliam checking a woman with no luggage into a hotel. No wonder this poor man had gotten the wrong idea. She was absolutely mortified.

"Of course she has luggage," Chance said. "Don't you?"

"Yes, it's . . . I left it at the station."

"I'll send someone right over," Deacon Cox said.

Chance nodded and took Elizabeth's elbow to draw her to the far corner of the room. After an awkward moment during which he looked extremely uncomfortable, he asked, "Do you need anything? Money or anything?"

Elizabeth was unexpectedly touched. He looked almost embarrassed at having to ask, and she knew his question could only have come from a genuine concern for her comfort. He had even been thoughtful enough to take her aside where no one could overhear. She was beginning to think perhaps she had misjudged her cousin. "No, thank you. I brought some money with me. I believe I have enough to meet my current needs."

He seemed relieved. "Well, then . . ." He paused, as if at a loss for words.

He really was an attractive man when he wasn't scowling, Elizabeth thought, and she wondered again what he would look like if he smiled. He was obviously waiting for her to say something, but for the life of her she couldn't think of a thing.

"Well, then," Chance repeated. She certainly did have the greenest eyes he had ever seen. "I'll be seeing you, I guess."

"When?" Elizabeth asked, knowing she sounded impertinent, but also knowing she needed the information.

"I . . . I don't know. I'll have Bill transfer your money to the nearest bank," he told her, forgetting he had already fired Bill. "I'll send you word. There'll be papers to sign probably."

Elizabeth nodded.

"And if you need me . . . need *anything*," he corrected, "just tell Deacon Cox or whoever is at the desk to send me word."

"I will, and . . . thank you, for everything." She gave him a small smile.

There it was, the smile he had been coveting all afternoon, except the sight of it wasn't making him feel at all good. Instead, he felt as if he'd gotten into a situation he could not control. He backed up a step. "You'll be hearing from me," he promised, and then he was gone.

Elizabeth sighed. He wasn't the Cousin Chauncey she had imagined, and he certainly wasn't the Cousin Chauncey her father had intended, but he was the only Cousin Chauncey she was going to get. For some reason, the thought pleased her.

Chapter 2

"Hello, Summer," Chance said after being admitted to her private quarters.

Summer Winters smiled grandly as she swept across the red plush carpet to greet him, her pale blue dressing gown fluttering around her. "What a delightful surprise, Chance," she said, reaching out to take his hands. "We don't see nearly enough of you lately."

"I was here just this afternoon," he reminded her, successfully avoiding her clutching fingers. She was, he admitted grudgingly, a very attractive woman. Not traditionally beautiful, of course, but appealing in an earthy way. Her blond hair had been artificially lightened, but the color was becoming, even to a man as fastidious as Chance. She had a good figure, too, full and lush, the kind a man could bury himself in. Chance had once found great pleasure in doing so, but no longer.

Summer batted her kohl-darkened eyelashes and puckered her generous lips into a pretty pout. "Yes, but you weren't here to see me," she reminded him, only a slight edge in her voice. "You never come to see *me* anymore."

It was true. At one time he had seen Summer frequently. She was an enthusiastic bed partner, and although she was the madam and did not have to sleep with any of the customers, she had chosen to sleep with him. He knew he was one of a privileged few and felt honored at the time. Then she had grown possessive.

Her interest in him had been piqued when she learned

of his monied background and of his family connections with upper crust Chicago society. She had apparently seen him as her ticket onto the right side of the tracks. The fact that their relationship had always been strictly a business deal, bought and paid for, ceased to matter. Suddenly she'd started professing a love he knew she didn't feel and hinting at vine-covered cottages and wedding rings. He liked Summer, but he didn't like her that much. He'd spent his first twenty years living with one conniving woman—his mother—and had come perilously close to marrying another. He wasn't about to repeat the mistake.

Chance gave Summer a small, cold smile. "Are you mad at me, Summer, because I visit the other girls now instead of you?"

He saw uncertainty flicker across her face and her blue eyes narrowed. "Of course not," she said with calculated indifference and turned away, swishing the skirt of her dressing gown with practiced provocation.

"You *are* mad at me, aren't you, Summer?" he prodded. "So you decided to play a trick on me."

Her shoulders stiffened slightly, but when she turned back to face him, she had assumed a puzzled expression. "I don't know what you're talking about."

"You know exactly what I'm talking about. Elizabeth Livingston."

She wrinkled her brow as if trying to recall the name. "I can't place her. Where does she work?"

"I'm not in the mood for games. If I don't get some answers pretty soon, Miss Winters, I'm afraid you'll find yourself plying your trade on the street, or have you forgotten I own this building?"

Although Summer owned the business herself, she knew she had best curry favor with Chance, who charged a far more reasonable rent than most landlords on the south side. "It wasn't a trick, Chance. I was only trying to help." Her face crumpled into a semblance of vulnerability, but Chance was unmoved.

"You may begin by explaining how you happened to get hold of my mail."

She hesitated, as if debating exactly what to tell him. "Well," she began, seating herself on a gilt-and-velvet chair, in a position calculated to reveal her décolletage. He foiled her, though, by seating himself opposite her in a matching chair.

Sighing with defeat, she continued. "One day when I was getting my own mail, I picked up yours, too. Don't you remember?"

"Ah, yes." Now he did, only too well.

"There was one letter in particular. It looked so official and important. The seal was broken, you see, and I just couldn't resist. Oh, Chance, I'm just like any other woman. I can't help myself sometimes!"

Chance grunted, letting her know she was wasting her time with that ploy.

"I admit it," she continued, "I read the letter. I felt so sorry for the poor child, left all alone in the world and you her only relative. And I knew what you'd do. You'd send her off to some fancy school, and she'd never have a home or a family. I thought maybe once you'd seen her, you'd decide to let her stay. Oh, Chance," she pleaded, retrieving a lace handkerchief from the deep cleft between her breasts and dabbing her eyes, "I know what it's like to be an orphan, to know nobody wants you. I was only thinking of the poor little girl."

Chance frowned. So she had thought Elizabeth was a child. He could guess what else she had been thinking: if he had a child to take of, he'd need a wife to help him. Summer, of course, would be only too willing to volunteer for the job. Fortunately for her, Chance was not a man to surrender to violent impulses or he might have been tempted to reward Miss Summer Winters for her meddling. He did know of a way to punish her without having to exert himself, however. "She's not a little girl," he pointed out.

Summer's vulnerable pose vanished instantly. "So I've

heard,'' she snapped, rising regally to her feet and strolling with apparent nonchalance to the large gilt-framed mirror hanging by the door. She pretended to make some adjustments to her elaborate coiffure, but she was really watching his reaction in the glass. ''I've heard she's quite beautiful,'' Summer remarked casually.

''Yes, she is,'' Chance told her, and actually allowed himself to picture Elizabeth's lovely face so he would have a faraway look in his eyes.

Summer whirled on him. ''Is she going to share your room over the saloon, or are you going to set her up in style?'' she demanded snidely.

Chance widened his eyes in feigned shock. ''Why, Summer, I'll have you know Cousin Elizabeth is every inch a lady—a very proper lady. The kind of lady a man dreams about having grace his home and table.'' Chance assumed a faraway look again. ''The kind of lady he wants to be mother to his children . . .''

He ducked just as the vase came sailing past his head. Glancing over his shoulder to where it had smashed against the wall, he managed to look only mildly distressed. ''Have I said something to upset you?''

''Get out of here, Chance Fitzwilliam,'' she ordered, pointing toward the door.

He studied her heaving bosom, savoring her fury before rising to his feet. ''I hope I don't have to warn you not to read my mail again,'' he said blandly. ''Ordinarily, I would be angry, but considering how things have worked out, I'm inclinded to forgive you this time. You see, without your interference, I might never have had the opportunity of meeting Cousin Elizabeth.''

''*Out!*'' she shrieked.

Chance smiled as he moved toward the door. He had been correct in assuming that pretending a romantic interest in Elizabeth would be the perfect revenge on Summer. He only hoped word of it never got back to his cousin. He would hate to have to explain his motives.

As he closed the door behind him, a voice called to him from the shadows down the hallway. "Is she very angry?"

He made out the figure of a woman standing by the stairway. "Yes, but she's mad at me, so I don't think you have anything to worry about, Hettie."

The girl came forward hesitantly. She was a small, frail thing, and her china blue eyes seemed too big for her face. "I'm real sorry about what happened, Mr. Fitzwilliam. I didn't know Miss Winters was playing a trick on you. She only told Lottie and me to pick up the little girl at the station. We thought you knew."

"It's all right, Hettie, I knew you weren't to blame. Miss Livingston said you ran away when you found out who she was," he added with a teasing grin.

Hettie smiled. "We were awful surprised to find out she was a grown woman. We didn't know what else to do, so we skedaddled back here to tell Miss Winters."

"I would have liked to have seen her face," Chance remarked wryly.

Hettie's smile grew conspiratorial. "She took a fit. I thought she'd pop her corset when we told her how pretty Miss Livingston was."

"Yes, she did seem disturbed about that fact," Chance said. "But don't worry about it, and if she gives you any trouble you come to me. Understand?"

Hettie's expression grew hopeful. "Maybe you'd like to go upstairs with me?"

Chance felt his own smile fading. Hettie was pretty enough, but she was simply not his type. Her big eyes held a sadness, a vulnerability, that warned him away. He'd been hurt too deeply himself to even consider hurting someone else. Consequently, he only chose women as jaded as he, women who understood that his fleeting interest promised no tomorrows.

"I'm in a hurry right now," he hedged. "Maybe next time."

* * *

Elizabeth stared down at the blank sheet of paper before her and very carefully wrote "Dear Cousin Chauncey." She smiled, knowing how he would detest such a salutation. Although she had mentally composed this note a dozen times, she was still uncertain how to word it. At last she settled for "Please meet me at Mr. Bates's office at two o'clock this afternoon. We have some business to discuss." She signed it simply "Your cousin, Elizabeth."

"Who're you writing to?"

Elizabeth glanced up from sealing the note to see her new hired companion, Barbara Jenks, standing in the doorway. "To my cousin," she said with a small frown.

Barbara Jenks chuckled as she came into Elizabeth's hotel room, closing the door behind her. She was a large woman, tall and raw boned, and although she was only thirty-three, hard living had aged her another ten years. Her graying brown hair was pulled into a practical but unflattering bun. Only her dancing blue eyes revealed her youthful spirit. "Are you asking him to meet you at Mr. Bates's office?"

"Yes," Elizabeth replied, trying not to notice Barbara's amusement. The two women had liked each other the moment they had met at Reverend Folger's home, and in the few days since Barbara had sold her farm and moved into the hotel room next door, they had become fast friends. "I only hope he comes."

Barbara seated herself on the bed. "He'll come," she said with a certainty Elizabeth wished she shared.

"He hasn't called all week," Elizabeth said, then could have bitten her tongue. For seven days she had tried to pretend she didn't mind that her guardian had not once stopped by to see how she was getting along.

"He's only been waiting for an invitation."

Elizabeth made a skeptical face. "He certainly doesn't need an invitation to see his own cousin, his own *ward*." It was an argument she had made to herself a hundred times. She had not wanted to believe it, but the facts spoke too clearly for her to deny them any longer. The man was a rude and selfish boor who cared for her not one whit.

After all, how much effort would it have taken for him to walk the block and a half to the hotel and come in for a minute or two to see if she was comfortable? Common courtesy dictated as much.

"Maybe he's just thinking about your good name," Barbara suggested. "Wouldn't do you no good at all for folks to be reminded he's your relation."

Elizabeth sighed. "After all I've heard about him, I find it difficult to believe he could be so noble."

"Pshaw. Just because he owns a saloon—"

"And a bordello!"

"He only owns the building. That Winters woman runs the business."

"Still," Elizabeth insisted stubbornly, "several people have told me how heartless he is."

"Who?"

"Well . . . some of the ladies at church."

"Those busybodies," Barbara scoffed. "Did Mrs. Claster also tell you how he gave her a hundred dollars when he found out her husband spent all their money on drink?"

"Yes, but she told me he lied about her husband being in his saloon and refused to send him home."

"I don't reckon you can expect a saloonkeeper to drive off paying customers, now can you?"

"You seem awfully determined to find some good in him, Barbara."

"And you seem awfully determined to find some bad."

This was not a subject Elizabeth cared to discuss further. She rose. "I'll take this note downstairs and have someone deliver it."

She was halfway to the door when Barbara's voice stopped her. "If you wanted to see him, all you had to do was send him the word, you know."

Elizabeth whirled on her new friend. "I never said I wanted to see him," she declared, but her irritation was directed more at herself than at Barbara. Elizabeth might not have *said* she wanted to see him, but that didn't mean she did not want to, no matter what her avowed opinion of his character. The truth was she had more than once sat down with pen in hand to scribble a message to him. He had, after all, told her to send word if she needed anything.

Unfortunately, she did not need anything. Barbara Jenks had acquainted her with the town and the townspeople. Reverend and Mrs. Folger gave her all the moral support she needed, and Bill Bates called every day to escort her and Barbara to both midday dinner and supper. Bates kept her informed about the arrangements for her trust—Chance had asked him to act as her attorney in spite of the fact that he had fired Bates in Elizabeth's presence—and had even helped her locate a place to live. Everyone else had been so helpful, she simply had not needed to consult her guardian.

Barbara was grinning from ear to ear. "You might not have *said* you wanted to see him, but I reckon you did. I know I do. I've heard he's a handsome devil."

" 'Handsome is as handsome does,' " Elizabeth quoted primly. "My cousin's behavior thus far makes it easy to forget how good-looking he is."

Barbara raised her eyebrows in disbelief. "Maybe for you," she said.

Refusing to rise to Barbara's bait, Elizabeth carried the note downstairs to have it delivered. Alone in her room a short while later, however, she began to have second thoughts about the meeting. What was Chance going to say about the house she wanted to buy? And, more important, what would he say about her "project"?

The project had seemed like such a good idea when Reverend Folger first suggested it. She clearly remembered the day she and Barbara had gone to the parsonage for tea.

"Reverend Folger, I'm accustomed to doing charity work in my church at home," she had told him, "so I want you to feel free to call upon me."

"What kind of charity work, dear?" Mrs. Folger inquired.

"Oh, the usual things, I suppose. We knitted and collected food and clothing for the poor, visited the sick."

Reverend and Mrs. Folger exchanged glances. "Have you ever wanted to become more personally involved?" the reverend asked.

"How so?"

"We're organizing a branch of the Women's Christian Temperance Union here in Dodge," he explained.

"We would so appreciate your help," Mrs. Folger added. "Your joining in the work would be an inspiration to us all."

"I'm so sorry, but I just couldn't," Elizabeth said, hating to disappoint them. "Although I admire the WCTU's goals, I'm afraid I don't see much hope for their success. Perhaps I've been unduly influenced by my father, but he always said no law would stop him from taking a drink in the privacy of his own home, and he doubted it would stop anyone else, either." She shrugged apologetically. "I'm sorry. I know you need my help, but I think I would prefer to spend my time actively doing good rather than trying to stamp out evil."

The Folgers took her refusal in good grace, and Barbara helped smooth over the awkward moment. "Do you have any idea what kind of work you'd like to do here?" she asked.

"Well, my father always said the greatest good was to help someone in need. He wasn't born wealthy, you see. He earned every cent of his fortune and never forgot his humble beginnings or the people who aided him. I guess he always felt he had a debt to repay, and my mother and I were only too happy to help him do so."

Reverend Folger rubbed his chin thoughtfully. "You say you like to help those less fortunate than yourself?"

"Elijah, don't even think about it," Mrs. Folger chastened. "Miss Livingston would never consider such a thing."

"We won't know unless we ask her," Folger pointed out.

"Ask me what?" Elizabeth wanted to know.

"There are some women in town—"

"Elijah!"

"—who need help in the worst way—"

"Worst is right!"

"—but no one else will help them," he finished, frowning at this petite wife.

"Who are they?" Elizabeth asked.

"Soiled doves," Mrs. Folger informed her primly.

"Oh, my," Barbara murmured.

Reverend Folger leaned forward, ignoring Barbara's disapproval. "A few of these women have come to me privately, seeking help. They lead a terrible life, worse than any decent woman can imagine. Some of them live in louse-ridden tents where they are forced to entertain their customers. And the men treat them cruelly."

"Why do they tolerate it, then?" Elizabeth asked. "Why don't they simply leave or find another type of work?"

"What type of work would you suggest?" the reverend asked. "You must admit there are precious few jobs available to women, and even if these women might once have found some sort of respectable employment, who would hire them now?"

Elizabeth had never given the matter a moment's thought but now found herself intrigued by the problem. "Are there many of these women in town?"

"At least a hundred, I should think," Folger replied. "Only a handful have had the courage to come to me, but if we had someplace for them to go . . ."

"What kind of place?"

"Elizabeth! You aren't really considering this, are you?" Barbara asked, but Elizabeth waved at her to be silent.

"A refuge of some kind," Folger explained, "here on the North Side where they could be safe."

"Are they in danger?"

"Without doubt," Folger said. "The men and women who employ them are ruthless. If they were to run away, they would be hunted down and severely punished."

"Oh, dear," Elizabeth murmured as she digested this information.

"Elizabeth," Barbara tried again, "you can't possibly become involved with women like this. Think of your reputation. Your father would turn over in his grave."

Elizabeth suspected Barbara was right, but she refrained from saying so. On the other hand, her father *had* always encouraged her to help others less fortunate than herself, and who was less fortunate than a prostitute? "Barbara, you know as well as I do these women were forced into a life of shame. I'm sure you've heard tales of white slavers kidnapping innocent young girls, and wicked men seducing and abandoning young women and leaving them with a baseborn child to rear. No woman would *choose* that kind of life. If some of them have sought release, how can we turn them away?"

"Well, when you put it like that . . ." Barbara shrugged helplessly.

"Dear," Mrs. Folger tried, laying a hand on Elizabeth's arm, "you must think this idea through very carefully. These women are not like the women you know. They're hardened to life. They've seen and done things you can't even imagine. And who knows what the other people in town will say? At the very least, you will be snubbed."

"I've been snubbed many times by the Main Liners in Philadelphia. It never caused me a moment's distress."

"But you'll be going against every code of conduct for respectable young ladies," Barbara warned.

Yes, Elizabeth acknowledged silently, thinking that the prospect of rebelling against such codes sounded much more interesting than it should have. Only once had she behaved in a less than perfectly respectable manner: on her arrival in Dodge City when she had brazenly entered the Last Chance Saloon. The consequences of that one incident had been far from dire. In fact, in retrospect she viewed the incident with amusement and a certain satisfaction because she had met a challenge squarely. Perhaps the time had come for her to meet another one.

"Exactly what type of refuge did you have in mind, Reverend Folger?" she asked.

The discussion had continued for several hours, with Mrs. Folger and Barbara playing devil's advocate. In the end Elizabeth convinced them both of her fervent desire to create a home for reformed prostitutes, a desire she had previously never suspected she possessed.

Now she was wondering what her unorthodox guardian would think of her plans. Surely he would not have the same concerns for her delicate sensibilities that Mrs. Folger and Barbara shared. No, if Chance Fitzwilliam objected his reasons would concern more practical matters, like how much it was going to cost. He might even object to her luring away the employees of his own brothel.

Well, she decided after due consideration, she wouldn't risk his disapproval. He couldn't object if he didn't know what she was planning, so she would just wait until things were underway before telling him. With any luck at all, he wouldn't care.

Chance guessed immediately who the note was from. All week he had been waiting for Elizabeth to ask for his help in some matter. As many times as he told himself he should be grateful she hadn't bothered him, and that he didn't *want* to be bothered, he'd still been disappointed not to hear from her. Now he felt a slight irritation that she wanted to meet him at Bates's office instead of her more private hotel room.

He was even more annoyed when he entered Bill's office and once again heard Elizabeth's laughter coming from the back room.

"That must be him now," he heard Bates say. "Come on in, Chance."

Chance was vaguely aware of Bill standing behind the desk and of another woman sitting beside Elizabeth, but mostly he was aware of Elizabeth. She rose slowly from her chair and turned to face him. She was lovelier than he remembered, even with a forced smile on her face. Her eyes glittered like emeralds framed by curling lashes, but their expression was masked, almost as if she were hiding something from him. He let his own gaze skim over her. She was dressed all in green, in a silk dress designed to show off her figure to the best advantage.

"Hello, Elizabeth," he said.

"Good afternoon, Cousin Chauncey," she replied, grateful her voice did not tremble. How could the mere sight of him cause her heart to race and her breathing to all but cease?

Only when Barbara cleared her throat did Elizabeth realize she and Chance had been staring at each other. With what she hoped was creditable calmness, she said, "Barbara, may I present my cousin, Mr. Chauncey Fitzwilliam? Cousin Chauncey, this is Mrs. Jenks."

Chance dragged his gaze from Elizabeth's sweet mouth to acknowledge the introduction. His first impression of Elizabeth's new companion was her homeliness. That, combined with her graying hair, lined face, and worn gingham dress, made the contrast between the two women startling. After a moment's thought, however, Chance decided he approved. This was the perfect person to lend Elizabeth the respectability she needed to get along in Dodge City—and to scare off whatever fortune hunters might come sniffing around. "How do you do, Mrs. Jenks?" he said, bowing.

Barbara Jenks's lips quivered before she replied with perfect gravity, "Very well, thank you."

"Well, now, why don't we all sit down?" Bill Bates suggested. "Pull up a chair, Chance."

Chance took care not to place it too close to Elizabeth's. He looked expectantly at Bill.

"As you know," Bill began, "the bank in Leavenworth has received a transfer of funds from Eliz—Miss Livingston's trust, and we've established a line of credit for her at the stores in town. Between the two, she should be able to meet her living expenses while she is here in Dodge. Chance, Miss Livingston needs your approval before she can spend any of her money, of course, and that's why we're all here today.''

Everything seemed cut and dried, and Chance felt a slight sting of regret. Being careful not to let his feelings show, he turned to Elizabeth and asked, ''How much do you need?''

''Three thousand dollars.''

''Three thousand dollars! What in the name of heaven for?''

Elizabeth winced, but she did not back down. She had expected such a response. After all, in a country where the average laborer earned a dollar a day, three thousand dollars was a small fortune. ''I need a place to live,'' she explained with as much composure as she could muster.

''You don't need three thousand dollars for a place to live,'' he declared. ''I own a couple of houses. You can have one of them, rent free.''

Elizabeth bristled. ''I'm not a charity case. I can pay my own way, and besides, I've seen the houses you own. They are both too small.''

''Too small? How much room do two women need, for God's sake?''

Elizabeth briefly considered telling him the truth but instantly decided against it. She would concentrate on getting what she wanted today and break the news of her project later, when he was feeling more calm. She lifted her chin, deciding to play the injured party. ''May I remind you, Cousin Chauncey, that I have been accustomed to a certain manner of living? I have no intention of lowering my standards simply because circumstances have placed me on the outer fringes of civilization.''

''Far be it from me to ask you to compromise yourself, Cousin Elizabeth,'' he replied sarcastically, fighting an urge to shake the impudent look off her face. ''May I inquire exactly which house here in the outer fringes has caught your fancy?''

Elizabeth winced again, bracing herself for the next explosion. ''The Harris house.''

"That *barn?*" He looked to Bill Bates for confirmation, but Bates refused to meet his gaze. Chance tried Mrs. Jenks, but she looked far too amused for his taste.

"And, of course, I'll need some furniture," Elizabeth continued, drawing his forbidding gaze. "You can't expect me to have things shipped all the way from Philadelphia, especially when I don't know how long I'll be staying here."

"Which makes me question the wisdom of buying a house at all," Chance argued. "Wouldn't you do better to simply rent a small place?"

"Mr. Bates has told me how much property you own in town. You of all people should realize this purchase is a wise investment." Seeing she had him, she smiled sweetly. "And I'll need linens and kitchen utensils—"

"And a silver tea service, of course," Chance snapped in exasperation.

"I have no intention of being extravagant," she informed him. "Mr. Bates has an itemized list of all things I'll be needing. If you will examine it, you will see I plan to purchase only the essentials."

Chance turned his glare on Bill, but it was Barbara Jenks who spoke. "Elizabeth and I spent a lot of time on our list, Mr. Fitzwilliam," she said. "In spite of her upbringing, Elizabeth is very sensible about money. You won't find any silver tea services in our house."

Chance knew a potential ally when he saw one. "Thank you, Mrs. Jenks. I appreciate the way you're looking after Elizabeth in this matter, but I still find it difficult to believe she needs such a large house. Surely a practical woman like yourself can see how foolish it is."

Mrs. Jenks smiled back at him, making her face slightly less homely. "Ordinarily, I'd agree, Mr. Fitzwilliam. I know *I* wouldn't need such a big place just for me and a friend, but Elizabeth's different. She's used to having things nice. Why, just look at the dress she's wearing." Chance resisted the urge to do so. "Do you have any idea how much a silk dress like that costs?"

"No, I certainly do not. I am not in the habit of buying women's clothing."

"That's a comfort," Mrs. Jenks murmured. "Clothes like Elizabeth's cost a fortune, Mr. Fizwilliam. For someone like her, setting up housekeeping on only three thousand dollars is a small miracle."

Chance opened his mouth to argue again, but stopped. What was the point? From what Bill had told him, Elizabeth could spend ten times three thousand dollars and not make the slightest dent in her fortune, so there was no danger to her financially. Another factor was her unmistakable intention of buying the house even if he tried to forbid her to do so. Suddenly, Chance was tired of all the wrangling.

He turned his gaze back to Elizabeth, who was sitting still and straight and keeping a careful mask on her emotions. "Well, Cousin Elizabeth, it looks as if you made a good choice in companions," he remarked. "Mrs. Jenks has become your champion."

Elizabeth met his gaze squarely. "Will I *need* a champion in my dealings with you, Cousin Chauncey?"

"No, you won't," he told her with a conciliatory smile. "You've managed to convince me you aren't going to be irresponsible with the house. Besides, I imagine that in buying it, you'll be doing a good deed."

"A good deed?" Elizabeth echoed in alarm. Did he know? How could he have divined her plan already?

"Yes," he replied. "I understood Widow Harris is in difficult straits and has had some trouble finding a buyer."

"Oh," she said, hoping her relief didn't show. "Yes, she was very glad to sell." Elizabeth managed to return his smile and continued to hold his eye, blaming her accelerated heartbeat on the fright he had just given her.

It was odd, she mused as she continued to stare, how much his appearance changed when he smiled. His black eyes looked almost warm and inviting.

"Well, now, since we're all agreed," Bill Bates said,

startling her back to reality, "all we need to do is get Chance to sign these papers."

The formalities were quickly dealt with, and a few minutes later Chance realized he had no further excuse for remaining in Elizabeth's company.

When Elizabeth had thanked him for his cooperation, she heard herself ask, "When will I see you again?"

Chance expertly concealed the quick pleasure her question brought him. "I was hoping you, and your friend Mrs. Jenks, of course, would join me for supper tonight," he improvised.

"Oh, how lovely," Elizabeth said with more enthusiasm than was seemly. She caught herself, however, and turned to Barbara. "That is, unless you've made other plans."

Barbara grinned knowingly. "Oh, no, supper sounds fine."

"Well, then . . ." Elizabeth was turning back to Chance when she caught sight of Bill's disgruntled frown. Good heavens! What was she thinking? Bill had escorted her and Barbara to practically every meal all week. How could she have forgotten about him so quickly and completely? "Oh, but . . . I mean . . ." She faltered, facing Chance again. "Mr. Bates usually takes us to supper, but if you'd like to join us . . ."

Chance's smile vanished and his dark eyes hardened as he turned to Bill. "I wasn't aware Mr. Bates had been so attentive to you ladies," he remarked. If looks could kill, Elizabeth was certain Bill Bates would at that very moment be falling stone dead at her feet.

To his credit, Bill looked only mildly amused at Chance's disapproval. "Don't bother to thank me, Chance. It was no trouble at all," he replied coolly. "And about this evening, Elizabeth, I was just going to tell you I have some business to attend to, so I won't be able to join you for supper."

"I'm sorry—"

"Good," Chance said. Barbara made a strangled sound

that might have been a smothered laugh. Elizabeth was outraged.

"Really, Cousin Chauncey," she remonstrated.

But before she could say more, he gave her his most disarming grin and asked, "What time shall I call for you ladies?"

Barbara answered for her, which was just as well since Elizabeth was too angry to speak. She had been right all along. Her cousin was an insufferable boor.

Elizabeth did manage a civil parting. Perversely, she made a point of telling Bill how much she would miss his company at supper, earning another frown from her guardian, which she ignored as she and Barbara made their way out of Bill's office.

No sooner were they beyond earshot of the two men than Barbara said, "He's just jealous."

"Who's jealous?" Elizabeth asked, surprised out of her fury.

"Mr. Fitzwilliam. He's jealous because you've been spending so much time with Mr. Bates."

Elizabeth stopped in the middle of the sidewalk and stared incredulously at her companion. "Why on earth would he be jealous of poor Bill?"

"I reckon he wouldn't be if he heard you calling the man 'Poor Bill,' but he hasn't any way of knowing how you really feel about Mr. Bates. You've been spending a lot of time with him, so Mr. Fitzwilliam must think you like him, and so he's jealous."

"That's silly," she decreed and began walking toward the hotel once more. "Why should he care whether or not I like Mr. Bates?"

Barbara fell into step beside her. "For the same reason he wanted to have supper alone with you tonight."

"He did not!" Elizabeth denied. "He invited you along, too."

"Only because he had to. You notice how he made sure Mr. Bates wouldn't be joining us."

Elizabeth frowned, recalling the uncomfortable scene.

Bill had seemed almost amused, however. Perhaps he, too, suspected that Cousin Chauncey was jealous of their relationship. It was ridiculous, of course, but intriguing nevertheless. "In any case, I'm glad you'll be with us. I'm worried I'll let something slip about the house."

"Don't be. I won't desert you," Barbara assured her with a grin. "I wouldn't miss dinner with Mr. Fitzwilliam for anything."

From the doorway, Chance contemplated the way Elizabeth's pert bustle swayed with just a hint of provocation.

"You know, Chance, I might be wrong about the will," Bill said.

"Wrong about what?" Chance asked, forcing himself to face his friend, who was again sitting behind his desk.

"The will," Bill said with apparent reluctance. "I could be mistaken in what I told you. You might be able to break the will if you take it before a judge. That is," he added slyly, "if you still want to."

"Why wouldn't I want to?" Chance challenged, although he was suddenly aware of having absolutely no desire to do so.

"If you want another opinion on the matter, you can take the will to Judge Beverley. I'm sure he'd be glad to give you a ruling on it."

Chance pretended to consider this advice. "Maybe I will," he said, but he suspected Bill didn't believe him.

"I can't leave you like this," Elizabeth said several hours later as she handed Barbara a fresh cold rag to put across her forehead. "I'll send word to Cousin Chauncey that I can't come."

"Don't be silly. It's just a sick headache," Barbara assured her as she adjusted the new rag over her eyes to block what little light still filtered through the drawn curtains. "I get them all the time. There's nothing you can do. In fact, what I need most is peace and quiet. Now go out and have a good time."

Elizabeth wasn't fooled. Barbara was lying on her bed

and making a valiant effort to appear much better than she was so Elizabeth would not feel guilty about leaving her. "I couldn't possibly have a good time knowing how sick you are."

"I'm not really sick; the doctor himself told you so. It's just a sick headache. I'll be fine in the morning, *if* you will just leave me alone to get some rest. *Please* go!"

Elizabeth realized she was being a pest. "I'm just not certain I should go out with Mr. Fitzwilliam without a chaperone," she said.

Beneath the wet rag, Barbara's face twisted into a thoughtful frown. "Are you afraid of him?"

"Oh, no. I . . . I'm not sure it would be proper, though," she improvised, unable to verbalize the real reasons behind her hesitation since she didn't understand them herself. There was simply something about Chance Fitzwilliam she found disturbing.

"I can't think what's improper about it. You'll be meeting in the lobby, walking on a public street, and eating in a public restaurant. Not even a man with Mr. Fitzwilliam's reputation could manage much mischief under those circumstances. So long as you don't let him get you off alone anywhere, you've got nothing to worry about."

"I suppose you're right."

"Then go," Barbara said with good-natured impatience. "If you don't hurry, you'll be late."

Chance had just entered the hotel lobby when he caught sight of Elizabeth coming down the stairs. Every loiterer in the place was also staring at her. He was annoyed by their rudeness, but he also had to excuse them. Elizabeth Livingston was something to behold.

Then she saw him, too, and a smile flickered briefly on her exquisite face before she noticed all the attention she was receiving and schooled her expression into one of unconcern. She was wearing a burgundy dress under a black satin cape. The cape hid most of her well-remembered charms, so Chance contented himself with admiring her face and the intricate coils of her ebony hair, crowned with a concoction of feathers. "Good evening, Cousin Elizabeth," he said, bowing formally as she approached.

Elizabeth studied him for signs of mockery but found none. And he certainly looked handsome in the tailored black suit, stiff white shirt, and black silk cravat. She smiled, hoping he could not tell how apprehensive she was feeling. "Good evening, Cousin Chauncey," she said, determined to keep an emotional distance between them.

Chance noticed with slight surprise that her barb hardly bothered him. He was becoming almost used to being addressed by the hated name. He returned her smile. "You're a marvel, my dear cousin. How do you manage to look so astonishingly lovely without keeping me waiting for an hour?"

Elizabeth flushed. "I didn't want to waste your valuable time since I know you usually work in the evenings," she said tartly. "In fact, I'm flattered you were willing to spend this evening with me."

His eyes narrowed, as if he were considering an equally tart reply, then his elegant features softened once more into a smile. He was going to overlook the way she was mocking him. "Giving up an evening in a smoky saloon to spend it with a beautiful woman is no great sacrifice," he told her, his dark eyes glowing.

Elizabeth shifted uneasily and pulled her cape a little more tightly around her. She had seen that look in men's eyes before and had engaged in enough flirtations to recognize desire when she saw it. Never before had it rendered her speechless, however. In such situations, she was normally able to engage in a little harmless banter, laugh lightly, and defuse the situation.

But no harmless banter came readily to mind, and she certainly didn't feel like laughing. She should never have let Barbara talk her into coming without her. If he was already looking at her like that, what was going to happen when he saw her dress? Another terrible mistake, she realized now. She gave him a strained smile. "Shall we go?"

Chance lifted his dark eyebrows. "Aren't we going to wait for Mrs. Jenks?"

"Mrs. Jenks has a headache," Elizabeth explained. "She will be unable to join us."

Chance's eyebrows rose another notch. "I'm sorry to hear that. She seemed fine this afternoon."

Did he think Barbara's indisposition was a ploy? Did he think Elizabeth had put Barbara up to faking a headache so they could be alone? If he did, he would be absolutely certain when he saw Elizabeth's inadvertently provocative gown. She could have groaned aloud. "The headache came on rather suddenly," she said stiffly, "but the doctor assured me it was nothing serious."

Fortunately, he simply murmured his sympathy. When he offered his arm, she took it carefully and allowed him to lead her from the hotel. Elizabeth reminded herself there was nothing dangerous about having dinner with her guardian, but her heart rate speeded up alarmingly when she touched him. She liked the feel of his solid arm under her hand. His strength was exciting.

As they made their way up Front Street to Delmonico's Restaurant, he discussed the unusually dry weather and the amazing quantity of dust churned up by the trail herds being driven daily into town. Elizabeth began to relax. He was behaving like a perfect gentleman. Probably she had only imagined that look in his dark eyes.

Then they were in the dining room. He seated her at the table and was waiting to assist her as she slipped the cloak from her shoulders. Her fingers clumsy from dread, she loosened the gold frogs at her throat and allowed the black satin to slide onto the chair. She winced at his slight gasp.

Chance had certainly seen a woman's bare shoulders before, and the dress wasn't extremely low cut, just low enough to hint at the swell of her breasts and the shadowy cleft between them. Nevertheless, the dress revealed more of Elizabeth than he had been expecting. If her skin looked like alabaster silk in the warm glow of the lamplight, if the graceful curve of her throat invited the caress of a man's hand, and if his hand itched to make that caress, he wasn't going to admit it, not even to himself.

Keeping his eyes carefully on her face, and only on her face, he took the chair opposite her. "What a lovely . . . necklace," he remarked.

"Oh, thank you," Elizabeth replied, her hand going self-consciously to the gold chain as the waiter approached.

"We'd like a bottle of champagne first," Chance said, smiling at Elizabeth's surprise. "To celebrate your new house," he said by way of explanation when the waiter had gone to fetch their wine.

Elizabeth noted that Chance wasn't looking at the dress or her bare shoulders, and his behavior was impeccable. Her tension began to ease. After all, the sight of her shoulders was probably not at all shocking to a man who owned a saloon and several other questionable businesses, especially if she believed the scandalous rumors she'd heard about him. "I'd like to thank you for being so reasonable about the house," she said.

Chance studied the way the lamplight flickered warmly across her skin before he replied. "I've been wondering all day if I made the right decision. Tell me, would your father have approved the purchase?"

A guilty smile curved her lips. "My father never denied me anything within reason," she hedged, certain her father would not have approved of the way she intended to use the house. "Of course, he deplored waste of any kind, but I'm sure he would consider the house a sound investment."

"Then he indulged you?" Chance guessed.

"Hardly," Elizabeth replied with a laugh. "I said he didn't deny me anything *within reason,* like food, clothing, and shelter. He worked from the time he was twelve years old, so he frowned on unnecessary luxuries. He said they made people soft."

Chance's eyebrows lifted in comprehension. "No wonder he and my father were so close."

Just then the waiter arrived with their champagne, preventing Elizabeth from pursuing the remark. She allowed the young man to pour her half a glass of the bubbly wine. Of course, no lady would actually drink more than a sip or two in such a public place, and in fact, Elizabeth had never actually tasted champagne. Her father had believed women incapable of handling alcohol, champagne in particular. It turned them giggly and silly, he said. But, Elizabeth thought with a smile as the waiter filled Chance's glass, perhaps this was another situation in which she should no longer be ruled by her father's opinions.

When the waiter had departed, Chance proposed a toast. "To your new home," he said.

Home. As the bubbles from the champagne tickled her nose, Elizabeth realized she had made a commitment to live in Dodge City. Could this wild place ever be a home to her? Not wanting to consider the answer, she swallowed the tangy wine, glad for the distraction. A few moments later, she eagerly turned her attention to selecting her meal.

To her dismay, she was unfamiliar with most of the items on the menu. "I never expected such a choice," she hedged when Chance asked her preferences. "If you eat here often, perhaps you can recommend something."

"Why don't I simply order for us?" he suggested, and she readily agreed, wide-eyed as he selected oysters on the half shell, turtle soup, lobster farci, saddle of lamb Salvandi, green peas, artichokes, fresh mushrooms, and paradise sherbet.

"My father would have said we were eating our way into an early grave," Elizabeth remarked. "His idea of a fancy meal was turkey with stuffing."

"Do I sense disapproval?" Chance asked with amusement.

"Well, not disapproval exactly. Perhaps amazement would be more accurate. Why on earth did you order so many dishes?"

"Because, my dear cousin, each dish is an adventure unto itself, an adventure that should be savored. Life is short, and it provides only a few sensual pleasures, eating, drinking, and . . . others."

The suggestive gleam in his dark eyes brought warmth to her face, but she refused to admit he had embarrassed her. "I'm afraid my upbringing was far different from yours. I was taught simplicity is best."

"Ah, but I, too, was taught that lie. Which only proves there's still hope for your conversion, too."

His smile was both wicked and challenging, stirring the urge for rebellion that seemed to have possessed her since the moment she set foot in Dodge City. "Conversion?" she asked. "I would have thought corruption a more appropriate word."

His eyebrows lifted in mock surprise. "If you want corruption, my dear Elizabeth, you have certainly come to the right man."

Elizabeth was deeply grateful for the arrival of the oysters, which excused her from replying to his outrageous comment.

"Ice?" she asked, staring down at the shimmering crushed ice on which the shells rested.

"The oysters and the ice arrive daily by train, as do many of the dishes you'll be eating tonight. You see, you aren't as far into the 'outer fringes of civilization' as you thought."

"Apparently not," she murmured, realizing she was enjoying luxuries she had never dared dream of in Philadelphia. She waited, watching to see how Chance managed the oysters before she tried. She'd eaten them in sauces before but never like this. The first one was a surprise, but a pleasant one. "They're delicious."

"Yes, but as your guardian, I must warn you not to eat too many."

"Why not?" As soon as she saw his eyes, she knew she had made a mistake in asking.

"Because they're purported to make one feel . . . how shall I say it? Romantic."

Once again, she felt the heat in her cheeks, but this time it also swept over the rest of her, warming her in places she would have been embarrassed to name. "I suppose I'm lucky you take your responsibility as my guardian so seriously," she replied tartly. "Tell me, would your father have been as conscientious?"

Instantly, his smile vanished and his expression became guarded. "Oh, yes, he would have been entirely too conscientious, I'm afraid."

"What do you mean?"

"I mean he considered women valuable only in terms of how much money they could bring in. He married my mother for her dowry and used it to build his business. He might have succumbed to the temptation to use your fortune in the same way."

"Surely not!"

But Chance's expression was implacable. "My father was ruthless. Believe it or not, he considered me much too honest and idealistic to follow in his footsteps."

He smiled at the surprise Elizabeth could not hide. "You must take after your mother then," she said in an effort to make amends.

"God, I hope not," he murmured.

"I . . . I'm sorry," she stammered, nonplussed. "I didn't mean to pry."

"No, I'm the one who's sorry," he said quickly. "As you may have guessed, my family life was far from idyllic."

"How awful for you," she said, thinking she was beginning to understand why he might have left Chicago all those years ago. "I know how lonely an only child can be, and not to get along with your parents—"

"I was not an only child," he surprised her by saying. Somehow she had gotten the distinct impression he was as alone in the world as she. She waited, not daring to reply for fear of disturbing whatever impulse had prompted him to confide in her.

Chance recognized her curiosity and admired the way she kept it under control. Not many women were so disciplined. In fact, when was the last time he had encountered a female who could be ready on time and who respected a man's privacy? Whose beautiful face and shapely figure matched every man's dream of a courtesan, yet who conducted herself like a lady? A woman who had intelligence and a sense of humor yet was not afraid to stand up to him?

But he could not let her get too close. "My brother died when he was still a child," he said, his tone telling her the subject was closed.

The turtle soup arrived, breaking the awkwardness of the moment. They ate in silence for a few minutes until Chance thought of a less volatile subject. "Did you say you went to Vassar?"

"Yes," she said, grasping gratefully at this conversational straw. "I studied all the useless arts necessary to make me a perfect hostess, housewife, and mother."

He winced. "Sounds as exciting as my time at Harvard."

"You went to Harvard?" she exclaimed in delight.

"Only for two years, and then I . . ."

"Then you what?" she prompted.

"Then I left home."

The words hung between them for long seconds while Elizabeth berated herself for having managed to uncover another sensitive area of his life. But perhaps they were all sensitive. She forged ahead. "Why did you leave home?"

He looked as if he would like to tell her it was none of her business, then he sighed in resignation. "I told you, my father was ruthless. Nothing and no one stood in his way. I had visions of someday taking over his businesses and reforming them, but then . . ."

He considered whether or not to tell her. She was, he

realized, one of the few people who might understand, and her sensitivity in not demanding an explanation convinced him to tell her.

"Then I met a girl who worked in one of my father's factories. No, it wasn't like that," he quickly explained, seeing her knowing look. "She was only about twelve or thirteen. I was twenty-one and had just become engaged to a woman I fancied myself madly in love with, so it wasn't anything romantic. She was sitting at her loom one day when I was walking through, and she looked up and smiled. She was pretty, but it was more than that. She had a vitality I can't describe. Maybe I idealized her because I was in love myself. I don't know, but she had beautiful yellow hair that hung down past her waist like spun gold. It made me happy to look at her."

His hand opened on the table as if he were beseeching her to understand, but just as quickly he realize how sentimental he sounded and closed his fingers.

"Anyway, a week later she was dead."

"Oh, no," Elizabeth cried, her hand instinctively clasping his on the tabletop.

"Her beautiful hair caught in the machinery and . . . well, you can imagine. I saw her afterward. My father sent a few dollars to her family and hired another girl, but I could never forgive him for her death."

"But accidents happen."

"Yes, they do. In fact, people died there all the time. Sometimes children who worked twelve hours a day couldn't stay awake and fell into the machines. Sometimes grown men lost a hand or a foot and died of infection. Sometimes . . . What does it matter? They'd all been faceless beings to me until the yellow-haired girl died. I realized all my glorious plans would be too little, too late. I couldn't stand by and watch them die while I waited to take over."

"But couldn't you convince your father to change things?"

"I tried," he said with bitter irony. "We had some terrible arguments, but he wouldn't listen to me. Foolish and wasteful, he said. I'd realize it when I was older and got some sense."

He glanced down at where she still held his hand across the table. Self-consciously, she released his fingers and lowered her hand to her lap.

"I started thinking about setting out on my own," he continued, his voice void of expression "I knew I didn't want to end up the kind of hypocrite my father was, someone who observes all the social amenities but lets his workmen die like so many flies. Then my fiancée broke our engagement, and I no longer had anything to keep me in Chicago."

The waiter came to take away their half-eaten soup and replace it with the lobster. As Elizabeth watched Chance attack the lobster with practiced ease, her mind whirled. Chance had once been engaged. Did she dare ask about the woman he had thought he was in love with, or should she leave well enough alone? He had already revealed far more of himself than she had hoped to learn.

When the waiter left, the tension between them was almost palpable. She chose to break it. "So how did you come to Dodge City?"

He relaxed visibly and gave a hint of a smile. "I started working my way down the Mississippi River on a steamboat. I became a gambler, figuring that was the occupation most likely to embarrass my parents if they ever found out."

She shook her head in disapproval as she lifted a forkful of crabmeat stuffing to her mouth.

He grinned unrepentantly. "I was amazingly successful as a gambler, and when I heard about the Kansas cattle towns I came west. I soon realized I would make more money as a saloonkeeper, so I invested in the Last Chance and here I am."

"Still trying to embarrass your parents?"

"No, I gave that up long ago. I found I liked the life here. Some people consider men like me unscrupulous or dishonest, but in fact we're far more honest than men like my father. Everyone who comes into my place knows he'll get good whiskey and an honest game. And nobody dies.''

"What about the men who spend their money in your saloon and let their families go hungry?''

"No one goes hungry if I can help it,'' he said with a frown.

She studied him and decided he was telling the truth. He wasn't the kind of man to let others suffer. Yet she also sensed his reluctance to let people see that side of him. He would be the type to do his alms in secret and deny them for fear of appearing soft. Perhaps he was already regretting his openness to her. To put him at ease, she gave him what she hoped was a disarming smile. "I had no idea you were so generous, Cousin Chauncey. I'm having second thoughts about a silver tea service.''

For a second, his frown held, then he understood her ploy. "A silver tea service,'' he said, feigning outrage. "If I see one piece of silver in your house, I'll cut you off without a cent.''

"Bill Bates would never let you get away with it.''

"Then I'll fire him . . . *again.*''

They both laughed, the tension finally and completely broken.

The dishes came and went as Chance gave Elizabeth advice on where to shop for furnishings for her home. Then they discussed places they had visited and interesting people they had known. Chance shared anecdotes from his two year sojourn at Harvard, and she replied with stories from Vassar. Elizabeth taxed her wit to draw from him an occasional smile, while he, in turn, seemed bent on teasing her into showing a flash of temper. At last, when they had long since finished their dessert, Chance bestowed upon her his most magnificent smile. "Well, Lizzie, are you ready to go?''

"Lizzie!'' she cried, surrendering to the urge to please

him by bristling at his barb. "No one *ever* calls me Lizzie!"

"No one ever calls me Chauncey, either," he countered.

Elizabeth pretended to consider his words. "Well, then, yes, I am ready to go . . . Cousin *Chauncey,*" she added with a wicked grin.

But her feeling of satisfaction diminished when she realized she had just put an end to the evening. He also showed a notable reluctance to rise from the table.

He lifted her cape and placed it around her shoulders. Did his hand linger on her shoulder, or was it only an illusion invented by her overactive imagination? A shiver raced down her spine, and she swiftly fastened her cloak and turned to face him.

Chance looked into the green depths of her eyes for several seconds and found he had to clear his throat to speak. "Shall we go?" he asked, offering his arm. Going, he discovered with some surprise, was the last thing he wanted to do.

Elizabeth noticed his silence but did not remark upon it since her own thoughts occupied her mind. Vaguely, she heard the muted din from the saloons lining Front Street and those on the other side of the railroad tracks. Glancing at the elegant man beside her, she tried unsuccessfully to picture him in such a setting. Having seen the sensitive side of Chance Fitzwilliam, she knew his roguish air was only a protective mask.

Suddenly aware of how alone she was in the world except for him, she found comfort in this more thorough knowledge of his character. Her fingers tightened on his arm. Once more she noticed his strength and felt inexplicably drawn to it. Aware though she was of her dependence on him, she sensed his isolation, too. Did he also feel the need for someone?

As if in answer, he placed his hand over hers where it rested on his sleeve and squeezed gently. "It's early yet.

I keep a buggy at the livery stable. How would you like to go for a drive?''

A faint voice in the back of her mind whispered Barbara's warning not to go off alone with him, but she ignored it. ''I'd like to, very much,'' she replied.

Chapter 3

Elizabeth told herself the quick surge of joy she felt at his invitation was caused by the prospect of escaping the confines of Dodge City, however briefly. Once she was in the buggy and Dodge City really was behind her, however, she had to admit her other motives for agreeing to this ride. Being alone with Chance Fitzwilliam was by far the most exciting risk she had taken since arriving in Dodge. She sat back to enjoy it.

"The moon is beautiful tonight, isn't it?" she said, admiring the view.

"Please, Lizzie," Chance said in a pained voice. "The man is supposed to comment on the beauty of the moon to impress the lady with his appreciation of nature."

"Oh, I'm sorry. You could talk about how lovely it looks reflected on the water," she suggested, pointing toward the moon's glittering reflection in the Arkansas River, which ran beside the road.

"Good heavens. No wonder you're a spinster. You don't have the slightest idea how to behave like a proper young lady."

"I am not a spinster! I am as yet unmarried. And, I might add, by choice."

"Are you trying to tell me some reckless young man has already asked you for your hand?"

"Not merely *some* young man, but quite a few of them, I'll have you know. As my guardian, you will happy to learn I'm selective in my male companions and as yet have

65

not met the one with whom I anticipate spending the rest of my life in marital bliss.''

Chance made a choking noise. *"Marital bliss?* And what makes you think this news will please me? As your guardian, I look forward with great eagerness to the day when I pass my responsibilities onto your husband.''

"Why, Cousin Chauncey, you've hurt my feelings! If you aren't careful, you'll make me think I'm a burden to you.''

"Nothing could be further from the truth," he assured her. "Please, feel free to take your time in choosing your life's mate. I wouldn't want you to make a hasty decision. You know the old saying, 'Marry in haste—' ''

"And speaking of taking time, you certainly have been dragging your feet for a man who was engaged at twenty-one,'' she said, deciding the mood was now light enough to explore his romantic history. "Was your heart irreparably broken by a faithless woman?''

"Yes," he said without emotion, relieving her fears on that account. "And having once so narrowly escaped a fate far worse than death, I am determined never to tempt it again.''

She laughed, inordinately delighted by their friendly banter.

"There's a place up ahead where we can pull off and watch the moon for a while.'' His tone made the statement a question.

"All right," she said, knowing such a thing was improper, but once again willing to take the risk. Excitement tingled along her nerve endings, making her wonder how she had lived almost twenty-one years without ever doing anything so daring.

He pulled into a copse of trees and tied off the reins. The horse whinnied questioningly and, receiving no further instructions, fell silent.

Elizabeth stared out at the moon reflected in a thousand tiny ripples across the surface of the river. A warm breeeze teased at her face, and the soothing chirp of insects filled the night.

Chance cleared his throat. "The moon is certainly beautiful tonight."

"Oh, Cousin Chauncey, I'm deeply impressed. I had no idea you appreciated nature so much."

"Very good," he murmured, and then pretended to stretch, extending his arm behind her and letting it come to rest along the seat where it brushed her shoulders.

"Exactly what are you doing?" she asked, eyeing his arm askance.

"Testing to see how you respond to ungentlemanly advances. You've already made two serious blunders by going out unchaperoned with an unscrupulous rogue and by granting him permission to stop the buggy."

"I see. And now he's put his arm around me. I suppose next he'll try to force his attentions on me."

"Of course," he said calmly.

In the next instant he lunged at her with a comic roar that startled a squeal from her.

Her hands came up instinctively to ward him off, but even as his arms closed around her in a bear hug, she dissolved into laughter.

"Hysterics. A very good reaction," he commented, sending her into convulsions of giggles. His hands rested on her shoulders as she sagged against his chest, clinging to his lapels for support as hilarity shook her.

How long had it been since she had laughed with such abandon? Too long, she knew. The sensation was wonderful, cleansing and invigorating and thrilling all at once.

"Chance Fitz . . . william, you are a . . . an unscrup . . . ulous rogue!" she gasped.

"I warned you, didn't I? By the way, the scream was good, too. Always scream."

She tried to punch him but found she was too weak to do much damage. His chest vibrated suspiciously, as if he, too, were laughing, but he managed to do so silently.

His hands moved on her shoulders, rubbing, kneading, while Elizabeth regained control of herself.

Taking a deep, calming breath, she inhaled the fragrance of bay rum and cigars and the underlying male scent. Beneath her hands, his chest was hard and strong, his heartbeat steady. Awareness tingled over her. They were so close, practically in each other's arms. The heat from his body engulfed her, and once again she felt a surge of excitement only this man could stir in her.

"Chance?" she said, lifting her head to see his expression.

His eyes glittered in the darkness, and slowly his smile faded. "Lizzie?" he replied. Beneath her palm, his heartbeat quickened, and she heard his breath catch. Her own vital functions seemed to cease entirely.

His face came slowly down to hers, as if he were giving her time to consider his act, but she had no desire to pull away. Her every instinct was to meet him, and so she did. Tentatively at first, she lifted her lips until his mouth touched hers and removed all remaining doubt. Instantly, she knew this was what she had been waiting for since the first moment she had seen him.

This wasn't kissing as she had previously known it, a pressing of mouth to mouth until the man grew feverish with insistence and she grew impatient to escape. Chance's lips were firm and warm on hers, neither feverish nor insistent but patient and exploratory, as if she were some rare treat to be tasted and savored.

He touched her cheek softly, almost reverently, and she clutched his lapels, urging him closer still. Responding with a groan from deep within his chest, he slid his fingers around her neck and drew her to him. His tongue teased the opening of her lips until they parted instinctively for his invasion.

His other arms came around her then, pressing her to his chest and swamping her senses with the feel and smell and taste of him. Blood roared in her ears, drowning all rational thought as she strained against him, eagerly drinking in his kiss. His fingers stroked the sensitive cord of her neck, and a few seconds later her cape slid free.

His lips left hers, drawing a moan of protest until he touched his mouth to the throbbing pulse at her throat. She clung to him, throwing her head back to offer him access to the flesh that burned for his touch. He took what she offered, using lips and teeth and tongue to explore every inch.

Her breath was coming in labored gasps by the time he encoutered the barrier of her gown. Beneath the restricting fabric, her breasts swelled as longing blossomed into need. His hand caressed their aching fullness through the layers of fabric, promising unknown pleasures, pleasures she yearned to know.

His fingers began to tug impatiently at the neckline of her dress, jarring her back to reality. Suddenly, all the silent alarm bells she should have heard long ago started jangling in her brain. What on earth was she doing?

"Chance . . . no . . . wait . . ." she gasped, fumbling to grasp his hand and pull it away.

At first he resisted, and for one horrible moment she thought he meant to overpower her. She struggled more frantically, calling out his name again until at last he heard. She knew the instant he came to his senses. His body went still and then stiffened, and he jerked away with a terrible oath.

Chance stared down at her in horror. What on earth had he done? What could he have been thinking? The answers were not something he cared to consider. Instead, he lashed out at Elizabeth. "What in hell did you think you were doing? Don't you have any better sense than to go out buggy riding with a man you hardly know?"

"What?" The charge was so ridiculous Elizabeth could hardly speak. It was too dark to see his face, but his anger was a palpable force. She simply could not reconcile it with what had just occurred.

"Didn't that father of yours teach you anything about men? Don't you know what can happen?"

"You're my guardian!" she snapped. "I trusted you!"

"Then you're twice a fool! And you were asking for trouble wearing a dress like that."

"There's nothing wrong with my dress. If you hadn't attacked me—"

"I did not attack—" Suddenly, Chance realized how unreasonable he was being, and the angry words died on his lips. She was right, of course. The only thing wrong was the way he had lost control of himself. He drew a ragged breath and passed one large hand over his face as he fought to regain his usual calm. After a long moment, he was once again able to speak in a normal voice.

"You're absolutely right, Elizabeth," he said more rationally, not daring to look at her for fear he might be tempted to start kissing her all over again. "I had no business bringing you out here in the first place. Please accept my apology. I behaved abominably."

Elizabeth could hardly believe her ears, and her own conscience pricked her. Hadn't Barbara warned her? Hadn't she chosen to forget those warnings? Was she not equally responsible for what had just happened?

Chance was reaching for the reins when she clamped a constraining hand on his arm. "Wait," she commanded, but when she felt him stiffen once again under her fingers, she withdrew her hand immediately. His suddenly-acquired calm was nothing more than a thin facade. She did not know whether the knowledge should comfort her or not, but it was at least comforting to know he was human. "I . . . you aren't the only one to blame. I never should have come out here."

"I'm your guardian. You should be able to trust me."

"But we hardly know each other, and I never should have worn this dress."

"There's nothing wrong with your dress."

Their eyes met in the darkness, and the absurdity of the situation struck them both at the same moment, snapping the tension between them. They each smiled ruefully.

"I'm sorry, Lizzie," Chance said after a minute.

"Please don't say that again," she begged. "It hardly suits your image as an unscrupulous rogue."

"No, it doesn't, does it? Unfortunately, I'm feeling more like your guardian right now, and as your guardian, I'm wondering what your attorney would say if he knew I'd just tried to seduce you."

Had he really tried to seduce her? Elizabeth did not find the idea nearly as shocking as she should have. But she also knew Mr. Bates would say Chance was abusing his privilege and taking advantage of her dependence on him, and he would be right.

The knowledge depressed her because she suddenly realized she didn't want anything to stand between her and Chance as man and woman. Tonight she had seen a Chance Fitzwilliam she wanted to know better. He had stirred feelings in her she hadn't known she possessed, feelings she wanted to explore, but as long as Chance was her guardian, such an exploration was impossible. If only there was some way to get around the legalities separating them, some way they could be on an equal footing . . .

The solution came to her with lightning swiftness. It was so obvious she felt stupid for not having thought of it before. "You could turn over control of my money to me. Then you would no longer be my guardian . . ." She let her voice trail off as she sensed his will hardening against her.

He stared down at her for a long moment. The intensity of his silence frightened her. At last he said, "Is that what this was all about?"

"What are you talking about?"

"Your change of attitude. Until tonight, you've barely been able to tolerate me, and suddenly you act like I'm the most fascinating man you ever met. Did you think you could charm me into giving you control of your money? Is that why you let me kiss you?"

"Don't be ridiculous!"

"I should have known. Proper Miss Livingston from

Philadelphia would never let herself be pawed by a lowly saloonkeeper unless she had a very good reason.''

Proper Miss Livingston! The accusation stung, more so because she knew it was true. She *did* have a good reason, although it was not the one he thought. "Chance, listen to me—"

"No, you listen to me, Cousin Elizabeth. You're out of your depth here. I was raised by a woman who learned how to manipulate men before she could walk, and I almost married a woman who shattered what little was left of my illusions. There isn't any female trick I haven't seen, so if you think I'll give you your own way in exchange for a few kisses, you've got another think coming."

"That's not why I let you kiss me!" she insisted furiously.

He ignored her and reached for the reins. He slapped them sharply, startling the horse and forcing Elizabeth to grab onto the side panel to keep from being thrown against Chance when the buggy lurched into motion.

Seething with indignation, she drew her cape around her and slumped back against the seat. Although she would like to have control of her own money, of course, nothing had been further from her mind when she had been in Chance's arms. But how on earth could she convince him of that? And could she do so without compromising her own pride? She didn't think so.

They made the trip back to town in silence, absorbed in their own concerns. Chance stopped the buggy in front of the hotel, got out, and helped her down. No one watching them would ever have guessed that less than an hour ago they had been kissing passionately.

"Elizabeth, I think we'd better forget this evening ever happened," he said, his handsome face as solemn as she had ever seen it.

"By all means," she replied. Turning on her heel, she walked into the hotel and up the stairs, wondering with every step if she was capable of forgetting.

* * *

Chance frowned as he glanced over the sheaf of documents Bill Bates had just handed him. There were lists of assets, summaries of holdings, and company prospectuses, along with a cover letter requesting Chance's instructions concerning the acquisition or liquidation of various stocks and bonds.

"It looks as if my Cousin Elizabeth is going to be even more trouble than I feared," he remarked, shifting in his chair.

Bill grinned across his cluttered desk. "My offer is still good."

"What offer?"

"To take her off your hands," Bill explained cheerfully.

Chance's frown deepened. "That isn't funny."

"I'm not joking," Bill assured him. "Even if she were penniless, Elizabeth would be the most eligible young lady in town. I'm already half in love with her. If I could get her to fall in love with me . . ."

Vaguely, Chance realized he should have been grateful for Bill's offer. In a town where males outnumbered females three to one, and where precious few of those females were both single and respectable, a woman of Elizabeth's obvious charms was a rare commodity indeed. She would soon be swamped with suitors, and Bill was probably the only one whose intentions Chance could trust.

Chance looked down at the papers he still held, papers that represented the extensive obligations that came along with Elizabeth. Remembering how much he hated the paperwork and decisions involved with managing business concerns, he knew he should have felt relief over the prospect of making her someone else's problem. But, amazingly enough, the thought produced exactly the opposite reaction. Marveling at this unexpected attack of conscientiousness, Chance shook his head. "'Elizabeth is *my* responsibility," he said, a little more sharply than he had intended. Bill's eyes widened, but he made no comment. "Besides," Chance added to soften his statement, "she's too young to be thinking about marriage."

"Young?" Bill echoed in disbelief. "She'll be twenty-one in a few months. Many women are mothers by that age."

Chance raised his eyebrows. "I hope you aren't going to offer to make Elizabeth a mother."

Bill's face turned a dull red. "Be reasonable, Chance. Look at this stack of papers. It'll take us all day just to go through them, and then you'll have to make some decisions, and you know how much you hate that. You said it yourself: looking after Elizabeth is going to be a lot of trouble. In the two years I've known you, you've avoided unnecessary obligations like the plague."

Bill was right. In keeping with Chance's usual philosophy, he should have put Elizabeth on the first train back to Philadelphia. Why hadn't he?

"Unfortunately, it seems I have no choice about being involved with Elizabeth. So," he said, laying the sheaf of papers purposefully on Bill's desk, "I think we'd better get started."

For a moment Bill looked as if he intended to say something more, then he appeared to think better of it. Turning to the task at hand, he began to explain the extent of Chance's duties as Elizabeth's trustee.

Later, when all the decisions had been made and duly recorded, and Chance was walking back down Front Street toward his saloon, he once again considered Bill's observation. Chance didn't need to be reminded about his uncharacteristic behavior toward Elizabeth. In the week and a half since she had arrived on his doorstep, his attitude had undergone a remarkable change. Suddenly he was once again concerned with propriety and obligations, two things he'd sworn upon leaving his father's house he would never again consider as long as he lived. He knew only too well how these social niceties were often used to cover a multitude of sins, and he had no intention of becoming the hypocrite his father had been.

Still, the fact that he'd kissed Elizabeth—and wanted to do a whole lot more, if the truth were told—weighed heavily on a conscience he'd thought immune to any torment. He'd even reconsidered his original opinion as to her motivation for returning his advances.

At the time, he'd believed she was trying to trick him into freeing her from his guardianship. It was, he had to admit, exactly the type of thing a woman like his mother or his former fiancée would have done. His mother had been an expert at using her beauty to bend men to her will, attracting young lovers with which to humiliate her husband and even playing her own sons against each other as they vied for her attention. Sybil, the girl he had almost married, had used her body to gain access to the Fitzwilliam fortune and influence.

In the years since leaving Chicago, Chance had encountered many women just like them. Summer Winters was simply the last in a long line. It was no wonder he'd attributed those same motives to Elizabeth. But had he been unfair to do so?

He still wasn't certain, but having seen the intricacies of administering her trust, he knew he could not possibly turn over its control to a naïve young woman, no matter what her personal wishes. He also knew if he was going to serve effectively as Elizabeth's guardian, he would have to mend their currently strained relationship.

And if his original suspicions about her proved correct and she did hope to use her charms to change his mind about relinquishing control of her estate, he would take great pleasure in allowing her to try.

"I've changed . . . my mind . . . about housework," Elizabeth reported breathlessly as she and Barbara Jenks wrestled the huge Oriental rug up over the clothesline.

After a few more moments of struggle, the rug at last sagged over the rope and the two women stood back to catch their breaths. "Have you now?" Barbara inquired skeptically.

"Yes, I have," Elizabeth replied with a grin as she dusted her hands. "I used to dislike it, but now I absolutely loathe it. I still don't see why you won't let me hire someone to do it for us.''

The two women were standing in the backyard of what had formerly been known as the Harris House. They were dressed in calico Mother Hubbards covered with long white bib aprons. Their hair was wrapped in large bandannas for protection against dust. They had spent the better part of the last three days cleaning in preparation for the delivery of the furniture Elizabeth had ordered from Wright, Beverley & Company, Dealers in Everything.

Barbara shook her head in feigned disgust. "I told you, it'd be a sin to waste good money paying somebody to clean when we're both able-bodied. Besides, when folks find out who's going to live in this house, you won't be able to keep no help anyhow."

Elizabeth frowned, unable to believe people would be so narrow-minded about her project. "Even temporary help would be fine. If my servants from back home could see me now." She made a deprecating gesture at her dust-covered attire.

"I wonder you didn't bring some of them with you, at least a maid for a companion on the trip."

"I would have if any of them had wanted to come," Elizabeth reported. "Most of our servants were with us for years, and when Father died, I pensioned them off. The few who were young enough to consider such a move were terrified of meeting up with wild Indians or some such. My poor maid actually cried when I asked her about coming."

"Oh, pshaw!" Barbara scoffed. "What a bunch of lily-livered cowards. We haven't seen a wild Indian around here in years . . . except from time to time some of the men in town'll dress up to scare a highfalutin' visitor from the East," she added with a twinkle.

"I certainly hope they don't consider me highfalutin'," Elizabeth said with a laugh just as the shrill ring of the doorbell sounded from the front of the house. "I wonder who that could be."

"I'll get it," Barbara offered. "And I'll tell whoever it is to come back later when we're receiving visitors. Meanwhile . . ." With a smug grin, she picked up the wire rug beater and placed it in Elizabeth's hand.

"Thank you," Elizabeth replied sarcastically as Barbara hurried off to answer the door. Elizabeth eyed the rug for a moment before preparing herself to assault a year's worth of dust and dirt.

Whap. There was, Elizabeth had to admit, something deeply satisfying about physical labor. *Whap!* One could work off one's frustrations while at the same time accomplishing a worthwhile task. *Whap!* Not that Elizabeth had an overwhelming number of frustrations, of course. *Whap!* Except perhaps her confusion over her feelings for Chance. *Whap! Whap!*

During the five days since their disastrous buggy ride, she had seen neither hide nor hair of him, yet his presence had haunted her every hour, both waking and sleeping. *Whap!* In her sleep, she had relived his fevered kisses—*Whap!*—with a clarity that left her aching with want. *Whap! Whap!* What did it mean? *Whap!* And where would it lead? *Whap! Whap! Whap!*

"Have some pity, Cousin Elizabeth."

Elizabeth jumped, almost dropping the rug beater.

"It's just a rug, after all."

Slowly, so she could gather her wits, Elizabeth turned to face him. He was standing on the back stoop, hands on his hips, suit coat flung back to reveal a glittering gold watch chain stretched across the vest that covered his broad chest. On his handsome face was a sly grin, as if he had caught her doing something indecent. Her cheeks burned even as she reminded herself he could not possibly have guessed her thoughts.

"Cousin Chauncey," she managed. Barbara appeared behind him and gave a shrug that said she'd tried her best to keep him out. "What a surprise," she murmured.

"So it would seem," he said, giving Elizabeth's ensemble an amused perusal. "But, as I told Mrs. Jenks, there's no need to stand on ceremony with me, is there?"

"Do you have some business with me?"

His dark eyes continued to twinkle. "Not exactly. I've brought you a gift to brighten your new home."

"Oh," Elizabeth replied in dismay. How awkward! How did one dismiss a man who had brought a present? "How . . . how thoughtful," she stammered, growing ever more self-conscious. "Barbara, would you take my cousin inside and serve him some tea while I get cleaned up?"

"There's really no need," he started to protest, then understanding flickered in his dark eyes, and he turned to Barbara with uncharacteristic meekness. "I'd really prefer coffee, if you have some," he said as he followed her into the house.

Chance had hardly begun to sip his coffee when Elizabeth appeared in the front parlor a scant ten minutes later. Quickly setting aside the cup, he rose to his feet, his eyes riveted on her.

He'd thought her charming when she'd looked like a scullery maid just minutes ago. Now she was irresistible. She'd removed the rag from her head and taken off her apron, but her uncorseted figure was still wrapped in the calico Mother Hubbard, a style he had never before found so appealing.

"Once again you amaze me with your promptness, Cousin Elizabeth," he said, resisting the urge to sweep her into his arms.

Elizabeth self-consciously smoothed her dress, aware of the poor picture she still made in spite of a liberal application of soap and water to her hands and face. She'd made what repairs she could to her hair, but she'd disdained changing her dress. She didn't want him to think his opinion was all that important to her. "I only wish you'd waited a few more days so we could have welcomed you in style," she said with a polite smile as she seated herself beside Barbara on the sofa.

Chance resumed his seat on the wing chair opposite the

two women and glanced around the ornately furnished room with its rich carpeting and heavy drapes. Even the tables had doilies underneath each piece of bric-a-brac. "It looks to me like you're already set up in style. Did you do all this?"

"Oh, no," Elizabeth assured him. "Mrs. Harris is moving to a much smaller place, so she sold us the furniture she could no longer use. She left us this room completely intact."

An uncomfortable silence fell as Chance's dark gaze held Elizabeth's. She tried to read his thoughts, but his expression was guarded, almost wary. She felt her pulse leap under his intense scrutiny, but in spite of her efforts, she could think of nothing else to say.

At last Barbara cleared her throat. "I can see you two have something important to discuss, so I know you'll excuse me." She rose, seemingly oblivious to Elizabeth's desperation, and left the room.

Reluctantly, Elizabeth turned back to Chance.

"Well . . ."

"I . . ."

They both spoke at once, and she indicated he should go ahead.

He smiled perfunctorily. "As I told you, I brought you a housewarming gift." He reached down and brought up an enormous package.

"My goodness," she murmured as she accepted the box. "You really shouldn't have." Inside, her mind was racing. Would a man who ran a saloon know what was a proper gift for a young lady? Hoping against hope that the box did not contain a statue of a nude woman with a clock in her stomach or some equally horrid item, Elizabeth tore into the wrapping paper.

In moments she had pried the lid off the box and pulled out the first of several articles securely encased in layers of tissue. She gasped aloud.

"A silver tea service!" she exclaimed, pulling the gleaming teapot from its tissue paper nest. In astonishment, she lifted her gaze to catch a look of anxious anticipation in his face.

"This was the only thing I felt certain you didn't have," he said.

Elizabeth stared at him. As surprised as she was by the generosity of his gift, she was even more surprised at the uncertainty she sensed in him. The gift was more than a polite gesture. He was making her a peace offering, taking the first step in reestablishing their friendship.

She was only too happy to help him. She sighed elaborately. "I'm afraid I can't accept it."

"Why not?"

"Because my cruel and heartless guardian warned me that if he saw even one piece of silver in my home, he would cut me off without a cent."

Chance coughed to cover a chuckle. "The man is despicable."

"Cruel and heartless," she agreed.

"Perhaps if you explain to him—"

"Oh, he never listens to my explanations, and besides, we had a terrible argument the other night. I don't think he's happy with me at the moment."

"And are you unhappy with him?"

She gave the teapot a significant glance. "I'm thinking it over."

"Lizzie, about the other night . . ." He paused, looking uncomfortable. "I want you to know I regret what happened."

"What do you regret?"

He gave her a blank look.

"Do you regret kissing me," she explained, "or do you regret acting like a jackass afterward?"

His face reddened. "Both. I should never have accused you of trying to influence me, and I certainly should never have kissed you, not when I'm your guardian. You have my word it will never happen again."

Elizabeth frowned. Was she supposed to express relief when the most exciting man she had ever known promised never to kiss her again? "Then you admit you were wrong to suspect me of ulterior motives?"

Clearly he did not enjoy admitting such a thing, but he nodded.

Inordinately pleased by his discomfort, she smiled. "Well then, I suppose I'll forgive you. However, we still have a small matter to settle about silver in my house."

He gave her a self-mocking grin. "I think I might have some influence with your cruel and heartless guardian. You may keep the tea service."

"I can't tell you how relieved I am," she said primly, but she could not keep her lips from twitching.

Elizabeth enthusiastically proceeded to unwrap the other pieces of the tea set. In addition to the elaborate teapot, which had its own warming stand, the set consisted of a matching hot-water urn, syrup pitcher, sugar bowl, creamer, waste bowl, spoon holder, and tray. By the time Barbara returned, Elizabeth had finished arranging the last piece on the tray on a side table.

"Good heavens," Barbara cried when she saw the display.

"Cousin Chauncey felt certain we didn't already have one," Elizabeth said wryly.

"Nobody has one like this," Barbara declared, approaching with an air of caution. "I never saw anything so pretty."

"I'm glad I've pleased you," Chance said, and Elizabeth's searching look found no trace of his previous uncertainty. This was the old Chance Fitzwilliam, confident and cocky. The smile he gave Barbara would have melted butter. It certainly melted Barbara. "I was wondering if you ladies would like to take a day off from your labors and go on a picnic with me tomorrow."

Barbara's eagerness was obvious, but she deferred to Elizabeth with a questioning look.

Elizabeth considered the matter for only a moment. "I think a picnic is exactly what we need."

* * *

Chance called for them in his buggy early the next afternoon. He had explained that theirs would have to be a supper picnic since his late hours forced him to sleep until noon. He was wearing his usual black suit and vest and a bowler hat, the kind Texas cowboys occasionally tried to shoot off the heads of unsuspecting gentlemen. Elizabeth suspected no one had ever tried to shoot off Chance's.

"We have a lovely day, don't we?" Elizabeth said as Chance escorted her and Barbara to the buggy. "I'm so glad it didn't rain."

"Actually, I'm not," Barbara said. "The farmers are desperate for rain."

Feeling a little selfish for not having considered the farmers' needs, Elizabeth frowned. "Are things really that bad?"

"This is the driest spring I can remember."

"I'm sure the rain will come," Chance said, handing Barbara into the buggy. "Didn't the land agents promise it would?"

Barbara made a face at him, aware he was teasing. "Drought isn't a joke, Mr. Fitzwilliam."

"It's too early to be predicting drought," he scolded. "Let's be grateful for the sunshine, shall we?"

His smile was irresistible, and Barbara had no desire to be difficult. "All right."

Chance's grip was properly impersonal as he helped Elizabeth into the buggy, but she felt the now-familiar tingles of awareness nevertheless. She wanted to know all sorts of things about Chance Fitzwilliam, and she had every intention of learning them before sunset. Secure in the knowledge her chaperone's presence would prevent anything untoward from distracting her from her purpose, Elizabeth happily anticipated the day ahead.

In the light of day, the Arkansas River lost its magic and became an ordinary stream cutting through the barren prairie. Still, Elizabeth found much to admire beneath the seemingly endless canopy of sky. Chance and Barbara called her attention to points of interest along the way, a circling hawk, a scurrying jackrabbit, an unusual plant.

In this treeless land, a copse beside the river stood out for miles, and Elizabeth wondered if it was the same one in which she and Chance had kissed.

"It's the best picnic spot around," Chance volunteered, as if sensing her question and making an excuse. A quick glance at his twinkling eyes confirmed her suspicions.

"You must picnic often," she replied, trying to imagine whom he might have brought on past expeditions. Saloon girls, perhaps?

"Actually, I don't picnic at all," Chance told her wryly. "Unscrupulous rogues seldom do. It's much too wholesome an activity."

"Really, Mr. Fitzwilliam," Barbara chastened, "you make yourself out to be such a scoundrel when we all know different."

"Do we?" Elizabeth inquired with interest.

"Yes, do we?" Chance asked, equally interested.

"As much as I hate to admit it, yes," Barbara explained. "Although I despise what you do for a living—"

"You're the president of the WCTU, aren't you?" Chance asked.

"Not president, corresponding secretary."

"My mistake," he apologized. He was melting Barbara with his smile again.

"Anyway," she continued, "as much as I disapprove of your profession, we all know that keeping a saloon, at least on the North Side, is a perfectly respectable occupation in Dodge City. Even our mayor owns a saloon."

"He's only half owner," Chance corrected.

"My mistake." Barbara grinned back at him.

Elizabeth smiled inwardly. Barbara had been dropping hints all morning about what a nice man Mr. Fitzwilliam had turned out to be. She was obviously smitten by his charm and even more obviously expected Elizabeth to fall victim to it, too. Suspecting Barbara's matchmaking tendencies, Elizabeth planned to let her do her best today.

"So you see, Elizabeth," Barbara was saying, "Mr. Fitzwilliam is really a pillar of the community."

Chance winced, and Elizabeth had to stifle a giggle. This was a little too much to swallow, even for someone as eager to be impressed as Elizabeth was. "He certainly knows how to choose a nice picnic spot," she allowed as they neared the copse.

"Some friends recommended it," he demurred.

Elizabeth wondered for what purpose it had been recommended but refrained from asking.

The spring grass made a delicate carpet beneath the newly leaved trees, and Chance spread out a blanket for them to sit on. Refusing their offers of help, he bade them be seated and began to carry the other picnic items from the buggy.

Barbara gave the brown stoneware jug a disapproving look, but Chance said, "Lemonade," and her smile returned. The hamper he brought out was overflowing with paper-wrapped items. Remembering Chance's penchant for good food, Elizabeth could hardly wait to see what he had selected.

"Caviar!" she exclaimed in disbelief as she unwrapped a jar. "For a picnic?"

His black eyes twinkled. "I had to bring things that could be served cold."

"What's caviar?" Barbara asked, eyeing the dark mass suspiciously.

"Fish eggs," Elizabeth said in disgust. She had seen it served at a party once.

"Have you ever tasted it?" Chance asked, amused by her reaction.

She shook her head and set the jar aside while she reached into the hamper again. She and Barbara continued to unwrap the food he had brought, and when they uncovered a package of crisply toasted bread, Chance relieved them of it.

"You both must taste the caviar before you decide you don't like it," he said, finding a knife with which to spread it on the toast. He handed one piece to Barbara and one to Elizabeth.

Elizabeth stared at hers dubiously. "I suppose this is one of those dishes you consider an adventure."

"Think of yourself as a pioneer into new territory," he suggested.

Gingerly, she took a bite while Barbara did the same. Barbara swallowed hers quickly and reached for the lemonade jug. Elizabeth tried to be more open-minded, chewing slowly. It wasn't as bad as she had expected, but she didn't think she'd ever eat any more.

"It's better with champagne, but I didn't want to incur the wrath of the WCTU," he told them.

"I'd like to try some lemonade, too," Elizabeth said, pursing her lips against the salty aftertaste.

"At least now when you say you don't like it, you'll be telling the truth." His grin was infectious.

"How many people did you tell Delmonico's to pack for?" Elizabeth asked as they continued to unwrap delicacy after delicacy. In addition to the caviar, there was cold beef and lamb, a veal-and-ham pie, a basket of salad, several jars of stewed fruit, a few dozen biscuits, a plum pudding, a cheesecake, a blanc-mange in a mold, a few jam puffs, cheese, and crackers.

"I told them to pack a little of everything."

"They packed *a lot* of everything." She glanced into the now-empty hamper. "What, no sherbet?"

He shrugged. "Doesn't travel well."

"My goodness," Barbara said, not for the first time. "I never saw so many things I didn't know the name for."

Chance leaned back on his elbow. "We'll be glad to teach you, won't we, Cousin Elizabeth?"

"We certainly will." And they did.

Elizabeth tried to be sensible, considering the number of dishes to be sampled, but even so she was unable to do justice to the numerous desserts. When all three of them were full to the point of misery, enough food remained to feed a dozen more people.

"You can take it home with you," Chance said. "You won't have to cook tomorrow."

"We won't have to cook for a week," Barbara exclaimed as she helped Elizabeth rewrap the uneaten food.

Chance stood up and stretched. "I think I should try to walk off a little of this feast. Would you ladies like to join me?"

Barbara groaned. "Not me. I think I'll sit here real quiet like until everything settles."

"I'll walk with you," Elizabeth said, flashing Barbara a grateful look. The woman was behaving like a perfect matchmaker.

Chance offered his hand to help Elizabeth rise. His fingers were warm and strong, but he released her the instant she was on her feet. Knowing he was taking pains to be proper, she did not tease him about his caution.

"I was just wondering," she said as they strolled along the riverbank, "what my father would have said about our feast today."

"Probably the same thing my father would have said, something like 'waste not, want not.' "

She nodded. "I'm sure he would have a few words to say to you about being a responsible guardian, too."

She was referring to the picnic, but he took a different meaning. "I told you, Lizzie, what happened the other night isn't going to happen again."

"Chance, I'm not nearly as upset by it as you seem to think."

"Then you should be. What do you think your father would say if he knew you were getting involved with a saloonkeeper? And what would your attorney think? Or your friends back in Philadelphia? Or Mrs. Jenks for that matter?"

"Barbara would be delighted. She thinks you're a pillar of the community, remember?"

"Well, she's wrong. Outside of Dodge City, no one considers a saloonkeeper respectable."

"You don't have to be a saloonkeeper."

His dark brows shot up. "Trying to reform me, Cousin Elizabeth?"

"Could I?" she countered.

"No. I like being a saloonkeeper. I don't have to pretend I'm something I'm not. I don't have to be nice to people I can't stand. I can say what I think and throw someone out of my place if I don't like his looks. No one tells me what to do or when to do it, and I don't have a lot of people depending on me to save them."

"Save them?" she echoed, thinking how strange the phrase was. His quick frown told her he regretted his choice of words. "You mean save their lives? Like the girl you told me about?"

"It doesn't pay to get involved in other people's lives."

She gave him a considering look. "Have you always been so hard?"

"Yes, I'm cruel and heartless. Ask my ward."

She smiled in spite of herself. "You must have cared about someone once, before you lost your heart. Who could it have been?" She stopped, tapping her finger thoughtfully against her lips. "Not your fiancée. You only *thought* you were in love with her. Not your parents. What about your brother?"

He stiffened, and she knew she had struck a nerve.

"What was he like? Like you, cool and aloof and utterly charming?"

"He was utterly charming and not like me at all."

"Chance," she scoffed.

"It's true," he said, apparently thinking he had found a way to convince her of his own deficiencies. "Jamie was so full of joy, bright and beautiful, always smiling. Everyone loved him."

"Even you."

"I killed him."

She stared at him in stunned silence, wondering if she could have heard him correctly. His voice was expressionless, but his eyes held a pain past bearing. "You didn't really kill him,'' she insisted, not bothering to analyze how she could be so certain.

He made an impatient gesture with his hand. "I caused his death. It's the same thing. We were fishing on Lake Michigan. A storm came up, and the boat overturned. They didn't find his body for three days."

"How horrible for you," she cried, instinctively reaching out to him.

"I don't want your sympathy, for God's sake," he snapped, shaking off her hand.

"Why did you tell me, then? To shock me? To disgust me? Did you think I'd believe you murdered your own brother?"

"My *half* brother. As I told you, my parents' marriage was not happy. My mother amused herself with a series of protégés. Some were artists, some musicians. She even found an occasional actor or two. One of these charming young men fathered Jamie, which explains why he was so different from my father and me. My mother took great pleasure in reminding me I was a difficult child, dark and brooding like the Fitzwilliams, while Jamie was exactly the opposite. She wanted children who could openly adore her, like Jamie did. I never could."

"What an awful woman!"

"You miss the point," he told her coldly. "I let my brother drown because I was jealous of him."

"Did she say that?"

"Of course. Everyone thought so."

"Oh, Chance!" Impulsively, she threw her arms around him, holding him close against the agony she knew he must feel. No wonder he had longed to do some good in the world to make up for the ugliness he had known within his own family. And no wonder he was no longer willing to give other people a chance.

For several seconds he stood still, stunned by her embrace, and then he stiffened in reaction. "Lizzie, don't do this." He took her arms as if to push her away, but she clung to him defiantly. After a second or two, he surrendered to her comfort and his arms slipped around her, too. He held her to him with desperation.

Her eyes swam with unshed tears, and she blinked furiously to keep them from falling. Beneath her ear she could hear the unsteady rhythm of his heart. "You must have felt so alone, losing your brother and then being accused of causing his death."

He let out a bark of mirthless laughter that brought her head up. "Not completely alone. My father admired my ruthlessness in ridding myself of a rival."

"No!"

"Lizzie, I didn't tell you all this to win your sympathy."

"I know. You thought I'd be shocked and horrified and that I'd hate you."

He made an impatient noise. "I wanted you to understand the kind of man I am. After Jamie's death, I decided to do something useful with my life. I was going to save all the other children, but when I saw the job was too big I ran away. I've been running ever since."

"I don't believe you."

"Then you're a fool," he said, pushing her away, "and much more naïve than I suspected."

"If you're trying to hurt my feelings, you're wasting your time."

"Damnit, Lizzie—"

"Chance, for heaven's sake, be reasonable. You don't have to convince me you're a despicable human being. I'm not some simpering schoolgirl who's going to go into seclusion because a man kissed me. You've promised never to do it again, and I trust you. Can't we simply be friends?"

"I . . . yes," he said, a little taken aback. "But why did you put your arms around me just now?"

"Because I wanted to comfort you," she said, telling only part of the truth. She had also wanted to put her arms around him for an entirely different reason.

He considered her statement for a moment and apparently accepted it. "I just didn't want you to have any romantic notions about me. You aren't going to save me from myself or reform me or—"

"I don't want to." This much, at least, was true. She liked him exactly as he was. "Now, can we be friends?"

His grin was slow in coming and dazzling when it arrived. "Friends." He gave her his hand and she captured it with both of hers.

"Shall we finish our walk?" she asked, releasing his hand with regret.

They strolled along in comfortable silence and then turned back.

"Lizzie, how much do you know about your father's financial dealings?" he asked suddenly.

"Father kept things pretty much to himself. He didn't have much confidence in—"

"—a woman's ability to handle her own affairs," he finished for her. "I know, you told me. In other words, you don't know anything at all."

She shook her head.

"I met with Bill Bates the other day and made some decisions about the estate. I sold off some stock and—"

"You did *what!*"

"You owned stock in two competing railroads," he explained. "I didn't see any point in that, so I sold off your investment in the one I think is going to go under."

Elizabeth frowned, not liking the helpless feeling she was experiencing. "I see."

"I did some other things I think I should explain to you. Perhaps . . ."

"Perhaps what?"

"I'd like to . . . that is, if you're interested, I'd like to go over everything with you."

For the second time that afternoon, Elizabeth stared at him incredulously. No one—not her father, not her attorneys back in Philadelphia, not even Bill—had ever considered the possibility she would be interested in learning about her estate. "When?"

"When what?"

"When would you like to meet with me?"

"Will you be receiving tomorrow afternoon?"

"I most certainly will."

He smiled at her eagerness. "Then I'll call on you."

Pleased beyond measure, Elizabeth basked in the warm glow of success as they made their way back to the copse where Barbara was resting. She had learned some important secrets about Chance's past, and by offering to explain her finances to her, he had proven once again he was not the unscrupulous rat he claimed to be.

The ride back to town went far too quickly, but Elizabeth comforted herself with the knowledge she would see Chance again tomorrow. The sun was an orange ball on the horizon when they reached Front Street, and the plaza was filling with would-be revelers.

Chance glanced over them, and his face hardened when one man in particular lurched into the street in front of them. Wrestling the horse to a precipitous halt, Chance glared after the staggering man until he disappeared into the Last Chance.

"Is something wrong?" Elizabeth asked.

He instantly resumed his charming manner. "No. I just saw someone undesirable going into my saloon. As I told you, one benefit of my profession is being able to throw out the customers I don't like."

"Is he a troublemaker?"

"You could say that." Chance slapped the horse into motion again.

"It's Abe Claster," Barbara informed her.

Elizabeth needed a minute to place the name. "Mrs. Claster's husband." Barbara nodded.

Elizabeth's gaze flew to Chance, but his expression told her nothing. Claster was the man Chance had refused to eject when his wife had come looking for him. "What will you do with him?"

"See that he gets home. It wouldn't do any good to throw him out in the street. He'd only go someplace else."

"Watch out, Chance. Your heart is showing."

He gave her a sharp look, frowning at the expression he saw reflected in her eyes. "I don't care what happens to him, but his wife comes looking for him. Having weeping women hanging around my front door is bad for business."

"I'm sure it is. Either way, Mrs. Claster will be grateful."

"I don't want her gratitude."

No, of course he didn't. He didn't want any involvement at all, and knowing what she did about his life up to now, Elizabeth could understand why. Her smile grew smug. "You're a very nice man, Chance Fitzwilliam."

He scowled as if she'd insulted him.

Chapter 4

For the tenth time in an hour, Elizabeth stopped in front of the hall mirror to check her appearance. She had dressed with more care than usual this morning in anticipation of her meeting with Chance. Since she had never attended a business meeting before, she wasn't certain what to wear, but she knew exactly what clothes would attract a man's attention. In contrast to the simple skirt and shirtwaist she had chosen for the picnic yesterday, today she had selected an elegant, green silk afternoon dress that hugged her fashionable hourglass figure and swept back into a tidy, flounced bustle.

Examining her reflection, she wondered how Chance would react to seeing her again. They had parted friends last night, but Elizabeth had high hopes of a closer relationship with him. Of course, her more sensible side knew she was only indulging in feminine fantasies of taming a rogue, but even her sensible side was eager for the challenge.

"You look fine," Barbara told her.

Elizabeth put a hand over the excited flutter in her stomach. "Do you think I'm too pale?"

"Flushed is more like it. You got some sunburn yesterday."

"Oh, dear. Maybe I should use some rice powder."

Barbara rolled her eyes. "I doubt he'll care," she said as Elizabeth hurried up to her sparsely furnished bedroom, which still awaited the delivery of the furniture she'd ordered from Wright, Beverley & Company.

Her order arrived at exactly the same moment Chance did. They had time only for a hurried greeting, but Elizabeth saw the glitter of appreciation in his eyes as he appraised her from head to toe. To her surprise, Chance removed his suit coat and pitched right in to help the workmen unpack and carry in the furniture, arranging it to her specifications.

"You must plan on having lots of company," he remarked as he returned from one of his many trips upstairs.

"What makes you say that?" Elizabeth asked guiltily. She was standing just inside the front parlor doorway, out of the line of traffic but where she could still see to direct the furniture to the proper rooms.

He moved closer. "I was only wondering why you chose to furnish all five bedrooms when there are only two of you. Are some of your friends from Philadelphia going to visit?"

She still didn't dare tell him about her project, not until it was too late for him to stop her. "Oh, yes. My friends from school all love to travel," she explained, telling herself it wasn't a lie. They really did love to visit new places, just not Dodge City.

He came closer still. At some point in his labors, he had removed his vest, too, and rolled up the sleeves of his once-pristine white shirt to the elbows. The sight of his muscular forearms with their thick dusting of ebony hair was disturbing, but pleasantly so.

"Make way," a voice called. The two workmen were coming in the front door carrying a large wardrobe between them. Chance hastily stepped out of their way, right into Elizabeth.

A startled cry escaped her as they collided. His bare forearms came up, and powerful hands steadied her as she braced against his chest. His shirt was damp beneath her palms, his body hard. She drew a quick breath, and his scent engulfed her.

Behind him, the workmen lumbered up the stairs and out of sight. "I'm sorry," Chance murmured hoarsely. Her gaze flew to his face, and her heart lurched to a halt.

His dark eyes glittered with unnamed emotions. A muscle twitched in his jaw, and his fingers tightened on her arms. "Lizzie . . ." he whispered, his face close to hers. His heart thundered against her hand, and her eyes slid shut.

His mouth covered hers, hot and hungry. She opened to him joyously, welcoming his seeking tongue, tangling it with her own. Snaking her arms around his neck, she pulled him closer. His arms closed around her, pressing her yielding softness against his unyielding strength with an eagerness that bordered on desperation. Her body responded with a need of its own, turning her blood to liquid fire and igniting a rampant desire.

"Elizabeth?"

Barbara's voice was like a dash of cold water. Elizabeth jerked free of Chance's arms to find her own dismay mirrored in his dark eyes. He released her instantly, and she backed away.

"I'm in the front parlor," she called, her voice breathless.

Chance released his own breath in a disgusted sigh. "I broke my word to you." Before she could assure him she didn't mind at all, he turned on his heel and strode from the house.

Barbara stopped in the parlor doorway, staring after him in confusion. "Is something wrong?" she asked.

Elizabeth drew in a deep breath and let it out slowly. "No, why should there be?" she replied, surprised she sounded almost normal. She only hoped her lips did not look as thoroughly kissed as they felt.

Quickly, before Barbara could form another question, Elizabeth asked, "What did you want me for?"

Effectively distracted, Barbara turned to Elizabeth again. Elizabeth hardly heard her friend's question, though; she was too busy watching Chance cross the hall carrying part of an iron bedstead upstairs. From the set of his jaw, she knew he was still furious with himself.

She resisted the urge to go after him. What could she say? That she forgave him? He hadn't apologized, and she certainly couldn't tell him to feel free to kiss her anytime the mood took him. Even her newly developed sense of adventure would not allow such brazenness.

Chance and the workmen made several more trips while Elizabeth supervised from the parlor doorway. Then the workmen were gone, and Chance came downstairs one last time, his hands and face washed, again wearing his vest and coat. Even his hair was neatly combed, but when he joined Barbara and Elizabeth in the parlor, Elizabeth could still smell the musky maleness of him. The scent belied his neat appearance and set her stomach to fluttering again.

"It was nice of you to help us, Cousin Chauncey," she said, grateful they could now, finally, be alone together for their meeting. Elizabeth had some business of her own she wanted to discuss.

"I'm glad I could be of assistance," he replied, his tone painfully formal. "I'm sorry we won't have time for our discussion."

"We won't?"

"I was thinking it might make more sense to have our meeting at Bill's office," he continued, ignoring her question. "Then he can explain anything you don't understand."

Apparently he no longer trusted himself to be alone with her. The knowledge was gratifying but also annoying. "That would be fine, but surely you can stay for a few more minutes."

"We have some lovely cheesecake left over from the picnic," Barbara added.

The remark surprised him, as if he had forgotten Barbara was there. "I'm afraid not. I've got some business to attend to. Maybe next time." He turned to Elizabeth. "I'll send word when Bill can give us an appointment."

"All right," she said, already experiencing the sense of loss she knew would flood her as soon as he was gone.

She thanked him once more as she escorted him to the door. He replied in stilted phrases without looking at her again. Pressing her lips together in irritation, she resisted the urge to kick him.

"What's bothering him?" Barbara asked when he was gone.

Elizabeth smiled mysteriously. "His conscience."

Chance strode quickly down the street, letting his long legs carry him as fast as propriety would allow, short of breaking into a run. He was thoroughly disgusted with himself. God in heaven, couldn't he keep his hands off her for one single minute? After the picnic yesterday, he had begun to believe they really could be friends. So much for that.

And so much for his plan to increase Elizabeth's confidence in him. She might overlook one lapse, but certainly not two, and not when he'd promised there would be no repeat performance. Well, he'd learned his lesson. He would make a point of never being alone with her again, not even for an instant . . . now that he knew an instant was all it took.

He reached Front Street and turned toward the Last Chance. Yes, he thought, he was her guardian, and he would protect her. Elizabeth was special, naïve and innocent, a totally different type of woman from any he had known. He would do everything in his power to see she remained innocent, even if he only had to protect her from himself.

"They're a likely looking pair," Barbara said, frowning in disapproval as she peeked through the drapes at the two women coming up the front walk with Reverend Folger. Two days had passed since Chance's visit, and Elizabeth had filled her days preparing for her new borders.

"It's rude to spy," she said.

"Pshaw! Those two wouldn't know what rude was," Barbara countered.

Standing behind Barbara, Elizabeth did not have a good view of her first two boarders, but from what she could see Barbara's assessment was correct. Still, Reverend Folger had vouched for their sincerity in wanting to start a new life, and Elizabeth was anxious to give them a chance.

"You stay here," Barbara commanded when Reverend Folger's knock sounded. "I'll bring them to you."

A few moments later, Barbara ushered a group into the lavish front parlor.

"Gawd almighty!" exclaimed the taller of the two women, gazing with amazement at the room's luxurious appointments.

"Please, Miss Stone," Reverend Folger said with a pained expression, "I'll thank you not to use the Lord's name in vain."

"Excuse me, Reverend," Miss Stone replied. "I forgot where I was for a minute. How about this place, Molly? Ever think you'd be working for a classy outfit like this?"

Molly was a mouse of a woman, short and plump and plainly ill at ease. Her small hands twisted nervously.

At Elizabeth's elbow, Barbara stiffened. "Neither one of you will be working while you're here. I hope Reverend Folger made that clear to you."

Molly made a soft mewling sound, but Miss Stone guffawed loudly. "He sure did. That's why we're here. It'll be pure pleasure to be off my feet and not on my back, if you know what I mean."

Barbara knew exactly what she meant, and Elizabeth had a very good idea, too, although neither of them confirmed their knowledge. Still looking pained, Reverend Folger took the opportunity to make some introductions.

"Miss Livingston, Mrs. Jenks, I'd like you to meet Miss Mavis Stone and Miss Molly Wilson."

"Pleased to meet you," all four women mumbled in unison.

Elizabeth studied Mavis Stone. She was almost as tall

as Barbara, and big all over. The thick hair under her stylish bonnet was an unnatural shade of red. Elizabeth had never known anyone who dyed her hair.

Neither Mavis nor Molly could be termed pretty, but they both possessed a certain robustness that Elizabeth guessed must be attractive to men, or at least to Texas cowboys. Outside of their buxomness, however, they seemed to have little in common. Mavis was dressed in the height of fashion, though the cut and material of the dress showed it was a cheap, ready-made garment, and the color was a garish orange no respectable woman would have chosen. Molly's Mother Hubbard was slightly faded and more suitable for cleaning house than for making a formal call.

"Mr. Shilling wouldn't let me bring any of my clothes," Molly said when she noticed Elizabeth staring.

Elizabeth's cheeks burned with humiliation at having been caught. "Who is Mr. Shilling?" she asked to cover her embarrassment.

"He's the son of a bi—" Mavis began but caught herself just in time. "He's the fellow who runs the dance hall where we worked. He told us we'd have to leave our clothes behind if we went away with the Reverend. I told him to stick it up his—" She gave Reverend Folger a sidelong glance and continued. "I told him I was taking my clothes whether he liked it or not. Molly here was too scared to stand up to him. I'm always telling her she's too nice for her own good."

Embarrassed, Molly hung her head.

"Well, now, there's nothing to worry about," Elizabeth hastily assured her. "I'm sure we can find some clothes for you to wear." No one responded, and suddenly Elizabeth noticed they were all still standing. "Please, everyone, sit down. Make yourselves at home."

Mavis and Molly showed a notable reluctance to make themselves at home in such splendid surroundings, but after a little encouragement, they allowed themselves to be seated. The newcomers took the sofa, Reverend Folger the wing chair, and Elizabeth and Barbara perched on the armchairs by the front window.

Reverend Folger spoke first. "I've told Miss Stone and Miss Wilson all about you, Miss Livingston, and of course, I've told you all about them, or at least as much as I know. I trust you'll get to know each other. Miss Stone and Miss Wilson have a few rough edges, but I truly believe they want a better life for themselves. It took a lot of courage for them to come here."

"Courage?" Elizabeth asked, directing the question to Mavis and Molly. She would not have thought the decision required bravery so much as common sense.

Molly was too flustered to answer her and hung her head again, but Mavis said, "Shilling wasn't real happy about us leaving him, miss. He might've slapped us around some to change our minds if Reverend Folger hadn't been there."

"He'll still do it if he gets the chance," Molly added, and then instantly dropped her head again.

"What an awful man," Elizabeth exclaimed, exchanging a shocked look with Barbara. "Well, you needn't worry. Nothing will happen to you while you're in my house."

"No," Mavis agreed matter-of-factly. "I don't reckon even Shilling would dare tangle with Chance Fitzwilliam's woman."

"His *woman?*" Elizabeth echoed, glad she was blushing so no one would guess the surge of pleasure the appellation gave her.

"Oh, I didn't mean it that way," Mavis hastily explained. "I just meant he has the charge of you and all." She cast a beseeching look at Reverend Folger, who nodded encouragingly.

"I explained your situation with Mr. Fitzwilliam, too, Miss Livingston. I'm sure these ladies understand everything is perfectly proper." Reverend Folger's smile was reassuring. Elizabeth wondered what he would think if he knew Chance Fitzwilliam had once, by his own admission, tried to seduce her.

She bit back a smile. "Well, let's get acquainted, shall we? Where are you from, Miss Stone?"

"Oh, call me Mavis," she insisted, and without further encouragement launched into a detailed story of her life. When she was finished, Elizabeth and Barbara coaxed a skeleton outline out of Molly. The stories were remarkably similar. Both women came from pitifully poor families in distant cities. They'd both had to support themselves when their parents turned them out on their own, but neither had an education or fortune to fall back on. Without other options, they had chosen the only profession open to them.

Elizabeth's surprise must have shown on her face. "Not exactly the story you were expecting, was it, miss?" Mavis asked with a knowing grin.

"I . . . I didn't really know what to expect," she said, but Mavis wasn't fooled.

"You thought you'd hear about the wicked men who promised marriage and then abandoned us far from home and family, forcing us to degrade ourselves. Am I right?"

She was exactly right, but Elizabeth didn't want to say so. "That's the way it always happens in novels," she said lamely.

Mavis cackled. "I expect lots of things happen in novels that ain't true in life, Miss Livingston. They're made up stories, ain't they?"

Elizabeth supposed that was true, but before she could say so, Barbara announced it was time to get their guests settled in their rooms. Reverend Folger carried Mavis's bags upstairs, and Elizabeth directed them to the proper rooms.

As Barbara took Reverend Folger back downstairs and saw him out, Molly tugged on Elizabeth's sleeve. "I guess you'll want us to help around the house, won't you?"

"I . . . I really hadn't thought about it," Elizabeth admitted, aware she had given far too little thought to the details of her project. She and Barbara had discussed where the women would sleep, but not what they would do. "I suppose making your own bed and keeping your room clean will be enough."

But Molly was shaking her head. "We should do more, though I don't know if I should offer to help clean or not. I'm afraid I might break something."

"We'll work things out, I'm sure," Elizabeth said, laying a reassuring hand on Molly's arm.

Molly glanced at the hand in surprise, and Elizabeth realized by touching Molly she had crossed some invisible social boundary. Self-consciously, she pulled her hand away. Did she imagine it or was there a fleeting expression of hurt in Molly's doelike eyes? Before she could decide, Molly had turned away. "I'll go down and see if Mrs. Jenks needs any help is the kitchen," she said.

Elizabeth frowned as she watched Molly descend the stairs. Behind her she could hear Mavis humming off-key as she unpacked her substantial wardrobe. Soon she, too, would be wanting to know what her rolé here was to be. Unfortunately, Elizabeth had absolutely no idea. The plan had sounded so simple: provide a home for women who had no place else to go so they could escape their lives of shame.

In their naïveté, Barbara and Elizabeth had not thought much past that point. Even more strange was discovering these women were flesh-and-blood people with unique personalities, people who would intrude on Elizabeth's privacy and her time and her energy. They were also people with needs, needs she might not even be able to comprehend much less meet. She was already disturbed to learn all her preconceived notions about these so-called soiled doves were not necessarily true.

Elizabeth could not imagine being desperate enough to sell her body. The very idea was appalling, yet she couldn't help recalling Mavis's painfully honest excuse: "I was hungry." Elizabeth had never been truly hungry.

Mavis came out into the hallway. "Well, what should I do now?"

Elizabeth winced.

* * *

Chance idly shuffled the cards as the other players joined him in the back room of the Last Chance for their weekly high-stakes poker game. Dog Kelley was the first to arrive. The mayor was an unprepossessing man, slightly built and rather unkempt, with a receding chin, heavy-lidded eyes, and a handlebar mustache. As usual, a greyhound followed at his heels.

"Evening, Chance," Kelley said as he took his accustomed place. The dog curled up contentedly beside his chair.

Chance returned the greeting, inquiring politely about business down at the Alhambra, Kelley's own saloon. While Kelley was exaggerating his business success to Chance, two other players came in: Nicholas Klaine, editor of the *Dodge City Times*, only one of several newspapers currently thriving in town, and an ardent supporter of the Kelley administration; and Michael Sutton, an attorney who handled business for Kelley and his cronies.

The men greeted each other by exchanging friendly insults. "Our peace officers will not be joining us tonight," Sutton reported as he took his seat. "There's a bunch of Texans out for blood over on the South Side, and they figured they'd better be on the streets."

"That's Earp's job, not Masterson's," Kelley objected.

"Bat's probably getting bored with no horse thieves to chase," Chance said, referring the sheriff's widely publicized success of the summer before. "Let him have some fun."

The four men quickly settled down to play. An hour passed with only desultory conversation interrupting their concentration.

"I'm out," Chance said, throwing down his hand.

"Oh, hell, so am I," Mayor Kelley announced, slapping his own cards on the table in disgust.

Sutton grinned and raked in the pot. "Thank you, boys.

You've just saved me from having to overcharge some poor sodbuster on his legal fees.''

Everyone laughed except Chance, who frowned his disapproval. ''Cheating the farmers has ceased to be a joke in this town, Mike.''

''It certainly has,'' Klaine agreed cheerfully. ''I intend to do an editorial on the subject next week.''

Chance gave him a skeptical look. ''I suppose you're going to criticize the mayor for allowing all these land frauds to continue.''

Klaine grinned. ''Of course not. I'm going to blame it all on some unnamed but unsavory characters who should be run out of town on a rail.''

''You won't fool anybody,'' Chance pointed out.

''No, but I'll sell a lot of papers. Everybody will want to read what I've said firsthand so they can call me a hypocrite and argue against me.''

''Chance, you're not turning into one of those reformers, are you?'' Mayor Kelley scoffed. ''Has Folger made a convert out of you?''

Chance should have felt annoyance at the charge. He'd cultivated his image as rebel against the so-called respectable element for a long time, but now, looking around the table at the men who made up the leadership of the gang that ran Dodge City, he realized he no longer relished being part of this unsavory group. ''I've always been against crooked gamblers and con men. They give the town a bad name and keep settlers away.''

Attorney Sutton made a rude noise. ''Who needs settlers anyway? They don't have any money to spend, and they're always trying to shut down the saloons.''

''They might succeed if the Kelley administration doesn't clean up the town a little. Dan Frost has been giving all of you hell in his paper for not prosecuting the confidence men,'' Chance reminded them, referring to the editor of the reformers' publication. ''They're planning to run somebody against Masterson for sheriff in the fall, and they won't stand for the kind of shenanigans you used to get Dog reelected this spring."

Kelley chuckled. "Let them try. We know how to get out the vote, don't we, boys?"

"That's just the kind of thing I'm talking about, Dog. The farmers will only stand for so much graft and corruption before they rebel. Fred Zimmerman already has the Germans stirred up." Zimmerman was one of the original residents of Dodge and owned the hardware store.

The mayor shook his head. "We'll take care of the settlers, don't you worry. We've already decided to build a new school in town, a nice big brick one, and we'll remind everybody the Texans' fines paid for it. That'll make everybody happy."

"Besides," Mike Sutton added, "we might not have to worry about the farmers at all if it doesn't rain soon. This is the driest spring anyone can remember, and one lost crop will wipe out most of the sodbusters. Then we won't have any opposition. We can run the town just the way we like it."

"Some of us would like it a little less corrupt," Chance remarked acerbically.

"All right, Chance, I'll speak to the boys about keeping things more undercover," Kelley said placatingly. "I swear to God, I think Folger's got to you."

"He's just feeling the weight of his new responsibilities," Sutton theorized with an understanding grin. "He's starting to worry about making Dodge safe for respectable ladies."

Chance shot Sutton a warning look. No gentleman would mention a lady's name in a saloon, and he certainly did not want to discuss Elizabeth with these men. Still, the charge struck a nerve. Before Elizabeth's sudden appearance in his life, he had never given a thought to the crime in Dodge City unless it directly affected his business. And since when had he cared about what happened to the settlers? Since meeting Barbara Jenks, he admitted reluctantly.

"Speaking of Folger," Kelley said, discreetly changing the subject, "Shilling came bellyaching to me a couple of days ago. Seems Folger kidnapped a couple of his girls."

"No!"

"What in the hell for?"

"I don't have any idea," Kelley admitted. "Shilling thinks Folger is a front man for some other brothel."

"That's ridiculous," Chance said.

"I know, but don't it sound peculiar? What would Folger be doing with a couple of whores?"

"What any man would do," Sutton suggested.

"Not Folger," Chance contradicted. "He's straight."

"Then he's probably going to make temperance workers out of them," Klaine said, drawing a raucous laugh. "Whose deal is it?"

Much later, when his fellow poker players and most of the other customers had gone and Chance had retired to his rooms, he reconsidered his new attitude. He supposed he was a convert, all right, but no preacher had reformed him. He pictured Elizabeth's lovely face and sighed with self-loathing at his own weakness.

He'd worked long and hard to cauterize what was left of his conscience, but in a few short weeks Elizabeth Livingston had resurrected it to pulsing, throbbing life. If he wasn't careful, he'd be closing down his saloon and urging grown men to drink buttermilk. Smiling at the thought, he prepared for bed.

He didn't think he'd been asleep long when the most god-awful pounding woke him. At first he thought it was some noise from the street, but gradually he came to realize it was coming from his outside door. Slowly, groggily, he pushed himself out of bed, unpleasantly surprised to discover it was broad daylight, and groped for the trousers he had discarded the night before.

He was still buttoning them when he reached the door. "What the hell do you want?" he demanded as he threw the door open.

"Just a moment of your time," Summer Winters informed him sweetly, giving his bare chest a provocative glance. She was wearing a respectable navy blue dress and matching hat, and looked as if she were on her way to a church social. The sedate ensemble warned him she was up to something.

"Come back later," he said, in no mood to play her games.

He had almost shut the door when she called, "It's about your precious Elizabeth."

The door flew open again. "What about her?" he asked suspiciously.

"I'm sorry to bother you so early, but I thought you'd want to know: your ward has opened a brothel, and she's over on the South Side right now recruiting whores for it."

Chance scowled. "If this is your idea of a joke, you picked a bad time to pull it."

"I wish it *was* a joke, darling boy, but at this very moment Miss Elizabeth Livingston is standing outside my house trying to entice my girls into working for her. I think you should go and stop her."

Chance ran a hand wearily over his face. If only he could be sure this was a bad dream, then he could slam the door on Summer and go back to bed. Unfortunately, he had the sinking feeling he was wide awake and that he was going to have to go across the tracks and prove Summer's ridiculous charge wrong.

"I'll be happy to wait while you get dressed, sweetheart." Her smile became a smirk as she gave his bare chest another leering glance and sidled past him into the room.

"Have a seat," he offered sarcastically. "I won't be long."

"Oh, do hurry! Your Elizabeth is putting on quite a show, and you won't want to miss any of it," she called as he shut the bedroom door behind him.

Chance would have preferred having time to bathe and shave, but he consoled himself with the knowledge that

Summer was probably leading him on a wild goose chase. Elizabeth couldn't possibly be putting on anything even remotely resembling a show on the South Side, and he would have staked his immortal soul she wasn't over there recruiting prostitutes either.

Not bothering with a tie or collar, he was still pulling on his suit coat as he left the bedroom. "Let's get this over with," he said, resigned.

Summer practically had to run to keep up with his purposeful strides. Luckily the traffic was light, because he seemed oblivious to the oncoming vehicles. Dodging past them, Summer followed in his wake across the broad Front Street plaza and the railroad tracks, and on down First Avenue.

At first Chance didn't connect the raised voices with his mission to locate Elizabeth. The two seemed incompatible, but the closer he got to Summer's house, the stronger his impression that there must be some sort of relationship became. When he turned the corner onto Summer's street, he stopped dead, unable to believe what he was seeing.

"Folger! I should have known!" he muttered.

In the middle of the street was a spring wagon. The Reverend Elijah Folger stood on its bed, preaching repentance at the top of his considerable voice and urging all the lost lambs—or in this case, ewes—to come back to the fold.

"Harlotry is a profession older than preaching!" he was saying. "I'm not here to point a finger at you and condemn you for your weakness. Those who keep you here are the true sinners. But you can rise above your circumstances like Rahab the harlot and like the woman taken in adultery whom we read about in the Good Book. Those women were sinners, too, but God forgave them. 'Go and sin no more!' the Lord told them, and they obeyed. Come out of your den of iniquity. Go and sin no more!"

"Tell 'em, preacher!" a cowboy yelled. A small group of inebriated Texans had assembled from the various dives lining the street. They all started shouting encouragement.

"That's right! Tell 'em to come out! Don't the Good Book say it's more blessed to give than to receive? Come on out, girls, and give me some!"

" 'God loveth a cheerful giver,' " another one quoted. "I'll sure love you if you spend some time with me."

Chance didn't pay much attention to what any of them were saying. He was far more interested in the slender, dark-haired female sitting on the wagon seat beside the good reverend's wife.

Elizabeth was clad in a sedate navy blue dress almost identical in design to Summer's. Her gloved hands were holding a ruffled parasol over her head and her eyes were fixed on some distant point, as if she wished herself any place but here. What in hell was Elizabeth thinking of, displaying herself on the South Side like some two-bit hooker?

"See? What did I tell you?" Summer inquired smugly.

Chance turned to her in exasperation. "It looks to me like she's helping Folger save souls. That's *not* what you told me."

Summer stood her ground. "Can't you see what they're doing? Folger's telling the girls to leave and go stay at *her* house."

Chance turned back to Folger and forced himself to listen.

"We know you're afraid, and you have a right to be. The very hounds of hell would pursue you were you to attempt escape. Where could you go? Where could you hide? *I'll tell you where!*" Folger's voice shook the windowpanes and startled the cowboys into silence. "God has sent a deliverer! She has come to us a wayfarer and a stranger, but she offers you her home and her heart. Any woman who seeks to escape from this life of shame and degradation can come, penniless and forsaken, and find a refuge and a sanctuary. Miss Elizabeth Livingston offers it freely, willingly, gladly, accepting God's promise that 'Inasmuch as ye have done it unto one of the least of these my brethren, ye have done it unto me.' "

Chance stared, incredulous.

"It's the best racket I ever heard of," Summer said indignantly. "They skim off all the best girls in town and set them up in style over on the North Side—"

"Summer!" Chance's warning silenced her, but only for a second.

"You don't believe all that nonsense about wanting to help the girls, do you? Nobody takes in a bunch of hookers out of the goodness of their hearts."

Nobody, Chance realized, except someone as naïve as Elizabeth who had come under the influence of a fanatic like Folger. Well, Chance wasn't going to allow anyone to take advantage of her innocence. He would put a stop to this right now.

Elizabeth glanced over at the house again. She could see faces looking out the windows—pale, curious, sleepy faces. Perhaps it had been a bad idea to come so early in the morning. Mavis had warned them the girls wouldn't be thrilled about being rousted out of bed when they'd been up half the night, but Reverend Folger had pointed out that they would not be busy doing anything else at this hour either. At any rate, none of the women had made a move to take Reverend Folger up on Elizabeth's offer, although the reverend was promising them safe passage and protection from retribution.

"Elizabeth!"

She almost jumped off the wagon seat. Her heart made a painful lurch in her chest, and she jerked around to see Chance striding toward her in a menacing manner.

Reverend Folger stopped in midsentence. "Chance, it's good to see you—"

"Shut up, Folger. I'll deal with you later. Elizabeth, just what in hell do you think you're doing on this side of the tracks?"

Mrs. Folger gasped. Elizabeth stared down at Chance, willing her heart to stop pounding. She certainly had nothing to be afraid of. Never mind that she had never seen his face quite so white nor his eyes quite so black. What could he possibly do to her, after all? "I'm helping Reverend Folger."

"We're doing the Lord's work," Mrs. Folger offered, but Chance silenced her with a look.

"No lady does *anybody's* work on the South Side of Dodge City," Chance informed them. "I want you to get down from there right now, Elizabeth. Mrs. Folger can do what she wants, but I'm taking *you* home."

"Really, Chance," she protested, painfully aware of the small but exceedingly interested crowd observing their exchange. "This is none of your concern."

"That's where you're wrong," he said, reaching for her. She started to resist, but instantly saw she would only create a bigger show and surrendered to the inevitable. He swung her effortlessly to the ground amid cheers from the drunken cowboys.

The moment her feet touched the ground, she wrenched out of his grasp. Straightening her dress and adjusting her parasol, she raised her chin haughtily. "I have no intention of leaving until our work is finished."

Something flickered in his eyes, something primal and frightening, but she willed herself not to flinch. His hands closed into fists, and his nostrils flared as he drew in what she hoped was a calming breath. Only then did she notice how different he looked—the unshaved whiskers, the collarless shirt, the mussed hair. This was not the dapper, mannerly Chance Fitzwilliam she was used to. She knew he normally didn't arise until noon or later, and it was now only a little after nine o'clock. From the looks of him, he'd had little sleep the night before.

Instinct told her she would be a fool to challenge him head-on when he was in this mood. Immediately she changed tactics, managing a placating smile and a beseeching tone. "Please, Chance, you're making a scene—"

"No, *you're* making a scene by coming down here with this lunatic." Chance made a contemptuous gesture at Folger, who uttered an indignant protest. "I am going to put an end to the scene by taking you back where you belong. Now, will you come along quietly or not, because if you won't, I'm perfectly willing to throw you over my shoulder and carry you home!''

Elizabeth gasped in outrage. As strongly as she wanted to defy him, to tell him exactly what she thought of his brutish threats, the truth was she believed him capable of doing just as he had threatened. The very idea of being so publicly humiliated horrified her.

Having no alternative, she drew herself up to her full height and gave him her most imperious look. ''Very well, Cousin Chauncey. I will allow you to escort me back to my home.'' She lifted her gaze to a distressed Reverend and Mrs. Folger. ''Please forgive me, Reverend.''

''Of course, Miss Elizabeth. I understand your guardian's concern . . .'' The preacher's powerful voice trailed off under Chance's glare.

Chance turned back to Elizabeth. ''Shall we go?'' He made a mocking bow and offered her his arm.

She turned up her nose and marched past him, heading north. He quickly caught up and took possession of her elbow in a grip she didn't try to break.

Elizabeth did not notice the blond woman standing off to one side until they had almost passed her. ''Good luck, honey,'' the woman said. ''His bite is even worse than his bark.''

Elizabeth stared at the woman, amazed at her audacity, but the amazement became something else entirely when Chance muttered, ''Shut up, Summer.''

Summer. This was the infamous Summer Winters, the person responsible for Elizabeth's journey to Dodge City. Unfortunately, Elizabeth got no more than a fleeting impression before Chance dragged her inexorably on.

The journey to Front Street seemed inordinately long to Elizabeth. Several times she stumbled, trying to keep up the pace Chance set. At first he didn't appear to notice her difficulty, but when she inquired, ''Are we in a foot race?'' he slowed down.

At last they crossed the tracks and headed back into the respectable part of town. Elizabeth hoped he would leave her there to make her own way home, but his grip on her arm tightened as he proceeded down the north end of First Avenue toward her street.

"Chance, I know I made a mistake," she said in an attempt to placate him. "I should never have gone over there, but it seemed like the right thing—"

"Shut up, Elizabeth," he said through gritted teeth. "I have a thing or two to tell you, but I don't want to do it out in the middle of the street, so don't tempt me."

Biting back her own outrage, she followed him dumbly until at last they reached her house. He didn't bother to knock. The front door wasn't locked.

"Chance, let me explain," Elizabeth began when they were inside, but he gave no sign of having heard her. The eyes that glared down at her expressed far more anger than she would have expected over a social indiscretion, and she felt a small shudder of alarm. "Barbara!" she tried. Barbara would help her calm him down.

"Mrs. Jenks went looking for you . . ." Molly began, poking her head out of the front parlor doorway, but her words died in a strangled sound when she saw Chance's expression. "Mavis went with her," she croaked, her eyes like saucers.

"Who are you?" Chance demanded.

"M-M-Molly," she managed, and then without another word frantically slid the parlor doors shut between them.

Chance glared down down at Elizabeth. "A friend of yours from Philadelphia?" he mocked.

"Chance, listen to me," she began, but he didn't hear. He was looking around as if he'd lost something.

Chance was searching for a quiet place where he could talk to Elizabeth without interruption. His glance strayed to the stairway and inspiration struck.

"Chance! Where are you going? Stop this instant!" Elizabeth's cries were useless. He was going up the stairs, and because he hadn't released his deadly grip on her arm, she was going with him.

The next thing she knew, they were in her bedroom. Chance maneuvered her in ahead of him and slammed the door.

"This is highly improper," she informed him, wrenching from his grasp and rubbing her numb elbow.

"You lied to me!" The words were hardly out of his mouth before he realized they were the true reason for his unreasonable fury. Elizabeth, the one woman he had begun to believe was different from all the others, had deceived him.

"I did not lie to you," she denied, appalled he would accuse her of such a thing.

His fine mouth twisted in savage mockery. "Oh, no?" he challenged, slipping into a falsetto imitation of her voice. "Oh, Cousin Chauncey, I need a big house so I can live in the style to which I'm accustomed. Oh, Cousin Chauncey, I need all these bedrooms so my friends can come to visit me."

Elizabeth bit her lip, speechless. He was right, she *had* lied to him, and some sixth sense told her the lies were what had enraged him, not her ill-advised trip to the South Side.

"I'm sorry, Chance. I didn't want to lie to you, but I was afraid you wouldn't let me have the money if you knew."

"You're damn right I wouldn't! And just what did you think you were going to do, empty out all the brothels on the South Side?" He crossed his arms in silent challenge, and his eyes glittered like shards of glass.

Elizabeth winced but stood her ground. "Ideally," she admitted.

"Ideally! Do you have any idea how many women there are over on the South Side?"

"Reverend Folger estimates around one hundred."

Chance snorted derisively. "Probably closer to two hundred. Did you think they'd all just fall in line behind your wagon and follow you back here?''

Elizabeth bristled at his sarcasm. He had no right to make fun of her efforts. "Of course not. We know it's going to be difficult—''

"How many do you have here now?''

"Two, but we haven't really started—''

"I can't believe how naïve you are! If you'll excuse my candor, I've had much more experience with ladies of the evening than either you or your Reverend Folger, and I've never heard one of them so much as hint about wanting to be rescued. You can't save people who don't want to be saved.''

Elizabeth's cheeks heated at his reference to his experience with ladies of the evening, but she didn't take the time to decide whether it was embarrassment or jealousy that caused her reaction. She lifted her chin stubbornly. "Even if we only find one or two, it will be worth it.''

"Oh, Lizzie,'' he said as all his anger boiled down into what felt like despair. He tried to tell himself he was only exasperated by her harebrained scheme and hard-headed stubbornness, but he knew he was lying to himself. The truth was far worse. He had begun to believe in her, no matter how tenuously and briefly, and she had crushed his belief. She was like all the others. The pain was like a knife thrust to his heart. "I thought I could trust you.''

Elizabeth heard the accusation in his words and for one fleeting instant glimpsed the same agony she had seen when he had spoken of his lost brother. Her own heart ached in response. "Oh, Chance, I'm sorry.''

She went to him as she had before, the urge to give comfort irresistible. But this time when she slipped her arms around his rigid body, she realized why the urge was so compelling: she loved him.

She loved him. The knowledge stunned her. Had she thought her heart raced because of the challenge of taming a rogue? Had she thought her nerves tingled because of the risk of angering him? And what would she do now? Loving him was the greatest risk of all.

And the greatest thrill.

Her hands found his face, tentatively touching his whisker-roughened cheeks. "You can trust me," she whispered. "I promise I'll never lie to you again." And she wouldn't, not if her life depended on it.

He tried to resist her touch. He'd heard such promises before without believing them. Why did he want so badly to believe them from this woman? Reason struggled with desire as he inhaled the fresh fragrance of her hair and stared into the emerald pools of her eyes, brimming with tearful repentance. Her cheeks were pink, flushed with emotion. Her breasts rose and fell unsteadily beneath her dress, and he almost imagined he could see the delicate fabric trembling with her heartbeats.

Without conscious thought, he reached for her. He wanted her, *needed* her, close enough to touch her and taste her and block out all the doubts.

His kiss was rough and demanding, almost desperate. Elizabeth responded willingly, glad to show him how much she loved him. His hands were urgent as he folded her into the cradle of his arm. Her arms went around him, up and under his coat, grasping and clinging and caressing. She felt the latent power of him and knew a primitive urge to release it. Opening her lips to him, she met his tongue with her own. He responded with a groan from deep in his chest.

He pulled her closer, flattening her breasts against him until she could feel his heart thundering along with hers. The blood sang in her ears, siren songs of sweet yearnings, haunting melodies of promised pleasures. The kiss went on and on, his lips ravenous, while his fingers stroked her, finding sensitive places and stirring new rhapsodies.

He lifted her high against his heart, and then she felt the bed beneath her, cushioning his weight as he bore down on her. She took him gladly, wishing she could absorb him into herself and keep him there forever. His mouth continued to devour hers, and his hands found new places to touch, places up under her skirt. The cadence of the music quickened, speeding heart and breath until the song in her head became a symphony.

Chance knew he should stop. This was wrong, so wrong, even for a man as inured to wrong as he was. He *would* stop, too, in just a moment. One more kiss, one more caress, and then he would have had enough. Except one more was not enough. She *was* different. She *wasn't* like the others: She would be his, completely his.

He couldn't stop. Kiss led to kiss, touch led to touch. The compulsion to possess her welled up anew, strangling out reason, choking out honor, and leaving only desire.

The dull sound of tearing silk jarred her as he tore away her pantalets. It was a discord in the melody, but then he touched her where she was hot and aching for him. The momentary break became a counterpoint for a brand new song. The cadence quickened again, catching her up in the racing, throbbing, pulsing beat.

When she was lost in it, he left her for a moment to loosen his own clothes. His voice came to her as part of the tune, whispering endearments, promising fulfillment, and then he was back. He touched her again with heat and strength, pushing and prodding until she opened to him.

The pain was swift and sharp, making her cry out, and the music ceased abruptly. Her eyes flew open, and she saw the haze of passion had lifted from his face, leaving only surprise and a strange regret.

Chance stared down at her in disbelief. What was he doing? Her cry had broken through to him, awakening him to the mad reality of his deed. He groaned in renewed despair. "Oh, Lizzie, I'm so sorry."

His voice was like warm honey pouring over her. The sweetness pooled in her loins, soothing the hurt. His eyes were close and dark, the pupils like ink spots on ebony. Beneath his regret she saw desire still smoldering, and the honey turned to fire inside her.

He was going to leave her. She could see it on his face

as he began to pull away, but she couldn't let him go, not yet. "Chance!" The word was half plea, half command, and he resisted both.

Her arms tightened around him, pulling him back. He came, reluctantly at first, and with him came the first tentative, lilting notes of the song again. Her lips brushed his, and the music swelled. This time his touch was coaxing, like gentle strumming, and once again the cadence quickened, faster and faster. The notes swirled inside of her, silent and compelling, building and building until the final, crashing crescendo overwhelmed her.

Elizabeth lay still for a long time, keeping her mind blank while the aftershocks echoed like grace notes. Her first hint that everything might not be perfectly, gloriously right was when Chance stirred and rolled away from her.

He thoughtfully drew her skirts down, but he refused to meet her gaze. He turned slightly away while he adjusted his own clothing, and when he finished, he did not turn back. The stiff set of his shoulders and the harsh way his breath rasped in his throat told her something was very, very wrong. The song in her heart slowed like a music box running down, dragging into a dirge.

Chance could hardly think. What in God's name had possessed him? Bitterly, he admitted God had had nothing to do with it. No, the demons that still haunted him from his childhood had driven him. For a moment possessing Elizabeth had seemed the perfect way to exorcise them forever, but it had been the devil's own lie. Instead of redeeming himself, he had corrupted her, too. He had destroyed in her the very innocence he had wanted so desperately to protect.

Now, ironically, the only way he could hope to make amends was to compound the outrage by offering to marry her. But how could he do such a thing to her? He knew he could never again live among the pharisees known as society who used their money to cover the evil they perpetrated on others. But neither could he ask her to leave the only kind of life she knew and share an existence he had deliberately stripped bare of meaning and importance.

"Chance?" Elizabeth tentatively touched his shoulder. She sensed his emotional withdrawal even before he turned back to face her, and she saw the shuttered look in his eyes. The lingering warmth from their lovemaking evaporated, leaving her chilled.

"Are you all right? Did I hurt you?" he asked, his voice husky.

"I . . . no, I'm fine," she assured him, uncertain whether the statement was true or not. Physically, she was only a little sore, but emotionally, she wasn't sure.

Chance pushed himself up against the headboard to a half-sitting position. "Lizzie, this was a terrible mistake," he began, uncertain exactly what to say.

Elizabeth hadn't thought she was making a mistake at the time, but she was beginning to change her mind.

Chance looked down into her eyes, but he couldn't stand to see the wary hurt reflected there. "I suppose you're expecting a proposal of marriage."

All her doubts coalesced into a cold knot of fear. "I'm not expecting anything. I've never been in this situation before," she reminded him, managing a semblance of her former dignity as she struggled up beside him.

He flinched at the reminder of what he had taken from her, but he could not let guilt tempt him to a greater wrong. "I'm not the kind of man a woman like you marries, Lizzie."

The knot of fear tightened. "Shouldn't that be my decision?"

His eyes were bleak. "I don't think so, especially after what just happened. You probably imagine you're in love with me, don't you?"

She wanted to tell him she *was* in love with him, but somehow she knew he wouldn't believe her.

"Yes, you do," he said, not waiting for her answer. "I can see it in your eyes, but it isn't real, Lizzie. You have to tell yourself you love me, or you couldn't justify making love with me.''

She shook her head in mute denial, unable to force the words of protest past her constricted throat. Fear was choking her now, blurring her vision and strangling her breath.

''Oh, God, don't cry! Please, Lizzie, don't!''

She didn't even know she was crying until he said the words, and by then it was too late. She wanted to run away, to hide her shame, but his arms slipped around her, tenderly this time. He drew her close, cradling her to his chest. His heart thundered in an uncertain rhythm beneath her ear, telling her of his own torment, but it was small comfort.

''Lizzie, don't cry. You've got to understand. Women like you don't marry men like me. You want a husband who'll be home for supper every night, who'll take you to church on Sunday and invite the preacher home for dinner. You want a man to raise a family with. Do you know what your life would be like with me, living over a saloon?''

''We don't have to live over the saloon. I have money,'' she argued, her words muffled against his chest.

''I don't want your money. I can't live in your world, where men lie and cheat and steal and kill, and no one cares so long as they maintain appearances. I turned my back on all that a long time ago, and I won't go back, not for you or anyone else. And I won't drag you into my world, Lizzie. You don't belong there, and you certainly don't deserve it.''

She didn't want to hear this. Every word was like a dagger in her heart. ''Stop it!'' she cried, pulling slightly away and clutching at his lapels in a desperate attempt to make him listen. ''We can work this out. There must be a way. I love you, Chance, and you love me. I know you do. You just proved it.''

''No! You're confusing love and lust, Lizzie. You think you love me because I'm the first man who ever made you feel like a woman, but that's not enough reason to throw your life away. The excitement of sex wears off much too quickly, and then you'd hate me.''

"I'll never hate you, Chance. I love you. I really do! You must believe me!''

But he couldn't let it be true. Gently but firmly, he pried her fingers loose and pushed her away from him, holding her hands tightly lest she reach for him again. "Listen to me, Lizzie. I'm the man who was charged with protecting you. I'm also the man who just seduced you, who took your virginity without a thought in the world. By God, if I don't do anything else right as your guardian, I'll keep you from marrying a bastard like me. I can't change what I did to you, but I can prevent you from making it worse.''

"Chance, wait." But she was too late. He was off the bed and heading for the door. "Chance, I love you.''

He stopped and turned slowly back to face her, his hand still on the doorknob. "You're going to be sorry you said that, Lizzie, so I'll do the kindest thing I can and forget I ever heard it.''

Quickly, before he had time to change his mind, he opened the door. Leaving her was like tearing out his heart. The pain literally took his breath, but he did not stop, and he did not look back.

Until the door clicked shut behind him, Elizabeth held out a feeble hope that Chance would change his mind and take back all the horrible things he'd said. The sound of the latch closing was like a gunshot penetrating her very soul.

Chapter 5

Alone now, she surrendered to the tears. They flooded down her cheeks as if they could wash away her pain. Then came the wrenching sobs. She buried her face in her pillow, ashamed for anyone to hear her anguish and terrified someone might guess her folly.

She'd been crying for a long time when she heard the knocking. She ignored it, hoping whoever was there would go away, but at last the door opened. "Honey, what is it? What's the matter?" Barbara's voice was full of concern. Elizabeth did not know if she could bear Barbara's pity.

Elizabeth lifted her face from the pillow and squinted at her friend through swollen eyes. She could see Molly and Mavis hovering in the doorway behind her.

At the sight of Elizabeth's face, Barbara hurried forward. "That pig! Did he hurt you?"

Elizabeth shook her head, still unable to speak.

Barbara sat down on the bed and gathered Elizabeth in her arms. "This is all my fault. I should never have let you go with Reverend Folger in the first place. After you left, Mavis convinced me I was right, and we went after you, but when we got there, the Folgers said Mr. Fitzwilliam had taken you home. I never thought, I never *dreamed*, you were in any danger. He's your guardian, after all, and he's always been such a gentleman."

"We didn't think there was any rush to get back here," Mavis continued, equally distraught. "We was just relieved he'd brought you back home where you belong."

Elizabeth wanted to absolve them of blame, but the words came out as another sob. Barbara hugged her more tightly. "I'll never forgive myself for not being here when you needed me."

Mavis made an impatient sound. "You said the same thing when she took off for the South Side. You said you'd never forgive yourself if anything happened to her, so we went after her. We went where we thought the danger was."

"Who would've ever guessed?" she said in despair. "He seemed so nice, but he's no better than an animal. We'll get the law on him, that's what we'll do. Hanging's too good for him."

Elizabeth had heard Chance vilified enough. She was angry with him, too, but beating some sense into him was more what she had in mind. She certainly didn't want to see him hanged.

"Barbara," she managed, straightening from her friend's grasp and clearing the tears from her voice, "it wasn't what you think."

"You mean he didn't . . . ? Oh, thank God!"

Hardly knowing how to explain, Elizabeth shot Mavis a silent plea for understanding.

Mavis registered mild surprise and nodded her comprehension. "Oh, I think he did, Mrs. Jenks, but I don't think he *raped* her. Am I right, Miss Livingston?"

Rape—an ugly word for an ugly deed. What had happened to Elizabeth had been awful, too, but it had not been rape. "Nothing happened that I didn't invite."

"Elizabeth?" Barbara's face was a mask of confusion, her eyes full of questions Elizabeth did not want to answer.

"I really don't want to talk about it," Elizabeth whispered as fresh tears filled her eyes. How could she explain she had given herself in love to a man who had rejected her?

"But you can't let him get away with it," Barbara insisted. "If he committed a crime—"

"You heard what she said, " Mavis interrupted. "He didn't force her."

"But why didn't you call for help, honey? Molly was here. She would've come."

Barbara turned to Molly, who stiffened in fright. "I would've for sure, only she didn't call," Molly insisted. "I snuck up the steps behind them, and I heard them arguing. He was saying how stupid she was for letting whores stay at her house, and she was saying he was wrong. I would've gone in, except then they got real quiet. I mean . . ." She looked around in silent appeal. "I didn't think it was my place to go busting in, and Miss Livingston didn't holler or anything."

"Don't blame yourself, Molly," Elizabeth said. "This wasn't your fault any more than it was Barbara's. You were right not to come in. I wouldn't have welcomed an intrusion." The admission cost her, humiliating as it was, but Barbara refused to accept her assurances.

"Then why are you crying like he broke your heart?"

Determined to prove Barbara wrong, Elizabeth hastily found the hankie she had concealed in one of her pockets and proceeded to blow her nose. "My heart isn't broken," she lied, trying to regain some of her lost dignity.

Mavis frowned skeptically. "Then why ain't he still here? Or did you two already set the wedding date, and these are tears of happiness?"

Elizabeth's cheeks went hot, but she met Mavis's gaze squarely. "No, he didn't propose. He said . . ." She faltered.

"Let me guess," Mavis offered. "He said he's not the marrying kind, but he offered to set you up as his mistress."

"No!" Elizabeth denied in outrage. "He said he wasn't good enough for me. He said if I married him, I'd ruin my life."

Her three companions stared at her in surprise. "That's a new one," Mavis muttered.

Barbara took Elizabeth's hands in a gentle grasp. "Honey, men will say anything in that situation."

"But he really meant it," Elizabeth insisted, knowing she must make them understand. "He really believes I can't possibly love him. He says I only *think* I do because . . . because of what happened, but it isn't true. I loved him before, and I . . . guess I still do."

"Oh, dear," Barbara murmured in dismay.

"Maybe you'd better let me handle this, Mrs. Jenks," Mavis advised, taking a seat on the other side of the bed from where Barbara sat. "Look, Miss Livingston, you ain't the first woman this ever happened to. You think you care for a man, you think he's the best thing to walk around on two feet, and you let him have his way. Then you find out he wasn't thinking happily ever after, the way you were. Maybe Mr. Fitzwilliam was lying about his reasons and maybe he wasn't, I can't judge. But the way I see it, you've got two choices: either you can wipe the slate clean and forget all about him, or else you can set out to make him sorry he threw you over."

"There's a third choice, of course," Barbara added, catching the spirit of Mavis's argument. "You can lock yourself in this room and cry your eyes out, but somehow I think you have too much spirit for that."

"You're right, Barbara. I've shed all the tears I'm going to." Elizabeth wiped her nose once more and turned to Mavis. "You probably think I should forget all about him."

Mavis shrugged. "I haven't known many men worth the powder it'd take to blow their brains out. When he said he wasn't good enough for you, he was probably right."

"I don't know. I'm so confused. When he said he wouldn't marry me because he would ruin my life, I had the oddest feeling he was telling the truth, or at least he believed he was. He sincerely thought he was doing the best thing by leaving me."

Barbara exchanged a perplexed look with Mavis. "He is a saloonkeeper," she tried. "Not exactly the kind of man your father would have approved of as a husband for you."

"Or as a *guardian* for me, either. But he *is* a responsible guardian, a *perfect* guardian," Elizabeth pointed out bitterly. "He said if he didn't do anything else, he would protect me from marrying a man like himself."

"Then he's a better guardian than he is a man," Mavis said.

Elizabeth sighed. "That's just it. By refusing to drag me down to his level, he proved he's really an honorable man."

Mavis and Barbara and even Molly were unconvinced, but they were not willing to disagree, either.

"Are you thinking about trying to make him change his mind about throwing you over?" Mavis asked with disapproval.

Elizabeth looked at the other women in dismay. "I know I shouldn't. I know I should hate him, and part of me does, but another part . . ."

"You really do think you're in love with him, don't you?" Mavis accused.

"Unfortunately, I *know* I'm in love with him, although at this moment I'd like to break a brickbat over his thick skull."

"Sounds like a good idea to me," Mavis said.

"We aren't going to let you make a fool of yourself over him," Barbara warned, once again assuming her authority as Elizabeth's chaperone.

"I have no intention of throwing myself at him," Elizabeth assured them. "I just can't stand the thought of . . ." She made a beseeching gesture, unable to think of the words to express her despair.

"She don't want to give up hope," Molly interpreted to the others. "She can't stand the thought that she let him have his way if he didn't care about her."

"Yes, that's it, Molly," Elizabeth said gratefully. "If I was wrong about him . . ." She hugged herself and shuddered.

"There, there, don't think about it now," Barbara urged. "Wait a few days until the shock's worn off. Things'll be clearer to you then."

"Barbara's right," Mavis said. "No use getting all worked up. We'll take care of you, and when you're feeling better, we'll talk again."

Elizabeth's eyes misted as she watched her other two friends nod their agreement.

Friends. The truth of the word registered unexpectedly. Barbara was her friend, of course. She had passed the stage of paid companion weeks ago, but what about Mavis and Molly? They'd come to her house as strangers, unknown people to whom Elizabeth had decided to extend a helping hand. How naïve she had been then. Somehow she had never imagined getting to know the women she had set out to help, much less growing to care about them.

Neither had she expected them to care about her in return, yet somehow they did. Mavis and Molly had just proven their concern, offering it without judging her or making her feel like a fool for having surrendered to Chance Fitzwilliam. Yes, she realized, Mavis and Molly were her friends, too.

Elizabeth's conscience pricked her. Had she treated them with the same understanding? Oh, she had been polite enough, but she had never accepted them as equals. She had maintained a distance, as befitted her station in life compared to theirs. How unfair she had been, both to them and to herself. She turned back to Mavis and squeezed her hand. "Thank you for being my friend."

Mavis's expression was almost comic, but she recovered quickly, resuming her usual brusqueness. "Well, now that's settled, I'd bet my bustle Miss Livingston would like to soak in a nice hot bath," she said, rising to her feet.

"Yes, I would," Elizabeth admitted, flushing when she remembered exactly why certain parts of her body needed soaking. But the other women pretended not to notice her embarrassment, endearing themselves to her even more. They quickly dispersed to procure hot water and a tub.

When all the preparations were made, Barbara and Molly filed out of the room, but Mavis hung back, waiting until the others were out of earshot before coming back to Elizabeth.

"There's one more thing. Maybe you haven't thought of it yet, but you probably will soon, and I don't want you worrying about it. There really ain't much chance you caught yourself a baby."

Elizabeth gasped as she thought of this new complication and all it might mean.

"Now stop fretting," Mavis scolded. "I told you not to. Getting a baby ain't as easy as the preachers want us all to think. Look at poor Barbara, married all those years and nothing to show for it. Then there's me and Molly. We been busier than any married woman, and we ain't never got one, either." She patted Elizabeth's arm reassuringly. "Anyway, you let me know if your next monthly is late. I've got some medicine will fix everything."

"I wouldn't want to do anything to . . . to harm it," Elizabeth protested, knowing she could never hurt her own child.

Mavis smiled with understanding and patted her arm again. "You let me know anyway, you hear?"

Elizabeth nodded numbly, and Mavis left her. She stared down at herself for a long moment, imagining her stomach swollen with child and wondering what on earth she would do in such a case. But Mavis had said the possibility was remote, and surely she should know. Elizabeth shook herself, consciously pushing all the fears from her mind. *The possibility was remote,* she told herself sternly. Like Mavis had said, there was no use in worrying about it, at least not yet. She already had enough to occupy her mind. Resolutely, she began to strip for her bath.

Much later, when Elizabeth had bathed and changed, she ventured downstairs again. She had hidden the torn pantalets, embarrassed for anyone to know just how wanton she had been. She'd burn them at the first opportunity.

Barbara was serving up the noon meal when Elizabeth

entered the dining room a little later, and Mavis and Molly were already in their places. Elizabeth took her own seat, noting with a flash of embarrassment that someone had placed a cushion on her chair. More thoughtfulness from women to whom she had been thoughtlessly condescending. But she would remedy the situation immediately.

When Barbara had asked the blessing, they began to eat. After a few moments, Elizabeth said, "Mavis, what do you think would be the best way to get women to come here to stay?"

Mavis glanced up in surprise, and Elizabeth could guess what she was thinking. That morning, she and Reverend Folger had not sought Mavis's advice. Looking back, Elizabeth realized how foolish they'd been not to ask people who had already made the move about how to get others to make it, too.

"Are you sure you still want to do this? I mean, the trouble's only just starting."

"I want to do this," Elizabeth insisted. Looking back, she knew her original motives had been nothing more than a shallow need to do something worthwhile with her life. Now she realized only a fine line separated her from the women on the South Side. Mavis and Molly had reached across it to her, and Elizabeth wanted to return the favor if she possibly could.

Mavis read the determination on her face. "Well, if you're still set on it, I think the best way would be to send me and Molly out to talk to the girls. They ain't likely to believe you or even Reverend Folger, but they'd trust us. Anyway, it's worth a try."

Elizabeth thought so, too.

What she didn't think about until later in the day was the possibility Chance might spoil everything by cutting off her funds. He had certainly expressed his disapproval of her project and might well decide the quickest way to end her involvement was to make it financially impossible. If he decided to cut back her allowance—the generous amount she had requested hoping she would be supporting a houseful of people—then she would be forced to turn Molly, Mavis, and whoever else sought refuge with her back out on the street.

She expected any minute Chance would send word he was cutting her allotment and ordering her to dismiss her visitors, but after several days of silence, she began to realize that if he'd decided to reduce her allowance, he was not going to inform her of it. Although she hated to give him the idea in case he hadn't already thought of it himself, Elizabeth decided she would have to write and ask him what his plans were for her. She made her note as impersonal as possible, giving him no clue as to the current state of her emotions. If she was still pining for him, if the thought of seeing him again made her quiver, he need not know.

His reply was equally formal. "Dear Cousin Elizabeth," he wrote. "I will continue to provide you with the allowance previously agreed upon, but only if I have your solemn promise you will never again venture south of the railroad tracks, either alone or in company." He'd signed it simply "Chance."

"It won't be any hardship to stay away from the South Side," Barbara pointed out after Elizabeth had read the note aloud to her three housemates. "You've already decided you shouldn't go back anyway."

"He's being pretty nice about everything, too," Molly added. "He might've cut you off without a cent."

"He'd have some gall to do that," Mavis said. "He owes Elizabeth more than money after what he did."

Elizabeth stared down at the bold scrawl, and for a moment the letters blurred as tears clouded her eyes. She blinked them quickly away, unwilling to let the others see how much his rejection still hurt. Mavis was right, she reminded herself. Chance did owe her. His generosity might be nothing more than a feeble attempt to make amends, but she would not question his motives. She would even let him think his mandate kept her north of the railroad tracks.

The next day Molly and Mavis went over to the South Side, and Molly came back with a girl named Alice. She was a tall, awkward girl with dingy blond hair. Large blue eyes brightened her otherwise plain face, but her defensive expression robbed her of any other claim to attractiveness.

"I'm so happy you're here," Elizabeth said with genuine joy, taking both of Alice's hands and giving them a welcoming squeeze.

Alice looked at her as if she were demented. Then she seemed to sense Elizabeth's sincerity, and slowly her expression changed to surprise. "It's . . . nice to be here," she replied hesitantly.

"Please come in. We were just going to have some tea. Would you like some?" This time she entertained in the kitchen where they all sat informally around the table and talked while they sipped tea from mismatched, chipped cups Mrs. Harris had left. Alice barely spoke at first, but the others kept up a stream of friendly conversation.

After a few minutes, Alice, too, ventured to join in the talk. Skillfully, using all the social graces she had been taught, Elizabeth drew the girl out until she was chatting as freely as the others.

How different this was from the day she had met Molly and Mavis, Elizabeth reflected as the talk swirled around her. They had been formal and awkward with her for days. They hadn't really become her friends until after she and Chance had—

Elizabeth's heart convulsed in her chest. The thought of Chance and what he had done still caused her pain. But, she reminded herself sternly, she had at least one thing to thank him for. If he had never hurt her, she might never have realized what good friends women like Mavis and Molly and Alice could be.

Looking at them seated around her kitchen table, she remembered how only a week ago she would have judged them unworthy of her notice because of the turns their lives had taken. Now she truly understood the old saying, "There but for the grace of God go I."

Elizabeth noticed the conversation had turned to the topic of men, as it often did when the women in her house talked.

"I married young," Alice was saying. "I grew up poor, and I figured getting a husband would solve all my problems."

The others groaned sympathetically.

"Are you widowed?" Barbara asked.

Alice snorted. "I hope so. I'd sure like to think that son of a bitch was dead. He took off one day and left me with a sick baby and a pile of bills."

Mavis was shaking her head. "A woman sure takes a chance when she lets a man run her life."

Elizabeth listened in fascination as the others chimed in with horror stories about their own mothers or sisters who had chosen the wrong men. The tales were enough to make a woman swear off marriage forever, yet Elizabeth knew marriage was the only real option for most women unless they were independently wealthy or relied on the charity of relatives. Lacking such resources, as many women did, they must find some other means of keeping themselves, but jobs for females were scarce and those available were often in unpleasant and even unsafe factories.

Or in prostitution.

"If you think about it," Mavis was saying, "getting married ain't much different than whoring. I mean, you let a man bed you and in exchange he keeps you."

"There's more to marriage than that," Barbara argued. "There's love and companionship and sharing."

"If you're lucky," Alice corrected. "I reckon your man was some different from mine."

"And the trouble is, you never know which kind you've got until it's too late," Mavis said.

"I suppose you're right," Barbara mused, glancing at Elizabeth.

Elizabeth had no trouble interpreting her friend's thoughts. In fact, Mavis and Molly were giving her similar looks, warning her to be careful about entrusting her heart to Chance Fitzwilliam. Unfortunately, she had already done so.

Anxious to change the subject, she turned to Alice with a smile. "Would you like to see your new room now?"

Chance sat alone at a table near the rear of the Last Chance's main room. He was going through the motions of playing solitaire, but his mind was far away. He kept thinking back to the note he had received from Elizabeth the day before and wondering if he had done the right thing in continuing her allowance. Worrying about that distracted him from dwelling on what he had done to her. He'd already tortured himself enough wondering what effect such a traumatic experience would have on someone who had been as sheltered as she.

Guilt had compelled him to continue her allowance, of course. He had seduced an innocent young woman who had been entrusted to his care. Then he had refused her the protection of his name. What could have been more despicable?

His only consolation was remembering how much crueler it would be to sentence her to a life with him. Oh, he cared for her, no question, and he would treat her as well as he could, but Elizabeth deserved more than material comforts. She deserved a real husband, a man able to give her his whole heart. Once, Chance could have given her that kind of devotion, but love had betrayed him one time too often. Since then he had closed himself off from every tender feeling until now he sometimes wondered if he still possessed a heart.

Since making love to Elizabeth, he wondered all the more. Something very like his heart ached constantly, a torment he could only escape in sleep and then only because his dreams were full of her. There they were together and happy, but when he awoke with empty arms, the pain would start afresh, stronger than before. He cursed himself for his weakness and allowed guilt to overrule his common sense and permit her to continue her harebrained scheme to save the prostitutes of Dodge City.

In disgust he tossed down the card he held and swept the rest of them back up to be reshuffled.

"Can I buy you a drink, Chance?"

Chance looked up to find Daniel Frost, editor of *The Dodge City Globe*, standing over his table. Grateful for the distraction, Chance smiled a welcome. *"I'll buy you* one. Sit down, although I warn you, if you're looking for a good story, you've come to the wrong place."

Frost grinned as he took a seat. "So I see," he said, looking around at the quiet crowd. "I can't even report that you cheat at solitaire."

"Our games are honest here at the Last Chance," Chance reported with mock gravity as he stacked the cards and set them aside. He motioned to his swamper, Joey, to bring them a bottle and two glasses.

"An honest game is something to brag about in this town nowadays," Frost replied. Chance could see his solemnity was not feigned.

"I read your editorial last week. I think you were exaggerating about the number of rigged games."

"I wish I were. Oh, things aren't so bad over here, but on the South Side, the cowboys are robbed blind, and I don't mean at gunpoint."

"The cowboys come to town expecting to lose their money," Chance pointed out.

"I'm not just worried about the cowboys, and you know it. There's land fraud going on, too. Settlers come here in good faith and find out they've been fleeced. I heard you've been talking to the mayor about cleaning up the corruption."

Chance should have known his remarks to Dog Kelley would not go unreported. "I was only saying that letting the town get a bad name—or maybe I should say worse name—is bad business for everyone, especially him. You reformers almost beat Dog this last time."

Dan Frost nodded grimly. "We would have, too, if Kelley and his cronies hadn't stuffed the ballot boxes."

Joey arrived with their drinks, and Chance grasped the opportunity to change the subject. "I'm sure you didn't come here to discuss politics."

"Oh, but I did. You've been making noises like a reformer, Chance. I know a potential convert when I see one."

Chance raised his hands in a defensive gesture. "Wait a minute, Dan. I'm nobody's idea of a reformer. I'm a saloonkeeper, remember? It's not in my best interests to clean up the town."

"It's in everyone's best interests to do away with the corruption of the Kelley administration and their handpicked lawmen. I think you realize that, Chance. I also think you're in a position to convince Kelley."

Chance frowned. "What makes you think Dog would listen to me?"

Frost shrugged. "I don't know if he'll listen to anyone, but if he won't, we're going to run somebody against him next spring, somebody who can beat him. We'll have the settlers behind us, and all the townspeople who are fed up with lawmen who look the other way when their cronies break the law."

"A fight like that could tear the town apart."

Frost's smile told Chance he'd played right into the editor's hands. "I know you'll want to avoid such an unpleasant circumstance. It would be bad for business, yours and everyone else's."

Since Frost had echoed Chance's own concerns, Chance could only agree.

The editor's smile broadened. "Then we can count on your help?"

"Yes, you can count on my help," he said, resigned.

"I'm sorry I can't get more enthusiastic about the temperance movement," Elizabeth told Barbara as they left the Folgers' front yard. Mrs. Folger had hosted the regular meeting of the WCTU, and Barbara had taken Elizabeth along as a guest. "I do think it's a good cause. It's just . . ."

"I know, it's just not *your* cause, and that's fine. But I wanted you to get to know the other women."

"They're very nice and so dedicated. I'm impressed."

"I only hope we're dedicated enough to get the state legislature to pass the prohibition amendment."

"Do you really think even a constitutional amendment will close Dodge City's saloons?" Elizabeth asked skeptically.

"To tell you the truth, I have my doubts," Barbara admitted. "Folks in Dodge have always done pretty much whatever they pleased, and as long as the cattlemen come through, they'll probably keep on selling liquor, law or no law."

Elizabeth decided she was probably right as they strolled silently down the street toward home.

Barbara and Elizabeth could hear the screaming coming from their house from half a block away. They exchanged worried looks and quickened their pace. In the two weeks since Alice had arrived, three more women had sought refuge in the house, but not all of them had proven as easygoing as Molly and Mavis. Elizabeth had already served as peacemaker more times than she cared to remember.

"Here they come," they heard Molly call from her post on the front porch. She must have been watching for their arrival.

"What's going on?" Elizabeth demanded breathlessly as she hurried up the steps.

"Sally and Fanny are at it again," she said, naming two of the new girls. "They quit for a while after you broke them up this morning, but now Sally says Fanny stole her necklace or something. I can't get it straight."

A shouted obscenity and the sound of a scuffle made them all flinch.

"Heavenly days!" Barbara exclaimed.

Elizabeth was already heading for the front door, but by the time she got to the bottom of the stairs, she could hear Mavis shouting orders.

"That's enough! Are you two gonna bring the house down around our ears?"

"She stole my locket, the one my mother gave me!" a second voice screamed. Elizabeth started up the stairs.

"You never had a mother, you bitch!" a third replied.

"Stop it!" Mavis's voice rose above the others. "Is this how you thank Miss Livingston for giving you a place to stay? Maybe you'd like to go back to living in a lousy tent behind the Lady Gay. It'd serve you both right if she threw you out."

Elizabeth paused for breath at the top of the stairs, and Fanny was the first to notice her there. "Miss Livingston!"

The other two turned to face her. Elizabeth could sense Sally and Fanny were now afraid of her, probably because of Mavis's threat. The knowledge fell like a weight on her heart. She didn't want their fear, and she would certainly never consider sending them back to their old lives. "Is there a problem, Mavis?"

Mavis sighed in disgust. "You could say that. See, Sally here—"

"I think I heard enough to understand what the dispute is about." Elizabeth turned to Fanny, a short, plump girl of eighteen with a pretty face and a belligerent attitude. "I am sure this is all a mistake and you didn't really steal anything from Sally, but I'm also sure you understand why Sally is upset over misplacing her necklace." She paused, waiting for Fanny's reluctant nod. "Why don't you go back in the room and look around? Perhaps you can find it for her."

Elizabeth was fairly certain Fanny *had* stolen the necklace, but with her eyes she told Fanny she was giving her a chance to redeem herself.

"Yeah, I'll be glad to look," Fanny agreed after a moment's thought. As Fanny ducked back into the bedroom,

Elizabeth glanced at Sally. A willowy girl with big brown eyes and a put-upon expression, she looked skeptical, but she didn't offer any arguements.

Meanwhile, Elizabeth was busy working out the real problem in her mind. Earlier in the morning the two girls had been arguing over where to hang their clothes. Tomorrow it would be something else. The answer was to separate them. As Elizabeth had discovered, all her guests were fiercely protective of their belongings and their living areas. As awful as their previous places of residence had been, the women were still accustomed to having a private room. Doubling them up had been a bad idea.

"Sally, it wasn't fair of me to ask you to share your room. After all, you were here first."

"Oh, Miss Livingston, I don't mind," she said, apparently unwilling to lodge even the slightest complaint as long as Mavis's eviction threat still hovered.

"It's very nice of you to say so, but I know you're only being polite, and I'm planning to remedy the situation. How would you like to have my room?"

"You mean share with you?" Sally asked in surprise.

"No, have the room all to yourself."

Sally's eyes lit up, but she looked to Mavis before expressing an opinion.

Mavis scowled in disapproval. "Miss Elizabeth, there's no call for you to—"

"Certainly not," Barbara agreed, having come up the stairs behind Elizabeth in time to hear the last part of the conversation. "She can have my room."

Mavis plainly thought this, too, was absurd. "Where would you sleep?"

"The back parlor," Barbara replied, having given the matter a moment's thought. "We never use it much."

"Then I'll take the library," Elizabeth said. "We don't have many books anyway. Then we can separate Alice and Kate, too." Alice and Kate had fought bitterly the day before about whether or not Alice snored. "And Mavis, the music room is empty if you want—"

"No, I'll just keep on bunking with Molly, if she doesn't mind." The two had moved in together when the new girls had arrived.

Molly had come up the stairs behind Barbara and nodded vigorously. "I don't mind at all."

Mavis turned back to Elizabeth and frowned. "It just don't seem fitting for you to give up your room. After all, it's your house."

"Yes, it is," Elizabeth agreed. "And because it is, I decide where everyone sleeps, so I'll be sleeping in the library."

"Here's your damn locket," Fanny announced, strutting importantly out of her bedroom to present the necklace to Sally. "It was under the bed."

"In a pig's eye," Sally replied, snatching it from Fanny's hand. "You'd steal the coins out of a blind man's cup."

"And you'd—"

"Enough!" Elizabeth announced. "We will now go down to dinner, and this afternoon we will move into our new bedrooms. Barbara and I will go downtown and see about getting some cots from Wright and Beverley until we can order more beds."

She waited a moment to see if anyone would give her an argument. No one did, so she started herding people downstairs. Mavis lagged behind until only the two of them remained on the landing.

"You did a good job with them," she told Elizabeth.

Elizabeth rolled her eyes. "It's difficult to know how to treat them. Sometimes they seem so worldly-wise, they scare me half to death, and other times they're like children."

Mavis grinned. "You did just fine, 'mama.' ".

Elizabeth grinned back in spite of herself. "Yes, *this* time, but what happens when we run out of rooms?"

After they had arranged to have the cots delivered later that day from Wright and Beverley, Elizabeth and Barbara went over to McCarty's Drug Store to pick up their mail. Elizabeth found a letter from an old school friend, a lovely young woman married to a fellow who was handsome and charming but a hopeless ne'er-do-well. Saundra was one of those women who had made a poor choice in life.

Suspecting the letter was a humble plea for a loan, just as her last one had been, Elizabeth tore it open and read it right there in the store. Sure enough, her friend needed a small amount to tide them over until her husband found work. Elizabeth pictured the husband standing over Saundra dictating the plea, which did not sound like her friend at all, and she experienced a rush of impotent rage at the man who was making this woman's life such a mess. Like Elizabeth, Saundra had also fallen violently in love and was paying a price for having done so.

With a frown, Elizabeth folded the letter and put it back in the envelope. She noticed it had been forwarded from Philadelphia. Probably Saundra didn't know about her move yet. She must write to her at once and explain her new situation. The thought made her frown deepen. Like Saundra, Elizabeth was also at the mercy of a man. In order to help her friend, she would have to get permission from Chance.

"Bad news?" Barbara inquired, having glanced through her own mail.

"No, not exactly," Elizabeth replied. "Just a business matter I need to take care of." And the sooner the better, she added mentally. "While I'm here, I think I'll stop by Bill's office and turn it over to him." Perhaps Bill could convince Chance to make the loan, and Elizabeth could help Saundra without actually having to see Chance. She didn't want her next encounter with him to involve yet another plea for money. "You go on back to the house and make sure the peace is holding. I won't be long."

The two women parted company on the sidewalk, and Elizabeth turned up Front Street toward Bill Bates's office. As always, the outer office was empty. The inner office door was slightly ajar. "Hello," she called.

The door swung open and Bill appeared, smiling in delight. "Elizabeth, what a pleasant surprise. Please, come in." He hurried forward to escort her.

"I don't want to bother you if you're with a client," she said as they walked toward the rear office.

"Oh, this client won't mind," Bill assured her, conducting her through the door.

As she entered the room, she looked up and came face to face with Chance Fitzwilliam.

Elizabeth felt as if all the blood had rushed from her head, leaving her dizzy, and for one awful moment she feared she might actually faint.

"Hello, Elizabeth," Chance said, his voice maddeningly void of expression. From his tone, they might have been perfect strangers.

"Hello," she managed. She could not quite speak his name. His eyes glittered with a nameless emotion, but his face was perfectly composed. Her cheeks grew warm, but she refused to look away. She wanted him to think she was as unaffected as he was.

Bill, seemingly oblivious to the undercurrents, was still smiling. "Is this a social call, or did you have some business to discuss?"

With difficulty, Elizabeth broke eye contact with Chance and turned to Bill. "A little business, I'm afraid." Did she sound breathless?

If so, Bill was politely pretending not to notice. "Well, since it's probably something Chance will have to approve anyway, we might as well all sit down and discuss it."

He pulled up a chair for Elizabeth, who sank into it gratefully. Annoyed by her weakness, she made a conscious effort to gather her wits and restore her composure.

Chance resumed his seat, moving carefully because suddenly he felt almost weak. He'd been glad for the warning, glad he'd had a moment to compose himself before seeing her for the first time since the morning they had made love. Still, the sight of her had been a shock, and from the look on her face, she'd felt much the same. He must handle this situation with delicacy. It would never do to let Bill suspect what had happened between them.

"What is it you need, Elizabeth?" Bill asked cheerfully, but Chance could tell that behind his smile, Bill was already wondering why Elizabeth had turned chalk white at the sight of him.

Elizabeth took an unsteady breath. "It concerns a friend of mine, a Mrs. Martin. We knew each other at school. She and her husband are in difficult straits, and she has asked me for a small loan."

Without looking she could sense Chance's resistance radiating from him in invisible waves. Bracing herself, she turned to face the brunt of it.

"Are you in the habit of sending money to all your friends?" he asked, not bothering to hide his disapproval. He'd already decided he could no longer let guilt color his judgement in dealing with Elizabeth. He would have to resume his role as responsible guardian, no matter how distasteful the role might be.

"Mrs. Martin is the only friend who has ever needed help," Elizabeth replied stiffly, disturbed by the way his dark eyes seemed to see past her formal pose and even her clothes to what lay underneath. Not just her body, but even deeper, down to her soul. Was this why the Bible referred to the act of sexual intimacy as "knowing" someone? Because it stripped away all the normal social barriers and left the lovers so strangely exposed? If so, she reasoned, feeling reassured, then sooner or later Chance would surely sense her abiding love for him.

"Are you planning to make it your mission in life to help every woman less fortunate than yourself?" Chance asked. He hated the way she was looking at him, her green eyes searching his face as if she could see the deepest, darkest corners of his soul. If so, she could not help but see how hollow his soul was, how devoid of human feeling.

"I can't help *every* woman less fortunate than I," Elizabeth replied. "But I do intend to reach as many as I can."

"Well, then, would you mind explaining to me how someone from your Philadelphia social circle has managed to go broke?"

Elizabeth sensed his challenge and rose to it. "She married a man unworthy of her. He squandered her dowry, and now he is forcing her to beg from her friends."

"I see," he said, wishing he didn't. Here was a perfect example of what happened when a woman married the wrong man, just as he had warned her. He should have reveled in his triumph, but instead he felt an irrational urge to defend the reprobate who had illustrated his own prophecy so neatly. "How much money will satisfy this scoundrel?" he asked instead.

"Only a few hundred dollars." When his eyebrows lifted, she added, "Saundra knows that's just pin money to me."

"Do you think it's a good idea to encourage this fellow to be irresponsible?" Bill asked, jumping into the breach. "I mean, if he can't get money any other way, he'll be forced to get a job."

"Or else he'll let Saundra starve."

"Doesn't she have any family she can turn to?" Bill asked.

"Her family has told her they'll take her in, but only if she leaves him for good."

Chance sniffed in disgust. "Maybe she should."

Elizabeth turned to him in triumph. "Perhaps so, but she claims she can't bear to. For some inexplicable reason, she still loves him, and for some women love matters far more than money and comfort."

He flinched at her words. She smiled benignly.

"Such devotion is . . . is commendable," Bill offered.

"Or insane," Chance snapped.

Pleased to have rattled him at last, Elizabeth ignored his implied insult. She folded her hands and cocked her head to one side as she waited for his decision.

Chance sensed she had somehow scored a point on him, and he shifted uncomfortably. "All right, Elizabeth, I'll authorize a draft for your friend," he said, responding to an undeniable compulsion to placate her, but he could not afford to placate her too much. "I will write to her husband, however, and explain such requests should be directed to me in the future."

Elizabeth's feeling of victory evaporated. "He'll never do that."

"I know. Which means you will never again be dunned for handouts by a worthless scapegrace." Now he had scored a point on her, and if her glowing cheeks and blazing eyes were any indication, she didn't like it any more than he did.

"Elizabeth," Bill hurried to intercede, "it's Chance's duty as your guardian to protect you from things like this. If he started giving your money away to everyone who asked, I would have to question his fitness to be your guardian, and so would you."

Bill was right, of course, but it didn't reassure Elizabeth, especially when she knew Chance thought the rogue he was really protecting her from was himself. Still, she also knew she would gain no ground by resisting. "Thank you for reminding me of what a good guardian Chance is, Bill," she said sweetly, giving Chance a telling look which made him frown.

She handed Bill Saundra's letter, which bore her return address. "You'll need to know where to send the money," she told him and waited while he wrote down the information.

Although she made a point of not glancing at Chance, she was aware of his scrutiny, and she could almost feel his wariness. As she thanked Bill and prepared to leave, her only concern was whether Chance would let her go or try to prolong their meeting. He rose when she did, but she pretended to be adjusting her gloves and did not look directly at him when she said, "Thank you for your help, Cousin Chauncey."

At first she thought he would not stop her. Indeed, she had already taken a step toward the door when he called, "Lizzie."

His voice was soft, but it had more power than a physical restraint. A viselike force squeezed against her lungs. She lifted her chin in a feeble attempt to hide her rush of anticipation and turned once more to face him. "Yes?"

The words died on his lips when she looked up at him with those enormous green eyes. He knew the glimmer of fire in them could be fanned into an inferno of passion, and a man could warm himself forever in the heat of it. With difficulty, he recalled what he had been about to say. "How are things going with . . . your ladies?"

"Fine," she lied. The vise squeezed tighter as she gazed up at him. He seemed even taller than before. Dressed in his custom-tailored black suit and his hand-tooled leather boots, he looked every inch the respectable saloonkeeper. His face was freshly shaven and his hair combed perfectly. She remembered him with stubble-covered cheeks and rumpled clothes and his hair hanging in his eyes as he lowered his mouth to hers. Yearning flickered back to life and filled her with a warming glow.

"Lizzie, there's been some talk." The hard glitter of his dark eyes softened. "A lot of people don't like what you're doing for those women."

"Who doesn't like it?" she asked, not really caring, as the warm glow spread.

"People on both sides of the tracks." His voice was deep and resonant, striking a responsive chord within her. "The dance hall owners, of course, and men like Shilling who run the brothels, but people on the North Side, too. They don't like you bringing those women over here."

She stiffened. "I don't give a tinker's damn for what people say or think, and you can tell them so for me."

Chance would have, and gladly too, but there was more to it than that. "They're doing more than talking and thinking, Lizzie. They're making threats."

Threats! Look who was warning her about threats! "If

you're trying to frighten me into sending those women back, you're wasting your time, Chance Fitzwilliam. As long as I have a roof over my head, those women will have a home. Are you going to tell me I no longer have a roof over my head?''

The stubborn tilt of her chin stopped his breath for a second, and the frown he gave her was as much in disapproval of his own reaction as it was of her defiance. ''Just be careful, Lizzie, that's all.''

His tender concern touched her heart, and her annoyance vanished as rapidly as it had appeared. Her lips quirked into a secret smile. ''Not on your life, Chance Fitzwilliam. You've already taught me how interesting life can be when I'm *not* careful.''

She turned on her heel and left.

Chapter 6

When Elizabeth arrived home, the cots she and Barbara had ordered from Wright and Beverley were being delivered. She was grateful for the confusion because it meant the other women would be too busy to inquire about her meeting at Bill's office. Chance's name was sure to come up, and she wasn't ready to discuss him again with them just yet.

She had no time to even think about the meeting until much later, when she was comfortably ensconced in her new bed in her new room. There, in the privacy of the darkness, she had to admit she still felt the pain of his rejection. But when she recalled his tender concern for her that afternoon, she began to suspect her deepest longings to have Chance love her as she loved him might one day be fulfilled. On that comforting thought, she fell asleep. She was in the midst of a dream when she heard the scream.

Elizabeth struggled to wakefulness, aware of the thuds of running feet on the floor above. Grabbing her dressing gown, she dashed into the hall to join the others. Continuing howls drew them to the back of the house where Sally stood in the kitchen, scrubbing her face and chest frantically with a tea towel.

Barbara reached her first. "What's the matter? Where are you hurt?" she demanded, searching for signs of injury. The others quickly joined them, gathering around.

Sally shuddered violently and paused only long enough

147

in her wiping to point toward the open back door. There, hanging just outside by a rope tied securely around its neck, was the dead body of a cat.

"Lord and Savior!" Barbara exclaimed over the more colorful expressions of the other women. Elizabeth only gasped.

For a long moment everyone simply stared at the disgusting object swinging slowly back and forth in the predawn light.

At last Elizabeth found her voice. "Who would do such an awful thing?"

Sally shuddered again. "Damn cat," she muttered. "I hate cats. The stinking thing hit me right in the face, too." She took a few more swipes at herself with the towel. "I was just going to the outhouse, minding my own business, and *bang!* right in the face. I near peed myself." She looked pleadingly at the ring of faces surrounding her. "Can't somebody get it down from there?"

No one seemed disposed to do so, but then Mavis mumbled something profane and snatched a butcher knife from the counter. She strode to the doorway, cut through the rope with swift, sure strokes, tossed the cat's body out into the shadowed yard, and slammed the door shut on the gruesome sight.

She snatched the towel from Sally and wiped her hands. "Well, I reckon they've started."

"Started what? And who's 'they'?" Elizabeth wanted to know. She had a strange feeling the other women were not as surprised to find a dead cat hanging on the back porch as she was.

The others all exchanged uneasy glances. "You know there's been some talk in town about how folks don't like us being here," Mavis finally said.

Elizabeth closed her eyes as the memory of Chance speaking almost those exact words swept over her. "Yes," she replied wearily. "But surely they can't think hanging a dead cat on our porch will scare you back across the tracks."

The others gave her a puzzled stare, making her certain she was missing the point. At last Mavis said. "They're telling us they think this is a cathouse."

"You mean they think we raise cats here?"

Someone giggled and promptly received an elbow in the ribs. Mavis sighed. "A cathouse is what they call a whorehouse."

Elizabeth's widened eyes sought Barbara's. She looked as outraged as Elizabeth at the very thought.

"They can't really think that," Elizabeth said. "Not after we've been so circumspect."

"Face it, Miss Elizabeth," Mavis said. "You've got a houseful of whores. What else are the decent people gonna think?"

"They can think the truth! You've all given up your past lives, and you've changed." The others dropped their eyes before her enthusiasm. "Barbara, do you think the so-called decent people in town could have hung that cat there?"

Barbara shrugged. "Could be. The older I get, the less surprised I am at the things people do."

Elizabeth considered her comment. "Well, then, we'll show them we aren't scared. Tomorrow is Sunday, isn't it?" Nobody disputed her claim. "We are all going to church."

"What?" the women asked in horrified unison.

"You heard me. We are going to get dressed up in our Sunday best and march right up to the Good Shepherd Church and force those people to look us in the eye. If they have something to say to us, let them say it to our faces." Elizabeth crossed her arms in silent determination.

"You may not like what they have to say," Mavis warned, but Elizabeth was adamant.

Sally shuddered yet again. "Is somebody gonna bury that old cat?"

Business at the Last Chance Saloon was just as good on Sunday night as on any other. Reverend Folger had circulated petition after petition to get the saloons to close on the Lord's day, but so far he had been unable to convince the town fathers to pass such an ordinance. Considering how many of the town fathers owned saloons, this wasn't surprising.

Chance stood in his customary place at one end of the bar and surveyed the clientele. Most of the men present were either townsfolk or cattlemen. A few cowboys and one or two farmers mingled with them, but for the most part, the working men sought their pleasures on the South Side where they could find female companionship. Chance's customers were men who wanted a glass of real Kentucky bourbon, an honest poker game, and maybe a lively game of billiards. Young Jacob Schaefer was playing tonight, and Chance had half a mind to challenge him. The boy was getting good.

The saloon doors swung open, and Chance raised a hand to greet Bill Bates, who came straight over to him, grinning.

"Evening, Chance." Bill signaled the bartender for two whiskeys. "You'll need a drink before you hear the story I have for you."

Chance frowned as he watched the bartender fill two glasses.

Bill lifted his up and saluted Chance. "To the female of the species, God bless 'em all." He drained his glass and set it back on the counter with a smack. Chance took a polite sip and set his down, too, waiting uneasily for Bill's news.

"You really ought to get to church more often, old hoss," Bill confided good-naturedly. "There's no telling what you might see."

"What did Elizabeth do now?" he asked with a sense of foreboding.

Bill's eyes literally sparkled with mischief. "She brought her whores to church with her, every last one. You should've seen them, all spit-shined and gussied up, like they were going to a wedding or something.'' Bill shook his head as Chance fought down a groan.

"I don't suppose the good people were too happy to see them.''

"You know the old saying, 'As alone as a whore in church'? Poor Elizabeth must've felt like she'd been quarantined. The church folks left a good three rows empty just so they wouldn't be contaminated.''

"You sat with her, didn't you?'' Chance asked, wondering why he should care if Elizabeth had been ostracized for doing such a damn fool thing.

Bill gave him a look of mock horror. "I most certainly did not sit with her! What do you think folks would've said if a man had sat down with that bunch? Elizabeth had enough problems without my adding fuel to the flames.''

Chance muttered a curse, knowing Bill was right but hating the truth of it.

"Folger was great, though. You should've heard him. He preached on the prodigal son. When he'd finished explaining how happy the good Lord is over one sinner who repents, there wasn't a thing anybody could say about Elizabeth's crew. Of course they didn't say anything *to* them either. Poor Elizabeth, she looked like she was about ready to spit nails.''

Chance could imagine. Almost against his will, he felt a twinge of admiration at her audacity. He was angry and disapproving, of course, the way a proper guardian should be, but he couldn't help grinning when he thought of her turning up her pretty nose at the whole lot of those hypocrites. He would have liked to have seen her.

He glanced back at Bill, surprised to see him frowning. "Now comes the part you aren't going to like," Bill said.

"I didn't like the first part.''

"Then you'll like the second part even less. I called on Elizabeth this afternoon to see how she was doing, and she told me the reason she took her girls to church was because somebody hung a dead cat on their back porch on Friday night.''

Chance swore again. "Do they know who's responsible?"

"They suspect some of the good Christians of Dodge City who don't like having a houseful of whores in the respectable part of town."

Chance rubbed his chin thoughtfully. "Shilling and his bunch could also be responsible. They'd be more likely to try something to scare the women."

Bill shook his head. "Those fellows are rough. A dead cat seems pretty mild for them."

"Maybe this is just the first step."

"Maybe," Bill agreed, "but they'll have to do a whole lot more to scare Elizabeth. All they did was get her fighting mad."

"Damn. I told her this was going to happen. It would be different if she were doing something worthwhile, but this!" He waved his hand in a dismissing gesture.

Bill stared at him in surprise. "Don't you think what she's doing is a good thing?"

"You can't change those women. You watch, they'll lay around her place for a few more weeks until they get bored or want some money for a new dress, and then they'll be back across the tracks. She's putting herself through all this aggravation for nothing."

"I don't think so, Chance. I saw those girls. Some of them looked mighty determined. It took a lot of guts to walk into that church this morning."

Chance studied his friend's face, unable to believe what he was hearing. "Has she made a convert out of you, too?"

"I admit I was skeptical at first, but after hearing her talk, I've changed my mind. I think she may actually have a chance of getting some of those women started in new lives."

Chance chuckled at his friend's gullibility and signaled the bartender for another round, draining his glass as he did so. This time he proposed the toast. "To men who see

miracles where there are none," he said with a good-
natured grin.

"To men who refuse to see them where they are."

Chance had called himself seven kinds of a fool long
before he reached Elizabeth's street, but his self-criticism
hadn't stopped him. He was still headed for her house even
though he knew he was probably asking for trouble by
seeing her again so soon. The afternoon sun was high, so
he blamed the heat for the dampness of his shirt as he
strode purposefully toward her gate.

His step slowed when he made out the figure kneeling
by the side of the house. A broad-brimmed straw hat
blocked his view of her face, but he would have known
her anywhere. She was working in a flower bed, pulling
weeds. He opened the gate slowly so it wouldn't squeak
and eased it closed so it wouldn't slam.

His heartbeat quickened with anticipation as he approached her, although he told himself once again this was
only a business call. He was going to avoid any mention
of personal matters or anything remotely sensitive, like
how the delicate skin on the back of her neck below her
hat just begged to be kissed.

She continued to work, oblivious to his presence. He
stopped three feet away, surprised to find himself as short
of breath as if he'd run all the way over from the Last
Chance. He cleared his throat. "Hello, Lizzie."

Elizabeth froze at the sound of his voice, hardly daring
to trust her ears. She took a moment to gather her wits
and regain her composure, all the while silently debating
whether to let him see her joy at knowing he hadn't been
able to stay away. Deciding he would be delightfully nonplussed by her happiness, she lifted a beaming face to
him. "Hello, Chance."

His breath lodged in his chest. The heat had given her
skin a sheen, and her radiant smile seemed to outshine the
sun. Her eyes sparkled with warmth and welcome and
something more, something he didn't dare name.

She was rising to her feet. He automatically reached to help her, taking her arm. A serious mistake, he decided as soon as he touched her. Through the fabric of her sleeve, he could feel the softness he had dreamed about more nights than he cared to remember. He dropped her arm and jammed his hands into his pockets. "Warm day," he remarked.

"Yes, but these weeds were getting bad." She studied his expression. Beneath the brim of his stylishly cocked hat, his dark eyes reflected conflicting messages, desire and restraint, need and resistance. "What brings you to my humble home?"

Her beautiful eyes were laughing at him, as if she knew about the undeniable impulses that had drawn him here. And she actually looked happy to see him. Too damn happy for a woman who had been seduced and abandoned. Dear God, why didn't she hate him? Instead, it was as if she knew some secret, some *amusing* secret. He reminded himself he had some serious business with her. "Bill told me about the cat incident."

The laughter vanished from her eyes. "Yes, someone sent us an unpleasant message, although we aren't quite sure what the sender's intention was."

Chance sighed impatiently, curling his hands into fists inside his pockets as he resisted the urge to reach out and brush away the strands of ebony hair clinging damply to her forehead. "I warned you this could happen." He'd intended to sound stern but fell somewhat short.

"Yes, you did, so your conscience is clear," she said with another smile. "And no one was hurt, after all, except the cat, but Barbara thinks it was dead before they hung it up, so at least the poor thing didn't suffer."

"Elizabeth, I don't think you're taking all this seriously enough. The cat was only a warning. If you ignore it, God only knows what might happen next."

"You're certainly developing into a conscientious guardian. And to think I once doubted your suitability."

"Elizabeth!" he said in exasperation, forgetting to leave

his hands in his pockets and grabbing her arms. "Don't you understand? You could be hurt!" Her upper arms were supple, yielding to his grasp. Her eyes kindled with the fire that had haunted his dreams.

"Is it my guardian who's worried, or my lover?"

He released her abruptly. "Dammit, Lizzie, don't you have any shame?"

"Don't you?" she replied. "And don't try to tell me you came by today to commiserate with me over a dead cat."

"I won't because I didn't," he insisted. "I came to warn you about these women you've taken into your home. They're running a con on you, Lizzie. They'll take you for everything they can get, and then they'll be gone. They're making a fool out of you."

"Only one of us is a fool, Chance Fitzwilliam, and it's not me." Elizabeth planted her hands on her hips, prepared to defend her boarders with the ferocity of a mother bear. "I know these women. I know what they've been through, and I know how much they want a different kind of life. I'm going to help them get what they want, and nothing's going to stop me, not your threats or anyone else's."

"I'm not threatening you," he said in frustration. "I'm warning you. I'm trying to *protect* you, for God's sake."

His tortured expression touched her heart, and her irritation faded. How could she fault him for such an urge? If only he could understand how ridiculous his fears were. "Oh, Chance," she said with a sad smile, "don't you know that *you're* the only one in this whole world who can truly hurt me?"

Her words struck him like the sting of a lash. He backed up a step, knowing he had somehow crossed into dangerous territory. What did she mean? He *had* hurt her. He'd hurt her past forgiving, or so he'd thought. Was she playing some kind of a game? He would have sworn his years of experience had taught him all the ruses women used, but this was something new. He no longer understood the rules. "I should send these women back where they came from," he said halfheartedly, knowing she couldn't possibly take the threat seriously.

"You're wrong about them, Chance. You'll see."

That oppressive ache was starting in his chest again. Instinct told him he could only soothe the hurt by taking Elizabeth in his arms. She alone would fill the miserable void. But he couldn't use her for his own comfort, not when he had nothing to give her in return. He took another step away. "Just be careful, Lizzie," he begged.

Seeing his pain, Elizabeth wanted to run to him and throw her arms around him. She wanted to hold him to her breast and tell him how wrong he was to want to protect her from himself. But she couldn't, at least not until she could make him see himself as she saw him, not unless she could convince him they really did have a future together.

"Don't worry about me. Nobody in this town is going to hurt Chance Fitzwilliam's woman."

His sharp intake of air told her she had scored another hit. His hastily muttered farewells confirmed it. Watching him walk out the gate and down the street, she sighed, blinking back tears. "Oh, Chance," she whispered. "Why can't you just love me? Then everything else would work out, I know it would."

By the time Chance reached Front Street again, a casual observer would never have guessed Elizabeth Livingston's razor-sharp tongue had cut him to the quick. To his everlasting surprise, he realized he actually preferred her sarcastic anger to this new, biting honesty.

And how could he convince her she was wasting her time with those women? Or could he possibly be wrong about their ability to reform? Bill had certainly changed his mind on the subject. What Chance needed, he supposed, was some proof one way or the other. He turned his steps toward the South Side of town.

Summer Winters's professional smile turned genuine when she saw who was waiting outside her door. "Chance!

How nice to see you. Do come in and make yourself at home.'' She waved him into her sitting room. ''Are you here on business or pleasure?''

''Business,'' he replied, already regretting his impulsive visit. ''I thought I'd collect the rent in person.'' She was sure to be suspicious. He never collected the rent himself.

Summer closed the door and looped her arm through his to lead him farther into the room. ''I'd be glad to let you take it out in trade,'' she purred.

''That's a lot of trade.''

''I'm able if you are,'' she replied without hesitation, leaning close so the décolletage of her dressing gown gaped enticingly.

He chuckled to cover his uneasiness. Normally, such banter came naturally to him, but today he felt strangely awkward, like a schoolboy at his first social. His discomfort probably stemmed from the schoolboy idiocy behind his visit. ''If you don't mind, Miss Winters, I'll settle for cash.'' With what he hoped was casual unconcern, he disengaged his arm and took a seat on a gilt chair.

He expected Summer to be piqued at his refusal to succumb to her charms. Instead she was studying him with more than usual interest. ''There's something on your mind, isn't there?'' she surmised. ''Go ahead, spit it out.''

''As a matter of fact,'' he admitted, ''I've been wanting to ask you something.''

Summer's gaze grew cunning. She pulled the matching gilt chair closer to his and sat down. ''Ask away.'' Her smile held an invitation.

''Would you . . . I mean, are you happy doing this?'' He gestured to include her house and her business.

Her smile faded as she carefully considered her answer. ''I make a good living, but . . .'' She paused, toying absently with a frill on her dressing gown as her expression faded into a soft vulnerability that Chance suspected she had practiced in front of a mirror. ''I'd rather have a home and a family. What woman wouldn't? I'd retire in a minute if the right man came along.''

Chance winced at his own stupidity. Plainly, Summer thought *he* was the right man, and his poorly worded question had led her to believe he was starting to agree. He'd stepped right into that one, and he'd better step out in a hurry.

He nodded his understanding. ''Do you think you're pretty typical of other women, in, uh, your line of work? I mean, are most of your girls looking for a way out of the business, too?''

Summer's sweetly puzzled expression slowly hardened as understanding dawned. ''You bastard! You're thinking about *her,* aren't you?''

''Who?''

''Your precious little Elizabeth, that's who,'' she spat. ''You want to know if she's wasting her time making a home for hookers. You weren't really interested in my feelings at all!''

Chance felt her accusation was much harsher than his innocent inquiry merited. He'd certainly had no intention of hurting her feelings. From past experience with her, he was almost certain she had none. ''I'm truly sorry, Summer,'' he said, trying to sound sincere. ''I meant my question in a general sense. I never thought for a minute you would think I wanted . . .''

He let his voice trail off, his reluctance to mention marriage completely genuine.

Her carefully made up face turned an unbecoming shade of red. ''I should have known. You haven't thought of anything but her since the minute she showed up here. In fact, now that I think about it,'' she added, her eyes narrowing speculatively, ''you haven't come to visit any of the girls since then either. Tell me, Chance, are you getting serviced these days at your very own private brothel?''

''Summer . . .'' His voice was heavy with warning.

She instantly realized she had gone too far, but her own pride had been wounded. She could not allow him to escape unscathed. "As to your question, the answer is no, most whores *don't* want to leave the business. Those women she's got over there are a bunch of lazy bitches who know a good deal when they see one. They'll take her for all she's worth and then come crawling back to this side of the tracks. If you were any kind of an advisor at all, you'd run them off and send little Miss Elizabeth packing back to wherever she came from. Her kind don't belong in Dodge."

Chance stiffened. Her words echoed almost exactly what his own common sense had been telling him for days. Philadelphia was where she belonged, not here in Dodge City where anything could happen to her.

He'd resisted, however, because he didn't want her to go. The desire to keep her close had driven him to Summer on a fool's errand. He'd wanted her to tell him all whores were innocent victims who would jump at the chance to escape their degradation. He'd wanted a reason to allow Elizabeth to continue her work so he would have an excuse for keeping her here.

He rose slowly, letting Summer see none of his inner turmoil. "Thank you for your advice, Summer. Now, if you'll give me the rent, I'll be on my way."

She made a sound that was part fury and part disgust, but with a swish of her dressing gown she turned and went to her safe. Muttering imprecations, she turned the dial with short, jerky motions and swung open the door. A minute later she rose and slapped a small sack of gold coins into his hand.

"Thank you again," he said, ignoring her murderous glare, and let himself out of her room.

He stopped in the hall outside, absently dropping the pouch into his coat pocket.

"Mr. Fitzwilliam, is something wrong?" Hettie approached him timidly. She'd been sitting in the front parlor, waiting for customers, when he had first come in. Now she came out into the hall, her head tilted quizzically.

He studied her small face, her diffident manner. She

seemed less suited for the life she had chosen than any other woman he'd met. If there was one woman south of the tracks who needed rescuing, it was Hettie.

"Is there something I can do for you, Mr. Fitzwilliam?"

Suddenly, Chance believed there was. "Would you go upstairs with me, Hettie?"

Her large eyes lighted up at the invitation. "I sure would." She took his arm and led him to the staircase. On the way up, he recalled Summer's charge that he was servicing himself at his own private brothel. With a grim smile, he thought of how she would take the news of this assignation.

Hettie's room was exactly like all the others on this floor, furnished with a brass bed, a washstand, a screen and two straight-backed chairs. A cheap brush lay on the washstand, but he could see no other personal articles to mark the room as specifically hers. It was simply a room, a cubicle designed to provide privacy for a hasty coupling between one eager person and one willing. The eager one would pay and leave, but the willing one had to stay behind and be willing for the next man who came along. Hettie lived in this cold, impersonal room day in and day out. Although he had been in rooms like this many times with other women, for the first time in his life he felt a quiet horror imagining what Hettie's life must really be like.

She was already working the buttons of her dress when he closed the door. "Don't undress," he said quickly. "I just want to talk."

"But . . ." Plainly she was confused.

"I brought you up here because I wanted Summer to think we went to bed and because I didn't want anyone to overhear our conversation."

Her frown was a little hurt. "Don't you like me, Mr. Fitzwilliam? You never . . ."

"I like you too much, Hettie. That's why I never brought you upstairs before."

Her frown deepened. "I don't understand."

"Hettie, ha̱ you heard about Miss Livingston?"

"Sure. I was the one who met her at the train, remember?"

"No, I mean, do you know what she's doing for the girls who work on this side of the tracks?"

Hettie nodded and her eyes grew wary. "Yeah, I've heard. I saw her the day she came down here with Reverend Folger and you took her back."

Chance cleared his throat, not wanting to think about that day. "Would you like to leave here and go stay at her house?"

Hettie's hand came up as if she could ward off his question. "Is this some kind of trick?"

"Trick? What do you mean?"

Her chin lifted in a way that reminded him too much of Elizabeth. "Miss Winters put you up to this, didn't she? She's testing all of us, to see if she can trust us."

"No, of course not. You know I'd never do Summer's dirty work for her." He was annoyed she could even think such a thing.

Hettie apparently decided he was telling the truth. "Then why are you asking?" Her suspicion was almost palpable.

He gave an impatient sigh. "Because I want to know. Would you like to leave here and make a new life for yourself?"

"Well . . . yes," she admitted hesitantly. "I mean, doesn't everybody?"

His relief was swift and heartfelt. Hettie wanted to leave, and she wasn't the only one. *All* the girls did, regardless of Summer's claims to the contrary. Elizabeth was right, and Bill was right, and Chance was glad, so glad he felt almost weak. "Then pack your clothes. I'll take you to Elizabeth's right now."

Her wariness turned instantly to alarm. "Oh, no! I couldn't!"

"Why not?"

She seemed at a loss as she searched for an explanation. "I just couldn't. Miss Winters would have a fit."

"You don't have to worry about Miss Winters. I'll take care of her."

"You might get me there all right, but you couldn't protect me all the time," she pointed out. "She might send someone over there at night. Besides, how do I know Miss Livingston won't get bored with this whole idea, or just decide to go back home and turn all the girls out again? What would become of us then? I'd be afraid to come back here, but where else could I go?"

"Elizabeth isn't going to get bored," he promised rashly, certain that she'd never simply turn the women out.

"I can't take the chance, Mr. Fitzwilliam. This is all I have. Miss Winters is mean sometimes, but she feeds us and takes care of us when we're sick. There's plenty of worse places to work. Believe me, I know. I guess you've seen those tents where some of the girls live."

Chance nodded, hardly able to believe what he was hearing. He was offering her a chance for a better life, but she was afraid to accept for fear of ending up even worse off than she already was. He tried to think of an argument to help her see the error of her logic, but there were too many counts on which she was right and too many more unknowns.

"Listen, Hettie, if you ever change your mind, let me know. The offer is always good. I'll even come over here myself to make sure you get to Miss Livingston's house safely."

She gave him a sad smile. "I won't change my mind. Miss Winters would skin me alive."

He resisted the impulse to deny her allegation. For all he knew, she could be right. Summer must be holding something over their heads in order to keep the women here.

"Just remember," he said, laying a reassuring hand on her arm.

She came to him at once, drawing close and slipping

her arms around his waist. "You're sure nice to think about me like that. Maybe you do like me some."

She pressed against him, and he felt an urge to recoil from her touch. Controlling it, he gently removed her arms and stepped back. "As I said, I like you too much to use you, Hettie. But don't look so disappointed." He pulled out a twenty-dollar gold piece and pressed it into her hand.

"But I didn't do anything," she protested.

"You were honest with me," he replied, knowing what she had told him was worth ten times twenty dollars. "Take care and don't forget to tell Summer I came up here with you."

He hoped Hettie's lie would satisfy Summer's curiosity as to where he was fulfilling his sexual needs. She didn't have to know, he reflected solemnly as he made his way out of Summer's house, that Elizabeth's patrician beauty and blazing passion had ruined him for anyone else.

"Fanny, what are you doing?" Elizabeth demanded in alarm, rushing into the girl's bedroom. Mavis had summoned her from her gardening to deal with a brand new problem.

"I'm leaving," Fanny replied, not even glancing up from her packing.

Elizabeth watched her stuff a petticoat into the worn carpetbag. "But why? Aren't you happy here?"

"Happy?" Fanny said the word as if she'd never heard it before. "I'm bored stiff is what I am. Nothing but cleaning house and cooking and sewing. I got all the disadvantages of being married with none of the advantages. You won't even let us have a little nip now and then. I'm going back where I can have some fun."

Fun? Elizabeth could hardly believe her ears. "You said you hated your old life."

"Yeah, well, this one's even worse."

Elizabeth absolutely did not believe anything could be worse than selling one's body to strangers, but Fanny sounded certain. "You don't have to go back to church again if you don't want to," she said. Fanny had complained the loudest of anyone about the experience.

Fanny laughed derisively. "As if you could even drag me back there with all those old biddies looking down their noses at me when I've spread my legs for half their precious husbands."

"That's not true and you know it," Mavis declared from the doorway.

"I have for one or two," Fanny insisted, and stubbornly turned back to her packing.

Elizabeth watched helplessly. "Maybe if you'd tell me what changes you'd like made around here, we could make things better. I'd like for all my guests to be happy."

Fanny whirled to face her. *"Guests?* Is that what you think we are?"

"Why, yes," Elizabeth replied, surprised by the girl's vehemence.

"We aren't your *guests,* Miss Livingston. We're your charity cases. Oh, you treat us nice and everything," she hurried on when Elizabeth would have argued, "but we're still living on your handouts. Me, I just can't take it anymore. If I was the kind who could take handouts, I never would've become a whore in the first place."

Elizabeth turned to Mavis with a silent plea. Surely the older woman could think of some way to stop Fanny. But Mavis seemed lost in dark thoughts of her own.

Fanny strapped the carpetbag shut, gave the room one last cursory inspection to see if she had forgotten anything, and hoisted the bag off the bed. "Thanks for putting up with me and for pretending you're sorry to see me go."

"I really am sorry to see you go," Elizabeth said in frustration.

Fanny shook her head in wonder. "I truly believe you are. You know, Miss Livingston, you're about the only real lady I've ever met. If there was more like you, this world would be a better place."

With that, she left, shouldering Mavis out of the way

and heading down the stairs. Elizabeth would have gone after her, but Mavis stopped her.

"Let her go."

"But she—"

"She's old enough to make up her own mind, and she needs to keep her pride."

"Pride?" Elizabeth didn't understand. She had never done anything to cost Fanny her pride.

"She's right about you giving us charity. We all feel it, and I reckon the rest of us would go back too, if we weren't too scared of what Shilling would do to us for leaving in the first place."

"Mavis, I thought we were friends," Elizabeth said in dismay.

"Friends are equals, Miss Elizabeth. We can't be equals if you're paying for every bite of food we eat."

"Friends help each other," Elizabeth argued.

"Yes, *friends* do. You can help us, but we can't ever help you back. That makes your help charity."

"You've helped me. You know you have," Elizabeth insisted.

"Not enough."

Elizabeth stared at her in despair. Instead of making these women's lives better, she had somehow made them worse. They couldn't go back to the old way, but they would never be accepted into respectability, either. Their experience at church had proved as much.

How long could this situation last? Soon another girl would work up her courage and pack her bags, too. If Elizabeth wasn't careful, she and Barbara would once more be alone in the house and she would have a double burden to bear: guilt over having failed her friends and pain from knowing the kind of life to which those friends were doomed.

She had to do something, and quickly. The problem was, she didn't have a clue as to what that something might be.

* * *

Chance walked slowly back to Front Street, trying to decide what his next step should be. If Elizabeth was right about the prostitutes in town needing to be rescued—and the evidence seemed to support her claim—what could he do to protect her while she did her work?

Lost in these perplexing ruminations, he almost didn't see Fred Zimmerman standing outside his hardware store. "Afternoon, Chance," he called.

"Hello, Fred," Chance replied, startled back to the present. "How's business?"

Zimmerman grinned, stroking one of his prodigious sideburns which hung down to the middle of his chest. "A man who sells guns will never go broke in Dodge City."

Chance returned his grin. "A man who sells liquor will never go broke, either."

The shopkeeper's smile faded. "Dan Frost told me he had a talk with you the other day."

"Not you, too, Fred. Like I told Dan, I'm not anybody's idea of a reformer."

Fred Zimmerman studied him silently for a moment. A Prussian who had come to Dodge by way of Paris, New York, Wyoming, and Colorado, he had a special rapport with the German settlers, many of whom had come here at his own instigation. Along with Dan Frost and liquor wholesaler George Hoover, he was one of the leaders of the reform movement. "Are you busy right now, Chance?"

"No, not particularly," he replied.

"How would you like to go for a ride with me? I have something to show you."

Intrigued, Chance agreed. The two men crossed the railroad tracks and fetched their horses from Ham Bell's livery stable. Zimmerman took him to an isolated spot on the outskirts of town where a lone wagon was parked. The canvas cover on the vehicle marked the occupants as movers, and from the looks of things, they had been camped there awhile.

Zimmerman called a greeting in German, and a tall

young man appeared from the back of the wagon. He was blond and robust, with the rosy-cheeked look of a foreigner. Zimmerman gave him some explanation, still in German. From the way the storekeeper kept gesturing at him, Chance figured he was making some sort of introduction.

"Chance, I'd like you to meet Hans Dietzel," Zimmerman concluded, switching back to English. "And his family is probably hiding in the wagon."

Chance nodded a greeting, and Dietzel told them in accented English they were welcome to get down from their horses. He spoke a gentle command in the general direction of the wagon, and an attractive young woman, as blond as Dietzel, climbed gingerly out. Two tiny, tow-headed children followed. Shyly curious, they clung to their mother's skirts while peering at the visitors. Chance judged the oldest to be no more than four or five, and he noticed the gentle swell beneath Frau Dietzel's apron.

Silently, he cursed Zimmerman for doing this to him, though the storekeeper could not possibly have suspected Chance's weakness for any woman who was with child. He managed a polite smile in response to Zimmerman's continued introductions, and accepted the offer of a camp stool and a cup of coffee. Though he felt certain these people could hardly spare even a cup or two of coffee, he also knew he had to accept their hospitality or risk insulting them.

Chance smiled at the smallest child, a girl named Gretel. She giggled and hid her face in her mother's skirt. Chance wished he had a peppermint stick to offer her.

"These folks came out here to farm," Zimmerman explained. Chance had already guessed as much. "They bought some land, but when they got here to claim it, they found out the land company did not exist."

"They were swindled." Chance sighed. He'd guess that, too. "But there's plenty of land available. Why are they still here?"

"They already bought all the land they could afford.

They have enough money for seed and to carry them through to their first harvest, but not enough to buy more land.''

"And not enough to go back where they came from either,'' Chance surmised, remembering why he had always made a point of avoiding getting close to people. He was too softhearted—soft*headed,* his father would have said. If he didn't know about other people's problems, he wouldn't feel compelled to do something about them. "What about the people who swindled them? Any chance of recovering their money?''

Zimmerman shook his head. "They got caught, and the Dietzels were going to testify against them, but they escaped.''

"Escaped?''

"Yes,'' Zimmerman said grimly. "The swindlers turned out to be friends of our illustrious mayor and his cronies. Somehow our law enforcement officers accidently let them go.''

Chance swore aloud before he could stop himself. An anxious glance at Mrs. Dietzel showed she had not understood, however, so he turned his attention back to her husband, whose frown showed he was following the discussion.

Chance's intention must have shown on his face because Zimmerman said, "They don't want charity, Chance. Besides, that's too easy.''

"What do you mean easy?'' Chance challenged, although he suspected he already knew. A portion of the Last Chance's nightly proceeds would set these people up in style. Helping them would cause Chance no hardship, and even if it did, he would be buying himself a clear conscience. He wouldn't mind paying richly for such a luxury.

Zimmerman smiled as if reading his mind. "They'll be insulted if you offer them money. They still have some pride left.''

"Then why did you bring me out here? What do you expect me to do?"

"I expect you to get angry. Nobody feels sorry for a cowboy when he gets rolled by a clever prostitute or when he falls into a crooked faro game. But what people forget is the cowboys aren't the only ones suffering from the rampant corruption in town. I want you to be outraged. I want you to confront your friends in the Kelley administration and demand some action."

Chance had already promised Dan Frost he would take a role in Dodge City politics, but so far he had procrastinated about doing so. He'd told himself he was waiting for the right time. Chance realized the right time had come.

He drained his coffee cup and rose to hand it back to Frau Dietzel. "Thank you, ma'am," he said, tipping his hat. "A pleasure meeting you."

She took the cup and mumbled something incomprehensible. She wasn't conventionally pretty, but her face had the special glow he'd seen in other pregnant women, or at least in the ones who were happy with their condition. Chance looked down at the children still clinging to her skirts. Gretel flashed him a grin before ducking out of sight again.

Sighing, he turned to face Dietzel. He stuck out his hand, and the German shook it vigorously. "I can't make you any promises," Chance said.

"*Ja*, I know," the German replied.

As they rode away, Chance caught a glimpse of Gretel scrambling up on the wagon seat for a better view of their departure. Next time he would bring some candy.

Elizabeth stepped into the cavernous building that housed Wright, Beverley & Company. She took a minute to allow her eyes to become accustomed to the dim interior and inhaled the mingled fragrances of leather, tobacco, cloth, bacon, pickles, and the hundred other scents permeating the room.

"Miss Livingston, what can I do for you today?" Bob Wright inquired. He was purported to be the richest man in Dodge City. Of course he would be friendly to Elizabeth, who had purchased so much merchandise over the past few weeks.

"I'd like to speak with you in private about a matter of business," she told him with a smile. Having had a night to think about her problems with her ladies, she had discovered what she hoped was a solution.

He was more than happy to oblige her and escorted her to his small cluttered office in the rear of the store. "If this is a financial matter, you'd do better to talk to Mr. Newton. He serves as our unofficial banker, you know."

"Yes, I know," Elizabeth assured him when she had been seated across from his desk. Bill had explained how Wright, Beverley & Company ran a quasi-banking operation for the convenience of the cattlemen since there was no official bank in Dodge City. "I wanted to talk to you about something else entirely. I'm sure you've heard about the ladies who have come to stay with me."

Bob Wright was not a handsome man. His lanky form, receding chin, and bushy mustache gave him the look of a callow schoolmaster, and his scowl now did nothing to improve his looks. "Yes, I have. In fact, I was in church on Sunday when they made their appearance."

From his expression she could tell he did not remember the incident with pleasure. Elizabeth went resolutely on. "As you know, then, these ladies hope to make a better life for themselves. I have provided them with a place to live, but they need much more. If they are to succeed at changing, they must have a means of earning their livelihood. I was hoping you could be of some help to them."

Mr. Wright's face darkened alarmingly. "Exactly what did you think I could do?"

Elizabeth had not expected such a negative reaction. "I thought . . . I mean, I was hoping you could help me find some jobs for them, *respectable* jobs," she clarified when a vein started throbbing in his temple. "Perhaps you have something here in the store they could do?"

"Absolutely not!" His voice came out louder than he had intended, and he apologized for shouting. "Miss Livingston, please, you must understand. There are no jobs in this store for females. It simply wouldn't be right for a respectable woman to wait on the kind of men who come through here with the cattle drives, and if we had women who were less than respectable . . . I'm sorry, but I simply cannot allow prostitutes to ply their trade right here in my store."

"They are no longer prostitutes and would not be 'plying their trade'!" Elizabeth glared at him, but he did not appear moved by her outrage.

"I don't think you could guarantee their behavior, Miss Livingston, and if there was only one incident— I have my good name to think of and the reputation of my store, which is known all over Texas. If gossip ever got started, the drovers would stop coming, and I'd be ruined."

Elizabeth had expected resistance to the idea, but this was an argument she was not prepared to meet. Wright was correct; she could not guarantee the behavior of the women in a place catering mainly to Texans, the very men the girls were used to dealing with in their former occupation.

She tried a different tactic. "I can understand your problem, Mr. Wright, but surely you see mine as well. I cannot continue to keep these women in my home as guests. They are bored and unhappy. They need something with which to occupy themselves."

"Maybe they could take up knitting," he suggested with such naïve sincerity she could not take offense.

"They're bored with knitting and sewing and cooking and cleaning. In a household of women, there are only so many tasks to go around, and those tasks are spread pretty thin already. I was hoping to find the ladies something to do outside the house."

Bob Wright shook his head. "I wish I could help you,

but I think all the other merchants in town will feel the same way I do. The women certainly can't work at the saloons or teach school or work as maids either." He wagged his head again. "That doesn't leave many options, I'm afraid."

"That doesn't leave *any* options."

"I'm sorry. I wish there was something I could do."

Elizabeth doubted his sincerity—he looked far too anxious to end the conversation—but she was too well-bred to challenged him. Instead she thanked him politely and took her leave. Once outside, she impulsively turned left on Front Street and started walking down the block she usually avoided, the block which boasted the most saloons. Surely, nestled in among them was some sort of business which could use several able-bodied female employees.

At this early afternoon hour, the saloons were relatively empty. First she passed the Alamo Saloon, obviously named to attract the Texans. Next was the Long Branch, named, she had been told, for the beach resort in New Jersey at which she had once vacationed. From what she had glimpsed through the open doorway, the Long Branch was a rival to the Last Chance in luxurious appointments. A few more saloons, and then Zimmerman's Hardware, hardly a place for ladies to work. Next door was O.K. Clothing, which specialized in outfitting cowboys for their sojourn in Dodge and which was also unsuitable as an employer. Then came the Lone Star, yet another saloon seeking favor with those who remembered the Alamo, and next to that stood the Last Chance.

Suddenly Elizabeth's heart began to pound. What was she thinking coming down here? What if Chance were to see her walking by? Barbara had promised to warn her if she was making a fool of herself, and she in turn had promised not to chase after Chance. If he saw her here, what would he think? Their relationship was too tenuous to risk another accidental meeting, especially since he was likely to think she had planned it.

She quickened her step and averted her eyes, hoping against hope Chance was nowhere around. The hour was early for a man who worked all night. Perhaps he was not even up and about yet.

The thought sent her scurrying past the narrow alley where the stairs that led up the side of the building to his rooms were located. What if he was coming down those stairs at this very moment? With every step she expected to hear his voice calling her name. She would turn and her pounding heart would lurch to a halt, and if she were extremely lucky, she would not faint from sheer mortification. Her heels made an ominously hollow sound on the broad boardwalk, as if sending out a coded message heralding her approach.

But no voice called; no tall, dark man appeared; and then she was past the saloon. Delmonico's was up ahead. Maybe she should stop there, rest a moment, and catch her breath. Yes, and while she was there, she would ask if they needed any help in their kitchen.

She was reaching for the knob when the door opened. Elizabeth almost collided with a large man in a black suit coming out of the restaurant.

"Lizzie!" Chance said in surprise.

Chapter 7

Elizabeth's stomach did a nasty little flip and her breath caught in her throat. "Hello, Chance," she managed.

Chance was equally shocked. He cleared his throat and cast about for something to say. She looked so exquisitely lovely with her pink cheeks and shining eyes, he had difficulty thinking. "Are you meeting someone?"

"Oh, no," she assured him. Too breathless, she judged. She sounded as if she'd been running. "I was on an errand."

"This is a strange area for you to have an errand. You really shouldn't walk down this block alone, even in broad daylight." Did he sound guardianish and overly protective? Good, he thought. He needed to keep a distance between them.

Elizabeth knew he was right, of course. She had no business walking alone past all these saloons at *any* time of day. She felt compelled to justify her behavior. "I was looking for a job."

"A job?" His fine eyebrows lifted in what might have been amusement. "Don't I give you an adequate allowance?"

"Not for me, for . . . for the ladies who are staying with me."

She was adorable when she blushed, he noted. He had an almost overwhelming urge to stroke one reddening cheek. "Well, if you're forced to put them all to work, I *know* I'm not giving you an adequate allowance."

His eyes were soft, almost gentle, and Elizabeth felt the tension drain out of her. This was the Chance she loved, the kind man he tried to keep hidden most of the time. He didn't think this meeting meant she was chasing after him, although she was, and for some reason he no longer seemed disapproving about her boarders. He'd even made a joke about them. "They need jobs because they need something to do. They can't live on my charity forever."

Chance's amusement vanished. "Charity? Is that what you consider it?"

"Of course not, but that's what they consider it, or so they tell me. They're too proud to take any more handouts from me, but they don't have anyplace else to go, either, so I have to find something for them to do."

Chance frowned, remembering his conversations with both Hettie and Zimmerman. He knew Elizabeth was right. Her home could not be a final destination for these women, but where could their ultimate destination be?

Suddenly, they both became aware of the curious stares they were receiving from passersby forced to detour around them on the sidewalk. "Come along. I'll walk you home," Chance offered. When they had gone a few steps, he asked, "Have you actually spoken to anyone about giving them jobs?"

She studied his face for traces of mockery but still saw only the gentleness, mingled now with genuine concern. Her heart warmed. "Yes, but I haven't had any luck so far."

"Where have you looked?"

She sighed in frustration. "I asked Bob Wright for jobs at his store, but he didn't want a bunch of whores 'plying their trade' in his place of business."

Her outrage was as adorable as her blush, and Chance once again resisted the urge to touch her. He slipped his hands into his trouser pockets for safety as they turned the corner. "I'm afraid I can't help you either. I don't think you want your ladies working at the Last Chance."

"No, I don't." His eyes were like black fire, dark and

smoldering, and a tingling awareness sizzled over her body.

As their gazes held, they were unaware of passing pedestrians or even passing time. Elizabeth noticed how unusually handsome he looked and wondered vaguely if he ever went out wearing anything except a black frock coat. The derby cocked over one eye gave him a rakish appearance that set her pulse pounding.

Too soon they reached her gate. Chance knew he should leave her there, but perversely, he followed her up to the door. The porch was dark and cool, screened by fragrant vines of morning glory. He stood looking down at her for a long time as they each waited for the other to speak.

At last Chance said, "I hope you find some jobs for your charges."

Elizabeth smiled, recognizing the opportunity for which she had been waiting. "This is the first time you haven't given me a lecture on how foolish it is to try to help them. Have you changed your mind?"

"I finally decided I was wasting my time trying to deter you." He couldn't tell her the truth. She'd only see it as proof of the finer qualities she believed he possessed.

Her eyes were sparkling, as if she knew a satisfying secret. "Then you still think I'm wasting my time?"

"Let's just say I'm resigned, although I'd still like to get those women out of your house and as far away as possible."

"Your concern is touching," she said, taking his hands. Her touch was like a jolt of electricity, and her glittering eyes told him she knew it. "You're a very thoughtful guardian."

"Lizzie," he murmured, intending to warn her, but as if of their own accord his fingers closed possessively over hers. "We shouldn't . . ."

Then, somehow, his mouth was on hers, seeking and searching and devouring. Her arms slid around his neck, holding him to her while the touch and taste and scent of her ran riot over his senses. For one instant he teetered on the brink of sanity, and only by the sheerest force of will was he able to keep from toppling into the welcoming oblivion of desire.

"Lizzie," he said raggedly as he tore his mouth from hers. "For God's sake, what are you doing?" His hands put her away from him, but his gaze held hers, unable to completely break the contact.

"I'm kissing the man I love." Her eyes were even brighter now with triumph.

"Why?" he demanded, growing angry because she had such power over him. "Do you want me to take you inside and ravish you again?"

"Don't try to make it sound ugly, Chance," she warned him.

"Can't you understand? It *is* ugly! I used you, Lizzie, and I'd do it again if you'd let me."

"Would you?" she challenged. "Then why did you stop just now? Why didn't you take me inside and make love to me again?"

"Because . . ." He stopped. He had no reason, or at least none that didn't sound noble and honorable and all the things he wasn't.

"Can't think of a reason?" she taunted. "Then come inside with me now. Come on, you said you would if I'd let you." She reached for him, but he brushed her hands away in irritation.

"Stop it, Lizzie."

"Stop what? Stop trying to make you see the truth?"

"Stop trying to prove I'm something I'm not. You'll only get hurt."

"Elizabeth? Is that you?" Barbara called as the front door opened.

"Yes," Elizabeth replied, her annoyance at the interruption apparent.

"Oh, Mr. Fitzwilliam," Barbara said, obviously displeased by his presence.

"Good afternoon, Mrs. Jenks. I was just leaving." He

bowed politely and was halfway down the steps before Elizabeth stopped him.

"Cousin Chauncey?" When he turned warily back, he saw the same triumphant gleam still in her eyes. "If you hear about any job openings, you'll be sure to let me know, won't you?"

"Yes, I will," he said, knowing he wouldn't because he wouldn't hear of any jobs. Finding employment for her charges was a hopeless cause, almost as hopeless as his relationship with Elizabeth.

She had smiled, the picture of respectability. No one would ever guess that moments ago she had begged him to seduce her. No one would guess her prim exterior concealed a woman worth selling one's soul to possess. Chance only wished he still had a soul worth selling.

Chance looked at the men gathered around the table for their weekly poker game. Several days had passed since his last conversation with Elizabeth, and he had decided the best way to distract himself from thinking of her was to involve himself in something challenging enough to require all his attention.

The men assembled for the game were the most influential men in Dodge, and he suspected he should be concerned about the confrontation he had planned. After all, if they turned against him, they could make his life hell. Obscure statutes might suddenly be selectively enforced against his business enterprises. Law enforcement officers might neglect to patrol his property. The *Dodge City Times* might "discover" any number of unsavory details about his life.

Still, he did not hesitate. Snatching his derby from where it hung on the wall, he carried it over to the table and handed it to Mayor Kelley as he sat down.

"What's this?" Kelley asked, looking askance at the hat.

"You're familiar with the American custom of passing the hat, aren't you, Dog?" Chance inquired cheerfully.

Kelley raised his eyebrows. "Has business been that bad lately?"

Chance chuckled his acknowledgement of the barb. "I'm asking you to donate to a worthy cause. Seems there's a settler family camped outside of town. They were cheated in a land fraud scheme, and now they don't have anywhere to go." His companions stiffened noticeably, but he continued, undaunted. "I know you'll find this difficult to believe, but although the rascals who cheated them were caught, they somehow got away."

"Chance, this is none of your concern," Mike Sutton warned.

"Yeah, since when have you been interested in the poor, downtrodden settler?" Kelley wanted to know.

"Since now." Chance frowned as he remembered little Gretel and her gentle mother. "I told you before, I don't approve of this kind of thing. Cheating the Texans is one thing. They'll be gone tomorrow. But you can't take advantage of people who are going to be living and voting here, not if you want to stay in office, Dog."

Nicholas Klaine took a thoughtful puff on his cigar. "I heard Dan Frost had been by to see you. Have you gone over to the other side?"

Everyone waited tensely for his reply. "I don't think we should have sides when it comes to the good of the town. Everyone benefits when the permanent residents are happy with their government."

Dog Kelley tapped the derby impatiently on the table. "You didn't answer the question: have you changed sides?"

Chance met his gaze squarely. "Not yet. I'm giving you a chance to prove I don't have to. I don't want to turn on you, Dog, but I will if you give me no choice, and you know if I go over, others will, too. Even Bob Wright is unhappy with the way you've been running the town." Wright had been one of the staunchest supporters of having a wide-open town. His influence was important, if discreet.

"Are you making threats, Chance?" Mike Sutton asked. Chance suspected the attorney was already considering various legal subterfuges to keep him in line.

"I'm making a promise, to all of you. If the Kelley administration can't make Dodge City safe for honest citizens, then I'll throw my support behind someone who can."

Chance waited, grateful his years of training as a gambler enabled him to keep his true emotions private. He would not want any of them to guess he was bluffing; he doubted he could influence Kelley's followers to desert him.

The men around the table exchanged angry glances. After what seemed a long time, Kelley sighed gustily and lifted the derby he still held. "What do you expect us to do with this?"

"I expect you to fill it with money. If each of you contributes one hundred dollars, the Dietzel family will be able to purchase the farm they were cheated out of."

"A hundred dollars!" Kelley blustered. "Chance, we didn't make any money on that deal."

"I never thought you were personally involved. I'm only trying to make sure you have a serious stake in obtaining restitution from those who did."

Sutton leaned back in his chair, and Chance thought he detected a glint of admiration in the lawyer's eye. "In other words, you're giving us a little incentive to move onto the straight and narrow."

"Call it what you will."

Kelley looked down into the hat for a long moment and then sighed again, this time in defeat. "You drive a hard bargain, Chance. It's a good thing you're such a lousy poker player, or I wouldn't put up with you."

Chance felt no obligation to respond to the barb since Kelley had reached into his pocket and was dropping twenty-dollar gold pieces into the hat. When he had finished, he thrust it into Sutton's hands. This time the look the attorney gave Chance held unmistakable admiration.

"Maybe you ought to become one of those traveling preachers, Chance. Seems you have a gift for collecting money."

The derby was heavy when it came around to Chance again. He would have to check with Zimmerman to find out exactly how much the Dietzels had lost. He would make up any deficit himself. "Thank you, gentleman," he said, setting the hat aside. "Shall we cut to see who deals?"

To his relief, the others seemed almost amused at the way he had challenged them and won. Knowing how very differently things might have turned out, Chance felt a surge of gratitude toward whatever forces controlled politicians. By the time they had finished the first poker hand, all signs of strain had vanished. Only the hat full of coins remained as evidence of his victory.

As usual, the play lasted until late. Chance had all but forgotten the earlier events when Dog turned to him between hands. "Since you're so interested in cleaning up this town, there's a thing or two *you* can do to help, Chance."

"You know I'll be happy to be of service," he replied, growing wary when he saw Klaine and Sutton's satisfied smiles.

"A lot of people in town are unhappy about a certain situation," Kelley began, choosing his words carefully. "It involves your cousin."

Chance's first impulse was to tell Kelley to mind his own damn business, but he knew such a rash reply would alienate a man he could not afford to alienate. Restraining his temper, he replied calmly. "Someone has already expressed his disapproval by hanging a dead cat on her back porch."

"So I heard. Chance, *nobody* approves of what she's doing. The dance hall and brothel owners have been on my back. Oh, she hasn't exactly shut down the South Side, but even the few women who've gone over have stirred up the rest of them. All the chippies are talking about her, and they've started to threaten to leave, too, if things don't go their way.''

Chance thought this was good news, indeed, but he refrained from saying so and decided to be tactful instead. ''If Shilling and his bunch can't control their girls, I'm afraid I can't work up much sympathy.''

''Shilling isn't the only one who's complained. There's people on the North Side who are upset, too. They don't like having those women living with respectable people. They're stirring up trouble, too, but a different kind. You know how fanatic decent people can get when they feel threatened.''

Chance pressed his lips together in a tight line. ''I've heard all this before,'' he said when he could speak calmly. ''And let me put your mind at ease, Mayor. You may assure those who have complained that the situation will soon be rectified.''

''You're going to shut her down, then?''

''No, and I'm not going to send those women back to Shilling and his friends, either. I will, however, make sure they are soon out of Dodge. Do you think that will satisfy everyone who has complained?''

Kelley let his questioning gaze drift to his companions. They shrugged their uncertainty. ''I reckon it'll have to, won't it?''

''Yes,'' Chance said coldly. ''It will.''

Bill Bates glanced approvingly around the well-kept front yard of Elizabeth's house when he came to call a few days later. Colorful flowers bloomed in the warm spring sunshine, and the dirt in the yard had been recently raked smooth. The porch was freshly swept and the wicker furniture arranged neatly. No one would ever suspect the residents of this decorous home were anything but completely socially acceptable.

Bill made his way up the porch steps, frowning as he thought once again that Chance should have come with him for this meeting. Bill still couldn't understand why his friend was so determined to keep his part in all this a secret. Sighing in resignation, he rang the doorbell with a flourish. The door opened just a crack, and a single eye peered suspiciously out at him.

"Who are you and what do you want?" a woman's voice demanded.

Taken aback, Bill tried a friendly smile. "I'm Bill Bates. I'd like to see Miss Livingston, please."

The eye narrowed, and the door opened a bit wider to reveal a woman brandishing a shotgun. "Men aren't allowed in here. Now you git before I blow a hole clean through you."

Bill's jaw dropped in astonishment, but before he could protest, Elizabeth exclaimed, "Kate, please don't shoot my attorney!"

Bill was about to add his own encouragement to her plea when the door swung open to reveal Elizabeth. "Bill, what a pleasant surprise."

Kate frowned at her. "You said we wasn't to let any men come in here."

"Yes, I did," Elizabeth assured her, "but I didn't tell you to threaten anyone's life, did I?"

Kate looked Bill over and sniffed derisively. "No."

Bill bit back a sharp rebuke and glared at the woman.

Elizabeth patted Kate's arm. "He probably has some important business to discuss with me. We'll sit out on the porch."

Kate grudgingly stepped aside so Elizabeth could join Bill, then slammed the door shut. Elizabeth winced and gave Bill an apologetic smile. "I'm sorry for that, but we can't be too careful. We decided it would be a good idea to make certain no men are seen going into the house."

"The shotgun should do the trick."

"We thought so," she said with a sympathetic grin. "Won't you sit down?" she added, indicating the two wicker chairs nearby. "And can I get you some lemonade?"

"Yes, but first I do have some business to discuss with

you," Bill said as they seated themselves. "Have you heard of the Orients?"

"I don't believe I have."

"They're a group of businessmen in town who . . . well, they formed a sort of club. Many people think they did so just to have an excuse to socialize, and they *do* socialize quite a bit, but their main purpose is to perform acts of charity in the community. They are . . . interested in helping your boarders."

"Bill, they already have all the charity they can handle. What they need is jobs."

"Oh, we understand completely. I mean, the gentlemen understand the situation, and one of them has arranged to supply as many jobs as you might need."

"Where? Doing what?" Elizabeth leaned forward, hardly able to believe such a stroke of good fortune.

"Well, I'm sorry to say the jobs aren't here in Dodge. In fact, they're in Chicago."

"Chicago!" Elizabeth felt her first prickle of misgiving. Chicago was so far away.

"Yes, Chicago. One of the Orients owns a factory there. It makes men's clothing, I believe. At any rate, the owner has offered to provide jobs for as many of your ladies as want to make the move. He will set up a sort of dormitory for them to live in, complete with a female chaperone to ensure every propriety is maintained."

"I . . . I don't know what to say." A hundred questions spun in her mind. "Do you mind telling me who has made such a generous offer?"

Bill shifted uneasily. "The benefactor wishes to remain anonymous."

Elizabeth frowned as she considered the possible reasons a benefactor might want to remain unknown. He might not want gratitude, he might be painfully shy, he might even want to be able to deny any association with former prostitutes. *Or* he simply might not want Elizabeth to know who he was.

Chance was from Chicago, wasn't he?

He might be an unlikely patron, but Elizabeth couldn't forget the concern in his dark eyes the other day just before he'd kissed her. "I can't help recalling Chance is from Chicago," she ventured, carefully watching Bill's reaction.

"Is he? Oh, yes, I suppose he is, originally, although I don't think he's lived there for many years. What does that . . . Oh! You think Chance is the one making this offer?"

Seeing Bill's reaction, she felt silly for even suggesting it. She had no reason to believe Chance even owned a factory, and in the two weeks since Fanny had left, Elizabeth had approached every merchant in town about providing work for her guests. The benefactor could be anyone. "Oh, no, it's just . . . it's such a coincidence," she replied.

"I suppose," Bill allowed. "At any rate, no matter who's behind it, the offer sounds like the answer to your prayers."

Elizabeth only wished Chance *was* responsible. At least she would have some idea of his motives. How could Bill expect her to trust a mystery benefactor? "Please don't think I'm ungrateful, but I'll need far more information before I put anyone on a train for Chicago."

"But I've already explained I can't tell you who the man is who—"

"I don't need to know who owns the factory, but I do need to make absolutely certain a factory does, indeed, exist." At Bill's puzzled expression, she added, "I don't have any reason to expect help from the good people of Dodge City. I'm sure my houseguests would also be suspicious, and, well . . . please forgive my skepticism, but there are brothels in Chicago, too. How can we be sure this isn't just a ruse?"

"Because I intend to investigate everything thoroughly," Bill informed her. "I can understand your caution and the need for it, but I would never suggest this to you if I did not trust the individual involved completely. In addition, I'm leaving for Chicago on the noon train tomorrow so I can see the factory firsthand and make arrangements for the dormitory and see about hiring a suitable chaperone. I hope you trust me enough to know I would never—''

''Of course,'' Elizabeth hastily assured him, feeling awful for having suggested he would be party to anything even slightly shady. Now, if she could only shake the feeling Chance was somehow involved. Hadn't he said something about getting those women as far away from her as possible?

''Perhaps you and Mrs. Jenks would like to go to Chicago, too,'' Bill said. ''Then you could see everything for yourselves.''

''I'll wait for your report,'' she replied, wanting to soothe the pride she had inadvertently wounded with her doubts. Bill had been too good a friend to allow a misunderstanding to come between them. ''How long do you think you'll be gone?''

''I hope to be back in time for the Fireman's Ball on the Fourth of July.'' His eyes sparkled. ''Perhaps you'll go with me?''

''Of course I will.''

Bill gave a satisfied sigh. ''I guess now I'll take you up on the lemonade you offered.''

Elizabeth fetched them each a glass, and they chatted amiably for a few minutes until Elizabeth managed to work Chance's name into the conversation again. ''Does he know about these jobs in Chicago?''

''I mentioned them to him, of course. He is your guardian, after all.''

''Yes, he is,'' Elizabeth agreed. ''Does he approve?''

Bill made a vague gesture. ''I'm sure he'd be happy about any scheme to get these women out of your house.''

Elizabeth sighed, unable to hide her disappointment. She'd been hoping for more than that.

''Are you and Chance still not getting along?'' Bill asked. ''If so, maybe I can help.''

"No, Bill, really. We're getting along fine, all things considered."

"Elizabeth, I know you care a great deal for each other." Bill's blue eyes had seen much more than she had suspected, and Elizabeth gratefully ceased her polite protestations.

"I'm afraid you're right, or at least partly right. Although I care a great deal for Chance, he seems unable—or at least unwilling—to return my feelings," she admitted.

"But . . ." He paused, apparently debating whether or not to tell her something.

"What is it, Bill?"

"Chance probably wouldn't thank me for telling you, but there's something . . . I don't know if it has anything to do with your problems with him or not, but . . . well, Chance was engaged once, a long time ago. The woman jilted him. Maybe that could explain his caution."

"Oh," Elizabeth replied, unable to conceal her disappointment. "He already told me he wasn't really in love with her, so I know he's not still nursing a broken heart."

"Then you don't know the whole story. Something really awful happened between them. The night he told me about her we'd both had a little too much to drink, but even as drunk as he was, he wouldn't tell me exactly what she did. Whatever it was, though, it turned him against women. Between her and his witch of a mother, he learned not to trust females in general."

Elizabeth sighed wearily. If what Bill had said was true, it could explain at least some of Chance's behavior. But a broken romance long ago, no matter how unpleasant, would hardly explain his reluctance now when it came to love.

"Thank you for telling me, Bill, but I'm afraid it doesn't help me much. Now, let's talk about something else, like this generous offer for my boarders."

"I guess I should warn you this generous offer isn't quite as generous as it sounds," he admitted.

"What do you mean?"

"I mean the person making the offer isn't doing so out of the goodness of his heart. I think his main motivation is to get your ladies out of Dodge City. Their presence here on the North Side has offended a lot of people and . . ."

Elizabeth understood completely. Now the seemingly unbelievable offer made sense. "I see. When they couldn't scare us out—"

"The people who tried to scare you are not the same ones making this offer, Elizabeth," Bill assured her. "That isn't their style. But I do hope you'll be careful not to offend anyone else while I'm gone. For one, you could stop going to church."

Elizabeth's stubborn scowl stopped him, but he refused to be cowed. "At least be a little less conspicuous," he added. "There are people in this town who'd do a lot more than kill a cat to scare you off."

"I'm not afraid."

"Then you should be," he warned her and soon after took his leave.

When Elizabeth told her guests about the job offers, they were as skeptical as she was. They all decided to wait for Bill's return before allowing themselves to feel any excitement.

Bill had been gone only a few days when Elizabeth had occasion to remember his warning. The women were still at breakfast when noise from the street in front of the house drew their attention. A small crowd had gathered and people were staring at the street side of their picket fence.

Fighting a sense of foreboding, Elizabeth hurried to see what they found so interesting. The murmuring crowd of neighbors fell silent when she emerged from the house, and her feeling of alarm grew as she stepped through the gate to see the red paint splashed across the pristine white-wash.

After a moment she realized the paint formed letters, crude and sloppy letters to be sure, but letters nonetheless. They formed a word: *whorehouse*.

Elizabeth gasped aloud.

"Lord and Savior!" Barbara exclaimed, having followed Elizabeth out to the street. "Who could have done such a thing?"

Elizabeth scanned the crowd, but no answer was forthcoming. Some of her neighbors simply refused to meet her eye, and the rest stared back defiantly, silently saying, "I told you so!"

"Didn't anyone see anything?"

"The paint's good and dry, Miss Livingston," said Deacon George Cox, who lived across the street. "It must've happened late last night."

"My dog started barking around midnight," volunteered Mr. Wilson, Elizabeth's next-door neighbor. "I hollered out at him to hush and he did, but I didn't see anything."

Elizabeth searched the crowd again, hoping to see at least one sympathetic face, but she found none. Plainly they felt she deserved this outrage. Perhaps they were also offended because she had brought this indignity to their neighborhood. That, Elizabeth thought solemnly, was just too darn bad.

"I'm going to get the law on whoever did this," she declared. Now she saw a reaction: astonishment. She turned to a young boy in the crowd. "Would you run and fetch Marshal Earp, please?"

"He won't like being waked up so early, miss," the boy pointed out.

Elizabeth knew the town marshal's late hours would keep him abed until afternoon. He would hardly be eager to investigate a case of vandalism at this hour. "Thank you for reminding me. Would you go to his office, then, and leave word that I would like to see him as soon as he goes on duty?" The boy shuffled his feet, making no move to obey. "I'll give you a dollar," she offered. The boy flashed her a grin and took off running.

Elizabeth noticed the crowd was now staring with disapproval at something behind her, and she turned to see her other houseguests had come out on the porch. None of them dared approach this assembly of "decent folks."

The knowledge filled Elizabeth with impotent rage. How could she fight such prejudice and hypocrisy, hatred and mistrust? As much as she detested the vandal who had defaced her fence, she knew he or she was only part of the forces intent on keeping an invisible gulf between the so-called good people and bad people of Dodge City. Ironically, in the very crowd of neighbors gathered here to gloat were men whose appetites had taken them to the South Side on more than one occasion.

Once again the injustice of it all struck her. If a woman engaged in intimacy with a stranger, she was evil. If a man did so, he was only being a man. Her temper rose until she thought she might explode with fury. Knowing she could no longer trust her tongue, Elizabeth strode back into the sanctuary of her own home, leaving those who would stare to do so.

Marshal Earp finally made his appearance just as the household was sitting down to supper. Elizabeth had long since given up hope he would come, and she could see by his expression he thought he was wasting his time.

"Do you have any idea who did it?" he asked after he had surveyed the damage under Elizabeth's watchful eye.

Marshal Wyatt Earp was an attractive young man with neatly styled ash blond hair and an imposing handlebar mustache. Without his brace of pistols and the silver star pinned to his lapel, his well-made suit might have marked him as somewhat of a dandy. However, no one seeing the cold expression in his eyes would ever make that mistake. Elizabeth met his expression squarely, refusing to be intimidated.

"I don't have any idea who is responsible, and my

neighbors all claim to have seen and heard nothing last night."

"Then I don't think there's anything I can do. If you had a witness . . ." He shrugged, plainly convinced that even if he caught the culprit, the crime was hardly worthy of punishment.

Elizabeth gritted her teeth, reminding herself she would be wise not to alienate the marshal if she wanted his help. "Perhaps if *you* questioned my neighbors, they would remember having seen something. I have a feeling they're being selectively forgetful because they do not like my houseguests."

The marshal's expression conveyed his own disapproval. "Miss Livingston, maybe you ought to give some thought to sending your 'houseguests' back where they came from. There's nobody in this town who approves of what you're doing, and you're just asking for more trouble. This"— he gestured toward the paint-spattered fence—"is only the beginning."

"Actually, this is not the beginning at all, but the second step. The first thing they did was hang a dead cat from our back porch."

"Well, then, you know I'm right. So far, nobody's gotten hurt, but if you don't give up this fool notion—"

"It is not a fool notion!" Elizabeth snapped, forgetting her intention to hold her temper. "These women want help, and I intend to do everything I can for them."

Earp shrugged yet again. "Suit yourself. But remember, you're stepping on plenty of toes around here, and there's nothing anybody can do to protect you. If you were my woman, I'd—"

"Well, I'm not your woman or anyone else's, so I will do as I see fit," Elizabeth informed him as she felt her cheeks flame in reaction to his distasteful reprimand. "I'll certainly remember your warning, marshal. Thank you for your concern."

If he noticed her sarcasm, he gave no sign. He simply replaced his broad-brimmed hat, nodded a farewell, and sauntered off toward Front Street. Elizabeth muttered a few imprecations about pompous men before she walked back into her house.

"What did he say?" Mavis asked as soon as Elizabeth entered.

"Just about what you predicted he would say. He can't find the culprit without evidence, and he's not interested in looking for any evidence."

"Wouldn't surprise me none if he already knew who did it."

"What makes you think so?"

"He don't think much of women, especially whores. Fact is, a few years back he got arrested for beating one up. That was before he was marshal, of course."

Elizabeth stared, too shocked to speak.

"It's true," Mavis insisted. "Frankie Bell was her name. She was drunk and they got into a terrible row. He slapped her around and somebody called the law. He was found guilty and fined, too, but only one dollar. Frankie had to pay, oh, twenty dollars, I think, for being drunk and disorderly. I guess that shows you what this town thinks of women like us."

It certainly did. Once again Elizabeth felt impotent rage flood her senses. Until coming to Dodge City, she had been sheltered and coddled, living under the delusion that men would protect her simply because she was female. Now she knew exactly the opposite was true. She and all other women were at their mercy. She would be protected if they felt like protecting her, but she would be persecuted if she displeased their sense of what was proper.

"Elizabeth!"

Chance Fitzwilliam's outraged voice snapped the last tenuous control on her temper. What right did he have to be angry? She whirled to the door and threw it open just as his fist connected with the wood. He snatched his hand back in the nick of time to avoid striking her in the face, but she didn't flinch. "What do you want?" she demanded.

"What's been going on here? Who did that to your fence?"

"You mean you don't already know?" she asked in mock surprise. "I thought surely this was all part of a master plan by you and your male cronies to frighten me into sending my houseguests back to their old jobs."

His shock was too great to be feigned, and Elizabeth felt a pang of guilt for having accused him, especially when she recalled his concern for those very houseguests at their last meeting.

His expression grew guarded. "Elizabeth, we need to talk. Alone," he added with a significant glance at Mavis and the other women who were lurking nearby, listening intently.

Mavis snatched up the shotgun standing in the corner by the door. "Men ain't allowed in here anymore. Especially you."

Chance's face turned dull red, and Elizabeth quickly intervened. "We'll talk outside on the porch," she said, pulling him toward the wicker chairs and closing the front door in the women's curious faces.

Once on the porch, Elizabeth discreetly dropped Chance's arm, although he hardly seemed aware of her touch. "I'm sorry. Mavis is a little overprotective of me."

"Someone should be. Would you mind telling me what happened to your fence?"

Wearily, Elizabeth sank into one of the wicker chairs. "I believe that is fairly obvious. Someone took it into his or her head to make a false accusation. No one in my house saw or heard anything, and no one else on the street will admit to having seen anything. I called in the marshal, but he didn't think he could be of much help in catching the vandal."

"I know," Chance said. "I passed him on my way here." He was still smarting from Earp's suggestion that he take Elizabeth more firmly in hand. What Earp knew about women wouldn't fill a thimble. "Elizabeth, I warned you what would happen if you persisted in taking in prostitutes." Suddenly, the question of whether what she was doing was right or wrong had ceased to matter. He only knew he had to remove her from danger.

"Really, Chance, if you think I'm frightened by a little red paint, you're sadly mistaken. 'Sticks and stones,' you know."

"This time it was only paint and an ugly word. Next time someone might not stop at name-calling." He was gratified to see her surprise. "You're a bunch of women living alone without male protection. What's to stop someone from . . . from . . ." He cast about for some horrible examples. "From grabbing one of you on the way to the outhouse, or setting your house on fire, or even from sneaking inside and doing God only knows what?"

"We have a gun," she offered uncertainly.

"Yes, you do," he said, feeling heat crawl up his neck at the memory. "It's just fine for intruders who walk up and very politely knock on your front door."

"Your knock was hardly polite," she pointed out, annoyed at the way he had unnerved her. The dangers he had mentioned were real possibilities, ones she should have considered herself. Still, she could hardly believe anyone would take such drastic measures to stop her from rescuing a few women no one cared about. "I think you're exaggerating the dangers—"

"Exaggerating! Prostitution is a violent business, Elizabeth. I'd be willing to bet every one of those women you have in there could have been responsible for at least one killing. That's right," he asserted when her eyes widened in disbelief. "Oh, they didn't do the killing themselves, but men kill each other over women every day. The desire for sex seems to bring out the worst in people."

His words hung there for a long time as they stared at each other in appalled silence.

After what seemed an interminable time, Chance tore his gaze from hers and spun around to face the street. Staring out with unseeing eyes, he jammed his hands into his trouser pockets and drew a steadying breath as he fought to block out the image of her agonized expression.

How could he have said such a thing to her? Hadn't he vowed not to cause her another moment's heartache? And how could he apologize without making matters worse?

He cleared his throat, determined to salvage what was left of her pride by pretending they weren't both remembering something neither of them could ever forget. "You'd better accept that offer Bill made you the other day, Elizabeth, and send those women away immediately. It's for your own good."

He turned back to face her, once again in control of his emotions and grateful to see the anguished look was gone from her eyes.

"I will, if and when I find out everything is in order. I'm certainly not going to just send them away where they might be in danger—"

"Damnit, I don't care about them!"

Elizabeth blinked at his vehemence and heard herself ask the question uppermost in her mind. "Do you care about *me*, Chance?"

Care about her? God, yes, he cared about her. Too damn much for his own good. Or hers. "Of course I care what happens to you," he hedged, using all his years of experience at self-protection to keep his voice carefully neutral. "I'm your legal guardian. Bill Bates would have my head if I shirked my duty."

"Oh, of course," she said tightly, determined not to let him see her disappointment. She fixed her gaze on a point somewhere beyond his left shoulder and lifted her chin stubbornly. "I won't send them to Chicago until I know the situation there, Chance."

He fought down the unreasoning rage he felt at her defiance, knowing it was only caused by his own helpless frustration. Dear God, didn't she realize the danger she was in? "You may *have* to. Don't forget, I control your money. If you don't obey me, I can sell this house out from under you and cut you off without a cent."

He saw the flash of fear in her eyes, but defiance quickly

replaced it. "Bill would never allow you to do such a thing."

"Bill is in Chicago," he reminded her ruthlessly, and saw he had scored a hit. Uncertainty flickered in her eyes again, and her mouth turned down in a troubled frown. "Think about what I've said, Lizzie. I'll give you a chance to find someplace else for the women you have here now. You can send them up north or wherever, but when they're gone, it's over. Your days as a crusader are finished."

He turned and marched down her front steps. He slapped the gate shut behind him and spared only one last, derisive glance at the paint-spattered fence.

Watching him go, Elizabeth resisted the urge to call him back and demand to know exactly what he meant by his threats. Would he really cut her off without a cent? Would he really sell the house?

"Miss Livingston, what'd he say to you? You're white as a sheet." Mavis took her arm and led her back into the house as if she were a child, Barbara on her other side.

"He just warned me to expect more trouble," she lied, disturbed to hear how faint her voice sounded.

"He must've said something else," Barbara insisted. "You look like you've had a shock."

Elizabeth glanced at the women who had gathered around. The eyes staring back at her were jaded, having seen far too much in the few years each woman had lived. Was Chance right? Had they even seen murder? She did not want to know. "He threatened to cut off my allowance," she explained, instantly regretting her hasty confession. The other women were frightened, and rightly so. "He won't, of course," she quickly assured them. "He was only trying to scare me into sending you away, but of course you'll all be going to Chicago soon, anyway." She tried to smile, but it felt stiff on her lips, and no one smiled back. They were even more skeptical of the Chicago jobs than Elizabeth had been, placing not the slightest hope in them.

Mavis muttered a profanity. "That sonofabitch. Ain't there some way you can get out from under his thumb?"

The other women murmured their shared frustration as Elizabeth shook her head. "My father's will was very clear. Chance Fitzwilliam is my guardian until such time as I marry."

"Then you oughta get married," Molly decided, only to earn the frowning disapproval of the rest of the company.

"She'd be going from the frying pan into the fire, peabrain," Kate informed her. "You think any husband is gonna let her take in whores for a hobby?"

"Maybe he would," Molly insisted, but even she didn't sound sure. The others simply glared her into shamefaced silence.

The sharp ring of the doorbell brought an abrupt end to their futile conjectures. For a moment Elizabeth thought perhaps Chance had returned to apologize, but instead Mavis admitted a young woman carrying a carpetbag.

Elizabeth hurried forward to greet her.

"Am I in the right place?" the woman asked, staring in awe at the lavish furnishings.

"If you're looking for Miss Livingston's house, you are," Mavis said.

"Hello, I'm Elizabeth Livingston," Elizabeth added, extending her hand. Only then did she see the bruise discoloring the woman's left eye. Her smile of welcome froze on her face.

"Pleased to meet you. I'm Amy Waters," the woman replied, taking Elizabeth's hand gingerly, as if she were not accustomed to social niceties. Then, seeing how Elizabeth was staring, Amy let go and reached up to cover her bruise. "I . . . I had a little accident. Walked into a door, of all the stupid things."

"Did Shilling do that to you?" Mavis demanded.

"Oh, no, he never . . . well, he sometimes does," Amy admitted, "but this was an accident. I swear!"

"It doesn't matter," Elizabeth said, giving Mavis a warning look. "What matters is you're here, and we're happy you are. In fact, we were just about to sit down to supper. I hope you'll join us."

"I'd be pleased to," Amy said with a timid smile.

Amy was a lovely girl in spite of the bruise. She had large blue eyes that still seemed innocent in spite of the life Elizabeth knew she had led. Her hair was the exquisite shade of golden blond a brunette always covets, and she was young enough so the rigors of her work had not yet robbed her of her beauty. Her figure was trim and her calico dress neat.

Elizabeth recalled Chance's words of warning about taking in any new boarders. The smile she gave Amy was one of silent rebellion against him. "Good, just set your bag right here for now. We'll decide where you're going to sleep later."

Chance ignored the curious look his bartender gave him when he asked for a refill. He didn't need anyone to remind him he was drinking more than usual. "I'd forgotten how good our whiskey is," he said in explanation.

The bartender nodded. "They say a couple whiskeys from the Last Chance will raise the price of a trail herd a dollar or two a head."

"You're a mighty dangerous man," Chance replied, lifting his glass in a salute.

"So they tell me."

Chance drank a long swallow and set his glass down to take another look at the early evening crowd. Idly, he wondered how much time would have to pass and how many whiskeys he would have to consume before he forgot the wounded expression he had seen on Elizabeth's face today.

And how much time and alcohol would finally blot out the knowledge that he loved her.

Love, he thought with despair. Almost a decade had

passed since he had last thought himself in love. Sybil had been everything he'd ever wanted in a woman: beautiful, intelligent, witty, and sensuous. Their fathers had introduced them for the purpose of making a marriage of convenience. He'd found the idea of marriage to Sybil the most convenient thing he could imagine.

She, too, had known of their fathers' plans and been equally smitten, or so he had believed at the time. Their engagement party had been the social event of the Chicago season, and later, when Chance had kissed her with all the fervor of his youthful passion, she had responded with ardor. Her surrender then and on subsequent nights had been the stuff of a young man's fantasies.

Now that he was older and wiser, he realized she had been much too experienced to be a virgin, but such a thought had never entered his head in those days. She had intoxicated him, blinding him to reality and making him believe all his other dreams could come true, too. She'd laughed the first time he suggested leaving Chicago, scolding him for teasing her. He'd persisted, however, and at last she'd had no choice but to believe his plan to escape his father's influence. They would run away together, he told her. They would be poor, but at least they would have their integrity.

The problem was, Sybil did not want to be poor. Her plans revolved around his taking his rightful place as his father's only heir. She used all her considerable influence to change his mind and convince him he would be a fool to turn his back on the Fitzwilliam fortune. Failing to dissuade him, she had broken their engagement, leaving him devastated. He'd thought no pain could be worse than her rejection until he discovered her ultimate betrayal.

"Hey, Fitzwilliam, where's the dancing girls?"

The drunken inquiry jarred Chance from his memories. The question had come from a cattleman Chance remembered vaguely from previous visits. "You know we don't allow dancing girls on this side of the tracks, Cartwright.''

Cartwright's broad mouth stretched into a lascivious grin. ''That's not what I hear. I hear Chance Fitzwilliam's got the best girls in town. In fact,'' he added with a broad wink, ''I hear he keeps his own private whorehouse right here on the North Si—''

Chance's fist cut off the man's drunken ravings, sending him crashing into a nearby table. The table, Cartwright, and a cuspidor went flying, each in different directions, but Cartwright came bounding up again. He reached inside his coat, but before he could draw, he came face to face with the double barrels of a shotgun Chance had pulled from behind the bar.

''Your manners need some polishing, Cartwright,'' Chance said, his voice deadly calm. ''I'll be happy to shine them up with a load of buckshot, but maybe you'd like to take care of the task all on your own.''

Cartwright cautiously withdrew his hand from inside his coat, holding it up so Chance could see he was unarmed. ''I didn't mean no disrespect.''

''You folks from Texas must have a strange idea of what's respectful, then. I'll accept your apology, and thank you to get the hell out of my saloon.'' Chance was so outraged, he would have welcomed a further confrontation. Fortunately, the rancher had better sense than to tempt fate. He dusted himself off and made as dignified a retreat as possible.

When the doors had stopped swinging behind the rancher, Chance handed the shotgun to the bartender, who placed it back under the bar. ''You'd better be careful when you go out tonight, boss. Some of his boys're liable to be laying for you.''

Chance nodded, realizing with surprise that he might enjoy such an encounter. Since when had he found the prospect of violence so inviting?

Since Elizabeth Livingston made your life a living hell, an inner voice replied. She's got you so frustrated you're ready to take on the world in a bare-knuckle brawl. Well, maybe not the whole world, he allowed with a self-mocking grin, but at least the portion that had painted the word *whorehouse* on her fence. The very thought made his blood roar in his ears, and he knew if he got his hands on the culprit, he would gladly throttle him.

Chance decided not to analyze the situation further. After all, he knew how to solve the problem. He only needed a little more time.

Summer Winters walked slowly across the now-empty dance floor of the Lady Gay Saloon. Her professional eye took in the curtained alcoves where Oliver Shilling's girls were expected to entertain their customers after they got warmed up by the dancing. In the glare of the noonday sun, the room looked exactly the way it was: ugly and dirty. The smell of cheap whiskey, cheaper perfume, and stale tobacco smoke mingled with the lingering scent of unwashed bodies and other odors with which a madam was only too familiar.

Her heels made a hollow clatter on the scarred wooden floor as she strolled over to a tall, gaunt man sitting alone at a table nursing a glass of Kentucky bourbon. The eyes he lifted to her were bloodshot and hostile, but she did not hesitate for a moment.

"Good morning, Oliver. Fine day, isn't it?" she inquired, pulling out the chair opposite his and sitting down uninvited.

"If you're looking for a job, Summer, I can put you right to work," he said, giving her a leering smile. His teeth were yellow below his ragged mustache.

"Well, thank you, Oliver. You're sweet to offer, but I only came to commiserate. I understand you lost another girl to Miss Livingston yesterday." The smile Summer returned to him held no trace of sympathy.

Shilling muttered a curse as he ran a hand through his thinning brown hair. "I don't reckon there's any secrets in this town, is there?"

"Now, now, Oliver, there's no need for secrets between us anyways," she assured him, patting his arm with false solicitude. "We're all in this together, and we have to help each other."

"You're going to help *me?"* His tired expression lightened at the novelty of the idea. "What's it going to cost me?"

"Whatever you're willing to spend," she replied, refusing to be insulted. "All *I'm* going to do is give you some ideas, absolutely free of charge. You obviously need some. Honestly, Oliver, a dead cat and a painted fence? Don't you have any more imagination than that?"

"They wasn't my doing," he informed her, pushing his whiskey glass aside. "I haven't done nothing to the Livingston woman."

"You aren't afraid of Chance, are you?" she asked. "What could he possibly do to you?"

"He could have me shut down is what. He's in tight with Mayor Kelley and Earp and Masterson. They'd drum up some charges against me and—"

"Chance isn't going to shut you down, Oliver, or even be angry at you," she told him with a conspiratorial smile. "In fact, I happen to know he'll be *grateful* if you do a little something to discourage Miss Livingston from her sacred mission. He feels she's already been scared so much, she only needs one more incident to put her right out of business."

Shilling's homely face screwed itself into a suspicious frown. "Grateful? Why?"

"Because he wants all those whores out of her house just as much as you want them back in yours, that's why. You can't think he approves of what she's doing." Summer's kohl-darkened eyes widened in wonder at such an outlandish suggestion.

"Well, no," he admitted reluctantly, "but I didn't think he'd want anybody messing with her either."

"Oh, he doesn't want *her* hurt, of course, but he doesn't care about the others. Anything you want to do to them is fine, so long as you put the fear of God into Miss Livingston. Do you get my meaning?''

Shilling's leering smile slid slowly back into place. "Yeah, I get your meaning, and I know exactly who has a personal interest in the job.''

Chapter 8

Except for the distant din from the saloons along Front Street and beyond, the backyard was quiet as a wraithlike figure in a white nightdress emerged from the outhouse and started back up the walk to the house.

"Pssst, Amy, is that you?" a voice called out from the darkness.

Amy recognized the voice immediately. "What're you doing here?" she asked in alarm.

"Hey, don't be scared. I just want to talk. Come closer. I promise I won't hurt you."

"I said I didn't want to see you no more."

"Aw, Amy, just for a minute. I gotta tell you something real important."

Amy hesitated another moment, then stepped into the deeper shadows of the yard, following the voice until two strong arms reached out and grabbed her.

Elizabeth wasn't certain what disturbed her, but suddenly, she was wide awake. She lay still for a long time, listening to the silence and searching the shadows for something unfamiliar, but she heard nothing. She rolled over, trying to settle into a more comfortable position on the cot that had been her bed for the last few days, ever since Amy had come to stay.

All the rooms in the cavernous house were occupied now except the kitchen and dining room. Elizabeth had moved into the front parlor, the last room to be taken over, when it became obvious no one else felt comfortable there. She and Barbara had packed up most of the knickknacks to store in the shed out back, but the ponderous furniture remained. All hunched together now to accommodate her bed, they made horrendous shapes in the darkness.

Elizabeth tried to close her eyes, but memories of Chance's warnings teased her, forbidding the relaxation necessary for sleep. What if someone really did decide to sneak inside and do them harm? Every creak and groan in the big house took on an ominous meaning as Elizabeth strained for signs of an alien presence.

She tried to concentrate on something else, forcing herself to recall the note she had received from Bill that evening. He had arrived back late in the day, his train having been delayed by a wreck farther down the line. He'd kept his promise to return before the Fourth of July by only one day, but his note said he hoped she would still attend the Fireman's Ball with him. He also promised her good news about the Chicago jobs. She tried to dwell on this pleasant prospect instead of listening for the sound of footsteps on the stairs.

After a while, she rolled over again, wondering if she should put the pillow over her head to block out what her common sense told her were the normal sounds of the house settling. She had not yet decided when she heard the scream.

Elizabeth bounded from her bed and raced for the door, not bothering with a dressing gown or slippers. Above her she heard other bare feet hitting the floor and racing along the hallway toward the stairs. The scream sounded like it came from the rear of the house, but when Elizabeth reached the kitchen, she found the room dark and empty.

The scream must have come from outside. She ran to the back door, but just as she reached it, it flew open and a wild apparition lumbered into her. Elizabeth screamed as the impact drove them both to the floor. Instinctively, she fought to free herself from the tangle of arms and legs even as her brain began to register certain nonthreatening facts about her assailant.

Vaguely she was aware of other people pouring into the room, their shouts of alarm, and their attempts to free her. A light suddenly appeared, and someone cried, "It's Amy and Miss Livingston!"

Amy? Elizabeth peered up into her attacker's face and saw blue eyes as filled with terror as her own must be. "Amy!"

The girl's blue eyes rolled back, and she instantly went limp. "She's fainted!" Elizabeth cried, gently easing Amy off of her and onto the floor. A half-dozen hands hurried to assist her.

"What on earth . . . ?" Barbara burst out. "Why were you and Amy fighting?"

Elizabeth took several deep breaths to still the pounding of her heart. "We weren't fighting," she said. "I heard her scream like the rest of you did, and I rushed out here. She was coming in the back door just as I was trying to go out and we collided. I thought she was an attacker, and she must have been too hysterical to know who I was."

Amy moaned softly.

"Somebody throw some water in her face and wake her up so we can find out what happened," Mavis instructed.

Elizabeth gave Mavis a disapproving look and promptly bent over Amy and gently slapped her face to revive her. "Amy, can you hear me?"

Amy moaned again. Her big blue eyes flickered open and for an instant were filled with terror. "Oh, God," she murmured, closing her eyes again.

"Amy, are you hurt? Can you tell us what happened? Why did you scream?"

"If she's fainted again," Mavis said, "maybe we *should* throw water in her face."

Amy's eyes instantly opened, and she flashed what might have been a dirty look in Mavis's direction. Then she moaned more loudly and looked beseechingly at Elizabeth. "It was awful, Miss Livingston," she said. "There was this man . . . no, *three* men, and they grabbed me and . . ." Her voice trailed off into a sob.

"Good heavens!" Elizabeth's oath was by far the tamest one uttered. "Did they hurt you? Should I call a doctor?"

"No! No doctor!" Amy's voice was shrill, and Elizabeth feared she might be getting hysterical again.

"All right, no doctor, if you're sure you're all right," she said, speaking softly and reassuringly. "Barbara, would you get the bottle of cooking sherry and pour Amy a glass? She looks as if she could use some."

Everyone in the room turned toward the door with renewed terror at the sound of running, booted feet outside. Before Elizabeth could lament not having thought to close the door, Mr. Wilson appeared, a Winchester rifle in one hand and a Colt Peacemaker in the other. His eyes were wild. "Where are they? Which way'd they go?"

"Did you see them, Mr. Wilson?" Elizabeth asked, scrambling to her feet.

"Not really. A scream woke me up. When I got to the window, I saw a shadow running down the alley. I looked around outside just now before I came in, but I didn't see anybody. I was afraid maybe one of 'em came in here." Elizabeth noticed he had stuffed his nightshirt into a pair of hastily donned pants. His boots were unlaced. She had an almost overwhelming urge to kiss his wrinkled cheek. At last *somebody* was attempting to help them.

"I guess the attackers got away," Elizabeth said. "But we surely appreciate your help, Mr. Wilson."

He glanced at the women staring at him and suddenly grew beet red. "I'm just sorry we didn't catch anybody. Is . . . is there something else you'd like me to do?"

Elizabeth felt an urge to ask him to sit outside and guard the house for the rest of the night, but she knew she was being cowardly. Instead, she said, "If you wouldn't mind, I think the marshal should hear about this right away, whether he wants to or not."

"Herbert! Herbert, where are you? You get home this

minute!'' Mrs. Wilson's voice came screeching from their upstairs window.

"I'll fetch Marshal Earp just as soon as I tell Mrs. Wilson what happened," he promised, ducking out the back door.

When Elizabeth turned, she saw a look of abject terror on Amy's face. "Oh, Amy, it's all right," she said, rushing to the girl's side. "You're safe now. You don't have to be afraid anymore. Marshal Earp will come and—"

"I don't want to see no lawman!" Amy said, her face chalk white.

"But you have to," Elizabeth explained. "How else are we going to find out who these people are and stop them?"

"She's right, Amy," Mavis said, but Elizabeth thought her tone was anything but reassuring. "You'll have to tell the whole story to Marshal Earp."

"But I can't!" she wailed.

"Why not?" Elizabeth asked, all solicitude to make up for Mavis's harshness. She would have to speak to Mavis about being so mean to poor Amy.

"Because," Amy said, glancing at the curious faces peering down at her in the flickering lamplight. She paused, as if considering. "Because one of them raped me. I *can't* tell that to the marshal!"

"Oh, Amy!" Elizabeth cried, tears starting from her eyes. Only now did she notice Amy's disheveled appearance. The dirt and grass in her hair and on the back of her nightdress told a silent story. No wonder Amy had been so frantic to reach the safety of the house. If there had been three attackers . . . Elizabeth shuddered and impulsively took Amy in her arms and pulled her close for comfort, acutely aware that any one of them could have been the victim instead.

The girl stiffened in reaction until she divined Elizabeth's intent. Then slowly her own arms came up, and she hugged Elizabeth back. How unfair, Elizabeth thought. After all Amy had been through, how terrible for her to be attacked in the very place where she had sought safety.

After a moment, Elizabeth realized the other women were still standing and staring. Amy must feel doubly humiliated at being the object of their curiosity. She shot Barbara a beseeching look, hoping she would take the hint.

She did. "Well, now." Barbara's authoritative voice broke the silence. "If the marshal is coming, we'd better get ourselves decent. We can't greet him in our nightclothes. Mavis, close the door, will you? Everybody else, go on upstairs." In a matter of moments, Barbara had cleared the kitchen. Only she and Mavis remained behind to help with Amy.

Reluctantly, Elizabeth released the girl. "Do you think you can walk? You probably ought to be in bed after your ordeal, and I do wish you'd let me call a doctor."

"No, no doctor," Amy insisted, her eyes wide, "and I think I can walk . . . if you'll help me."

Mavis made a funny noise, but before Elizabeth could glance at her, Amy was struggling to her feet, occupying all her attention. They easily got Amy to the front parlor where Elizabeth tucked her up on the sofa after determining it would be improper for the marshal to interview her if she were in a bed. Elizabeth and the other women put dresses on over their nightdresses, but they had time for little else before Marshal Earp came pounding on the door.

Mr. Wilson was with him, and so was Bat Masterson, the county sheriff. If Wyatt Earp looked like a dandy, Bat Masterson *was* a dandy. Someone had once described him to Elizabeth as "the finest looking young man in Dodge City," and the description was certainly apt. Not only was he handsome, but his clothes were immaculately tailored, and he wore a jaunty derby hat similar to Chance's. He had a charming smile for her even though Marshal Earp looked disgruntled.

"Mr. Wilson says you had some more trouble here, Miss Livingston," Earp said by way of greeting.

"Yes, three men attacked one of my guests in the backyard not long ago. Please come in, and she'll tell you the whole story."

Earp went into the parlor where Mavis and Barbara waited with Amy. The other women either stood in the hallway or sat on the stairs. Earp did not even spare them a glance. Masterson started to follow him into the parlor, but paused for a moment to say to Elizabeth, "I hope you don't mind my tagging along, Miss Livingston. This isn't my jurisdiction, but I'm always concerned when someone breaks the peace in town."

"I'm sure Marshal Earp is grateful for any help you can give him," Elizabeth said with a smile.

Mr. Wilson walked in behind Masterson, but his wife's voice came screeching once again. "Herbert? Are you there? You get yourself home this instant! I don't want to hear of you going into that house."

Mr. Wilson winced and gave Elizabeth a look of pained apology.

"Perhaps you'd better go on home, Mr. Wilson. We don't want your wife to worry about you."

"No, no, we don't," he agreed in an agony of embarrassment.

"And, Mr. Wilson, I want to thank you again for trying to help us tonight. I appreciate it more than I can tell you."

He shrugged. "Any decent man would've done the same."

"Yes, but there are too few truly decent men in this town. I'm proud to have one of them for a neighbor." When Wilson left, he was once more blushing profusely.

Elizabeth followed the two lawmen into the parlor, painfully aware they were entering what was now her bedroom. Amy huddled under the blanket Elizabeth had thrown over her and stared fearfully at the two men. Elizabeth bade them be seated, and when they had, she sat at the foot of the sofa where Amy lay to lend the girl moral support.

"Please tell the marshal what happened," Elizabeth said, giving Amy a meaningful look. They had all agreed the men did not need to know about the rape, only that Amy had been waylaid.

Amy took a shaky breath and said, "I was coming back from the necessary house. It's dark back there, so I was kind of nervous, but I didn't see anything out of the ordinary. Then, all of a sudden, somebody grabbed me and pulled me into the bushes. I tried to yell, but he clamped a hand over my mouth so I could hardly even breathe."

She paused, looking to Elizabeth for encouragement.

Marshal Earp cleared his throat impatiently. "Miss Livingston said there were *three* men."

"Oh, there were," Amy insisted as if she had just remembered. "I tried to fight, but they held my arms and my legs, and they forced me down on the ground. I'll probably be black and blue all over."

Earp and Masterson exchanged glances, and Elizabeth imagined they were silently debating the advisability of asking to see the bruises. They must have known Elizabeth would never permit such a thing, however, because Earp asked, "What happened next?"

"Well"—Amy looked down at the floor for a long moment, idly toying with the edge of her blanket—"first one of them says, 'Are you one of the whores?' but he had his hand over my mouth, so I couldn't answer. I tried to shake my head no, but another one says, 'Sure she is. The Livingston woman's got black hair, and this one's a blonde.' "

Amy glanced at Elizabeth again, as if for approval. This story was completely new to Elizabeth and the other women, who had heard nothing beyond the fact that one of the men had forced himself on Amy and the others had manhandled her. Elizabeth nodded, and Amy continued, warming now to the tale. "The first one says, 'We got a message for you, and you can tell all the other whores, too. There's people on the South Side who don't like you being over here, and if you don't leave, this is what you're all gonna get.' And then he pushed up my nightdress and did it to me, right there on the ground."

Both men started at the frankness of her confession, and Barbara and Elizabeth grasped aloud.

"Amy, you don't have to—" Elizabeth began, but Amy did not seem to hear.

"And when he was finished, the other two took their turns, and I can tell you, I ain't never been treated so rough. Then they slapped me a couple of times and turned me loose. That's when I screamed and ran into the house."

"Oh, Amy!" Elizabeth saw the girl through the haze of her own tears. How hardened to brutality Amy must be to tell such a horrible story so calmly. Elizabeth's heart ached for the suffering she had endured, the horror she had experienced. When Amy turned to her and saw the tears streaming down Elizabeth's face, her own composure finally broke. She fell sobbing into Elizabeth's arms.

Sheriff Masterson coughed discreetly until he had obtained Elizabeth's attention. Remembering her manners, she realized how uncomfortable all this must be for the lawmen. With stern gentleness, she managed to calm Amy and dry both her own tears and Amy's with a handkerchief Barbara supplied.

When she was satisfied Amy was all right, she turned again to the men. "I hope you think *this* crime is serious enough to be investigated," she told Earp tartly.

Earp frowned and exchanged another look with Masterson, who quickly covered his mouth and coughed nervously. When Earp looked back at Elizabeth, he said, "As a matter of fact I don't, Miss Livingston."

"What! Are you telling me that when a woman is attacked in this town, the law does nothing?"

Earp's frown deepened, and his eyes flashed dangerously. "When a *lady* is attacked, we hang the son of a bit—we hang the man responsible. But in a case like this . . ." His voice trailed off.

"A case like what?" Elizabeth demanded.

Earp sighed. "Miss Livingston, it's a well-known fact a whore can't be raped." He ignored Elizabeth and Barbara's outraged gasps. "Even if I found the men responsible and took the case to court, I'd be laughed out of Dodge. Maybe the men would be fined for not paying her . . . *maybe*, but that's the worst punishment they'd get.''

Elizabeth stared at him in stunned silence.

Amy sniffed loudly and wiped her nose with the back of her hand. "See, I told you, Miss Livingston. They ain't gonna do nothing."

Masterson seemed to have recovered himself, and now he gave Elizabeth an apologetic smile. "Look at it this way, Miss. With tomorrow being the Fourth of July, there's an awful lot of strangers in town. We wouldn't even know where to start looking. Tell me, Amy, could you describe any of the men?''

Elizabeth noticed Masterson called Amy by her given name with the ease of long familiarity, but she chose not to think about the implications. Instead she listened hopefully to Amy's reply.

But Amy shook her head dolefully. "Only that they smelled of whiskey."

Masterson turned back to Elizabeth. "Most of the men in Dodge smell of whiskey tonight, Miss Livingston. It's not much to go on.''

Once again Elizabeth felt impotent rage course through her. This time she had been so certain the law would *have* to help. Surely men who attacked women were the dregs of society, those most fiercely despised by men and women of every class, but now she understood only men who attacked *decent* women were despised. The other kind of women didn't matter. Hurting them was no crime at all. In fact, it was actually some sort of dirty joke if she could judge by Bat Masterson's ill-concealed amusement.

Masterson quickly rose, urging Earp to do the same. "Amy, if you remember anything else, you let Wyatt here know. We can at least run those skunks out of town if you can tell us who they are.''

Amy simply glared at the two men as they took their leave. Elizabeth let Barbara see them out. Only when they were gone did Elizabeth notice the strange way Mavis, who had been uncharacteristically silent through the interview, was staring at Amy. Before she could ask Mavis the reason for her odd expression, however, Amy burst into tears again.

"All I wanted to do was go to the outhouse," Amy wept into Elizabeth's shoulder.

With shocking clarity, Elizabeth heard Chance's earlier warning echoing in her head.

"What's wrong, Elizabeth?" Mavis asked. "You've gone stark white."

"I . . . I just remembered something Mr. Fitzwilliam said to me," she admitted. "He said if we weren't careful, somebody might grab one of us on the way to the outhouse."

Mavis frowned. "Why'd he say a thing like that?"

Even Amy pulled slightly away, awaiting her reply. "He said we were asking for trouble. He was trying to frighten me, I suppose, and he said our gun wouldn't scare away anyone truly bent on doing us harm. He even suggested someone might burn down the house."

This sent Amy into a new fit of weeping, and Elizabeth drew her close again. Mavis patted Elizabeth's hand where it rested on Amy's back. "Don't fret about it. Like you said, he was only trying to scare you. I suspect he'd like to see you shed of the lot of us."

Elizabeth nodded absently, but she could not shake the uncomfortable prickle of suspicion. How could Chance have predicted so accurately what had happened tonight?

The morning of the Fourth dawned bright and warm with the promise of intense heat before the afternoon parade was over. Elizabeth had slept poorly even after assuring herself Amy did not need medical attention and seeing everyone else off to bed. The house had still creaked ominously, as if invisible intruders crept through it searching for new victims.

When the rising sun turned the sky pink, she managed to drift off at last, only to be awakened shortly afterward by the pop of firecrackers and the shouts of young boys in the street. The celebration had officially begun.

With sleep now impossible, the women gathered listlessly in the dining room for coffee and toast. Elizabeth was surprised to see Amy come in dressed, smiling, and apparently none the worse for her ordeal.

"Sounds like the fun's already started. I can't hardly wait for the parade. I just love parades," Amy informed the group as she waltzed over to the ornate sideboard and poured a cup of coffee.

When she turned back to face the others and saw their stunned expressions, her smile froze. "Something wrong?" she asked.

Mavis's lips curled in contempt. "You must be feeling some better this morning, Miss Amy. Ain't you even a little sore?"

Amy's pretty mouth pursed. "I've felt worse," she admitted. "I'm bruised up some, like I said I would be, but I reckon I'll live. Anyways, I ain't the kind to sit around crying about what's over and done. Best to think about today and get as much fun as you can, 'cause there's no telling what'll come tomorrow."

This was, Elizabeth had to admit, a practical philosophy, but in light of what had happened to Amy the previous night, Elizabeth couldn't begin to understand how the girl could forget so easily. Memories of Elizabeth's one sexual experience haunted her still. If she was so disturbed by an encounter with a man she loved and to whom she had surrendered willingly, how must Amy feel at having been forced by three strangers? But then, Amy was used to intimacy with strangers. Perhaps one became inured to that kind of horror when one lived with it on a daily basis.

She glanced at Barbara, whose expression said she was as puzzled over Amy's quick recovery as Elizabeth was, but none of the other women seemed particularly surprised, so Elizabeth had to assume her theory was correct. She had thought no one would feel much like participating in the Fourth of July celebration, but now she realized she had been wrong. In fact, celebrating the holiday seemed to be exactly what everyone needed to make them forget their troubles. With mixed emotions, Elizabeth joined in their plans for viewing the afternoon parade.

Bill Bates came calling in a rented buggy just as they were preparing to leave the house. After welcoming him home, Elizabeth eyed the vehicle apologetically. "I promised my friends I'd go to the parade with them."

"But I had to move heaven and earth to get this buggy. You can't turn me away and break my heart," Bill argued.

"Go with him, for heaven's sake," Barbara said when Elizabeth hesitated. "You'll have a lot more fun than you will with a bunch of women."

"Besides," Mavis added with a twinkle, "it'll be nice for us to meet somebody in the crowd who'll speak to us."

Elizabeth could not argue, knowing her friends would be snubbed equally by representatives from both sides of the tracks. Still, she was afraid Amy's apparent recovery was just bravado that might not sustain her once she began to mingle with the crowds. "I don't know . . ." Elizabeth hedged.

The other women shouted down Elizabeth's remaining objections and pushed her out the door to join Bill, who whooped triumphantly at her capitulation.

Seeing she still had misgivings, he tempered his enthusiasm somewhat. "This is really a business meeting," he informed her with mock solemnity as he helped her up into the buggy. "I have to report to you on my trip."

He was right, of course. They did have some important things to discuss, but was this the proper time? "Do you normally conduct business while watching a parade, Mr. Bates?" Elizabeth asked skeptically.

"No, but we have at least half an hour before the parade actually starts. We have to get there early if we want a good spot, and while we're sitting in the sun, baking our brains, I can tell you all about what happened in Chicago."

"I have no intention of baking my brain," Elizabeth said in feigned outrage as she put up her parasol. The midday sun was merciless, but the stiff breeze off the prairie and the shade from both the buggy top and Elizabeth's parasol made it almost bearable. She had selected a fine lawn gown in deference to the heat, and she decided if she had not been burdened with her corset and drawers, she might even be comfortable. At least she wasn't required to wear a suit coat, she thought with a sympathetic glance at Bill.

Most of the townspeople and those who had come in for the day were already situated along the parade route, and many of them called a greeting to Bill and Elizabeth as they rode past. Bill was unconcerned by the crowding and quickly found them a choice place from which to view the event. Then he went to procure them each a cool glass of lemonade from a vendor. While she waited, Elizabeth entertained herself by watching the crowd, hoping to catch sight of Chance.

Chance sensed her presence even before he spotted her green parasol sticking out of the buggy. He sat his horse overlooking the crowd and, without conscious thought, kneed the animal toward her. She hadn't seen him yet, which gave him a opportunity to study her unobserved. Her magnificent ebony hair had been swept up beneath a pert bonnet, leaving her neck exposed above the modest neckline of her dress.

Against his will, he imagined cruel hands closing around the vulnerable white flesh, the nightmare that had haunted him all night. After hearing about the attack on one of her boarders, Chance had barely been able to resist the urge to go to her, to make certain she was all right, the hour and propriety be damned. But hadn't Earp and Masterson assured him of her safety? Hadn't they even, at his insistence and unbeknownst to Elizabeth, placed a deputy on guard at the house in case the attackers returned?

In spite of all that, even in the light of day, the thought of Elizabeth coming so close to danger still had the power to make his blood run cold. If she saw him, surely she would guess his torment. He should ride away, but before he could, she glanced in his direction.

Elizabeth lifted her eyes, and there Chance was, not five feet away. To her surprise, in that one unguarded instant she glimpsed not outrage but naked longing in his eyes.

Instantly, all expression except polite interest vanished from his face. ''Good afternoon, Cousin Elizabeth,'' he said, tipping his hat.

''Good afternoon, Cousin Chauncey,'' she replied, thinking how striking he looked astride the big bay gelding. ''It's a nice day for the parade, don't you think?''

His lips quirked at the banality of her remark, but he said, ''Personally, I'd prefer cooler weather, but I suppose we can't hope for much better than this in July.''

Her own lips twitched, although she managed to resist the urge to smile. From the corner of her eye, she saw Bill approaching carrying two glasses.

''Chance! Nice to see you. I was just going to tell Elizabeth all about my trip. Why don't you join us?'' Bill's smile was guileless. Chance gave only a hint of the wariness she knew he must be feeling as he swung down from his horse and came closer.

Bill handed Elizabeth her lemonade and climbed up beside her in the buggy while Chance tethered the bay to the back wheel. As Chance came up to stand at her other side, Elizabeth took a sip of the tart-sweet liquid to cover the surge of excitement she felt at his nearness. She turned to Bill expectantly.

''The factory is everything I'd hoped for and more,'' he began. ''The working conditions are much better than I've seen anyplace else, and the pay is above average. The man who owns the factory seems as interested in his employees' welfare as he is in making a profit.''

''A very enlightened attitude,'' Elizabeth remarked, still not able to believe such an idyllic situation could exist, much less that it had fallen into her lap.

''I met with your benefactor's man of business,'' Bill

continued. "A shrewd fellow by the name of Ebenezer Cooper. Mr. Cooper is utterly disapproving of your bene-factor's insistence on 'coddling' his employees, as Cooper put it, but he accepts it." Bill smiled conspiratorily. "He took me to see the dormitory. It's a perfectly respect-able hotel fallen on hard times due to poor management. Cooper grudgingly admits the building will be more than adequate to house all the ladies you can send plus any of the other single females who work at the factory and want to live there for reasons of economy and safety. All the place needs is some cleaning to put it in perfect condition. The man who owns the factory has purchased the building and intends to charge the women room and board, but he'll only charge them his own costs. He's not planning to make a profit on the feeding and lodging of his employees."

Elizabeth still could not credit what Bill was saying. What would her father have thought if he heard such generous terms being offered to employees? He was an honest businessman, but shrewd enough never to run any enterprise without turning a profit. In fact, no one of her acquaintance would even think of making such a magnanimous arrangement. The person behind all this must be some sort of saint. As much as she loved Chance, Elizabeth could hardly credit him with sainthood.

She looked up at Chance, still hoping to discover he was the benefactor. "What would your father have thought of these business practices?"

Chance raised his eyebrows in faint amusement, dashing what remained of her hopes. "He would have agreed with this fellow Cooper, I'm sure. He would have thought the owner completely mad."

"And what do you think?"

"I'm *sure* he's mad."

Disappointment formed a leaden lump in her stomach. Surely, if Chance were the owner, he would at least defend himself to her. She told herself she was silly to be so upset. After all, what did it matter *who* the benefactor was? And did she love Chance any less because he didn't own the factory? Of course not.

She turned back to Bill and gave him a smile that must have reflected her disappointment because the satisfied gleam in his eye faded a bit. She hastened to justify her lack of enthusiasm. "I think Chance may be right. This all sounds too good to be true. Why would anyone want to be so generous to women most people would hardly consider deserving?"

"As Mr. Cooper explained to me—and please understand, he absolutely refuses to condone such irrational behavior—the owner believes the workers will be more loyal and productive if they have a decent place to live and wholesome food to eat, rather than living in the rat-infested hovels most factory workers inhabit and eating catch-as-catch-can."

"The idea has a certain logic," she conceded. Perhaps the factory owner was not as saintly as she had first thought. Perhaps he was equally as shrewd as her father, only smarter since he had considered the human element of business, an aspect too many entrepreneurs overlooked. But did her new analysis of the situation mean Chance might be the benefactor after all?

"Elizabeth, is something bothering you? As I said, if you don't trust my judgement, you can go to Chicago yourself. I'm sure you'd find Ebenezer Cooper delightful and—"

"Oh, no, Bill. Of course I trust your judgement. I wouldn't think of insulting you by checking up on you. I guess it's just . . . well, I'm thinking how difficult it will be to say good-bye to all my houseguests," she improvised, coming up with another painfully true reason for her lack of enthusiasm. "We've become close friends."

Bill's expression reflected his astonishment, and Chance frowned. "Oh, I know they aren't the sort of women I would have met in the normal course of my life, and some of them are difficult to like. Still, others are as good and loyal and kind as anyone I've ever known." Parting with

Mavis and Molly and poor little Amy would be painful. Suddenly, Elizabeth noticed a skeptical quirk on Chance's mouth.

"Tell me, Elizabeth, do you consider that harridan with the shotgun a good and kind friend?"

"She wasn't really going to shoot you," Elizabeth said. "I told you, the gun is only to frighten off intruders . . ." Her voice trailed off as she realized the ploy had not worked, just as Chance had warned.

"Elizabeth, what is it?"

"I was thinking about—" She caught herself just in time. If Chance didn't already know about last night, she certainly didn't want to inform him.

But she didn't have to. "You were thinking about the attack last night, weren't you?"

Elizabeth stared at him in astonishment. *He knew!*

"Attack? Who was attacked?" Bill asked.

"One of Elizabeth's guests was attacked outside her house last night," Chance explained grimly.

"My God!" Bill exclaimed. "Was she badly hurt?" Elizabeth was vaguely surprised Chance had not already told him.

"She just got some bruises, thank heaven," Elizabeth hedged. Propriety forbade her to explain exactly what Amy had endured. "She made a miraculous recovery, and she's even coming to the parade today."

Bill looked as surprised by this news as Elizabeth had been. "This is very serious, Elizabeth. You really ought to report it to the authorities."

"I *did* report it," she informed him angrily. "Marshal Earp explained to me that an attack on a prostitute—even a former prostitute—is not considered a crime in Dodge City."

Bill opened his mouth to protest, but after a quick look at Chance, closed it again. Watching the emotions play across his face, Elizabeth began to suspect he and Chance might sympathize with Earp's opinion. "Surely you don't think so, too," she demanded of both of them.

"Of course not! Every woman should be safe in her own backyard," Bill quickly demurred. Too quickly, she thought.

"Don't blame Earp for not taking this too seriously," Chance explained. "You can't believe the stories women like that tell just to stir up trouble."

"You believe she wasn't really attacked?" Elizabeth challenged.

"I have no way of judging," Chance replied, wishing he could find a way to be certain. He would sleep much more easily if he could be sure Elizabeth was in no danger. Now the best he could do was put out a warning that anyone harming her would have to deal with him, something he should have done long ago, he realized bitterly. He had foolishly expected the rougher elements to know his family relationship to her implied his protection.

Elizabeth sighed in frustration. She supposed she would get no sympathy from these or any other males. As Mavis had explained last night after the lawmen left, most men didn't see much harm in taking another slice off a loaf of bread that's already been cut.

She said to Bill, "I'm surprised you didn't hear anything about the incident. I thought it would be the town's main topic of gossip by now."

"It is," Chance said. The coldness of his tone sent a prickle of warning up Elizabeth's spine. "Bill left the Last Chance early last night, or he would have heard the news straight from Marshal Earp, too."

Again, Elizabeth studied his face, searching for signs of his true feelings. Where was the Chance who had ranted and raved over a painted fence and a dead cat? He should be furious because a woman had been violated, but instead he stared back at her calmly. Had he ceased to care?

Chance shifted uneasily under her scrutiny. Could she tell how tenuous his self-control was? Did she know he wanted to grab her and shout out his frustration? Could she tell he wanted to carry her off and lock her safely away where no harm would ever befall her? Had she guessed his guilt, the guilt he felt because he might have prevented the tragedy to Amy by issuing a few threats to the right people? In an attempt to distract her, he said to Bill, "Why don't you tell Elizabeth some more about the factory in Chicago. Exactly what kind of jobs would the women be doing?"

Acutely aware of Chance's continued presence less than an arm's length away, Elizabeth listened with half an ear to Bill's explanations. She tried not to think about the mysteries surrounding Chance and the many questions to which she had no answers. She especially avoiding asking herself what she would do if he really had ceased to care for her. Or if he had never cared at all.

For several minutes Bill regaled her with further tales of the Chicago enterprise. Unable to concentrate, Elizabeth was glad when Bat Masterson drew Bill's attention with a shout.

"Bill! I didn't know you were back in town!" he exclaimed, hurrying up to the buggy. He nodded a greeting to Chance and tipped his hat at Elizabeth, sparing them only a moment's attention.

"I got in late yesterday—" Bill began, but Masterson cut him off.

"You've got to march in the parade."

Bill chuckled, certain Masterson was teasing. "I've got the best seat on the street for *watching* the parade and the prettiest lady in town to watch it with. Why would I want to march in it?"

"Because Tom's dead drunk," he explained, lowering his voice discreetly, "and as assistant fire chief, it's your job to lead the men if the chief isn't able to."

"You're the assistant fire chief?" Elizabeth asked, delighted.

"It's only an honorary position," Bill said.

"The other men would be disappointed if they found out you wouldn't march with them," Masterson pointed out.

Elizabeth knew membership in the fire company was a

coveted honor. To have been selected for a position of leadership showed the respect the other men in Dodge had for Bill. "You can't let them down," she said.

She could see his indecision. "But I'm your escort," he reminded her.

"Chance'll look after Miss Livingston, won't you, Chance?" Masterson asked, not waiting for an answer. "Bill, you have just enough time to get into your uniform if you hurry."

At her elbow, Elizabeth sensed Chance stiffen at the sheriff's request, but he did not reply. Did he find the prospect of spending time with her so onerous? Perversely, Elizabeth seconded Masterson's request. "Don't worry about me, Bill. Chance will take good care of me," she said with a forced smile. "I wouldn't think of letting you shirk your responsibilities, and besides, I'm looking forward to seeing you in your uniform."

Still not convinced, Bill gave Chance an inquiring look. "Take my horse," Chance said. "You'll save some time." If his offer was less than enthusiastic, Elizabeth was the only one who appeared to notice. She barely heard Bill's apologies as he climbed out of the buggy, hurried along by Masterson.

Chance disappeared around the rear of the buggy to help Bill with the horse. In a few moments Bill rode away and Chance reappeared at the buggy's side, then hesitated, as if reluctant to take his friend's place on the seat. In silent invitation, Elizabeth drew her skirt closer to make room. With what sounded like a sigh of resignation, Chance climbed inside.

Chance cursed himself roundly. What was he thinking of to climb into a buggy with Elizabeth? The last time they'd shared one, they had ended up in each other's arms. Of course, they were more than adequately chaperoned today by the Fourth of July crowds. Unfortunately, with Elizabeth so close chaperones didn't seem to matter. Hadn't he kissed her the other day on her front porch in full view of anyone who might happen to look?

Elizabeth took a nervous sip of her lemonade as Chance's nearness seemed to raise the summer temperature by another ten degrees. She listened to him breathe for a minute, surprised at how loud it sounded, then she cast about for something to say to break the awkward silence. "Aren't you a member of the fire company?"

"Yes, but only insofar as the social events go. I draw the line at parading up and down Front Street in my underwear."

"Your underwear!" Elizabeth flushed. "Mr. Masterson said something about a uniform."

Chance tipped his hat back so he could see her better. "The uniform is a pair of red longhandles."

"Oh," Elizabeth said, and took another sip of lemonade. The parade should be very interesting indeed.

Chance watched her, intrigued by the startled vulnerability in her emerald eyes. The urge to gather her close and soothe it away was like a raging fire in his chest, and he curled his hands into fists in an effort to resist. Instead he said, "Would you like me to hire someone to guard your house?"

His voice was flat, just as flat as it had been before when she had thought he didn't care about the attack on Amy, but now she could see the intensity of his eyes, the smoldering anguish he was trying to disguise. Her own anguish melted into a sweet glow. "I . . . I don't know. Who would you hire?"

He shrugged. "I don't think I'd have much trouble finding a man to guard a houseful of women."

"Exactly the problem," Elizabeth said, foreseeing the potential for abuse of the job. "The wrong kind of man would be only too glad to apply. We have enough problems without worrying about a man who's being paid to hang around and spy on us."

Chance's control snapped. "Dammit, Lizzie, you could have been the one they attacked last night. Have you thought of that?"

"They didn't want me," she protested even as renewed

fear curled inside of her. "They said they wanted one of the 'whores.' "

"You don't believe that any more than I do. I can tell by looking at you. Your hands are shaking."

Elizabeth wrapped her betraying fingers more tightly around the glass she held. "You heard what Bill said about the jobs in Chicago. Now the women will be able to leave Dodge, and when they're gone, no one will have any reason to do me harm."

Chance drew a shaky breath and let it out slowly as he tried to remind himself Elizabeth would soon be out of danger. "How soon can they leave?" he asked bluntly.

"Chance!" Before Elizabeth could chasten him further, the blare of brass instruments announced the beginning of the parade. What with the music and the accompanying shouts from the crowd, conversation became impossible. With a resigned sigh, Elizabeth settled back against the seat and drained her lemonade glass. Doggedly focusing her attention on the spectacle of the parade, she reminded herself he was only concerned about her safety and she managed to regain most of the warm glow the realization had originally caused.

First Dodge City's Cowboy Band marched by, resplendent in their blue flannel shirts, silk scarves, leather leggings, and spurred boots. Large floppy sombreros protected them from the glare of the sun, and the huge Navy six-shooters and cartridge belts they wore would protect them from anything else. The blazing sunlight reflected dazzlingly off the silver and brass of the horns which blared forth a rousing rendition of "Buffalo Gals, Won't You Come Out Tonight?" The crowd gave a lusty cheer in response.

Behind the band came a collection of children of assorted sizes, each wearing a banner representing one of the states or territories that made up the United States of America. Unfortunately, as the parade went on with various and sundry social groups each represented by an exhibit mounted on some sort of vehicle, Elizabeth found it less and less of a distraction and she grew ever more aware of the man beside her.

In the close confines of the buggy, she was conscious of his every breath. Her own lungs strained as the taunting scent of bay rum and cigars and Chance Fitzwilliam swirled around her. His elbow bumped hers, and her gaze flew to his for one electric moment before ricocheting away again.

Chance watched the parade with unseeing eyes. God in heaven, why had he ever gotten into this buggy with her? The cursed thing seemed to be shrinking until he couldn't move a muscle without bumping against her. And those eyes! As green as the bottomless ocean and equally dangerous. A man could lose himself in them and not even mind. His shirt beneath his coat had grown damp. He wished he could blame the July heat.

Through the haze of his thoughts, Chance caught sight of someone waving. With conscious effort, he focused and saw Bill trying to catch their attention. "There's the fire company," he said.

Elizabeth waved at Bill, who was marching proudly at the forefront of the group. She had to admit the Dodge City Fire Company made an impressive sight wearing their red long-handled uniforms and pulling their shiny new hose cart. She tried not to remember Chance's remark about underwear, but she couldn't help wondering how he would look in the revealing outfit.

"You should have marched with them," Elizabeth said, her imagination making her smile. "Aren't you proud to belong?"

"Of course. They give the best parties in town."

"I've heard their drills are thrilling to watch."

"Drills are easy," he replied, refusing to rise to her bait. "What nobody knows is how we'd do in a real fire since Dodge City has never had one."

"Let's hope you never have to prove yourselves."

"Yes, let's," he agreed somberly.

They sat in silence, listening to the Cowboy Band playing "Red River Valley" to the tumultuous delight of the Texans as the tail end of the parade marched out of sight. The conductor, Professor Eastman, directed the group with a six-shooter, "to kill the first man who strikes a false note," or so he claimed.

Even before the song ended, the crowd was moving toward the southwest edge of town for the next event in the day's activities. Elizabeth wondered whether Chance would use the excuse to leave her. Didn't he feel the attraction drawing her to him? And how could he relinquish her to another man if he did?

He couldn't, she realized with delight as he turned to her with a rueful smile. "Are you ready to go see some *real* horseracing, Cousin Elizabeth?"

She was, but only under certain conditions. "Not if you're going to be disagreeable all afternoon."

Chance studied the stubborn tilt of her chin and the determined glitter in her eyes. He should run like hell. What little resistance he still possessed was rapidly evaporating.

But why deny himself a few pleasant hours with her, especially in public where nothing untoward could happen? Tomorrow was soon enough to take up the torture of living without her again.

Elizabeth watched his silent struggle and held her breath until his finely molded lips stretched into the utterly charming smile she saw all too seldom. "If I start acting disagreeable, you can pinch me."

The tension drained out of her, leaving her almost giddy. "Don't worry, I will."

Chapter 9

"Will the racing be the type I'm used to?" Elizabeth asked as Chance directed the buggy toward the tracks.

"Probably not. I imagine the good people of Philadelphia are too staid for the kind of racing we do here in Dodge."

"And what kind is that?"

"Wild and fast."

"Just like everything else in Dodge City."

"Exactly. The horses won't be Thoroughbreds, of course, but I think you'll be impressed with their fleetness."

"I'll let you know."

"The fire company is in charge," he continued, ignoring her barb, "so everything will be done in style. Look, you can see the tents from here."

Huge tents had been erected for the comfort of the audience, and vendors were selling all manner of culinary delights: ice cream, ears of corn, waffles with powdered sugar, pretzels, and beer. Chance found a spot not far away to leave the buggy, and as he came around to help Elizabeth down, she felt a quiver of anticipation.

"I suppose we should try to find Bill," she said when he released her.

"No, we shouldn't," he replied with a twinkle, offering her his arm. "He was unspeakably rude to desert you at the parade and leave you with a notorious saloonkeeper. We'll let him find us."

She took Chance's arm, feeling unreasonably proprietary in her possession. The first race was beginning, and Chance led her to a shady spot beneath a tent where they had a good view.

"I like the bay," Elizabeth said when she had looked over the horses being lined up for the race.

"You have a good eye, but the gray has more bottom."

"Would you care to make a small wager?"

Chance's eyebrows lifted. "How small?"

"Oh, I don't know," she said thoughtfully, eyeing him from head to foot.

"What are you looking at?"

"I'm trying to decide what you have that I want."

Chance made a choking noise. "Elizabeth, I can see your upbringing has failed to instill in you a certain gentility of manner."

"Are you changing your opinion of Philadelphians?"

"No, I'm sure they aren't all as wild and fast as you are," he said with mock sternness. "As your guardian, I'm afraid I'm going to have to—ouch!"

"You said I could pinch you if you became disagreeable," she reminded him.

"I didn't say it could *hurt,*" he complained, rubbing his arm.

"Sissy."

"Hoyden."

The crowd roared as the race began. Startled, Elizabeth drew closer to Chance's side. He responded by settling his free hand over hers where it rested on his sleeve.

Their eyes met, and suddenly it was as if they were alone. The crowd, the race, the noise all ceased to exist as Elizabeth watched Chance's dark eyes soften. "Have I ever mentioned how incredibly lovely you are?" he whispered.

Fierce emotions, joy and love and triumph, clogged her throat so that she could only shake her head.

His mouth curved upward while his eyes glowed with

admiration. He was about to speak again when someone called his name, shattering their private world.

"Chance, there you are!" Bill had changed back into his suit, and he was grinning broadly, at least until he saw Chance and Elizabeth spring guiltily apart.

"I see Chance has been taking good care of you." Bill's expression grew speculative as his gaze went from one to the other.

"We saw you in the parade," Elizabeth said brightly. "You looked very dashing in your uniform."

"I would rather have been sitting in the buggy with you."

"Don't bother to be gallant for my sake," she scolded. "I saw how proud you looked marching with the other firemen, and besides—"

"Besides, Elizabeth wouldn't know good manners if they hit her on the—ouch!" Chance glared at her, but she ignored him.

"Chance took excellent care of me," Elizabeth finished. "Of course I did have to remind him of his own manners now and again."

"So I see," Bill said, not bothering to conceal his amusement. "Have you two had any ice cream yet?"

"Not yet," Chance said, "but you're probably dying for something cold after marching around in the hot sun. Find Elizabeth a seat, and I'll get us something."

Elizabeth's gaze followed him until he was lost from view in the milling throng.

"I get the feeling you didn't miss me at all," Bill remarked. Taking her elbow, he directed her toward the center of the tent where benches had been set up.

"Of course I missed you," she lied politely. His eyebrows lifted skeptically, but he did not challenge her.

They were seating themselves on one of the benches when Elizabeth caught sight of Reverend Folger, who waved as he approached. She and Bill rose to greet him.

"How was your trip to Chicago, Mr. Bates?" he asked, shaking Bill's hand vigorously.

"Very successful. I think we may have found the perfect solution to Miss Livingston's problem."

"That *is* good news. I'd like to hear all about it."

"Why don't both of you come to luncheon tomorrow?" Elizabeth suggested. "That is, if Bill can come." Her inquiring look brought a nod from the attorney. "Bring Mrs. Folger, too. Bill can explain everything to everyone at once and answer our questions, too."

"We'd be delighted," Reverend Folger agreed. After they had decided on a time, he bade them good-bye and drifted away.

Just then Chance reappeared, wending his way carefully while juggling three dishes of ice cream. "Oh, dear," Elizabeth murmured as Bill rushed to his assistance.

"Sweets for the, uh, sweet," Chance said, offering her one of the dishes.

"What does the 'uh' mean?" she asked suspiciously.

"I was wondering if I shouldn't have gotten you a pickle instead."

Bill cleared his throat discreetly. "I know you two will excuse me for a moment," he said, and moved away to speak to some fellow firemen gathered nearby.

Chance warily took a seat on the bench beside her, but she made no move to punish him again. "Sweet pickles or dill?" she asked instead.

"Oh, sweet, but tart."

"You like them tart, don't you?"

He pursed his lips to keep from smiling. "Unfortunately. Now eat your ice cream."

"Yes, Cousin Chauncey," she replied primly and took a dainty taste, savoring the coolness.

"Good?" Chance asked.

"Mmmm, delicious."

"You've got some . . . wait." He touched his finger to the corner of her lip to capture a trace of the creamy sweetness. Elizabeth's heart lurched at the intimacy of the gesture, and it stopped completely when he licked his finger.

"Enjoying yourself, Chance?"

Summer Winters's caustic question jolted them back to reality, and Elizabeth felt her cheeks redden as she looked up to find the blonde glaring her disapproval. She was dressed as demurely as any other woman present, and except for her skillfully applied makeup and too-yellow hair, she might have passed for a respectable lady. Still, everyone knew who she was, and she had no business speaking to Elizabeth or even to Elizabeth's companion.

Something in Chance's expression must have reminded her of this because her own face mottled unattractively, and she flounced away without another word. Elizabeth watched her through narrowed eyes while her heart pounded in reaction to the look of hatred on the woman's face. Summer Winters was evil, and she meant Elizabeth harm. Elizabeth knew it instinctively and shuddered in reaction.

"Summer sometimes forgets her place," Chance said by way of apology.

"Don't worry, I'm not going to faint because Summer Winters spoke to me. I was just realizing that I haven't been able to lure away a single one of the women who work for her."

Chance frowned, and for a moment she thought he would remind her once again of the dangers of her mission. Instead he said, "You can't save the whole world, Lizzie. You've already done more than anyone else to help those women. You have a lot to be proud of."

"Proud?" she echoed. "Aren't you the same man who wanted me to throw those women out into the street, bag and baggage?"

"Only because they're a danger to you. God, I'd like to ship them off to Chicago tomorrow to make sure you'll be safe, but that doesn't mean I can't see you've done some good. I'll admit I was skeptical at first—"

"Skeptical! You told me they didn't *want* to be rescued," she reminded him.

"All right, I was wrong about them, but I still haven't changed my mind."

"Oh, Chance, thank you," she whispered, her eyes filling with tears of gratitude as she squeezed his arm.

"For what?"

"For admitting you were wrong."

"I wasn't *completely* wrong. It's still too dangerous—"

"Hush," she commanded.

"Are you crying?" he asked with some alarm.

"Don't be silly." But her eyes were swimming.

"Your ice cream's melting," he pointed out, obviously confused by her mood.

"So is yours," she replied with a teasing smile as she scooped up another spoonful. From the corner of her eye she caught sight of Molly waving frantically from where she, Mavis, and Barbara were sitting under an adjoining tent, also eating ice cream. Elizabeth called a greeting to them.

"What do they think about the Chicago jobs?" Chance asked when he saw to whom she was speaking.

"I don't know. I guess none of us really believed the offer could be as good as it sounded, so we haven't discussed it much. I think they were afraid to hope, and I can't blame them. There's been little enough in their lives to lead them to expect the best."

Before he could respond, Bill strolled back, his conversation apparently ended. "If you've finished your ice cream, we can take the dishes back on our way to the footraces," he said, apparently unaware of the emotional undercurrents.

Elizabeth relinquished her half-empty dish and allowed the two men to escort her across the field to where the races were being held. Bill seemed to assume she would prefer to take Chance's arm and didn't even offer his own. She wondered at his attitude, but when she caught another knowing glint in his eyes, she quickly turned her gaze back to Chance.

They hadn't gone far when a childish voice called, "Herr Fitz!" and a tiny blond blur propelled itself into Chance's leg.

"Gretel!" he cried in delight, releasing Elizabeth's arm to hoist the child onto his hip. "Where's the rest of your family?"

But three-year-old Gretel's command of English did not stretch to questions of such length. "Can-dy," she demanded, rifling his pockets while he chuckled.

"Who's this?" Elizabeth asked in amazement.

"This is Gretel Dietzel," Chance replied, scanning the crowd. "And I think she's probably escaped from her mother's watchful eye. Oh, yes, here she comes now. Gretel, my dear, I fear you are in grave danger."

Gretel grinned beatifically, oblivious to her mother's wrath. "Can-dy?"

"Sorry, sweetheart. I wasn't expecting to see you today."

Her face fell. Thoroughly enchanted, Elizabeth wished she had some candy to offer the child.

Gretel's mother made her way to them through the crowd, chastening her daughter in rapid German while pulling her small son behind her. She stopped in front of Chance.

"So sorry," she said, taking the child from him. "She run away." Frau Dietzel wore a frayed straw hat and her cheeks were flushed from the heat and exertion, but her blue eyes sparkled as she looked at Chance.

He stepped back, uneasily aware of her esteem. He did not think he would ever forget how grateful she had been the day he'd brought them the money he had collected. Dietzel had not wanted to accept it, thinking it was charity. Chance was glad he could explain honestly the money came from the men responsible for cheating him. Frau Dietzel had listened to her husband's translation and then, with tears in her eyes, had clasped Chance's hand and kissed it.

Unaccustomed to such displays, Chance had found himself blushing for the first time in over a decade. Gretel's gratitude for the peppermint sticks he'd brought had been much easier to accept.

Hans Dietzel appeared out of the press, having caught up with his family. "Mr. Fitzwilliam! I am happy to see you." The two men shook hands, and Chance introduced him and his wife to Bill and Elizabeth.

"The Dietzels are new settlers to the area," Chance informed them.

Gretel made a sad little face. "Can-dy?" she asked again, making everyone laugh. Thinking their smiles meant success, she clapped her hands. "Can-deee!"

"Nein," her mother said, and chastened her again.

"Perhaps she'd like some ice cream instead," Elizabeth suggested.

Plainly the Dietzels did not recognize the word, but Chance knew a good idea when he heard one. "Yes, ice cream," he repeated slowly for Gretel's benefit. She brightened at once and made a dive for him from her mother's arms. He caught her just in time as everyone laughed at her antics.

"Come on, Dietzel," Chance said, slapping the farmer on the back. "I'm going to buy your daughter some ice cream, and some for the rest of the family, too, if they want it."

Dietzel looked uncertain, but when he translated the offer for his wife, she was willing to go along with anything Chance suggested. To Chance's astonishment, he realized she trusted him. How on earth had he earned such an honor?

"Are we invited, too?" Elizabeth asked.

"I don't care if we're invited or not," Bill announced before Chance could reply. "I wouldn't miss this for anything. Would you?"

"Absolutely not," Elizabeth replied. Since Chance had his hands full with Gretel, she took Bill's arm as they all started back across the rough field toward the ice cream vendors.

About halfway across, Elizabeth leaned over to Bill and whispered, "Who are these people?"

"Settlers, like Chance said," he replied. "Oh, this must be the family he helped."

"Helped? How?"

"Land speculators cheated them, I think. Chance got their money back for them."

"Oh," was all she said, but her heart sang. This was the Chance Fitzwilliam she loved. Through a mist of love she watched him purchase a dish of ice cream and feed a spoonful to the skeptical Gretel.

The child's eyes widened as she tasted it. "Can-dy," she decreed, reaching for the spoon and bowl.

At Chance's insistence, the rest of Gretel's family experienced their first American ice cream, too. Amid the laughter and teasing, Elizabeth heard Dietzel say, "We have found a farm."

"Good, where is it?" Chance asked.

As Dietzel described the location, Elizabeth sidled closer so she could hear every word.

Chance congratulated him on his success, but he replied, "We would have nothing without your help."

Uncomfortable again, Chance glanced around to see if anyone had overheard the remark. Bill was engaged in instructing the little boy on the proper method of eating ice cream, and Elizabeth seemed intent on watching Gretel devour hers. "All I did was deliver the money. Anyone would have done as much."

Elizabeth doubted his assertion, but she kept silent. She glanced up to see Mrs. Dietzel smiling warmly at Chance. To Elizabeth's delight, he reddened slightly.

He quickly changed the subject. "Will you be able to get a crop in?"

"No, it is too late and too dry this year, but with the money you brought us, we can live until the next harvest."

Elizabeth's eyes misted again. After what he'd done for these people, how could Chance possibly think he wasn't good enough for her?

Frau Dietzel laid a hand on Elizabeth's arm. "You and Herr Fitzwilliam?" She made a gesture indicating she did not know the proper English words with which to ask her question.

Elizabeth smiled, feeling her cheeks grow pink again. She gave Frau Dietzel an eloquent shrug, and the woman nodded her understanding.

She patted Elizabeth's arm and smiled encouragingly. "*Ja,* it will be," she said.

Gretel interrupted their exchange with a frustrated cry. She was having trouble maneuvering a slippery spoonful of ice cream, so Elizabeth went to her aid.

Later, when they had parted company with the Dietzel family, Chance asked Elizabeth and Bill what they would like to do next. Bill gave his pocket watch an ostentatious glance. "I think Chance has a race to run pretty soon."

"A race?" Elizabeth echoed, intrigued by Chance's scowling disapproval.

"Yes, last year Chance carried off the honors in the hundred-yard dash," Bill explained. "The Dodge City Fire Company is depending on him again this year."

"I already told you I'm not going to run," Chance said.

"Oh, Chance, please do! I'd love to see you." Elizabeth touched his sleeve beseechingly.

With fascination, she watched him vainly try to assume his usual hauteur. She tilted her head coquettishly and purred, "Please?"

His eyebrows shot up. "Tart but sweet, eh, Lizzie?"

"When I have to be," she replied.

"All right, you win. *This* time," he murmured.

"We'd better hurry," Bill urged, taking Elizabeth's elbow and turning her in the proper direction.

"I had no idea you were a runner," Elizabeth said as they made their way back to the racing area.

When Chance did not reply, Bill volunteered, "He ran in college."

Elizabeth could see Chance's reluctance to brag about himself and suspected he believed it would be inconsistent with his claim of being unworthy of her. "Were you very good?" she wanted to know.

"I won a few ribbons."

"I knew it," she said smugly, earning a disapproving frown.

The other runners were already warming up when the three of them arrived at the starting line. Chance quickly stripped out of his coat and vest. After removing his shirt collar and cuffs, he rolled up his sleeves and sat down to dispense with his shoes and socks.

Elizabeth watched with wide-eyed and somewhat prurient interest. Never before had she considered a man's bare feet in any way attractive, but now she realized she had been much too narrow-minded. Chance's feet were long and slender, like his hands, and also sprinkled with the same dark hair. When he rolled up his pant legs, she saw the hair thickened on his muscular calves and found herself wondering if the rest of him was equally sexy. Her heart was fluttering unevenly when Bill said, "Let's go down to the finish line."

'Good luck!" she called to Chance, and then remembered a time-honored custom. Digging in her purse, she produced a lacy handkerchief. "A token," she explained, pressing it into his hand.

His eyes were like black fire as he lifted the delicate fabric to his lips and inhaled the scent of her perfume. Her stomach quivered in response, and she resisted with difficulty the urge to touch him. She wanted so much to feel of those lips on her own.

A crazy idea occurred to her, and she glanced around at the other runners preparing for the race. "A kiss for the winner!" she announced, giving Chance a smile that was half-promise and half-challenge. His gaze scorched her soul, and she hardly heard the whoop of approval from the other contestants.

"I'm starting to feel like the odd man out with you two," Bill said as he led her away.

Elizabeth's conscience pricked her. Bill was, after all, her escort, and she had been inexcusably rude by ignoring him. "I'm awfully sorry. I didn't mean—"

"Don't start apologizing," Bill begged in mock consternation. "I know you don't mean a word of it, and I'm not hurt in any case."

"You're not?" she asked, knowing he had every right to be.

"No," he said cheerfully. "I've always known why you encouraged my attentions."

Elizabeth stopped in her tracks and stared up at him in dismay. "You have?" she asked, not certain she knew herself.

"Of course," he explained. "You've been using me as a buffer between you and Chance. Obviously, you both love each other, but according to Chance you quarreled. By keeping me in the middle, you've been able to continue seeing each other without actually making up."

The analysis was oversimplified but remarkably accurate. Elizabeth had behaved reprehensibly toward Bill. "You're right, I'm afraid. I'm so sorry!"

Bill sighed impatiently. "Don't be silly. I haven't minded a bit. In fact, I've found watching you two highly entertaining."

Elizabeth frowned her disapproval, but he ignored it. "What I can't understand is what's keeping you apart, especially after seeing you together today. By God, I could light a cigar on the looks you've been giving each other!"

"Bill!" Elizabeth chastened him, blushing for what seemed the hundredth time today.

"Is it something to do with the trust? I know Chance can't ethically court you when he controls your money, but that can be worked out."

"No, it's not the trust," she said, wishing the situation were so simple.

"You know I'll help any way I can."

She managed a reassuring smile. "There's nothing you can do, really. This is a problem we have to work out ourselves."

"I hope you can, although I'll admit, I wouldn't have

minded if you and I had fallen in love. But I'm happy to be your friend, and I don't mind your using me."

"I never meant to use you, Bill," she told him earnestly.

Bill gave her an understanding grin. "I told you I didn't mind. In spite of your questionable penchant for befriending ladies of the evening, you're still the most eligible young woman west of the Mississippi. Being seen around town with you has increased my status considerably. There are a few other young ladies—not quite as lovely but certainly attractive—who have started to see me in a new light. I think once they discover I'm not really involved with you, I'll have my hands full choosing among them."

His grin was irresistible. "I have a feeling you'll take your time doing so."

"It's an important decision," he said, but his grin never wavered. "Now, we'd better get along or we'll miss the race."

With Bill's help, she shouldered her way into a place near the finish line. The contestants were lining up for the start, and she easily spotted Chance near the middle of the group. Behind her, Bill whispered, "Maybe you'd like me to find some other companions for the rest of the afternoon."

"Certainly not! I've treated you badly enough without deserting you."

Bill chuckled softly. "Don't worry. I think I know a sweet young thing who'd be happy to comfort me."

Before Elizabeth could reply to his outrageous statement, the starting gun fired, making her jump. The runners were off in a blur of motion, and for a second she couldn't find Chance. Then he emerged at the forefront, arms and feet flashing in the blazing sunlight, muscles straining beneath the fine linen of his shirt.

The shouts of the crowd drowned out her own yells of encouragement as he streaked by, his face set with grim determination. It was over almost before it started. Chance hit the tape and caught it, carrying it behind him like a streamer as he ran out the race, his arms held high in victory.

Elizabeth jumped and clapped and screamed with the rest of the spectators, her joy doubled because she loved the winner. Then she noticed the attention of the crowd had suddenly shifted to her and a murmur rose, louder and louder until the word "kiss" became a roar.

Good heavens! She had almost forgotten her impetuous offer. Several firemen had hoisted Chance onto their shoulders and were bearing him back to her to receive the victor's spoils.

"Kiss! Kiss!" the crowd chanted, and Bill gave her a gentle nudge out onto the racetrack.

Mortified at the attention, Elizabeth once more felt her face flame, but her embarrassment evaporated when she saw Chance's expression.

Flushed from the run and the heat, his face shining and his shirt clinging damply, he looked every inch the rogue he tried to style himself. But it was his eyes that caught and held her attention; the wicked, yearning, blazing passion there. He wanted her, and he was no longer able to hide it.

Feeling her own flush of victory, Elizabeth folded her hands in front of her and waited for the firemen to deposit their burden in front of her, her demure pose belying the riot of sensations inside her. All around them people were laughing and jesting and teasing, but Elizabeth was hardly aware of them. She saw only Chance. She heard only the ragged rasp of his breathing. She felt only the heat of his nearness.

His hands reached for her, and she went to him, her face lifted, her lips parted. His mouth was hot and wild and rough, the conqueror claiming his willing captive. She surrendered eagerly, knowing she was the true victor.

A deafening cheer parted them with a jolt, and Chance was torn from her by well-wishers. Bumped aside, she waited until he was free to claim her again, certain with every female instinct she had that he would.

A few moments later, still grinning from receiving congratulations, he found her with unerring accuracy. "Where's Bill?" he asked, surprised to find her alone.

"He seems to have abandoned me. I'm afraid I'm sorely in need of a male escort, Cousin Chauncey."

Chance's lips quirked. "Then I guess it's my duty as your guardian to look after you."

Elizabeth managed to look put out. "You should have been here earlier, then. Some ruffian grabbed me and kissed me right in front of the entire population of Dodge City."

His grin turned wicked. "He'd do it again, too, if he thought he could get away with it."

Laughing, Elizabeth gave him a playful swat. Joy bubbled through her like fine champagne. He offered his arm with exaggerated gallantry, and she took it with no pretense of reluctance. Together they strolled back to retrieve the rest of Chance's clothes, and in spite of all the hundreds of people milling around, they might have been the only two people alive.

For the rest of the afternoon, while they watched more footraces and horse races and the wheelbarrow race and the three-legged race and the greased pig contest, Elizabeth floated as if through a golden haze. Chance's dark eyes were alternately teasing and adoring, and his touch lingered on her arm or her hand with a lover's yearning.

The afternoon shadows were growing long when the last race ended. Chance glanced down at Elizabeth's beautiful face, still not able to believe she was here beside him. He couldn't recall ever feeling so happy and carefree, and Elizabeth was the source of his joy. He supposed if he hadn't already been in love with her, he would have lost his heart earlier today when Gretel had dripped a blob of melted ice cream on her dress and she hadn't even flinched. The memory of that moment still caused his heart to contract.

He knew he was tempting fate to spend so much time with her, but he could not resist the brightness she offered.

Tomorrow and all the dark, lonely days afterward would be more difficult to bear when contrasted to this time spent together laughing and teasing like lovers. Still, as they walked back toward the buggy, he knew he could not let the day end, at least not yet.

"There's Bill," he said, finding his friend in the crowd and changing their course so they could intercept him.

Elizabeth pouted prettily. "Are you going to give me back to him now?"

"Don't be a goose. I'm going to reprimand him for deserting you."

She found this prospect delightful, and Bill was equally glad to encounter them, although he should more properly have been mortified at being caught with a young lady on each arm when he was actually Elizabeth's escort. Chance drew Bill aside, leaving the women to make small talk.

"I'm going to use your buggy to take Elizabeth home," Chance informed him.

"I assumed you would," Bill replied. "What about the ball tonight? I was supposed to take her, you know."

"You won't mind if I do, will you?"

"No, and I don't think anyone else involved will mind either," Bill said with a significant glance at Elizabeth.

The two men exchanged a look of understanding, and relieved, Chance gave Bill a friendly slap on the back. "Thanks," he said.

"Just tell Elizabeth to save me a dance."

As Chance led Elizabeth toward the buggy again, she looked up at him inquiringly.

"I told him he'd behaved like a cad and that he had forfeited the right to take you to the ball tonight," Chance explained.

Her eyes widened in mock alarm. "Now I'll have to stay home."

Chance managed to look resigned. "No, you won't. I'll do my duty and escort you myself."

"You're very noble, Cousin Chauncey," she replied with a twinkle.

Chance only wished he were.

A few minutes later, Chance left her at her house so she could change for the ball. Half-expecting to encounter a crisis inside the house, she turned reluctantly toward the door, loath to be distracted from thoughts of Chance. However, she was pleasantly surprised to discover the other women had enjoyed themselves immensely, Amy most of all. Finding no problems, as soon as she and the others had finished comparing notes on the delights of the day's festivities, Elizabeth retired to the privacy of the front parlor and began to prepare for the ball.

She chose a gown of pale green silk that left her arms and shoulders bare. Although she'd left most of her jewelry in Philadelphia for safekeeping, she managed to find a gold collar set with a single emerald and a pair of earrings with emerald chips to go with it. Delicate lace gloves, a shawl, and a green painted fan completed her ensemble.

As she whirled for her friends' approval and saw their wistful smiles, she suddenly felt like the lone stepsister about to leave behind a houseful of Cinderellas. Amy especially looked disappointed.

"I wish all of you could go with me," Elizabeth said with genuine regret.

Mavis snorted. "Wouldn't that be a fine thing! You think we got trouble now, there's no telling what would happen if we showed up at the Fireman's Ball. They'd probably tar and feather us." All the women knew no gentleman who was sober and reasonably attired would be turned away from this gala event, but only the most respectable ladies in town would be welcome.

"I wouldn't mind getting dressed up real fancy, though," Amy said with a sigh.

"Really, ladies," Barbara scolded genially. "I thought you were all heartily sick of dancing with men. You've certainly complained enough about it."

"She's right," Mavis decided, recognizing Barbara's attempt to lighten the mood. "Me, I don't care if I never even hear music again."

"And we're going to have a good time this evening," Barbara added, having elected to stay with the others instead of attending the ball herself. "We'll go see the fireworks later, too."

The doorbell rang.

"I'll get it," Elizabeth said, unable to wait a second longer to see Chance again. They stared at each other for a long moment as eyes confirmed what memory had promised.

Chance looked dashing in his evening clothes. Holding his top hat properly in the curve of his arm, he sketched her a bow, but the glitter in his dark eyes belied his dignified behavior. Her heart gave a familiar lurch.

"Good evening, Cousin Chauncey," she said primly, although she knew her own eyes must betray her feelings.

"Good evening, Cousin Elizabeth. Are you ready to go?"

Elizabeth was more than ready. She also knew her housemates' attitude toward Chance might dim the glow she was experiencing if she invited him inside, so with a last pang of guilt, she called good-bye to them and stepped out onto the porch.

"I don't think I've ever seen you look lovelier," he said as they walked down the porch steps.

"You look rather handsome yourself," she replied, knowing her happiness must surely have enhanced her beauty a hundredfold.

"I didn't bother with the buggy since there probably won't be any place close to the Dodge House to leave it anyway," he said by way of apology for making her walk the short distance to Front Street.

"I don't mind," she replied. "It's a perfect night for a stroll."

He studied her for a moment. "Are you sure? You were probably up most of last night and after today, you must be tired. If you want to leave the dance early . . ."

"No, I'm fine, really," she said truthfully. Her anticipation of the evening ahead had cancelled any fatigue she might otherwise have felt. "I might look a little subdued, but that's only because I feel guilty for going off and leaving the others."

His hand closed warmly over hers where it rested on his arm. "Try to remember all you've done to help them back on the road to respectability, Lizzie. Without your help, they'd be entertaining customers over on the South Side tonight."

"Yes, and when they get to Chicago, they'll have the opportunity to become completely respectable again."

Chance's fingers squeezed hers. "So don't ruin our evening fretting because they can't dance in the same building you can . . . yet."

"Yes, sir, Cousin Chauncey," she replied with a mischievous tilt of her head.

"Somebody should kiss the impudence out of you, young lady," he said hoarsely.

Her eyes gave a saucy invitation. "Maybe somebody will."

Drawing an unsteady breath, Chance tactfully changed the subject to a discussion of the upcoming fireworks display, which they continued until they reached the Dodge House where the ball was being held.

A large crowd had already assembled in the dining room, which had been cleared for the occasion, and a group of musicians stood on a makeshift stage playing a waltz. Chance swept Elizabeth into his arms, and they joined the couples on the dance floor. Chance was an expert dancer, and they glided along as if in a dream.

Chance gazed down at her adoringly, his dark eyes mirroring the reaction his body was obviously having to her nearness. He pulled her close until her breasts brushed his chest and her temple rested against his chin. She slid her left hand up to touch the bare skin on the back of his neck and was rewarded by his sharp intake of air.

"God, Lizzie," he murmured into her hair, his breath, caressing her cheek.

Delicious shivers danced up her thighs as his arm tightened around her waist. Just then the music stopped. For a moment neither of them noticed, but suddenly, Elizabeth was surrounded by would-be partners eager to claim her for the next dance. With a smile of regret, Chance relinquished her to them.

As the dancing went on, Chance became less gracious. Risking bodily harm, he fought his way through to her more and more frequently, earning the animosity of her many hopeful dance partners. At last he appeared at her current partner's side and tapped him on the shoulder. With an apologetic smile, he took the man's place.

"It's about time you rescued me," she chastened him.

His eyes widened in feigned surprise. "I had no idea you needed to be rescued," he replied.

"Well, perhaps rescued is too strong a word," she conceded, "although all this dancing seems like an ordeal unless I'm dancing with you."

"Watching you with other men is somewhat of an ordeal for me, too, so I've decided not to let you dance with anyone else for the rest of the evening."

"How do you propose to manage that?"

"I simply won't let you go."

Elizabeth smiled her approval, thinking she didn't want him to let her go *ever.* She watched him watching her, and her blood began to heat. "I suppose the fireworks will be starting soon," she said inanely, thinking they would seem tame in comparison to the excitement Chance had stirred within her. As if reading her thoughts, his arm tightened around her waist, pulling her closer so the bodice of her gown brushed his chest.

His musky, male scent teased at her, sparking memories of the wild kiss they had shared that afternoon. Sparks danced along her nerve ends, and her nipples tautened painfully inside the silk of her chemise.

Chance watched her eyes kindle and her lips soften as if in preparation for his. Desire coiled in him, hot and urgent. She loved him. He could see it in her eyes and on her face and in every line of her body. He sensed her willingness, and his lonely heart cried out in silence for the solace her love could give.

The music stopped, although again neither of them noticed until Mayor Kelley mounted the stage and announced the fireworks would soon be starting. The couples around them began to move toward the door, and reluctantly Elizabeth stepped out of Chance's embrace.

"Shall we go?" he asked, offering Elizabeth his arm.

Elizabeth gladly took it, using both hands to cling to him and reveling in his strength.

Front Street was already crowded with people who had come from other parts of town to view the spectacle. Chance led her to the least crowded area, close to the Dodge House. The shadows here were deep, increasing the feeling of intimacy. Although hundreds of people mingled nearby, she and Chance once again felt alone in the universe.

The first rocket misfired, and the resounding boom made Elizabeth jump. Chance slipped his arm protectively around her, pulling her tightly against him. Her heart began to race as the heat from his body seeped through the thin fabric of her gown.

The second rocket exploded above them, showering the street with a burst of light that brought oohs and aahs from the crowd. Elizabeth hardly noticed. She was aware only of Chance and of his dark eyes shining down at her.

"Lizzie." He did not realize he had spoken aloud. The feel of her slender body against him overwhelmed his senses, and all he could hear was the roar of his own blood. He needed to touch her and taste her; he needed to press her softness against his aching heart to stop the pain.

In the square, a Roman candle spewed forth a blaze of glory, but it paled against the blaze of desire she saw in his eyes. This was the moment for which she had been waiting, the moment in which he wanted her beyond all reason. "Please kiss me, Chance," she murmured, knowing he could not refuse.

For one second, she thought he might, but then he whispered, "Come with me." A few steps carried them away from the crowd, which was shouting its delight at some new display of pyrotechnics. Elizabeth had eyes only for Chance, and in another second they truly were alone in the deep shadows of the alley beside the Dodge House. Behind them sparks streaked across the velvet sky, but here they were only faint flickers. Chance pulled her into his arms.

She heard the pounding of his heart against her ear and felt the rasp of his breath on her cheek. His hands moved over her back and shoulders in silent desperation, as if he were trying to convince himself she was really there, in his arms. Her own arms encircled him in response, holding him with equal fierceness. She needed him so much, needed him to love her. Yielding to the impulse, she lifted her face to his.

His kiss was urgent and devouring, demanding a response she willingly gave. She opened to him, granting him possession of her mouth in erotic imitation of the fulfillment her body craved. Sweet longing intensified into seething desire.

"Chance." She breathed his name in the instant when he lifted his mouth from hers. The word evoked a multitude of questions.

"Lizzie," he whispered back, answering every one of them.

His lips trailed down her throat to find the throbbing pulse. She threw back her head in abandon, and against her closed eyelids she could see the bursts of light exploding in celebration.

He found her full breasts straining against her dress. His palm closed over one, kneading gently and sending the warmth of his touch scorching through her until it settled between her thighs. As if sensing her response, he pulled her closer until she could feel his own turgid need hard against her belly.

Her lips parted in a gasp. Instantly, his mouth was there

to capture the sound and then to press against her lips with renewed hunger. His tongue plundered her mouth once more, leaving nothing of her unclaimed. She surrendered, confident of her ultimate victory.

His questing fingers slipped inside her bodice, finding her soft flesh. The rockets exploded inside her now, one after another, each brighter and more brilliant than the last. Someone made a moaning sound, but she could not have said which of them it was. He groaned her name.

"I need you, Lizzie. I need you so much."

Her aching heart responded. She needed him, too, in a thousand ways, but only one would satisfy this burning desire.

"Come with me." His voice was hurried, urgent, a moist breath against her skin. "We'll go to my place."

"Yes, yes," she whispered. She wanted to lie with him and love with him, to be with him forever. "We'll be so happy, Chance. You'll see. I don't expect you'll be a traditional husband, but we can work things out if we love each other; I know we can."

His body went perfectly still as the shock registered and sanity returned with a rush. "You think I want to marry you?"

"You . . . you asked me . . ."

"I asked you to go to bed with me.

Stung, she jerked away from him and hastily adjusted her dress. "Are you saying you don't love me?"

"I never said I did."

"But you wanted—"

"I wanted to make love with you. People make love all the time without being in love. Lizzie, for God's sake, listen to me!" he said, grabbing her arms as if he could shake the truth into her. "Don't you know what kind of man I am? I'm the kind of man who'd drag you off into an alley and try to seduce you! I'm the kind of man who'd ruin you just to satisfy his own lust!"

"No, you aren't! You're good and kind, and you're the man I want to marry."

"You don't know what you're talking about."

"Yes, I do," she insisted. "If you really were as bad as you say, you wouldn't have stopped just now. You would have lied so you could have your way instead of trying to convince me you're a cad."

He released her as if she'd burned him. Damnit, she could even make his sins sound noble! They had to get away from there, or he *would* be pouring out his heart like some lovesick swain. "Come on," he said, taking her arm in a deadly grip and heading back toward the square.

"Where are we going?"

"To watch the fireworks."

Something streaked across the sky with a shrieking sound before dissolving into a shower of sparks. The scream could have come from Elizabeth's own pain. She almost would have preferred being dragged off and ravished. At least then she might have had a chance of reaching him, of touching the emotions she knew lay hidden behind his rock-hard refusal.

She stumbled, trying to keep up with him, and he stopped, automatically assisting her. "Sorry," he murmured, but she jerked her arm from his grasp.

"I'm sorry, too. Sorry I ever fell in love with you."

His head snapped back as if she'd slapped him, and for one instant she glimpsed pain in his dark eyes. It vanished just as quickly, to be replaced by the neutral expression she had grown to hate. "I tried to warn you, Lizzie."

She wanted to scream and stamp her foot and rain blows on his head until she forced him to admit his feelings, until she forced him at least to admit the pain she had seen with her own eyes. Why did he persist in this madness when he was tearing them both apart?

In mingled fury and frustration, she marched down the alley and out into the street until she reached the edge of the crowd again. Chance followed at a discreet distance and made no further effort to touch her. She stood there feigning an interest in the latest shower of sparks overhead and blinking to ensure the image would not blur. She simply would not permit herself to cry.

When she felt more certain of her composure, she turned to him. "I'd like to go home now."

"Certainly," he replied, giving no clue as to his true emotions. In silence and still without touching her, he escorted her down the boardwalk to the corner where they turned toward her street. As the crowd noises faded and the explosions from the fireworks grew fainter, the magnitude of her problem loomed larger and larger. Here she was, not two feet from the man she loved more than life itself, and she would have cheerfully strangled him. The walk home seemed to take an eternity, but at last they reached her front gate.

"Good night, Chance," she said, turning to him, her voice flat with despair.

"I hate to let you go in there alone."

"Are you offering to go inside with me?" she snapped, out of patience.

"I don't think that would be a good idea," he replied with maddening calm. "I could wait outside until the others come back."

"Don't bother," she told him with false bravado. "I have my shotgun, and I'll stay inside with the doors locked until my friends return."

He nodded, and she waited in vain for him to speak again. Frustration bubbled up until she thought she would choke on it. "Chance—"

"Good night, Elizabeth." His voice held the finality of good-bye.

"Good night," she replied in defeat. Turning on her heel, she hurried up the walk. She closed and locked the door behind her and leaned wearily against it. Tears scalded her eyes, spilling over before she could stop them. Angrily she dashed them from her cheeks, but new ones fell.

Silently she damned Chance Fitzwilliam. Was there no justice? Chance was a man who had scorned the code of honor by which gentlemen lived, yet the same code forbade him to love her. She might have laughed at the irony if she hadn't been crying so hard.

Outside, Chance walked slowly back out into the street, resisting every step of the way the invisible forces compelling him back to Elizabeth. This was, he told himself, the best thing. He had no right to her. She deserved a man who still had his whole heart to give her. He realized he was being noble again and smiled at the bitter irony. Being noble should at least have provided him some measure of satisfaction. Instead, he felt as if someone had ripped him open with a dull knife.

As penance, he walked across the street until he reached the shadow of a large cottonwood where he could stand unobserved until Elizabeth's friends returned. He would wait and torture himself with visions of what might have happened tonight if he hadn't been so damn virtuous.

When she had finished crying, Elizabeth scrubbed the tears from her cheeks, snatched up the shotgun from the corner, and carried it into her room. She would pretend to be sleeping when her friends came home because if they saw she was awake, they would want to know why she was weeping. She couldn't bear explaining what a fool she had been.

Why couldn't she have given her heart to someone sweet and uncomplicated like Bill Bates? By now she would probably be married, and she would never have to see Chance Fitzwilliam again. It would serve him right.

She froze as the idea took shape in her mind.

At first she rejected it outright. Knowing how Chance mistrusted women in general, she would be foolish to give him a reason to doubt her love, wouldn't she? Or would she? Her faithfulness had certainly failed to convince him, so did she have anything to lose by trying another method? And jealousy was, after all, a time-proven way of forcing men off the mark.

She toyed with the possibilities as she prepared for bed, glad the other women were still out so she had this time alone to consider the ramifications. The plan was desperate and dangerous. She might alienate him completely.

On the other hand, how could the situation be any worse than it already was?

Chapter 10

"Then it's agreed," Elizabeth said, glancing around the dining room table where the Folgers and her boarders had gathered to hear Bill's explanation of the Chicago situation. "Barbara, you will make the trip with those who want to go. You will send us word within one week telling us what you've found and if everyone is satisfied. Anyone who isn't will receive a ticket back to Dodge. When everything is settled, Barbara will return home. Is that about it?"

"I think so," Barbara said. When Bill had nodded his agreement, he gave Reverend Folger an inquiring look in case the preacher had anything else to suggest.

"I know you wanted to go yourself," the minister said to Elizabeth, "but I hope you understand it's for the best. A young lady with your fortune can't be too careful."

The possibility that this whole thing was a trick to lure unsuspecting women up north still lingered in everyone's mind. Even Bill had become convinced that a bit of caution might be advisable. Consequently, Elizabeth felt those who were making the trip should have with them someone who could report back to them in the event of trouble. She wanted to be that person, but her fortune made her a prime candidate for kidnapping or blackmail. Reluctantly, she would stay behind and wait, meanwhile hoping to draw more women to the sanctuary of her home.

"You can stay with us while Barbara's gone," Mrs.

Folger said. "It wouldn't be right for you to rattle around in this big house all by yourself."

"You're very thoughtful." Elizabeth was more than grateful for this offer. The idea of staying there alone was terrifying. Ever since the attack on Amy, even last night when Elizabeth had gone to bed exhausted from the Fourth of July festivities and her encounter with Chance, she had slept poorly, imagining intruders in every creak and groan of the house.

Bill looked around the table again. "Does anyone have any more questions?"

"I'm still not sure about this sewing business," Mavis said. "I told you I never done it before."

"The manager assured me that learning to operate a sewing machine is simple, and for those who prefer, there are other jobs that don't require such skills. He needs pressers, and women to fold and pack the clothes for shipping, too," Bill explained.

Kate snickered. "Don't worry, Mavis. They'll probably make you the boss after the first week anyhow."

This caused a ripple of good-natured laughter. "You're probably right," Mavis agreed. "And when they do, you'd better keep your nose to the grindstone or I'll put you out."

More laughter followed, and Elizabeth's tension began to ease. She had been so concerned for so long about the future of these women that the relief of knowing they might soon be permanently settled was almost overwhelming. Her only lingering worry was about Amy, who sat with her eyes lowered, refusing to meet anyone's gaze. She hardly seemed to have heard a word of the discussion. Elizabeth sensed something was terribly wrong, but she would not embarrass Amy by questioning her in front of the others. Later, when they were alone, she would uncover Amy's problem.

In the meantime, she needed to discuss something completely different with Reverend and Mrs. Folger. A few minutes later the luncheon meeting broke up. When Eliz-

abeth had thanked Bill and seen him out, she asked the
Folgers to remain behind for a few minutes. At Elizabeth's
request, Barbara joined the three of them out on the porch.
The Folgers sat in the swing, and Barbara and Elizabeth
took the wicker chairs.

"Uh, as you know," she began, "my father's will de-
nies me control over my fortune. As you also know, my
relationship with my cousin has been somewhat, uh,
strained." The Folgers exchanged glances but did not
comment. Elizabeth did not dare look at Barbara. When
Barbara had cornered her this morning to learn what had
happened the night before with Chance, Elizabeth had told
her only that the two of them had quarreled irrevocably.
Barbara's subsequent relief had made further explanation
unnecessary. "After giving the matter considerable
thought, I have decided it would be to my advantage to
end my cousin's guardianship as soon as possible."

Reverend Folger frowned. "Can you do that? Legally,
I mean?"

"If I marry, I can. Control of my fortune would then
go to my husband."

Barbara made a startled sound, and the Folgers stared
at her in stunned surprise. Mrs. Folger found her tongue
first. "Are you engaged, Elizabeth? You haven't said anything."

"No, of course I'm not engaged. How could I be when
I've discouraged gentlemen callers in order to protect the
reputation of my home and my guests? I would, however,
like to correct the situation."

"And you want us to help you?" Reverend Folger asked
in some confusion.

"Yes," Elizabeth replied, lowering her eyes modestly.
"You see, it's hardly proper for me to announce I'm in the
market for a husband, Reverend Folger." She lifted her
gaze to his beseechingly. "I was hoping I could depend
on you to spread the word, so to speak."

The idea astonished him, but he was also intrigued.
"Why, I'd be delighted to oblige, Elizabeth. The news

will be most welcome, too. Your aloofness has wounded many a heart, I can tell you.''

Mrs. Folger was not quite so pleased. "This sounds awfully cold and calculating to me. Marriage isn't something you choose in order to get out of a bad business arrangement.''

"Oh, I have no intention of marrying someone I don't love just to get away from my cousin's authority," Elizabeth said truthfully. "Unfortunately, under the present circumstances, I'm not likely to meet anyone I could fall in love with, am I? All I want is to provide myself with the opportunity.''

"That seems reasonable," Reverend Folger decreed. "And it makes a good bit of sense, too. Much more practical than leaving things to chance the way most girls do.''

"I know she'll find the perfect man if she looks for him." Barbara said. "The only reason she hasn't already is because she's let *other things* distract her." Clearly Barbara considered Chance Fitzwilliam to be Elizabeth's primary distraction.

"There is one other favor I must ask of you," Elizabeth said. "I will need a place and a proper chaperone for entertaining these gentlemen callers. You know about our rule prohibiting men from entering this house, and especially with Barbara out of town, I don't think it would be a good idea for my suitors to call on me here.''

"Oh, certainly not!" the Folgers agreed in unison.

"You'll use our house," Mrs. Folger said. "Since you'll be staying with us for a while anyway, it's perfectly logical.''

"I was hoping you would offer," Elizabeth confessed.

"Good, then it's all settled," Reverend Folger concluded. "I'll make the announcement on Sunday—"

"Elijah!"

"Not from the pulpit, Mama," he assured his wife with a grin.

"*I* will make the announcement, Papa," she contradicted sternly. "I will discreetly mention the subject to a few anxious mothers, and the word will spread like wild-fire.''

''Oh, I wish I could be here,'' Barbara lamented.

Elizabeth patted her hand reassuringly. ''You'll be back in a few weeks. I couldn't possibly fall in love and agree to marry someone in such a short time, and even if I do, I promise to delay the wedding until you return.''

Barbara frowned at her foolishness, but she gave Elizabeth's hand a squeeze. ''I just want you to be happy, honey.''

''I will be,'' Elizabeth promised rashly, wondering how she would keep the promise if her daring plan failed to win the only man who could ensure her happiness.

Later that afternoon, Elizabeth found Amy alone in her bedroom, huddled on the bed. ''Amy, what's the matter?'' Elizabeth asked, hurrying to Amy's side.

The girl's cornflower eyes filled with tears. ''I can't go to Chicago, Miss Livingston. I'll be arrested.''

''Arrested! Whatever for?'' Certain the girl was exaggerating, Elizabeth sat down on the bed beside her, prepared to argue away her objections.

''For being a runaway wife!'' she said as large tears rolled down her fair cheeks.

''Wife? You're married?'' Elizabeth could hardly believe it. Why would a married woman work in a dance hall? ''Who is your husband?''

''Mike Loving,'' she said, waiting for Elizabeth's reaction. ''You've probably heard of him.''

''I don't think I have.''

''Well, he's pretty famous around here.'' Amy seemed a little surprised Elizabeth didn't know who he was. ''You must've heard about the gunfight. It happened right before you got to town. It was in all the newspapers.''

The Dodge City newspapers were always reporting on one sensational crime or another, although Elizabeth didn't pay much attention as long as the incident didn't take place at the Last Chance Saloon. "Maybe I'll recall it if you refresh my memory," Elizabeth said diplomatically.

"Well, it was over at the Long Branch," Amy began, brushing the tears from her face. "Mike was playing cards there. He's a gambler. I was working at Summer Winters's house back then, and this fellow, Levi Reynolds, took a shine to me. Mike was sweet on me, too—we weren't married then—and they got to arguing over me." Amy seemed proud of this revelation.

"Levi got real mad when he found out I liked Mike better, so one day he goes out looking for him. He found him at the Long Branch. Mike was minding his own business, but when Levi busts in and starts yelling and calling him names, he goes for his gun. Levi starts shooting, too, and they chased each other around the stove, shooting almost in each other's face!"

Elizabeth stared at Amy in speechless horror, unable to believe the way the girl's formerly tearful eyes were now shining with excitement. Amy did not seem to notice Elizabeth's dismay.

"I wasn't there, of course, but I heard they was so close their guns was almost touching, but neither of them even flinched. They just kept firing until their guns were empty. Mike got off all six shots, and Levi would have except his pistol misfired once. Eleven shots in all, and you'll never guess! Levi fell down, as good as dead with three bullets in him, but all Mike got was a scratch across the back of his hand. Levi never touched him!"

"A . . . amazing," Elizabeth managed, shaken as she recalled Chance's accusation about the women in her house having all been responsible for men's deaths. "Did Levi die?"

"Yeah, a few minutes later. He called for me, but Mike told them not to send for me. He was afraid I'd be upset. Mike's real considerate."

"I'm surprised he let you work at Miss Winters's house," Elizabeth murmured, thinking nothing Amy said quite made sense according to Elizabeth's understanding of the world.

"I told you, we weren't married then, so he didn't have any say in what I did. We didn't tie the knot until after the gunfight. After what happened, I realized how much Mike loved me. With a name like Loving, I should've guessed before, don't you think?"

Elizabeth nodded numbly. How could Amy sit there smiling with apparent delight as she explained how one man had murdered another over her?

"Anyway, we had a judge marry us after Levi died. Mike said he'd take me to New York City for our honeymoon, but we only got as far as Topeka. The cards went back on him there, and he lost all our money. He said we'd come back here for a little while, until we got a stake, and then he'd take me away for sure." Amy shrugged resignedly. "I didn't want to come back, but I didn't want to leave Mike either, so I came."

"How did you end up working for Shilling then? Did your husband desert you?"

"Oh, no, *I* left *him.*"

"Why? Did he mistreat you?" Elizabeth could think of nothing bad enough to drive her into a place like the Lady Gay Dance Hall, but possibly Mike Loving had not proven as loving as his name.

Amy shrugged again. "It wasn't that. Oh, he slapped me a couple of times for talking back to him, but he was nicer than most, I guess. What I didn't like was how he made me go back to whoring. Right away, as soon as we hit town, he made me go to Miss Winters and ask for my old job back. She wouldn't hire me, though. She said I made trouble, even though the fight was on the other side of town from her place. I never caused no trouble in *her* place," Amy reported indignantly. "So I had to work for Shilling, and I didn't like it one bit. Those cowboys'll smash your feet if you let them. They get plumb wild when they're drinking and dancing, and they stink, too, not like the men who come into Miss Winters's house.

"I told Mike I wouldn't work there no more, but he said I had to 'cause his luck was still running bad, and how would we live if I didn't work? I told him to go to hell, so he hit me in the eye, and then I came here."

"I'm so glad you did," Elizabeth said, taking Amy's hands in hers. Imagine living with a brute who beat her and made her sell her body to other men to support him. Elizabeth was only sorry Levi Reynolds hadn't been a better shot. A man as wicked as Mike Loving didn't deserve to live.

Amy smiled shyly. "Anyway, that's why I can't go to Chicago. Mike's been by here a couple times, wanting me back. He's pretty mad about me leaving him, but he figures I'll change my mind soon. If I went to Chicago, though, he'd know I was gone for good, and he'd put the law on me. I know he would."

Amy was crying again, so Elizabeth squeezed her hands reassuringly. "Don't be afraid, Amy. No one will force you to go. It's your decision, even if you didn't have to worry about Mike Loving. Under the circumstances, though, I think you should stay here, at least for a while. You might want to ask Mr. Bates about getting a divorce, too, so you'd be free from this man once and for all."

"Divorce! Nobody in my family was ever divorced. How could I bear the shame?"

Elizabeth stared in astonishment. Surely the stigma of prostitution was much worse than divorcing a man like Mike Loving, a man who had forced her to sell herself. "Of course, I would never try to influence you to do something you felt was wrong," she said.

"Oh, I know you wouldn't, Miss Livingston. You're such a good person yourself. And Mike's really not so bad. If he wasn't set on me working for Shilling, everything would be fine."

Elizabeth had her doubts, but she refrained from saying so. "Well, I must confess, I'm relieved to hear you'll be staying. I wasn't looking forward to being left all alone."

Amy's expression grew instantly wary. "Will I have to stay at the Folgers' house, too?"

Elizabeth hadn't thought that far ahead, but now she realized if Amy was remaining behind, there was no reason for her to stay with the Folgers. "No, we can both stay here." She wouldn't let herself think how active her imagination was bound to become with only the two of them in the house. She would probably sleep with the shotgun under her bed simply for peace of mind.

Amy was delighted at the prospect of being alone with Elizabeth. "We'll have lots of fun, just the two of us," she predicted.

Elizabeth's smile wavered only slightly as she nodded in agreement.

A few minutes later, she found Barbara and Mavis in the kitchen making plans for the trip. "Amy won't be going with you," she reported.

"Why not?" Barbara asked with concern.

"She can't. She's afraid her husband will send the law after her for being a runaway wife."

Mavis and Barbara stared at her in astonishment.

"She's married?" Mavis said in patent disbelief. "Who'd she say she was married to?"

"Mike Loving."

"Cockeyed Mike? She *married* that bastard?" Mavis's face twisted in contempt before she remembered her manners. "Oh, I'm sorry, Elizabeth. I forgot who I was talking to for a minute. I'd heard she went off with old Mike, but I never dreamed they'd gotten married."

"Cockeyed Mike?" Barbara repeated with some amusement.

"Yeah, he's cross-eyed. A skinny little runt, too. All I can say is he must have something that don't show when he's got his clothes on. I can't think of any other reason she would've taken up with him. Oops, sorry again, Elizabeth," she added when she saw Elizabeth's blush.

"In any case," Elizabeth continued, "she's afraid to leave the state, and I can't blame her. I mentioned divorce, but she won't hear of it, although I think she'll change her mind once she realizes he isn't going to change. In the meantime, I've told her she can stay here.''

''I wouldn't lose too much sleep worrying about Amy, if I was you,'' Mavis cautioned. ''She looks pretty fragile, but inside she's hard as nails. She can take care of herself.''

Elizabeth thought this an incorrect evaluation of Amy's character, but she didn't want to argue with Mavis. ''You may be right, under normal circumstances, but after what happened to her the other night—''

''I wouldn't worry about the so-called attack either. I don't like to tell tales out of school, but Amy isn't too partial about telling the truth if it ain't absolutely necessary.''

''You don't think she was lying about the attack, do you?'' Barbara asked.

Mavis gave a noncommittal shrug.

''But you saw her afterward,'' Elizabeth pointed out. ''Her gown was soiled, her hair was full of grass. She'd obviously been lying on the ground.''

''Oh, something happened to her all right,'' Mavis allowed. ''I'm just not sure it happened exactly the way she told it.''

''But why would she lie?''

''With Amy, there don't have to be a reason.''

Elizabeth pondered the charge for a moment. She tried to make it fit the sweet, delicate girl she had come to know, but without success. Obviously Mavis saw Amy in a completely different light. When Elizabeth considered the situation, she recalled how Mavis had been hostile toward Amy since the first day the girl had arrived. Could it be they had some past enmity which colored Mavis's opinion? Another possibility was jealousy. Jealousy was a petty emotion, and Elizabeth hesitated to assign it to her good friend, but she did know Mavis was impatient with any sort of weakness. Perhaps she perceived Amy as weak and consequently didn't like her.

Whatever the reason for Mavis's poor opinion of Amy, Elizabeth could not subscribe to it. But neither did she want to alienate Mavis. "I'll keep all that in mind when I deal with her then," she conceded.

The scene at the train station two days later was one of mixed joy and sorrow. The women who were leaving were excited and nervous, hopeful and fearful. Elizabeth shared their feelings. "Everything will be fine, I just know it," she assured them all as she bid each one farewell.

At last she came to Mavis, who had been hanging back, as reluctant as Elizabeth to put an end to their friendship. "I'll miss you," Elizabeth said in perfect honesty. For a moment they simply gazed at each other and then, impulsively, they embraced. Elizabeth blinked back tears, remembering how Mavis had guided her through some of the most difficult days.

When they parted, Mavis's eyes were tearful also. "I'll try to make you proud of me."

"I'm already proud of you. Try to make a good life for yourself."

"I will. Like Kate said, I'll be the boss in no time."

Elizabeth had no doubt of it.

The blast of the train whistle and the hiss of the brakes told them the time had come to board. Barbara promised for the hundredth time to telegraph as soon as they were all settled. Everyone had more hasty good-byes to call and last-minute instructions to give. After the confusion of the final minutes, Elizabeth felt bereft as she stood alone on the platform waving at the departing train.

When the last car had disappeared from sight, she heaved a weary sigh and headed back toward the house where Amy waited for her. She would have her hands full with the young woman, but Elizabeth was determined to help her make the right decision about her future.

If only Elizabeth could do the same for herself.

* * *

Chance swore softly as he straightened, stepping away from the billiard table. He'd missed a difficult bank shot which would cost him the game. He turned to Jake Schaefer. "Congratulations, Jake. You beat me again."

Jake beamed as Chance counted out the amount of their wager and dropped it into his outstretched hand.

"Are you sure you don't want to learn how to play poker?" Chance asked.

"No thanks, Mr. Fitzwilliam. My mother already thinks I'm hopelessly corrupted just from playing billiards. I can't help it if the best tables are in the saloons, but I promised her I wouldn't pick up any other bad habits."

"Beating me is getting to be a bad habit with you, Jake. If you're smart, you'll let me win every now and then as encouragement. Otherwise, I might stop playing you."

"I'll keep it in mind," Jake promised with a grin. "How about another game?"

"No thanks. My pride's taken enough of a beating for one day." Chance slapped the boy affectionately on the back and headed to the bar. Threading his way through the Saturday night crowd, he was surprised to find Bill Bates standing at the bar waiting for him. His friend was frowning thoughtfully.

"I didn't see you come in," Chance said.

"I didn't want to interrupt your game."

"Thanks. I need all my concentration when I'm playing Jake. What's got you so down in the mouth?" He signaled the bartender to bring him a beer and to refill Bill's.

"You can consider this a professional call. I've been wrestling with my conscience all day about whether or not to tell you, and I hope I've made the right decision."

Chance felt the first prickle of unease, but he waited until the bartender had delivered his drink and withdrawn before he spoke. "Spit it out, then."

"It's about Elizabeth."

"Of course."

"Do you know what's happening tomorrow?"

Chance searched his memory, but he could recall nothing significant. "No."

"I didn't think you did or you would have said something by now," Bill replied in a fatalistic tone. "Tomorrow afternoon, Miss Elizabeth Livingston will be entertaining gentlemen callers at the home of Reverend and Mrs. Elijah Folger."

Chance's beer mug froze halfway to his lips as he absorbed this astonishing information. Very carefully, he set the mug back on the bar. "To what purpose?" he asked, his voice void of expression.

"Rumor says she's in the market for a husband. The reason I called this a professional visit is because, according to the stipulations of her father's will, Elizabeth cannot marry without her guardian's consent. I thought you should be informed of the situation."

Chance saw Bill studying him for his reaction, so he did not dare reveal his true feelings—the searing anguish, the seething frustration.

Dissatisfied with Chance's lack of response, Bill said, "She hasn't confided in me, but it doesn't take much intelligence to figure out why she's doing it."

"It doesn't?" Chance inquired, instantly wary.

"No, it doesn't. I'm well aware of the problems between you two. I thought you'd worked them out last week, but Elizabeth tells me you quarreled again at the ball." Chance stiffened at this reminder, but he did not interrupt. "She might be thinking that if she gets married, she'll be out from under your thumb. I can't blame her for wanting to be free of you, but I don't think she realizes the trouble she could be getting into. Suppose she marries some profligate who squanders all her money? Or someone who mistreats her?"

"If you're so concerned, why don't you marry her yourself?"

Bill sighed in exasperation. "I'm afraid Elizabeth and I like each other too much to get married."

"What does that mean?" Chance snapped.

"That means we know we aren't in love. Therefore, we won't subject each other to a loveless marriage. The problem is, I'm afraid Elizabeth won't be as considerate to someone else.''

"You mean you think she'd marry someone she doesn't love just to be free of me?'' Chance asked as an unspeakable suspicion began to form.

"Yes, I think she might. What I want to know is whether you're going to let her.''

Chance hardly heard the question. He was too busy thinking about the other reason she might have for needing to make a hasty marriage, a reason having nothing to do with who controlled her money.

"Chance? You aren't going to let her do this crazy thing, are you?'' Bill prodded.

"No.'' Chance saw Bill's obvious relief, but he was too distracted to analyze it closely.

"Then you'll be there tomorrow, and you'll put a stop to this nonsense?''

"I'll be there. It's my duty, isn't it?''

The hot air was deathly still as Chance walked the few blocks to Reverend Folger's house the following afternoon. Even the ubiquitous Dodge City dust seemed weighted by the torpid air. It barely stirred as he strode determinedly down the street.

The stillness suited his mood. Ever since Bill had told him of Elizabeth's plans, he'd been nursing an almost unbearable anguish. All night he had replayed the scene with Elizabeth in the alley when she had said she wanted to marry him. Had his refusal forced her to turn in desperation to another man? The question had burned into his soul ever since Bill told him about Elizabeth's plans for this afternoon. Today he would learn the answer.

Chance wasn't sure what he expected to encounter when he arrived at the Folgers' house, so nothing should have surprised him. Still, he was unprepared for the number of men standing in the front yard. They milled aimlessly within the confines of the picket fence, reminding him of the cattle in the stockyards down by the tracks. Bill Bates separated himself from the group and called a greeting to Chance.

"Why is everyone standing around out here?" Chance asked with a sense of foreboding.

"Not *everyone* is, that's why we're out here. It's too crowded inside," Bill explained. "Mrs. Folger promised to flush out the first batch in a few more minutes and give the rest of them a turn."

"Good God," Chance muttered in exasperation. How many eligible young men were there in Dodge? Too many, he decided. He could easily think of an even dozen in addition to the ones standing before him. Many of them were blatant fortune hunters, and the others . . . well, the others certainly didn't deserve Elizabeth Livingston. Working his way through the group gathered in the yard, he reached the Folgers' front door and rang the bell.

"I'm sorry, but—oh, Mr. Fitzwilliam!" Mrs. Folger exclaimed with some surprise when she saw who was there. "I . . . I suppose you're here to see Elizabeth."

"Quite the contrary, Mrs. Folger," he lied with stiff courtesy. "I am the only man *not* here to see Elizabeth. I have come, instead, to see those who came to see her. As her guardian, I am duty bound to inspect her potential suitors."

"Then you must come in right away, mustn't you?" she decided, stepping back so he could enter. "I'm afraid we're a little crowded. We simply had no idea . . ."

But Chance had moved into the parlor and was no longer listening. Or at least he tried to enter the parlor. The room was jammed to capacity. Increasing his irritation was the musical sound of Elizabeth's laughter above the drone of male voices. She was apparently having the time of her life.

"Chance, good to see you," said someone at his elbow. Mechanically, he shook the man's hand as his gaze swept the room. Every fortune hunter, scoundrel, and crook in town mingled with boys barely old enough to shave. The murmur of conversation gradually ceased as the occupants became aware of his presence.

When all eyes were upon him, he turned toward Elizabeth, who was sitting on the sofa surrounded by a privileged few early arrivals who had procured the choicest seats.

"Cousin Chauncey, how nice of you to come," she said with apparent pleasure.

"Did you think I would shirk my responsibilities, Cousin Elizabeth?" he replied. "Since I have to give final approval on whomever you choose to marry, I thought I'd come by today and eliminate a few undesirables right in the very beginning."

He let his gaze settle meaningfully on a fellow who he knew was a professional gambler. The man's face reddened, and he slipped from the room without so much as a nod in Elizabeth's direction. In a matter of moments, half a dozen others had followed his example.

"Really, Cousin Chauncey, you've cast quite a pall over the afternoon," Elizabeth scolded. "Must you stand there and glare like that?"

"I don't see anyplace to sit," he said, purposely misunderstanding her.

"You mustn't let Cousin Chauncey intimidate you," Elizabeth advised the other gentlemen. "He takes his duties as my guardian quite seriously. In reality, he is most anxious to see me happily settled, isn't that right, Cousin Chauncey?"

Elizabeth smiled benignly in response to his murderous glower and turned to the man seated beside her. "What were we discussing? I'm afraid I've forgotten."

"The . . . the Centennial Exposition," he reluctantly said, glancing anxiously at Chance.

"Oh, yes," Elizabeth agreed, trying to recall something about the huge World's Fair that was held in Philadelphia during the summer of 1876. "I enjoyed it very much. Fairmount Park is so peaceful now, I can hardly remember how huge the crowds were."

"I'm sure," the man agreed lamely, still watching Chance from the corner of his eye.

As an awkward silence fell, Elizabeth wished she could remember the man's name. Her smile was beginning to feel stiff when she turned to the gentleman seated on her other side. "What do you do for a living, Mr. Simpson?" At least she knew this fellow's name.

"I own the harness shop. We do a real smart business this time of year, what with the Texas trade and all. But we don't depend on the Texans coming here. We do a good mail-order business all year round, too."

With dismay, she realized he thought she was inquiring into his financial stability. She tried changing the subject. "I should see you about purchasing a sidesaddle so I can go riding from time to time."

"I'd be proud to make you a gift of one, Miss Livingston," Simpson offered quickly.

Oh, worse and worse! "I'm afraid that would be most improper," she chided, softening her rebuke by patting his arm. Instantly, she knew she had made another mistake. His expression brightened at her unintentional show of favoritism, and the others in the room frowned their disapproval. She didn't dare look at Chance. Closing her eyes, she sent up a silent prayer for deliverance. It came in the form of Mrs. Folger.

"I'm sorry gentlemen, but your hour is up. You'll have to go now and make room for the others who are still waiting outside." Her announcement was met with protests which she quickly overruled. She began shooing the callers out, a process they attempted to resist. Only Mrs. Folger's tenacity enabled her to clear the room. Elizabeth had one bad moment when she noticed the determined Mr. Simpson grinning smugly, certain he would be exempt from the evacuation order.

Elizabeth gave him an apologetic smile. "I'm sorry you have to go now. Perhaps you'll call again." He seemed startled at being dismissed, but her invitation to return perked him right up again.

"I most certainly will," he assured her, apparently convinced she looked upon him with favor.

As Mrs. Folger escorted the last of her visitors out the front door, Elizabeth glanced at Chance, who still stood defiantly nearby. "This would be an excellent opportunity for you to find a chair."

The look he gave her would have curdled milk, and she felt the warm glow of satisfaction. He was absolutely livid, and it didn't take much imagination for her to decide why: he was jealous, pure and simple.

"Thank you, Cousin Elizabeth, but I prefer to stand," he said.

"Lovely day, isn't it?" she remarked after a short silence.

"It's hot as Hades."

Another silence fell. Elizabeth could hear the men in the yard shuffling toward the porch.

"Are you well, Elizabeth?"

The question surprised her. "I'm very well, thank you," she replied, puzzling over his narrow-eyed scrutiny. Did she look ill? Perhaps she was showing the effects of so many sleepless nights spent listening for imaginary intruders in her house. "Although I must confess I find so much company a little trying."

"You should have thought of that before you issued your invitation."

"I had no idea my invitation would draw so many interested parties."

His expression hardened perceptibly. "An auction of prize breeding stock always draws a crowd."

Elizabeth had barely gasped in response when Bill Bates appeared in the parlor doorway. "Good afternoon, Elizabeth," he said with forced enthusiasm. "How are you holding up so far?"

Elizabeth turned to him gratefully, glad to see the questioning way he was eyeing Chance, almost as if he suspected her cousin was tormenting her. She held out her hand to him.

Behind him followed the remainder of her suitors. She greeted each one in turn, although her cheeks were beginning to ache from the strain of holding her smile in place. Chance withdrew to a corner where he stood with arms crossed, a forbidding frown on his face. Conscious of his every change of expression, Elizabeth had a difficult time following the conversation going on around her.

Apparently aware of her problem, Bill carried the day for her, covering when she lost her train of thought and repeating questions she missed. She hardly noticed Mrs. Folger serving tea to this second group. Every nerve in her body was concentrating on the tall, dark man looming in the corner. His cold-eyed disapproval drove three more men from the parlor, and heaven only knew what he might say or do next. Surely he wouldn't make any of his snide remarks in front of witnesses, but she could not be perfectly certain.

At last Elizabeth looked at the clock to discover the time had come to bid her guests farewell. Mrs. Folger took her cue again and sent them on their way. Only Bill lingered. He seemed to be sending Chance a silent message, but try as she would, Elizabeth could not decipher it.

Chance had no such problem, however. Before her very eyes, he sloughed off his dour mood. When Mrs. Folger returned after closing the front door behind the last of her suitors, he flashed his most charming smile. "You are very kind to permit Elizabeth to do her entertaining in your home," he said.

Mrs. Folger blinked once in surprise at his sudden change. "I . . . I was only too happy to oblige."

"*We* were only too happy," Reverend Folger added, coming into the room behind her. He had been secluded upstairs until the visitors left, having announced his aversion to intimidating anyone with his presence.

Meanwhile Mrs. Folger was busy taking stock of the situation. Her perceptive gaze went from Chance to Elizabeth and back again. Elizabeth could actually see the older woman hatching a plot.

Mrs. Folger smiled serenely at Chance. "We are all astonished at how many gentlemen came today. I'm sure none of us expected such a turnout. As I tried to explain to Elizabeth, I can't believe this is a proper way of finding a husband." She gave Elizabeth an apologetic glance. "I'm sorry, my dear, but I think we can be frank with Mr. Fitzwilliam." She turned back to Chance. "I'm sure you see the folly of it. Perhaps you can convince your cousin?"

Elizabeth almost choked. She had laid her plans very carefully, hoping Chance would do exactly what Mrs. Folger was asking, and here she was, pushing him into it.

"Yes, Chance," Bill added, "as her guardian, your duty is to prevent her from making a terrible mistake. Don't you agree?"

"Absolutely," Chance said. "Perhaps Elizabeth will allow me to escort her home so we can discuss the matter."

Elizabeth bit her lip to keep from smiling.

"An excellent idea," Mrs. Folger was saying.

"Very well, then," Elizabeth said in feigned resignation, rising to her feet. "I'll be ready in a moment."

She needed less than a moment to put on her hat and gloves. By then Bill had gone. When she had thanked the Folgers once again for their kindness, she made her way regally out the front door to where Chance awaited her on the porch. Choosing to ignore the arm he offered, she picked up her skirt and descended the steps, leaving him to follow in her wake.

He waited until they reached the road before he started in on her. "Exactly what were you trying to accomplish with this . . . this . . ."

"Auction of prize breeding stock?"

"That was the most disgraceful display I've ever seen. Half those men should be in jail."

"All friends of yours, I suppose."

"I don't think you understand the seriousness of the situation, Elizabeth."

She batted innocent eyes at him. "Then explain it to me."

His jaw worked as he fought to control his temper. "Just tell me one thing. Why have you suddenly decided you need to get married?"

Elizabeth shot him a look of disgust. "Chance, does the expression 'dog in the manger' mean anything to you?"

"What are you trying to say?"

"I'm saying *you* don't want me, but you don't want anyone else to have me either. Some might consider you . . . what's the word I'm looking for? *Selfish.*"

"I'm your guardian. I can't let you ruin your life by marrying the wrong man."

"So you've told me, time and again."

"I'm referring to those men at Folger's house this afternoon," he said impatiently.

"Not all of them are the criminals you make them out to be. Some are perfectly respectable businessmen."

He seemed to be grinding his teeth. "Elizabeth, we need to talk. In private," he added as she shoved open her front gate and marched into the yard with him at her heels.

"I don't think this is a good time for us to talk, Chance. You're too upset."

"I'm not upset!"

"Perhaps you could call on me tomorrow," she suggested as she glided up the porch steps.

"Elizabeth, come back here!"

She closed the front door behind her with a decisive click and leaned against it, smiling smugly.

"Miss Livingston, is that you?" Amy appeared at the other end of the long entrance hall. "How did everything go?"

"Just fine. Too fine, in fact. Every eligible bachelor in the country came to call."

"How exciting!"

"Fatiguing, too, I'm afraid. I think I'll lie down awhile."

"All right," Amy replied. "When you feel better, you can tell me all about it."

Resisting the urge to peek outside to see if Chance still stood fuming in the yard, Elizabeth slipped quickly into the front parlor and closed the doors behind her.

The parlor was cool and dark, having been shuttered against the afternoon heat. Damp and sticky, Elizabeth sighed with relief, glad she had decided to retain this room as her bedchamber. The upstairs rooms would be like ovens on a day like today. With another sigh, she kicked off her shoes, tore off her hat and gloves, and proceeded to peel out of her clinging dress.

Chance stood in the front yard for what seemed like a long time. The summer sun blazed down on him, but the only heat of which he was aware was the rage scorching his soul. He had to know the truth behind her sudden search for a husband. Striding up to her front door, he hammered authoritatively. If some black-hearted witch opened it pointing a gun, he'd . . .

Amy opened the door cautiously, just a crack at first, until she saw who was there.

"Mr. Fitzwilliam," she exclaimed happily, throwing the door open wide. "What brings you here?"

The chit looked vaguely familiar, although Chance did not bother trying to place her. He swallowed what remained of his fury and smiled graciously. "I'd like to see Miss Livingston. Is she in?"

Listening from the parlor, Elizabeth could make out the dull rumble of Chance's voice obviously demanding entrance. She smiled, thinking that, of all her guests, poor abused Amy was the least likely to allow a male visitor inside. Chance would simply have to stew in his own juice awhile longer before Elizabeth put him out of his misery.

Having poured some tepid water into the bowl on her makeshift washstand, Elizabeth scooped up a handful and splashed it on her overheated face. The trickling water drowned out the murmur of voices in the hallway, but not the sound of the front door closing. Elizabeth took up a towel and began to blot her face dry.

Behind her, she heard the parlor doors open. After such a visitation, Amy would want an explanation. "Did he give you any trouble?" Elizabeth asked, turning.

"Not a bit," Chance Fitzwilliam replied, closing the doors behind him.

Elizabeth uttered a startled cry and quickly covered herself with the damp towel. Unfortunately, the small scrap barely concealed her bosom. "What are you doing here? Where's Amy?"

"She discreetly left us alone."

"Get out of here!"

"Not until you answer one question for me, Elizabeth. Are you pregnant?"

Chapter 11

"What?" Elizabeth demanded.

"I asked if you are carrying my child. Is that why you need a husband, Elizabeth, as a father for my baby?"

Elizabeth didn't know which was worse, the accusation or the realization that he thought her capable of such a thing. "Exactly what makes you think I'd be guilty of such a deception?"

His eyes glittered like broken glass. "You asked me to marry you the other night—"

"I did not!"

"—and when I refused, you suddenly invited every bachelor in town to court you. If you have another explanation for your behavior, I'd like to hear it."

Elizabeth stared at him in astonishment. Her outrage evaporated as she saw her actions through his eyes and realized how easily he could have put the wrong meaning to them. His fury wasn't jealousy at all, or at least not the kind she had hoped to inspire.

"I . . . no, I didn't . . . I couldn't . . . Chance, I'd never do a thing like that! I was only trying to make you jealous."

"Jealous?" He said the word as if he'd never heard it before.

"Yes," she said, closing the space between them and putting a hand on his arm. "I know it sounds idiotic, but I thought if you really did care for me and you thought I was going to marry somebody else—"

"Dear God," he murmured in relief, and then his eyes flashed with renewed anger. "When I think of what you put me through—"

"*Were* you jealous?"

"Insanely."

Elizabeth let her hand drift to his chest. "I suppose I should be sorry."

He drew an unsteady breath. "I suppose I asked for it."

"You did."

"Young lady," he said hoarsely, "somebody ought to kiss the impudence out of you."

Elizabeth slid her hand to his shoulder. "Maybe somebody will."

In the next instant, his mouth was on hers, hard and possessive. He crushed her to him, and she clung fiercely. The kiss went on and on until they were both breathless.

"You're a witch," he gasped against her cheek.

"I wish I were. I'd cast a spell on you."

"You have," he assured her, pressing her to his heart. "You're driving me crazy. When I saw those men today, I wanted to murder every one of them for even thinking about marrying you."

She smiled sadly. "Like I said, Chance, you're a dog in a manger. You don't want me, but you don't want anyone else to have me either."

"You're wrong. I do want you, Lizzie, more than I've ever wanted any woman."

"You *want* me," she mimicked. "And Chance Fitzwilliam always takes whatever he wants. Is that it?"

"No, that's *not* it," he snapped in frustration. How could he make her understand? "I love you, Lizzie. I *love* you. That's why I want you. That's why I can't stay away. That's why I can't stand to see you with other men, and that's why I went crazy when I thought you wanted to marry someone else!"

"Chance?" The word was a whisper of awe. He loved her! He really *did* love her. "Oh, Chance!" She flung her arms around his neck. His mouth found hers for another ravenous kiss as he silently confirmed his confession, worshiping her with his hands and lips and body.

"You were so mean to me," she marveled as her hands delved into the thick softness of his hair.

"I had to be," he said against the column of her throat. "How else could I keep us apart?"

Apart? She never wanted to be farther away from him than she was at this very minute. "There's no reason for us to be apart now," she murmured.

"Yes, there is," he murmured back, even as his hand found the swell of her breast. "Lizzie, stop me."

"Why?" she asked, pressing herself into his embrace.

"Because . . ." His mouth closed over hers for a long, lingering kiss. When he lifted his head, his breath was ragged. "Because if you don't, I'm going to make love to you, here and now."

"Good."

Chance froze. He tried to remember all the reasons why he shouldn't take her, all the reasons why it was wrong to love her. They'd seemed so important before, but now, with Elizabeth in his arms, her eyes dark with desire, he couldn't recall a single one.

Elizabeth waited, frightened she had gone too far. Was she too wanton? Had she shocked him? But no, the eyes looking down at her were soft with love and wonder. His fingers came up to gently graze her cheek. He whispered an endearment, his breath mingling with hers as he touched a kiss to her upturned lips. "Lizzie." He spoke her name in adoration, chanting it over and over while his fingers fumbled with buttons and hooks and ties and laces.

Her hands were busy, too, pushing off his jacket and vest and shirt to find the vital flesh beneath. She purred with delight when she discovered the dark hair blanketing his chest. He groaned when she raked her fingers through it. Beneath her palms his heart thundered, echoing her own.

"You're so beautiful," he said, lifting away the last of her garments so she stood naked before him. Any shame she might have felt evaporated in the heat of his adoring gaze, and she watched boldly as he stripped off the rest of his own clothes to reveal the urgency of his need.

She knew a moment's fear then. This was all so new, and his desire was so blatant.

"I won't hurt you, Lizzie," he promised, lowering her to the cot. "I'll never hurt you again. You're mine now, sweetheart, all mine."

His hands soothed away her fears as they moved over her body, searching for her secrets. This was so different from before, not a blinding burst of passion but a slow building. He teased and tantalized, stirring but never too much. Her arousal waxed and waned as he explored her from the top of her head to the tips of her toes, and before long the breathless tingle became an aching need.

She opened to him, but he did not come to her as she demanded. Instead, he settled between her legs, planting biting kisses on her sensitive inner thighs. She shifted restlessly, urging him on, but he resisted and pressed a kiss into the dark curls crowning her womanhood.

"Chance!" she cried, shocking by the intimacy.

"Hush," he said, and his tongue flicked out to caress her most sensitive spot. She moaned aloud as her body kindled. The smoldering heat in her loins pulsed and throbbed, swelling into molten waves that surged up and over until she was drowning in desire. Gasping, she called his name, clinging to his shoulders as the waves climbed higher. Then the white-hot ecstasy closed over her, shutting out all else, and she surrendered to its oblivion.

The aftershocks still thrummed through her when Chance's voice coaxed her back. "Lizzie, my love. Lizzie, we aren't finished yet."

Her weighted eyelids lifted slowly, and she saw his face above hers, his dark eyes alight with adoration. Her mouth curved into a blissful smile. "No, we aren't," she agreed languidly. She wanted *him* now, wanted him to be as weak and helpless with passion as she had been.

She slipped her arms around him, sliding her palms

down the satin smoothness of his back to clutch at the sinewy strength of his flanks. His surrender was as desperate as hers. With a groan, he possessed her, trembling in need. She welcomed him with kisses and caresses and whispered endearments, which he echoed back in a ragged, panting refrain.

Reveling in her power, she barely noticed her own excitement building again. Embers from her previous conflagration flickered to life, stoked by his thrusting urgency, and her breath quickened.

She gasped in wonder as his body tensed above hers, triggering her own release. New convulsions shook her even as she absorbed the hot rush of his spasms. "I love you," she said, the words a whispered sigh as she sank exhausted into the twilit afterglow.

"Lizzie." His voice was soft and coaxing, a teasing trickle against her ear.

She opened her eyes to find his face close, his eyes adoring. "I love you, Lizzie."

"I know," she sighed.

Tenderly, he brushed damp strands of hair from her cheeks. "I acted like a jackass this afternoon."

"You were provoked."

"Yes, I was, but I had no right to accuse you of someone else's sins."

Still lethargic from their lovemaking, Elizabeth had a difficult time deciphering his statement. "Whose sins?"

"My fiancée, a long time ago."

Slowly, the pieces fell into place, and Elizabeth's lethargy vanished. "Your fiancée? Did she . . . she passed your baby off on another man?"

"No, not quite. She didn't have time to find another man, so she killed my baby instead. She had an abortion."

His eyes clouded with anguish, and he didn't seem to hear Elizabeth's horrified gasp. She struggled upright, clutching the bedclothes to her breasts. "Oh, Chance, I'm so sorry."

She touched his cheek, and he turned toward it, pressing his lips to her palm. ''It must have been awful for you,'' she whispered. ''How did you find out?''

''She told me,'' he said bleakly, remembering. ''But not at first. When she found I had no intention of following in my father's footsteps, she simply broke our engagement. I was devastated, and I kept trying to see her. The servants told me she was ill, but I didn't believe them. I thought her parents were keeping us apart so I wouldn't be able to change her mind, and I finally forced my way inside.

''She was in bed, in her room, and I'll never forget how pale she was. At first I thought she was dead, but then she opened her eyes. She said, 'I killed your baby, Chance.' She said she'd had to because she was already too far along to be able to pass it off as someone else's.''

His pain and bitterness brought tears to Elizabeth's eyes. ''Oh, Chance!'' Murmuring words of comfort, she drew his head to her bosom. He clung to her while she stroked his hair and rained kisses on his face.

''We'll have lots of children, my darling,'' she promised. ''We'll be so happy, you'll forget it ever happened. I love you. I love you so much . . .''

He stirred and suddenly he was returning her kisses. His clinging became caressing, and his weight carried her back against the pillow. Desire flickered to life again, stoked by his searching hands and eager mouth. He touched her everywhere, breasts and belly, hips and thighs, until the flames raged out of control.

Gasping her name, he plunged into her welcoming depths. This time the maelstrom captured them both, swirling and boiling around them until they were swept away together.

Exhausted, Elizabeth nestled in the curve of his arm and slept. Chance held her for a long time, not wanting to break the physical bond between them. He nuzzled the fragrant curve of her neck, pressing tiny kisses into the tender flesh and letting the smell and taste of her engulf him.

Like one awakening from a trance, he suddenly saw the future clearly. The years left to him, the years that had once stretched before him devoid of love and tenderness, would now be filled with Elizabeth. He gloried in her loveliness, the perfection he had always admired, and wondered why he of all men should have been blessed with her love.

But he knew the why no longer mattered. What mattered was his reaction to it. He'd behaved like a bastard up until now, and he did not intend to compound his sins. If the Chance Fitzwilliam he had been for the last decade was unworthy of Elizabeth Livingston, then he would become a different man. He'd sell his saloon and turn respectable. Dammit, he would even go back to Philadelphia if that's what she wanted, although he would draw the line at rejoining the ranks of the robber barons.

Smiling at the thought of Elizabeth's reaction when she learned he was her mysterious benefactor, he touched a kiss to her lips. She would probably scold him, telling him it was more proof he was an honorable man. He would even let her believe it. He could easily grow accustomed to Elizabeth's admiration.

A distant sound disturbed his fantasies—the church bell summoning worshipers to evensong. Startled by the lateness of the hour—and by how long he had been in Elizabeth's house—he realized he should leave immediately. He had probably already done irreparable damage to her reputation. Of course, the announcement of their engagement would do much to allay any gossip, but for now, he'd best be on his way as swiftly as possible.

Carefully, he untangled himself from Elizabeth's embrace and eased off the cot. She murmured something in protest, but he drew the coverlet over her, and she settled again. Quickly, he donned his clothes, smoothing the wrinkles as best he could and hoping he would not look as if he had just come from Elizabeth's bed when he was finished.

Fully clothed once more, he stood over her, watching

her beloved face in repose. He wanted to wake her. He
wanted to tell her again how much he loved her and assure
her he had come to his senses at last. They would be married, and he would become the man she thought he was
or die trying. He wanted to see her joy and hear her pro-
fess her own love, but she was sleeping so soundly, he
didn't have the heart to disturb her. He'd let her rest now.
Tomorrow would be time enough, and then they'd have
their entire lives together.

Quietly, he slipped out of the parlor, sliding the doors
shut behind him.

"Where's Miss Livingston?"

Chance jumped and turned to see the woman who had
let him in the house hovering in the hallway. "She's sleeping," he said, keeping his voice low. "I don't think she
should be disturbed. She seemed to be exhausted."

The girl nodded, her blond curls bobbing. "She hasn't
been sleeping too good ever since I got attacked."

Chance's eyes narrowed as recognition dawned. This
was Amy Waters, the woman who claimed she had been
raped in Elizabeth's yard. He remembered her vaguely
from Summer's place, another of the girls he'd judged too
fragile for his attentions. She still possessed the same vulnerability, but something in her eyes told him it was only
a pose. "I hope you've recovered from your, uh, ordeal,"
he ventured.

She drew herself up and took a step closer. "I was hurt
real bad, but I'm fine now," she said with what he took
for pride. "In fact," she added with a provocative smile,
"I'm *real* fine, if you'd like to find out for yourself."

Chance could hardly believe his ears. When Wyatt originally told him of the attack, the marshal had expressed
some doubt about Amy's version of the story. Still, Chance
had been prepared to offer sympathy, not to hear her brag
about her experience, and he was especially not prepared
for her counteroffer. "I don't think so," he replied, trying
to hide his revulsion.

Her expression changed from provocative to contemptuous in the blink of an eye. "Oh, I guess you've had all you want for now," she said with a malicious glance at Elizabeth's door. "I guess she's no better than the rest of us underneath all them fancy clothes—ouch!"

Chance had her arm in a far-from-gentle grip, and he gave her a warning shake. "You keep your mouth shut about Miss Livingston's affairs, you hear me? She and I are going to be married."

For a second, her eyes glinted with what might have been hatred, then her pretty face crumpled and tears shimmered in her huge eyes. "I'm awful sorry, Mr. Fitzwilliam. I didn't mean . . . I'd never say anything against Miss Livingston, not after all she's done for me."

Chance looked for duplicity but found no trace of it. With a satisfied nod, he let her go. "Good. And like I said, let her sleep. When she wakes up tell her I'll be by to see her tomorrow afternoon around one o'clock."

"I sure will," Amy said, blinking at her tears and rubbing the arm he had held.

"I'm sorry I hurt you."

"I probably deserved it. I never should've said anything ugly about Miss Livingston. I won't ever again, I promise."

Chance couldn't ask for anything more. "I'll see you tomorrow, then."

"Yeah, I reckon you will." She opened the door and let him out. He did not see the narrow-eyed way she watched him as he walked away.

Elizabeth woke slowly. Her first realization was of her nakedness beneath the cover. Shocked to full wakefulness, she glanced around the room, trying to judge the time and remember something important.

Chance! She sat bolt upright and instantly regretted her hasty movement. Her body was once again sore in unusual places, and she moaned involuntarily.

"Chance?" she called, but received no reply. He was gone, as she had instinctively known. Disappointment welled in her, but she fought it down. Chance had said he loved her, that she belonged to him. He'd whispered a thousand endearments as he had worshipped her body with his own.

But why had he left her without a word?

She jumped up from the cot and grabbed her robe, shrugging into it as she headed for the door. "Amy! Amy!"

"What is it, Miss Livingston?" Amy answered, coming from the kitchen.

"Chance—Mr. Fitzwilliam—did you see him leave?"

"Oh, yes, ma'am, I did," she replied with a conspiratorial smile. "I didn't know things was like that between you two. You should've told me—"

"Did he say anything before he left?" Elizabeth interrupted, flushing with embarrassment at Amy's frank insinuation.

Amy's smile faded into a frown. "Well, yes, he did," she admitted reluctantly.

"What?" Elizabeth prodded uneasily. What could Chance have said that Amy would hesitate to repeat?

Amy shifted from one foot to the other. "He didn't . . . I mean, I know he didn't mean anything by it. You gotta remember, we've been friends for a long time now. I knew him way back when I worked at Summer Winters's place. Sometimes he used to pay to have me for the whole night, and we'd—"

"Amy!" Elizabeth stared at her, appalled.

"Oh, I'm sorry, miss. You can't let it bother you, though. He didn't even know you then."

Elizabeth felt as if she'd been dealt a blow that had knocked all the newfound joy completely out of her. "What did he say to you?" she demanded, afraid she didn't really want to hear.

Amy shrugged. "Like I said, he didn't mean anything by it. He was teasing, I know he was. He just said something about how good a time he'd had today, and how next time he came he'd give me some fun, too. Miss Livingston, are you all right? Don't take on so. I'd never steal your fella.''

The room had begun to spin, and Elizabeth leaned gratefully on Amy's offered arm. "I . . . I'd better sit down," she murmured. Amy led her to the hallway bench.

"I don't blame you for being upset, Miss Livingston. He's a man worth fighting for, I'll tell you. Sometimes after he'd been at me, I could hardly walk, but a girl doesn't need to walk when she's floating, now does she?''

Amy's secretive smile made the bile rise in Elizabeth's throat as she acknowledged the truth of the statement, a truth only a woman who had loved Chance could know.

"Can I get you something, miss? You look awful peaked.''

Elizabeth felt far worse, and she nodded. "Some tea, I think," she said, more anxious for the solitude the errand would afford her than for a drink.

"I'll get it right away.'' Amy started to turn, then stopped as if a thought had just occurred to her. "He said he loved you, didn't he?'' she guessed with a knowing smile. "He always does.''

Then Amy was gone in a swish of skirts, leaving Elizabeth to stare after her in horror. Her head felt as if it would burst. Nothing made sense anymore. She had been so certain Chance loved her.

Oh, dear God! A memory chilled her to her marrow. At the fireworks she had told him she knew he was an honorable man because if he was not, he would have lied in order to obtain her surrender. Today he had done exactly that.

Chance pulled out his gold pocket watch and checked it for the fifth time in as many minutes. It was still almost an hour before one o'clock, when he had told Amy he'd return to Elizabeth's. Why hadn't he told the girl he'd call first thing in the morning? He should have known how anxious he'd be to see Elizabeth again and get everything settled between them.

He stuffed the watch back into his vest pocket and began to drum his fingers on the table, glancing impatiently around the saloon. The Last Chance was virtually deserted at this time of day.

The problem was he simply wasn't used to considering propriety, but he supposed he would have to *get* used to it if he and Elizabeth were going to be married. He wanted to make her life perfect from now on, and if that meant he must once again learn to bend to the rules of society, he would do so.

His first obstacle would be overcoming the gossip that would inevitably surround their marriage. Part of it, he knew, would involve speculation about his trusteeship of her estate. Some people were bound to think he had used his position to pressure her into marriage in order to benefit himself financially. How anyone could believe he'd care a fig for her money when Elizabeth herself was so beautiful he didn't know, but he was sure they would. Consequently, he'd take immediate steps to ensure Elizabeth was not subjected to such conjecture. In fact, he realized suddenly, he should take those steps well before announcing their engagement.

Wondering if he had time to stop by Bill Bates's office on his way to Elizabeth's house, he was already rising from his chair when the saloon doors swung open to reveal Bill himself. Chance lifted a hand in greeting, but his welcoming smile froze when he saw Dan Frost and Reverend Folger enter behind him.

"Oh, hell," he muttered at the sight of the town's leading reformers.

"That's a fine greeting," Bill said in feigned outrage.

"Is it too much to hope you're only collecting for some worthy cause?" Chance asked, eyeing the preacher and the newspaper editor askance.

Dan Frost grinned. "Yes, but if you'd like to give us some money anyway, I for one won't turn you down."

Chance turned to Folger. "Aren't you afraid some of your flock will see you in here, Reverend?"

"I wouldn't expect any of my flock to be in here to see me. Besides, even the good Lord consorted with publicans and sinners from time to time."

"I don't think I have to ask which category I fall into," Chance remarked. "Won't you gentlemen have a seat? Can I offer you a, uh, drink?"

"Nothing for me, thank you," Folger replied cheerfully, taking a seat.

"It's early for me, I'm afraid," said Dan Frost, sitting opposite Chance.

Bill was grinning from ear to ear. "This isn't a social call anyway," he explained unnecessarily.

"So I gathered. You gentlemen are wasting your time if you think I'll support any candidate except Bat Masterson for county sheriff. Bat's a close friend of mine, and nobody can say he isn't doing a good job. Have you forgotten how he went after those horse thieves last year?"

"Nobody's asking you to support another candidate, Chance," Dan Frost assured him, but Chance wasn't listening.

"If you reformers really want to accomplish something, you ought to start organizing relief for the farmers. This drought is going to ruin them."

Dan exchanged a glance with Reverend Folger. "Exactly what kind of relief did you have in mind?"

"Every kind," Chance informed him, thinking of his recent visit to the Dietzels' new homestead. "Some of them are already on short rations. Come winter, they'll need food and clothes and fuel, and they'll probably need more help than the county or even the state can provide."

"You're right," Reverend Folger agreed, leaning back in his chair as if to get a better look at Chance. "The weather has affected farmers all over Kansas, but do you think we can persuade people in other states to come to our aid?"

"If we approach them correctly. We have to make them understand that if the farmers go under, everybody in the country suffers."

Bill frowned thoughtfully. "Isn't it a little early to start? I mean, the harvest isn't even in yet."

"We haven't had a drop of rain to speak of since early spring, and rain now won't help a bit. The crops are already dead in the field," Chance pointed out.

"Then we can't get started too soon," said Dan Frost. "All we need is someone to organize the effort."

Chance opened his mouth to agree, but he suddenly noticed all three of his companions were staring at him expectantly. "I'll be damned," he muttered as realization dawned. "You didn't come in here to talk to me about the election at all, did you?"

The three smiled smugly back. "I already told you we didn't," Dan reminded him.

Their motives were now crystal clear, but for some reason Chance didn't feel the least bit annoyed at having been manipulated. There was only one thing he didn't understand. "Why did you pick me?"

The other two men looked at Bill, who smiled sheepishly. "After I saw you with those settlers on the Fourth of July, I kind of figured you had a vested interest in the plight of the farmers."

"Rumor has it you're pretty good at collecting money, too," Reverend Folger added with a twinkle. "I've been thinking what a wonderful deacon you'd make."

"Whoa!" Chance said, lifting his hands. The others laughed, but Chance couldn't help thinking the idea was not as preposterous as it might have sounded twenty-four hours ago. Life with Elizabeth would include all the trappings of respectability, including church. A few days ago the prospect would have appalled him. Now he had no trouble picturing himself in the role of responsible citizen. His father must be turning in his grave.

Meanwhile, Dan Frost was already laying strategy. "I'll get you started by writing an editorial to stir folks up a bit. I suppose we'd better make some plans first though, so we'll have someplace to channel their enthusiasm."

"Yes, we should," Chance agreed, "but unfortunately,

I have an appointment in a few minutes. Maybe we can meet tomorrow sometime.''

Folger invited all of them to supper the following evening and promised to round up a few more volunteers before then. Folger and Frost rose to take their leave, but Chance asked Bill to remain behind for a moment. When the others had gone Chance turned to him, and Bill was ready with his explanations.

''I didn't tell them you were the one who provided the Chicago jobs, but I think they suspect. Whether you like it or not, you're getting a reputation around town as a man who gets things done.''

''Don't worry, I don't mind your interference. It's my own fault, anyway, I could have refused when Dan asked me to get involved in the first place.''

Bill was startled but pleased. ''I did think you took the whole thing rather well. I expected a fight when you found out what they wanted.''

''Well, somebody has to help those people,'' he demurred, uncomfortable with explaining the reasons for his change of heart. ''Anyway, I didn't ask you to stay so I could rake you over the coals. I need to consult with you about a matter of business. Do you remember you told me I could get Elizabeth's father's will overturned if I wanted to?''

Bill's eyes narrowed in concern. ''Are things that bad between you? I thought yesterday you were going to work out your differences.''

''We did,'' Chance assured him with a smile as he thought of just how thoroughly they had worked them out. ''But I'm a little reluctant to ask Elizabeth to marry me while I'm still her guardian.''

''Marry!'' Bill brightened instantly, but Chance stopped him with a warning gesture.

''Like I said, I haven't asked her yet, but I have reason to hope she'll accept. People are going to talk, though, when they find out she's marrying a saloonkeeper. I don't want them thinking I used my control over her money to force her into anything.''

''Of course not. I'm sure I can get a judge to appoint another guardian for her without any trouble. I'll have to contact her attorney in Philadelphia first. I'm afraid I'll need some time.''

''Anything you can do to speed up the process will be appreciated,'' Chance told him wryly.

Bill grinned. ''I understand. I'll do whatever's necessary.''

''Miss Livingston? Are you feeling poorly?''

Elizabeth turned from where she had been staring unseeing out the parlor window to face Amy's frowning concern. ''I'm a little tired, that's all,'' she lied. She'd hardly slept a wink all night, but in spite of her weariness, she did not dare close her eyes even now for fear of seeing visions of Chance Fitzwilliam.

All through the dark hours until dawn she had replayed the events of the previous day in her mind, trying to make sense of what had happened. She'd asked herself a thousand times why he'd lied to her, and the answer was painfully obvious: to get her into bed. Chance's failure to appear this morning gave silent affirmation to Amy's story. A man violently in love would have been on her doorstep first thing. Now it was after noon, and he still had not come.

Amy sighed impatiently. ''You can't sit here staring out the window forever, Miss Livingston. Life goes on.''

''Yes, you're right,'' Elizabeth agreed wearily. She recalled Amy's amazing recovery from the rape and wondered what reserves of strength the girl possessed that enabled her to bounce back so quickly. Elizabeth felt as if she would never have the energy to leave the house again.

''I know, why don't you make us a pie,'' Amy suggested. ''You really oughta do *something* besides just sitting.''

Elizabeth wanted to argue but simply did not have the

strength. "A pie," she repeated. "All right. I'll start on it in a little while." Barbara had taught her the rudiments of baking, and Elizabeth had gleefully mastered the art of pie making. Those carefree days seemed far away now.

"No, you won't start it in a little while," Amy said, taking Elizabeth by the arm and urging her out of her chair. "You'll start right now."

Amy looked so determined, Elizabeth had to smile. "Whatever you say," she replied as Amy marched her toward her kitchen.

"Then I say quit moping and get to work." In a few moments, Amy had her in the kitchen with an apron around her waist. Elizabeth had to agree the activity would do her good, although she was certain nothing would completely lift the weight of depression from her shoulders. Sighing, she reached for the pastry board.

Chance saw Amy come onto the front porch just as he passed through Elizabeth's front gate. She was carrying a broom and seemed about to begin sweeping when she saw him.

"Oh, my, is it one o'clock already?" she asked, smiling a greeting.

"No, I'm early," Chance said, thinking he could not have waited another minute. "Will you tell Miss Livingston I'd like to see her?"

Amy's smile vanished. "She . . . she ain't here."

"Didn't you tell her I was coming?" he demanded, knowing nothing less would have prevented Elizabeth from meeting him.

"Oh, yes, I told her all right, but she . . ."

"She what?" Chance pressed.

"She said she didn't want to see you, not ever again."

Even as Chance absorbed the blow, some part of him denied it. It couldn't be true. Elizabeth would never say something like that. "Where is she?"

"I . . . I don't know exactly. She went out." Amy toyed

nervously with the broom handle and her gaze refused to meet his.

"Out where? She must have at least told you where she was going and when she'd be back."

"Well, she went for a buggy ride."

"A buggy ride?" he echoed incredulously.

"Yeah, a buggy ride. Some man came and got her, and they went for a ride."

"Who was it?"

"I never saw him before. I think he was . . ."

"Who?"

"I think he was somebody she met at the Folgers' yesterday."

Chance could hardly believe what she was saying. "Elizabeth went for a ride with someone else when she knew I was coming to see her?"

Amy winced in distress, and he knew there was even more to the story than she'd told him.

"Tell me the rest of it," he commanded.

"She . . . well, when I told her you were coming to see her, she carried on something awful, and then she went and wrote a note to this man and . . . and . . . she sent it to him asking him to take her out today so she wouldn't be here when you came by."

Stunned, Chance could only stare. None of this made sense. Why would Elizabeth make love with him one day and avoid him like the plague the next? "Do you know how long she'll be gone?" he managed after a long moment.

Amy shrugged and shook her head.

"I'll be back later then," he said, turning on his heel.

Elizabeth looked up from rolling out the pie dough as a sound teased at her consciousness. She was a long way from the front door and the house was relatively soundproof, but she thought she could hear the murmur of voices. Was Amy talking to someone out on the porch?

Her heart made a funny little lurch as she pictured

Chance standing there, hat in hand, come to apologize and beg her forgiveness. Perhaps Amy was right and his suggestive remarks to her yesterday meant nothing. Perhaps Amy had misunderstood. Perhaps . . . Without conscious thought, she pulled off her apron and moved down the hall, wiping the flour from her hands with it as she went.

The front door opened, and Elizabeth's heart lurched again, but it was only Amy coming back inside. She started when she saw Elizabeth. "Oh, Miss Livingston, you gave me a scare."

"I thought I heard voices. Were you talking to someone?"

Amy's gaze darted guiltily away.

"Amy, who was there?" she insisted.

"Mike," she replied reluctantly. "My husband, Mike. He keeps coming by, like I told you before, trying to get me to come back to him."

Elizabeth's shoulders sagged in disappointment, but she was almost grateful for this new crisis to distract her from her own troubles. "Maybe we should speak to the marshal and have him tell your husband not to bother you anymore."

Amy opened her mouth to reply, but the doorbell rang shrilly, cutting her off. "I'll get it," Elizabeth said, brushing past Amy before the girl could move.

Without even looking to see who was there, Elizabeth threw the door open. A smile already trembled on her lips, but the man on the porch was not Chance Fitzwilliam. He was a stranger, average in height and slight of build, well dressed in a dark suit, although his vest was somewhat loud. He fiddled nervously with the hat in his hands.

"Could I see Amy Waters, please?" he asked. He was handsome in a florid way, Elizabeth supposed, but his eyes were not quite right somehow. The word *cockeyed* sprang to mind. Cockeyed Mike Loving.

Before Elizabeth could reply, Amy appeared at her elbow. "I already told you I don't want you coming around here no more, Mike," she said furiously.

"You seemed pretty happy to see me the other night,'' he replied.

"Please, Mr. Loving,'' Elizabeth tried, hoping to avoid an altercation. "I'm sure you can understand why Amy doesn't want to see you. You've treated her very badly.''

She expected Loving to at least show some remorse, but instead he looked mildly insulted. "I don't know what she told you, miss, but I've always treated Amy like a perfect lady.''

"Like the time you blackened my eye?'' Amy retorted venomously.

Loving looked aggrieved. "You drove me to hit you, Amy, always nagging me about money like you do, but I promise it'll never happen again. My luck's turned now, and I'm flush. We can go to New York like we planned.''

"Humph, I wouldn't go to Leavenworth with you, Mike Loving.''

"Mr. Loving, I think you'd better leave,'' Elizabeth said.

He turned his funny eyes on her, and to her surprise she saw genuine anguish in them. "Please help me, Miss Livingston. Amy's my wife and I love her. I'll treat her good from now on, I swear. She won't even have to work anymore if she don't want to. If she don't come back to me, I don't know what I'll do.''

Elizabeth gaped at him, unable to reconcile this dapper, brokenhearted man with the monster she had envisioned. Still, he had admitted striking Amy and making her work in a brothel. He might seem meek, but he must have another side. Grateful for the shotgun still standing nearby, she squared her shoulders and stared him in the eye. "I'm sure Amy will consider your offer and let you know her decision. Now I must insist you leave.''

He seemed to droop at this and looked back at Amy. "Amy, honey, you know I love you. I'll do anything you say if you'll come back to me.''

Amazingly, Amy seemed to be considering his offer. "How soon could we leave for New York?''

"Whenever you say. Tomorrow if you want."

Elizabeth stared at her in disbelief, and Amy seemed to change her mind again. "Well, you'd better go now. We don't allow no men in here, and we don't want you giving the place a bad name."

Reluctantly, Loving started to turn away, but he shot Elizabeth one last, pleading look. "I'll be real good to her. She'll never want for anything."

Deciding not to comment, Elizabeth closed the door and bolted it. "Amy," she chastened, "you aren't really going to go back with him, are you?"

Amy looked a little sheepish. "I've always wanted to go to New York. I've heard they got buildings seven stories high there."

"You'd go back to him just to see a tall building?" she asked in astonishment.

"I wouldn't have to stay with him if he didn't treat me right. There's lots of men in New York, I'm sure," she replied reasonably. "How's the pie coming?"

Amy was halfway to the kitchen before Elizabeth recovered enough to follow.

When the doorbell rang again later, Elizabeth did not allow herself to feel anticipation. Amy hurried to answer, but she found only Bill Bates. Elizabeth invited him to sit out on the porch, leery of his bubbling good humor. "I've brought you a telegram," he announced when they were seated.

This was perhaps the one piece of news Elizabeth would find exciting in her present mood. Eagerly she tore open the envelope as Bill explained he'd been in the telegraph office when it arrived and knew she'd want to see it immediately.

As agreed, Barbara was letting her know everything was settled. The women were satisfied with the jobs and the living conditions, and Barbara would be returning in a few days. Elizabeth felt relieved, both because her friends would be starting new lives and because Barbara would soon be home. She needed a friend so very badly.

"You must be happy," Bill said when she had finished reading.

"Yes, I am," she told him with a smile. "Not long ago I was wondering if this day would ever come. I feel as if a tremendous burden has been lifted from my shoulders."

Bill's smile grew conspiratorial. "I guess you'll feel even better when I tell you I've already set the wheels in motion to have a new guardian named for you."

"A . . . a new guardian?" Elizabeth managed to ask despite the constriction in her throat. "Did Chance ask you to do that?"

"Uh-oh," Bill said, aghast. "I can see I let the cat out of the bag. Hasn't Chance spoken to you today?"

Elizabeth shook her head, knowing she could not let herself comprehend Bill's statement just yet for fear of publicly humiliating herself.

Bill didn't seem to realize the extend of her shock. "I'd better get out of here, then, before I say anything else I'm not supposed to," he said, but Elizabeth barely heard him. Vaguely, she thanked him for bringing her the telegram and then he left. She could hardly believe it. Now that Chance had gotten what he wanted, he was washing his hands of her!

Chance strode briskly down the street toward Elizabeth's house, oblivious of the summer heat. He'd spent part of the afternoon trying to determine with whom Elizabeth might have gone buggy riding, but a trip to Ham Bell's livery had proved fruitless. No one had rented a buggy today, and no one recalled seeing Elizabeth. Frustrated, Chance endured the hours until he felt certain she would have returned home.

He slowed his step as he approached her gate, thinking he should not be short of breath when she first saw him. With great effort, he calmed himself, determined not to let his hurt and anger show. With cool deliberation, he made his way down her walk, up onto her front porch, and rang the bell.

Elizabeth knew instinctively it was Chance at the door. "I'll get it," she told Amy, who had already come out of the kitchen. Elizabeth was setting the table for supper and laid down her handful of silverware.

She felt strangely detached as she moved along the hallway. During the long day of waiting, she had prepared half a dozen speeches in which she told Chance Fitzwilliam exactly what she thought of him, but she couldn't recall a single one of them now. Steeling herself against the reaction she knew she would feel at seeing him again, she opened the door.

Chance winced at the sight of her. Her eyes held the wary, almost frightened expression he remembered from their very first meeting. "Hello, Elizabeth," he said at last. "May I come in?"

Elizabeth squelched her frisson of fear. "I don't think that would be a good idea," she replied, recalling what had happened the last time he had entered her home. "We can sit on the porch."

The porch was the last place Chance wanted to confront her, but he sensed her unease and acquiesced, stepping aside so she could come out. She moved stiffly, as if holding herself tightly in check, and Chance experienced a flash of annoyance.

She perched primly on the edge of a wicker chair and waited. She obviously had no intention of breaking the awkward silence, so he asked, "Did you have an enjoyable afternoon?" His voice betrayed a trace of bitterness, but she didn't seem to notice.

"I did until Bill Bates came by to tell me he was getting me a new guardian."

"He *told* you?" Chance asked in astonishment. Weren't things bad enough without Bill mucking them up even more?

"In all fairness, he assumed I already knew," she replied, folding her hands in her lap. Chance hardly recognized his Lizzie in this prudish pose.

"You don't look pleased," he observed, wondering if she understood the implications of the change.

"I'm thrilled," she informed him, sounding anything but pleased. "Now that I'm free of you, I'll be able to leave this godforsaken place and return to Philadelphia."

Chance could hardly believe what he was hearing and seeing. What had come over her? What could have happened to change her so completely and make her hate him as her eyes told him she did? Where was the woman who had professed her love for him only yesterday? "Lizzie . . ."

"Don't call me that," Elizabeth cried, jumping to her feet. "Don't ever call me that again!" She was already fighting tears and was very much afraid she might lose control completely if she let him charm her. "I know all about you, you and Amy and what you said to her yesterday. Do you think I'm a fool? Oh, I suppose I've given you reason to think so, but those days are over. I've finally come to my senses, albeit a little late. I never want to see you again, Chance Fitzwilliam."

She was almost to the door when he found his tongue. "Lizzie, wait!" he called, starting after her, but the door slammed shut before he reached it. He pounded on the wood and heard the bolt shoot home. "Lizzie, open this door!"

An ominous silence greeted his request. "Lizzie!" He wanted to break the door down with his bare hands, but he had already made enough of a spectacle. People in neighboring houses were coming onto their own porches to see what the disturbance was about. He twisted the bell savagely, but to no avail. Elizabeth obviously had no intention of letting him in.

Muttering a curse, he sent a glaring reprimand at the curious neighbors, who scurried back inside. A thousand questions taunted him, questions to which he had not the slightest hint of an answer. Only one thing was certain: something had set Elizabeth against him; something having to do with that girl Amy, something that made Elizabeth feel like a fool.

But how could he defend himself if Elizabeth wouldn't tell him what was wrong? And how could she tell him if she wouldn't speak to him? Cursing again, he stepped closer to the door, sensing Elizabeth was still on the other side. "I'll be back, Lizzie," he promised in a voice just loud enough for her to hear. "And we'll settle this once and for all."

On the other side of the door, Elizabeth held a clenched fist to her lips to stifle a sob.

The crowd in Summer Winters's parlor was small, even for a Monday night, and the gentlemen seemed to be taking their time about choosing partners. Deciding to encourage them to hurry along with their business, Summer put on her professional smile and began a leisurely stroll around the room.

Summer prided herself in running a first-class establishment. Her girls were fully clothed in modest calico dresses, not half-naked like the women at some parlor houses. Her customers sat on velvet-upholstered sofas and enjoyed the finest cigars and brandy. Of course, they paid handsomely for these niceties, and they had made Summer Winters a wealthy woman.

She had just opened her mouth to speak to the first gentleman when a loud thump followed by a woman's scream from the room above made her wince. "Excuse me, please," she said calmly even as her eyes were searching out the tall male figure standing discreetly in the corner. Her bouncer was already moving toward the stairs, and she followed.

Such disturbances were rare, given the quality of her clientele, but one could never predict how a man might act in the privacy of a bedroom. Sighing with resignation, she tried to place the noise to determine which of her girls was involved.

Hettie, she determined as she reached the second floor

and saw her bouncer throwing open one of the bedroom doors. She winced again at the sound of flesh hitting flesh.

"You goddamned whore! I'll teach you!"

Oscar, the bouncer, disappeared into the room to the sound of scuffling and another scream from Hettie. Summer sighed. Hadn't she told the girl a dozen times not to carry on so loudly when things like this happened? She might well drive away some of the customers downstairs, and heaven knew there were few enough of them to begin with tonight.

"Who the hell are you?" the customer yelled at Oscar. "Get out! This is private, between me and her."

Summer finally put the voice together with a face and remembered the well-dressed cattleman who had gone upstairs with Hettie a few minutes earlier. He'd looked harmless enough, but one never knew. He must have been drunk. With some men it was difficult to tell they'd had too much. Then, when the alcohol interfered with their sexual performance, they had an alarming tendency to blame the girl and take out their frustration on her.

"Get your pants on, buddy. It's time to leave," Oscar was saying.

The drunk started arguing, but Oscar continued to insist in his quietly determined way, wearing down the man's resistance. If the customer turned violent again, Oscar would handle that, too. He really was very good at his job, Summer thought idly, thinking she would reward him by asking him to share her bed later. He was good there, too.

A small figure came darting out of the room, interrupting Summer's thoughts. Hettie had grabbed a robe and was pulling it on over her nakedness.

"Are you hurt?" Summer asked with businesslike concern.

"He hit me in the face. I think my eye'll swell up," she said, plainly on the verge of tears.

"Go down to the kitchen and put some steak on it. And take the rest of the night off." She didn't need a battered, tearful girl casting a pall over the evening. The chit's screaming had caused enough trouble.

"Thanks, Miss Winters." Hettie disappeared down the hallway toward the back stairs.

Summer waited another moment until she was sure Oscar had the drunk under control, then descended the stairs again.

"Trouble, Summer?" asked one of the customers when she entered the parlor.

"Nothing serious," Summer said with a dazzling smile. "It seems some men can't hold their liquor."

A few men chuckled at her remark, and the girls quickly eased the awkward moment with lively chatter, as they had been trained to do. Taking a mental count, Summer saw with relief no one had left, and just then the doorbell chimed, announcing yet another customer. Her Negro maid escorted Mike Loving into the parlor.

"Mike, we haven't seen you around here in a month of Sundays," Summer said by way of greeting.

"When I married Amy, I didn't think I'd ever *have* to come back," he replied bitterly. "But that Livingston bitch has got her now, and I'll probably never see her again."

Summer had never cared for Mike Loving, but he had suddenly endeared himself to her. "You look like you could use a drink, friend. From my private stock," she added, slipping her arm through his and leading him from the room.

His astonishment was comic, but her provocative smile gave no hint of her amusement. An hour and several glasses of bourbon later, Mike was waxing eloquent on the subject of prissy do-gooders who thought they were better then everybody else and made it damned easy for women to desert their husbands.

"Amy's young and foolish, Mike. She doesn't know what's good for her. You ought to take a firm hand. I'll bet you could scare her out of there if you tried."

Mike grunted. "I did try. I went over there the other night and caught her alone out in the yard. She was all sweetness and light at first. She even let me take her right there in the grass, but when I said she should come home with me, she got mad. Said she didn't want to work for Shilling anymore and started calling me names, saying I should get a regular job. I slapped her, not real hard you understand, just to shut her up, and she started screaming bloody murder. I took off and next thing I hear is how three men raped her.''

Summer crooned sympathetically. ''Amy always was a liar. I thought she did it mostly to get attention, and I'll bet it's your attention she wants most. She wants you to act like a man, Mike. She wants you to go over there and drag her out by force. You ought to put the fear of God into Little Miss Prissy Face, too. Teach her not to mess with married women.''

She watched him carefully, hoping she hadn't miscalculated his state of sobriety. He had no trouble understanding her words so he wasn't *too* drunk. Now, if only he was drunk enough to act on them, she'd have her final revenge on Elizabeth Livingston.

Chapter 12

"Mr. Fitzwilliam?"

Joey approached his boss cautiously, correctly judging his dour mood.

"What is it, son?" Chance asked gently, hoping to ease the boy's misgivings. After all, he wasn't mad at Joey. He must look pretty forbidding, though, since no one else had yet approached the corner table where he'd been sitting all evening, lost in his broodings about Elizabeth.

"There's a lady to see you."

"A lady?" Chance rose quickly, hardly daring to hope. "Where? Who is she?"

"Well, maybe I shouldn't of said a lady," Joey demurred. "She's one of the girls from the South Side. I wouldn't of bothered you except she said you told her to come, and she said she wasn't gonna leave until she saw you."

Chance's hopes plummeted again, but the story intrigued him. "Lead on," he told the boy, and Joey headed for the saloon's back entrance.

At first glance Chance saw no one, but when he called, a small figure emerged from the deeper shadows.

"Mr. Fitzwilliam, is that you?"

"Yes," he replied, squinting into the darkness as he tried to make out the woman's face. "Hettie? What are you doing here?"

"You told me to come, remember? You said you'd help

me get to Miss Livingston's. I would've gone alone, but I don't know where her house is.''

Chance felt a pang at the mention of Elizabeth's name, but he put his own feelings aside. Hettie sounded as if she'd been crying, and he vividly recalled their earlier conversation about this subject. "Did Summer do something to you?''

"No, it . . . it was one of my customers. He . . . he hit me," she said, her voice quavering.

Chance reached out to comfort her. "How badly are you hurt? Should I call a doctor?'' he asked, laying a hand on her shoulder.

"Oh, no, he just bruised my face up some. I didn't mind that so much, but when he . . . when he called me a whore, I just couldn't . . .'' She dissolved into tears, and feeling helpless, Chance could think of nothing to do but pull her close and let her cry on his shirtfront.

"Does Summer know you're gone?'' he asked after a few minutes.

Hettie shook her head, pulling away from him at last and wiping her eyes with the sleeve of her dress while Chance searched his pockets in vain for a handkerchief. "She told me I could have the night off after what happened, and I sneaked out the back way. I don't think anybody even knows I'm gone yet. Can you take me right to Miss Livingston's?''

Chance would have liked nothing better, but under the circumstances, he doubted his reception. "I think it would be better if someone else took you," he said, quickly settling on the perfect escort. "I'll send for Reverend Folger. You can wait upstairs in my room in the meantime. You'll be safe there.''

"Th-Thanks, Mr. Fitzwilliam. I'll pay you back somehow.''

Chance sighed wearily. "Just say a few kind words about me to Miss Livingston, and we'll be more than even.''

* * *

Elizabeth and Amy were getting ready for bed when the doorbell summoned them. They were wary of opening the door until they heard Reverend Folger's voice. The last thing Elizabeth had been expecting was to receive a new boarder, but she was grateful for the distraction.

She immediately recognized the newcomer as one of the women who had met her train the day she arrived in Dodge City. Hettie was ashamed of the episode and begged Elizabeth's forgiveness, a favor Elizabeth gladly granted.

When Reverend Folger left, the three women gathered at the kitchen table over cups of tea. None of them felt like sleep, least of all Elizabeth. Putting all thoughts of Chance from her mind, she used her considerable conversational talents to draw Hettie out, choosing small talk in an effort to put the young woman at ease before inquiring into the details of her escape.

Amy, however, was not so patient. "Who smacked you around?" she asked baldly during a lull, making Elizabeth cringe.

Hettie gingerly touched her rapidly discoloring cheek. "A customer. He was drunk, I guess, although he didn't seem like it when I took him upstairs. Miss Winters is real careful. She don't let the customers get drunk because they cause too much trouble."

Elizabeth nodded politely, although her thoughts of Summer Winters were far from polite. Elizabeth's one comfort was in knowing she had finally rescued someone from her nemesis.

"Was it the beating that made you finally decide to come here?" she asked, hoping to discover Hettie's motivation and use the information to lure others away, too.

"Partly," Hettie allowed. "I guess getting hit was just the last straw, and after what Mr. Fitzwilliam promised me, I finally got up the nerve and ran."

"Chance?" Elizabeth asked, as her stomach did a little flip-flop. "What does he have to do with it?"

Hettie seemed alarmed by Elizabeth's intensity, so Elizabeth smiled and explained. "He's my guardian, so naturally I'm interested."

Somewhat mollified, Hettie continued. "He told me once a long time ago when he was visiting the house to let him know if I ever wanted to leave, and he'd see I got here safe and sound."

"Oh," Amy said, a little surprised. "Is he a friend of yours, too?"

Elizabeth's breath caught on a shaft of pain at the thought of having two of Chance's former conquests at her very own kitchen table.

"Yeah, he's a friend of mine all right," Hettie replied, "but I never noticed him giving *you* the time of day."

"He gave me a lot more than the time of day!" Amy declared, jumping to her feet.

"You're a damn liar, Amy Waters. You always were. Mr. Fitzwilliam never looked at you twice."

Amy's face mottled, but she planted her hands firmly on her hips. "He never looked at you *once*. And don't try to tell me you ever had him, either."

Hettie's triumphant smile sent a shiver of dread down Elizabeth's spine. "He said he liked me too much to ever use me like that," she bragged. "That's better than having a man pay for you, isn't it?" she demanded, turning to Elizabeth for confirmation.

"Yes," Elizabeth managed in reply. Her mind was racing, trying to make sense of what she was hearing. *Amy was a liar.* Everything Amy had said about Chance was a lie. Or was it? And how could she be sure?

"And when I went to his place tonight," Hettie was saying, "Mr. Fitzwilliam got Reverend Folger to bring me over here, just like he promised. He said he wouldn't let Miss Winters take me back, either. He said if I wanted, I could go to Chicago like the others and get an honest job."

Her eyes held a silent inquiry, and Elizabeth felt compelled to organize her wayward thoughts and respond. "Yes, you can. I had a telegram this afternoon saying they'd gotten settled and would be starting work in a few days.''

Amy sniffed contemptuously. "Sewing clothes all day in a factory. I'll bet they never have any fun."

Elizabeth stared at her in disbelief. "They didn't think their old jobs were fun either. At least they can hold their heads up now.''

"I've never been ashamed to hold my head up to anyone," Amy said haughtily, and stamped out of the kitchen.

Elizabeth and Hettie sat in uncomfortable silence while they listened to her footsteps fade as she mounted the stairs.

"I . . . I didn't mean to cause you any trouble, miss," Hettie said at last.

"You haven't," Elizabeth assured her, laying a comforting hand on her arm. Silently, Elizabeth speculated on the possibility Hettie had just *resolved* some problems rather than caused any. "Maybe you'd like me to show you your room now. The bedrooms upstairs are awfully hot. I'll let you look at the ones downstairs first. You pretty much have your pick."

Hettie chose to sleep downstairs, and Elizabeth soon had her settled in. Still a little numb from all she had heard, Elizabeth returned to the parlor and prepared to retire while she mentally replayed the revealing conversation Hettie and Amy had held in the kitchen.

In spite of the fact that Elizabeth could still think of no justification for it, she now knew Amy had lied. Elizabeth's mind reeled at the implications. Amy had never had a relationship with Chance, and if she hadn't, then she had also lied about his parting remarks to her yesterday. Elizabeth had doubted the man she loved and had sent him away with a promise never to speak to him again. Dear heaven, what had she done?

First thing tomorrow, she would go to him. *She* would pound on *his* door this time, rousing him from sleep if she had to in order to confess her folly and beg his forgiveness. How terribly hurt he must be. She would make everything up to him, though, even if it took the rest of her life. They would be so happy. This time her tears were of relief.

Comforted by these thoughts of rosy bliss, she drifted off to sleep, and Chance came to her in her dreams, to hold her and kiss her. For a while everything was perfect, but then some faceless woman with yellow hair appeared. She grabbed Chance's arm and tried to pull him away. Elizabeth clung to him desperately, but the woman was much stronger. Elizabeth felt him slipping from her grasp.

"He loves *me!*" Elizabeth cried frantically, but the woman only laughed, a terrible, bloodcurdling laugh, and something flashed in her hand.

A gun! The woman pointed it at Chance's heart and the roar sent Elizabeth bolt upright in bed. The room was as bright as daylight, although Elizabeth knew she had only been asleep a short time. The light danced grotesquely and after a moment she realized the roar was not in her head at all but outside the house.

"Fire!" The shouted warning from outside echoed in her mind, freezing her body in momentary terror. All the parlor windows were bright with it, even through the shutters. Dear God, the house was on fire, the *whole* house, and she, Amy, and Hettie were trapped inside!

"Fire!" someone outside shouted. "The house is on fire! Wake up in there!"

Responding to the cry, Elizabeth fumbled with the covers, throwing them aside so she could swing her legs to the floor. All her limbs felt heavy and wooden as she struggled to her feet. Her mind raced ahead to the front door and safety, but like someone still caught in the throes of a dream, she could not make her body catch up.

After what seemed a lifetime, she reached the parlor doors and slid them open. Smoke billowed in the hallway, flowing up the stairwell to where Amy slept. Elizabeth opened her mouth to yell a warning, but the sound came out as a choked whisper.

"Amy! Hettie!" she tried again, louder this time.

Living flames danced at the far end of the hall, telling her the kitchen was already engulfed. *"Amy! Hettie!"* Her voice was working again, but the smoke thickened with every second. Torn with indecision, she ran out into the hall, calling both names over and over. Why didn't they answer? Which one should she go after?

Just then, a door down the hall flew open and a flash of white nightgown told her Hettie was awake. A scream from upstairs told her Amy was, too.

"The door, miss! Open the door!" Hettie yelled as she raced toward her.

"Amy's upstairs!" Elizabeth protested, but Hettie grabbed her arm and dragged her along.

"She can get out on the porch roof. Quick, before we're burned alive." Hettie reached the door, but the smoke was too thick for her to see any longer. Coughing and choking, she fought frantically with the knob.

"Amy! Go out your window onto the porch roof and jump down!" Elizabeth yelled.

Amy screamed again as something exploded in the kitchen, sending a blast of flame and smoke into the hall.

"Miss! The door!"

Hettie was near hysteria as she twisted and tugged to no avail. Suddenly, Elizabeth realized Hettie did not know where the lock was or how to open it.

"Let me," she cried, trying to shove Hettie out of the way.

"Miss Livingston! Are you in there?" someone called from the porch.

"Yes! Yes! We're here!"

"Stand away from the window. We're coming through!"

Elizabeth wrestled Hettie away in the nick of time. The glass panel beside the door shattered as an impenetrable wall of black smoke closed around them . . .

Chance strolled slowly around the main room of the saloon, pausing to watch the billiard players. All evening he had been mulling over various ways to deal with Elizabeth. He had decided he was not the best person to make inquiries into why she was so upset with him. Instead, he'd send Bill around first thing in the morning. Bill would find out in short order, and once Chance knew what had made her so angry, he'd figure out how to placate her, even if he had to hog-tie her to get her to listen to reason.

He was reaching into his pocket for a cheroot when he heard the fire bell clanging. The last time he could remember hearing it was a year earlier as a harbinger of an Indian attack that never came. Since Dodge City had never had a major fire, Chance wondered idly why the bell was ringing at this hour of the night.

Everyone in the saloon fell silent at the unusual clangor, and a murmur of speculation had just begun when the sound of running, booted feet silenced them once more.

"Fire!" a voice called outside, and then the running began again until the messenger stopped in the doorway of the Last Chance. "Fire!" he echoed and ran on. In seconds, the doorway was clogged with men eager to see the excitement, but Chance stood, rooted to the spot as all his foreboding coalesced into stark terror.

Elizabeth. Knowing in his heart she was in danger, he headed for the back door where he would encounter no interference. No sooner did he reach the alley than he saw the orange flames licking against the black velvet sky, but he didn't pause a moment in his headlong flight. When he reached the street, he encountered a cowboy on horseback making his way through the surging crowd.

"I'll give you a hundred dollars for your horse," he shouted above the melee.

"A hundred dollars?" the cowboy repeated incredulously.

"Two hundred if you throw in the saddle and get down right now."

The cowboy blinked and complied with alacrity.

"Do you know who I am?" The cowboy nodded. "Come by the Last Chance later, and I'll pay you then."

Without waiting for a reply, Chance vaulted into the

saddle and headed the pony out into the center of the street where the going was a little easier. A few times his shouted warnings narrowly averted disaster; the patrons of Front Street exhibited little regard for life and limb as they surged forward to see the now-raging fire.

"Elizabeth!" he called when he reached her street, lit as bright as day by the towering flames. Her house was engulfed, fire belching from every window.

"No!" he cried as unwanted visions of her trapped inside, helpless, rose up before him. He couldn't lose her now, not when he'd only just found her. Not when he'd only just had the sense to admit he loved her. *"Elizabeth! Dear God, let her live. I'll do anything,"* he promised rashly, wildly, not even knowing if God still listened to his prayers. "I'll even let her go, if that's what she wants. Just let her be alive!"

The other members of the Dodge City Fire Company were already organizing themselves. They had hooked up their hose cart and, recognizing the futility of trying to put out the fire in Elizabeth's house, were pumping streams of water on the neighboring houses to keep them from burning, too. Firemen leaned out of every window, holding buckets with which to douse stray sparks. Others spread damp blankets on the roofs, while still others worked at holding back the curious crowd.

The horse beneath Chance balked, frightened by the flames. Chance stripped off his coat and flung it over the animal's head, awkwardly tying the sleeves to make an enormous blindfold. Then he urged the unwilling animal onward, forcing the crowd to part before him.

"There's a woman on the roof!" someone shouted, and Chance strained to see. Yes, a figure in a white nightdress was barely visible through the billowing smoke.

"Elizabeth!" Chance kicked the mustang mercilessly, heedless of the bystanders who bolted from his path.

Chance broke into the clearing the firemen had created around the burning building. Some of the men had a blanket stretched between them and were calling to the woman to jump, but she was screaming hysterically, unable to obey. Without hesitation, Chance rode up to them.

"Hey, get back, you fool!" someone commanded. Chance glanced down to see Bat Masterson waving him away. "Oh, it's you, Chance. What do you think you're doing?"

"I'm going to get her down. Here," he said, tossing the reins to Masterson. "Lead the horse over there and hold him steady."

The sheriff quickly grasped Chance's plan and drew the balking animal toward the house. Chance squinted against the blast of heat, trying to make out the woman's features, but she was swathed in smoke. "Elizabeth! Come here! I'll get you, Lizzie!"

Standing in the stirrups, he could actually touch the edge of the porch roof. "Lizzie! I'm here! Come to me!"

The woman's foot was only inches from his hand. "Closer!" he yelled to Masterson, who smacked the mustang's rump. The animal sidestepped in reaction, and Chance's fingers closed around a slim ankle. He jerked, and she came tumbling forward with a howl, straight into his arms. The impact nearly knocked him from the saddle, but he held on, cushioning her fall as best he could and clinging to his precious burden.

"Lizzie, Lizzie, are you all right?" The woman righted herself and blond hair blew everywhere.

"Oh, Chance," Amy cried, throwing her arms around him. "You saved my life!"

Chance was vaguely aware of cheers from the crowd and Masterson leading the horse away from the fire, but he ignored them. "Elizabeth! Where's Elizabeth? Did she get out?" he demanded frantically, prying the girl's arms from his neck.

Amy reared back. "How should I know?"

"Bat, where's Elizabeth? Did she get out?" Chance was already climbing down from the horse, leaving Amy in the saddle.

"I don't know, Chance," Masterson replied. "I've only

been here a minute myself. *Wait!*'' Bat grabbed him and held on when Chance would have bolted back toward the burning building. "Are you crazy! Even if she *was* still inside, you couldn't help her now."

The truth of the statement staggered him, and Bat, sensing he'd gotten through, released his grip. "Check around the other side of the house. If she got out, she might be over there."

Chance was off at a dead run before Masterson finished the sentence. "Stay away from the house. It's going to fall any minute now," Masterson called after him, but Chance barely heard.

His panicked eyes scanned the edges of the crowd, searching, searching. He registered many familiar faces, but not the one for which he searched. "Elizabeth!"

Then he saw her, standing in the shadows on the far side of the house, wrapped in Bill Bates's coat and Bill Bates's protective arms. Her black hair streamed down her back, and she trembled even as Bill's hands soothed her. Relief and joy and jealousy were like a hot blade thrust into his heart. "Elizabeth, thank God," he whispered. For a long moment he simply stared, too staggered by the intensity of his emotions to move.

"There he is! He's the one who set the fire!"

Chance turned, startled to see Amy Waters pointing an accusing finger at him. Wyatt Earp stood grimly by her side, contemplating the accusation.

"He told Miss Livingston somebody'd get attacked on the way to the outhouse, and I did! And he said somebody'd burn down her house and now somebody has!" Clad in her white nightdress and with her golden hair swirling wildly around her, Amy looked like an avenging angel.

Stunned by her absurd accusation, Chance could only gape, vaguely aware of the curious looks he was receiving in return. With crystal clarity, he recalled the conversation to which she referred, in which he had predicted with uncanny accuracy the fire now blazing behind him. The horror of it momentarily paralyzed him.

"Don't be a damn fool, Amy," Wyatt was saying. "Why would Chance burn down Miss Livingston's house?"

"Because he hates us, he hates all whores," she replied without hesitation. "And so he could get her money. If you don't believe me, just ask her yourself."

Chance looked back to find Elizabeth watching him from the haven of Bill's embrace. Her green eyes were wide with shock, her cheeks smudged with soot, but she had never looked more beautiful.

"Miss Livingston, is what Miss Waters said true?" Earp asked with obvious reluctance.

Elizabeth's gaze grew troubled, and Chance knew a wrenching anguish. Did she believe the lie? Did she think he had done this horrible thing?

Elizabeth couldn't look at Chance for another second. Her feelings were still too raw, and she couldn't let herself cry, not yet. Instead she turned to Amy, glaring fiercely at the girl. "She's lying."

Amy flinched as if Elizabeth had slapped her, but she recovered quickly. Her chin came up defiantly. "Are you gonna say he never warned you about those things? I know he did. I heard you telling Mavis about it."

Elizabeth took a deep breath to still her trembling anger. Amy had already done enough damage. Elizabeth would not allow her to do more. "Mr. Fitzwilliam warned me about the possible consequences of taking former prostitutes into my house," she explained to Earp. "To interpret his cautions as threats is totally ridiculous."

"Amy! Amy! Are you all right?" Mike Loving burst into the clearing and gathered the girl in his arms.

As if on cue, Amy began weeping hysterically. "Take me away from here, Mike," she begged between sobs.

Loving cast the others a baleful look and led Amy back into the milling crowd. Elizabeth noticed Earp watching them through narrowed eyes, but Chance's voice distracted her.

"Was the fire deliberately set?" he asked the marshal.

Earp nodded. "Somebody soaked the woodpile and the back of the house with coal oil. The whole thing went up with an explosion that knocked the neighbors right out of bed. Wilson next door says he went to the window and saw somebody running around the house still carrying the coal oil can and yelling, 'Fire!' "

"Did everyone get out all right?" Chance asked, his gaze returning gratefully to Elizabeth.

"Yeah, the other girl's over there with the Folgers," Earp replied, pointing. Chance glanced perfunctorily in the indicated direction, some part of him relieved to know Hettie was safe but most of his attention focused on Elizabeth. She had defended him, but was she still angry with him? Did she still hate him? Her solemn expression told him nothing.

"I'm going to ask some questions," Earp was saying to Elizabeth. "I might be able to solve this real quick. I don't want you thinking Dodge City peace officers can't do their job when they've got a real crime on their hands, miss."

Elizabeth nodded absently, no longer interested in giving Earp the upbraiding he deserved for his past failure to take her problems seriously. Her attention was focused entirely on Chance. What was going through his mind? His carefully shuttered expression told her nothing. Earp drifted away, leaving her and Bill and Chance in the clearing.

Bill's comforting hands still rested on her shoulders, and he gave her a little squeeze as if he expected her to leave him for Chance, but she did not move. Every nerve in her body screamed for the comfort of Chance's arms, but she had no reason to think he would welcome her after her ugly words to him the day before.

Chance wanted to reach for her. He wanted to snatch her away from Bill and hold her to his heart and never let her go. Suddenly, he realized what a fool he'd been not to have done so long ago. He'd wasted so much time, but he wasn't going to waste another minute. "Lizzie," he said, her name a command. He lifted his arms and took a step toward her.

It was all the encouragement she needed. Elizabeth flew into his outstretched arms. They closed around her like a vise, crushing her to him as if he would squeeze her into himself. She clung with equal ferocity, reveling in the thunder of his heart beating beneath her ear.

"Oh, Lizzie, thank God. Thank God you're all right," he murmured over and over into her hair. Chance caught a glimpse of Bill's approving smile as he moved discreetly away, and then he concentrated completely on the woman in his arms.

She felt so warm, so alive, and he closed his eyes against the horrible images that had haunted him on his mad dash to find her. *"Are* you all right?" he asked hoarsely after a long moment. "You weren't hurt, were you?"

"I'm fine," she said into his shirtfront, unwilling to let him go just yet, even to have a conversation, but he forced her a little away so he could lift her chin and see her face.

"How did you get out?"

Elizabeth shuddered at the memory. "The noise of the explosion woke me up. Hettie and I somehow got to the front door." Elizabeth began to tremble, not wanting to remember the nightmare she'd endured gasping for breath in the thickening smoke as her hands groped blindly for the door lock. "The neighbors were there by then, and they broke the window by the door. Amy climbed out her window onto the porch roof, but she was too frightened to jump. Bill dragged me away so I wouldn't see if . . . if the flames got her." Elizabeth shuddered again at the thought. "But then we heard that someone came by on horseback and got her down."

Chance drew a ragged breath. "I thought she was you."

"You saved her? Then why would she accuse you of setting the fire?"

"You don't think I started the fire, do you?"

Elizabeth's overbright eyes reflected her outrage at the idea. "No! How can you even ask?"

His handsome face twisted with pain, reminding her of the way they had last parted. "I didn't mean what I said yesterday," she hastened to assure him. "I thought . . . I mean, Amy told me some things to make me doubt you, but I know now she was lying."

"Amy? What did she tell you?" he asked, his voice hardening.

Elizabeth didn't want him to know she she had believed the ugly lies even for a minute, but she knew he'd never rest until he learned what Amy had said. "She told me the two of you had been lovers for a long time." His face registered his shock, and she hurried on. "She said when you left on Sunday, you told her next time you'd come to see her. Oh, Chance, I'm so sorry! I should have trusted you more but . . ."

"But what?" he demanded when her voice trailed off.

Elizabeth swallowed, seeing the pain in his dark eyes and knowing her words would hurt him even more. "You told me you loved me, but you never mentioned marriage or the future. Amy was very convincing, and all I could remember was what you'd said to me during the fireworks."

He scowled as he tried to recall the events of that evening, and when he did, his eyes blazed. "You thought I said I loved you just to get you in bed?"

"I didn't know what else to think," she defended herself. "You left without a word, and you didn't come back the next morning."

"You looked exhausted, and I didn't want to wake you, so I told Amy I'd be by at one o'clock the next day."

"Then why didn't you come?"

"I did, but you'd gone out buggy riding with some other man."

"What! I never went anywhere! I was in the house the entire day."

"But Amy said—"

Their eyes locked as understanding dawned.

"Why? What did we ever do to Amy?" Elizabeth asked in despair.

Chance shook his head, wondering if his anger at Amy's implied insult to Elizabeth could have triggered so much animosity. He tried without success to remember if he had offended her sometime in the past, if she'd ever approached him and been rejected back when she worked at Summer's house. "I intend to find out what her reasons were, but not now. You've already been through enough tonight."

He pulled her close, this time in a tender, cherishing embrace. "Oh, Lizzie, I love you so much. When I thought I'd lost you . . ."

"Shhh! Don't even say it. You didn't lose me. You'll never lose me."

They clung to each other for long moments, content simply to be together. Behind them the fire raged and men fought it, running and shouting commands, and Chance's conscience pricked him. "I should be helping with the fire."

"Please, don't leave me," she begged, tightening her embrace.

He felt her body trembling and soothed her with loving hands. "I'll never leave you again."

"Chance? Miss Livingston? Excuse me." Elizabeth reluctantly drew away from the haven of Chance's arms to confront Wyatt Earp. "I think I've found the man responsible for the fire."

He stepped aside to reveal a shamefaced Mike Loving in the custody of two deputies. "He still reeks of coal oil, and your next-door neighbor identified him," Earp explained.

"What in the hell were you trying to do?" Chance demanded of the gambler while Elizabeth stood beside him in stunned silence.

Loving squared his shoulders in a pathetic show of bravado. "I did it to get Amy back."

"By burning the house down around her head?" Chance

wanted to know. Elizabeth could feel the rage quivering inside him, and she tightened her grip on his arm.

"I didn't intend to burn down the house, or at least not so fast," Loving explained in a wheedling tone that set Elizabeth's teeth on edge. "I thought there'd be plenty of time to get everybody out, and with your house gone, Amy wouldn't have anyplace to go. Then she'd *have* to come back to me."

Elizabeth stared at him in mute horror, unable to comprehend a love so destructive.

"I figure he's telling the truth, ma'am," Earp was saying. "He probably didn't have any idea the fire would catch on so quick, and he did shout a warning to wake everybody up. I reckon his biggest crime is stupidity, but we'll try him for arson and attempted murder all the same."

"Murder! I never tried to kill anybody," Loving protested as the deputies started to lead him away. "Amy! Where'd she go? Amy, honey, where are you?"

"I'm here, Mike," she cried, bursting out of the crowd into the clearing. Someone had wrapped a blanket around her, and she clutched it tightly. "What's going on? Why are they holding you?"

"I set the fire, honey, but I only did it because I love you so much."

"You *what?*" she demanded shrilly. "You almost got me killed!"

"I only wanted to get you back, and if the house was gone, you'd have to come back to me."

Amy's eyes were wide as she watched the lawmen take Mike away. Then she turned her gaze on Chance and Elizabeth, who stood together. Elizabeth could almost see the girl trying to form a new plot, and she lifted her own chin in silent defiance. Amy's vindictiveness had almost separated her from Chance, but in the end Amy had failed. All of her schemes had failed, and now she stood alone.

"I reckon you'll be needing a place to spend the night,"

a man said as he came up beside Amy. She turned to him in gratitude.

"Oh, thank you, Mr. Shilling. You're awful kind," she said, taking the arm he offered.

Elizabeth shivered at Shilling's look of malicious triumph as he and Amy moved off into the crowd.

"Amy's back where she belongs," Chance remarked.

"How sad," Elizabeth replied. "She had the same opportunity as all the others to make a new life for herself, but she threw it away."

"Threw it away and alienated everyone who might have helped her. But she's not your problem anymore, Lizzie. Amy's made her own choice."

Elizabeth knew he was right, but the knowledge gave her little comfort. Suddenly she felt tired.

When Chance pulled her close again, he realized she was shaking. They both started when the house suddenly collapsed in on itself in a roar of flame and sparks. Elizabeth's eyes seemed to glaze over as she watched the terrifying sight. "My God," he muttered. "I've got to get you out of here."

Without another word, he scooped her up and lifted her high against his chest.

"Chance, what are you doing?" she protested weakly.

"I'm taking you someplace safe and quiet."

Already feeling much safer in his arms, Elizabeth laid her head against his shoulder. To her surprise, he stopped only a short distance away.

"Reverend Folger," he called, summoning the preacher from the crowd.

"What an awful thing," Folger said as he approached. "I'm so sorry, Miss Elizabeth. If there's anything I can do . . ."

"There is. I'm taking Elizabeth to your house. Will you follow us?"

"Of course," Folger replied. "We'll bring Hettie, too. What about the other girl? What's her name?"

"Amy." Chance spit out the word as if it were vile.

"A cat always lands on its feet. I don't think we have to worry about Amy."

"A cat?" Folger asked, puzzled.

"I'll explain later," Chance said, already turning away.

"The Folgers live in the opposite direction," Elizabeth observed when she saw where he was heading.

"I know. I left my horse over here someplace. If it's still here, we can get to the Folgers' much more easily."

They found the animal a safe distance away. Someone had thoughtfully tied it to a tree. Chance lifted Elizabeth onto the saddle, then mounted behind her. With relief, they left the noise of the crowd and the fire behind as Chance chose an indirect but less crowded route to the preacher's house.

After the roar of the fire, the relative silence weighed on Elizabeth's ears, making her feel as if she had slipped under water. Perhaps she was only beginning to feel the shock, she thought, snuggling more closely against Chance's strong chest. She only wished he wasn't leaving her with the Folgers. "I must confess," she said with a small smile. "When you said you were taking me away, I had something a little more scandalous in mind than Reverend Folger's house."

Chance gave her a measuring look, then his mouth quirked. "Oh, I fully intend to take you to my room over the saloon and have my way with you until we're both too tired to move, but I thought you'd want to get married first."

"Cousin Chauncey!" she cried with mock outrage, blushing furiously. Then the second part of his statement registered. "Married! Oh, Chance!" She turned and threw her arms around his neck, but then another thought occurred to her and she pulled back again. "Aren't you even going to ask me first?"

"No," he replied. "I'm not going to take the chance. We might have an argument about it, which would spoil my plans for spending the next few days doing nothing but making love to you."

"The next few days!" Elizabeth repeated, thoroughly scandalized and just as thoroughly delighted.

Several minutes later, the Folgers were equally scandalized. "You want to get married *now?* Good heavens, Chance, use a little judgment," Folger urged. "The girl's been through an ordeal tonight. She's not in any condition to make a decision like this."

"And she can't get married in her nightdress," Mrs. Folger pointed out. "That's hardly fitting for a wedding."

"It's fitting for a honeymoon, which we're going to have whether or not the good reverend consents to perform the ceremony," Chance informed her, making her blush.

"Really, I know exactly what I'm doing," Elizabeth said in an attempt to restore some dignity to the proceedings.

Hettie sighed longingly. "I think it's all real romantic."

After a bit more convincing, the Folgers came to agree, and Chauncey Fitzwilliam IV and Elizabeth Livingston were married that night in Reverend Folger's parlor. The bride wore her smoke-stained nightdress and Bill Bates's suit coat, and carried a bouquet of dried flowers Mrs. Folger took from her dining room table. Elizabeth's dirty bare toes curled with joy when Chance pressed his lips to hers after Reverend Folger pronounced them man and wife.

"Come by the Last Chance tomorrow, Reverend, and tell the bartender to give you a hundred dollars as payment for your services," Chance instructed as he once again scooped Elizabeth up in his arms and headed for the Folgers' front door, leaving the stunned pastor stammering his thanks.

"I'll go to Wright and Beverley's tomorrow and get you some clothes, Elizabeth," Mrs. Folger promised as everyone followed them out onto the porch.

"Elizabeth won't be needing any clothes for a while. I plan to keep her in bed for at least a week," Chance said with a wicked grin.

"Mr. Fitzwilliam!" Mrs. Folger reprimanded him, blushing again. Elizabeth punched him in the shoulder.

Chance feigned a look of innocent surprise. "After the shock she's had, she needs rest, don't you think?"

Hettie giggled. "I doubt she'll get much rest with you around." Elizabeth's cheeks burned again.

Reverend Folger cleared his throat and tried to look solemn. "I don't suppose you'll be joining us for supper then, will you, Chance?"

For a moment Chance could not recall why he had agreed to dine with the Folgers, and then he remembered the plan to help the farmers. "Maybe we can reschedule it for next week sometime," he suggested.

"Reschedule what?" Elizabeth asked with wifely interest.

Reverend Folger didn't give Chance the opportunity to respond. "Oh, a few of us are getting together to see if we can't talk Chance into running for mayor next year." His smile was guileless.

"Good God!" Chance muttered in genuine alarm. "We'd better get out of here before he has me up for governor."

Elizabeth was laughing too hard to speak her good-byes, so she settled for a wave as Chance carried her off and set her on the horse once again. They had not gone far when he reined to a stop.

"Maybe we should go to the Dodge House instead. Your wedding was outlandish enough without spending your honeymoon over a saloon."

Elizabeth considered the suggestion and shook her head. "We'll probably have more privacy in your rooms, and besides, I don't want to check into the Dodge House in my nightdress. What would people think?"

Under the circumstances, checking into the Dodge House in her nightdress would hardly rate a mention when the gossips recounted the scandals of the evening. Then Chance noticed the mischievous gleam in her eyes and realized she was teasing him.

"You're absolutely right, Mrs. Fitzwilliam," he agreed

with mock solemnity. "The last thing I'd ever want to do is shock the good people of Dodge City."

Elizabeth's laughter was sweet music as he kicked the horse into motion again. By the time they reached the alley behind the Last Chance, the first stragglers were making their way back to Front Street, having grown bored with the dying fire.

Chance swung down from the horse and called his bartender out into the alley. "My wife and I will be upstairs, and we do not wish to be disturbed, although you can send up some breakfast around, oh, say, ten o'clock tomorrow."

From where she still sat on the horse's back, Elizabeth had to bite her lip to keep from giggling at the man's expression. "Wife?" he echoed, looking up at Elizabeth in astonishment. "Ain't that Miss Livingston?"

"She *was* Miss Livingston," Chance corrected. "Reverend Folger married us a few minutes ago."

"Married! Good God almighty! Oh, excuse me, ma'am, but . . . *married!* Wait till word gets out." The man was already rubbing his hands in anticipation.

"Do us a favor and keep our secret for a few days," Chance said.

The man nodded, frowning. "Folks'll want to know where you two got off to, though."

"Tell them we left town or something. And send Joey over to Reverend Folger's house first thing in the morning with a hundred dollars. I told him to call for it himself, but somehow I don't think he will."

Chance had already started back for Elizabeth when the bartender said, "That reminds me. There's a cowboy inside says you owe him two hundred dollars for buying his horse."

"Oh, yes," Chance said, remembering. "This is the horse. Give him the money and give him back the horse, too. I don't need it anymore."

This time Elizabeth did giggle at the man's expression,

but Chance was reaching for her, and she quickly forgot all about the bartender.

"Come on, Mrs. Fitzwilliam," he said, his voice husky.

She slid eagerly into his arms. "I can walk, you know," she said when he carried her toward the outside stairs.

"I don't want you to cut those pretty little feet," he explained, nuzzling the sensitive spot just below her ear and sending delicious shivers coursing through her body.

His breathing was labored by the time they reached the top steps, but Elizabeth didn't think the strain of carrying her was the only cause since her own breath was coming in quick gasps, too. Chance kicked the door shut behind him, but he didn't stop until they reached his bedroom, where he lowered her carefully onto the unmade bed.

He would have straightened, but Elizabeth locked her arms around his neck and pulled his mouth to hers, having waited far too long to kiss him. He surrendered instantly. His weight pressed her down into the mattress, and she took it gladly.

She opened to him, and his tongue swirled in her mouth as if he would drink her very essence. Elizabeth's skin began to heat, as it had when she had stood in her burning house, but she was no longer afraid. These flames would not destroy her.

"You're mine now, Lizzie. All mine," he whispered, his breath a warm caress against the sensitive skin of her throat.

"And you're mine," she replied, caressing the back of his head with loving hands.

Her claim seemed to startle him for a moment, although the room was too dark for her to see his expression. His hands came up to cup her face, and even in the darkness, she could see the glitter of his eyes. "I've always been yours, Lizzie, since the first moment we met. I've just been too big a fool to admit it."

Joy exploded inside her, bubbling and fizzing through her veins. "Oh, Chance," she managed before his mouth closed on hers again, blocking all thoughts except one.

His hands were urgent, seeking for her beneath the few layers of clothes, and he disposed of them swiftly while she struggled with the simple task of removing his suit coat. Finally, he rolled away with an impatient sound and finished the job himself, stripping off his own clothing with little regard for fastenings.

Mere moments later, he lowered himself to the bed once again, as naked as she. His flesh was hot against her cooling skin, and she turned into his warmth. He gathered her against him, breathing words of love with every ragged breath.

This time his hands encountered no barriers in his quest to rediscover the delights of her body. She moved sinuously against him, glorying in the hair-roughened planes and angles of his body, so different from her own. She'd never had the time to learn about him before, but now they would have the rest of their lives. The knowledge made her giddy. And bold.

She snuggled closer, burrowing her swollen nipples into the hair on his chest. His moan of approval encouraged her, so she ran her hand down his back until she encountered the curve of his hip.

Chance rolled her onto her back and captured one taut nipple in his mouth and the other in the palm of his hand. Sensation streaked into her very core, igniting new flames of desire. She ran her hands over him, needing to inflame him, too.

He gasped when her fingers closed around the hard shaft of his arousal.

"Did I hurt you?" she asked in alarm, releasing him at once.

He gave a shaky laugh. "Not exactly, although the shock did some dangerous things to my heart. Feel free to shock me like that anytime," he added, guiding her hand back again. This time his intake of breath was pure pleasure, and he retaliated by running his own hand down until he grazed the sensitive apex of her thighs.

Her hips lifted to his touch, but he moved past to stroke

her thighs, first one and then the other, up and down, teasing and tormenting, stopping just short of the most intimate caress until she was writhing.

"Chance," she begged, and he needed no further encouragement. Delving into the dark curls of her womanhood, his fingers found the prize of her desire. He drank her gasping response with his own mouth while he worked his magic down below. Caught up in the spell, she forgot modesty and guided him to her until once again he filled the aching void.

"I love you," he breathed as he sank into her welcoming depths.

"And I love you," she replied, receiving him with wonder. The mystical words sounded strangely inadequate, no longer powerful enough to describe the feelings she had for him. Knowing no others, she showed him with her body the magnitude of her adoration.

Pleasures swirled, blurring into each other until her whole being was one mass of sensation. Sparks flickered behind her eyelids, tiny harbingers of the blaze yet to come. The sparks flared, larger and larger until they threatened to consume her, but she flung herself fearlessly into the purifying flames, letting the inferno engulf her with its seething, roiling heat until she was nothing but a brightly glowing ember of herself.

Chance fell with her, crying out his release as the shudders shook him. They clung to each other, helpless yet triumphant in the glory of their love.

For a long time they simply lay still, loath to break the sweet connection symbolizing the commitment they had made to each other. But finally, reluctantly, Chance stirred, shifting his weight from her while still keeping her firmly in his arms. "We need to talk," he said.

Slowly, he let her go, but only long enough to light the lamp and pull the sheet up over them. Back in his arms again, she rested her head on his chest while she waited for him to begin.

"I'm going to sell the Last Chance."

"What? Why?" Her head came up in surprise, and she searched his face for some hint of his motivation.

"Because I no longer have any reason to lead a scandalous life, and because I now have every reason to become a respectable citizen."

Elizabeth could not hold back a smile. "I thought being a saloonkeeper *was* respectable in Dodge City."

"It's not respectable in Philadelphia, though, and since that's where we'll be living—"

"We will?" she asked in dismay.

"Isn't that what you want? The other day you said you couldn't wait to get back there."

"Only because I thought you didn't love me."

She saw the regret shadow his eyes and was instantly sorry, but before she could go on, he said, "I've treated you abominably, Lizzie. I can't understand why you didn't give up on me long ago."

With gentle fingers, she traced the familiar contours of his face. "I love you, and I was certain you loved me in return. How could I give up on that?"

"But you stopped believing in me yesterday, didn't you?"

"Oh, Chance, I'm so sorry!" Tears of remorse misted her eyes, and she blinked them away. "I'd believed in you for so long, even when you told me you didn't love me, even when everyone else told me I was wrong, but I guess I was starting to weaken. When Amy told me you had been lovers, I had no reason to doubt her, and when she told me the other lies . . . Oh, darling, as awful as they were, I couldn't think of a single reason for her to lie! Why would she want to hurt me when I'd never done her any harm?"

"And you had every reason to doubt me after the way I'd treated you."

Elizabeth could not refute his claim. "When Bill told me you no longer wanted to be my guardian, I thought it was proof you wanted to break all ties with me. That's why I was so upset when you finally did call on me last evening.''

"Lizzie, I couldn't be your guardian anymore because I didn't want people to think I'd forced you to marry me. Many already know your father's will gives your husband control of your money. They would have thought I tricked you into marrying me.''

In spite of her tears, she smiled. ''You mean you were trying to be noble?''

"I suppose I was.''

Elizabeth shook her head in wonder. ''You have an odd sense of honor. You seduce me and then refuse to marry me because you don't think you're good enough for me. Then you make me miserable by pretending you don't love me, while all the time you're working to keep me safe.''

"Yes, I've acted like a gold-plated bastard, and I didn't even do a good job of keeping you safe,'' he pointed out. But Elizabeth shook her head again.

"You went to great lengths to get my houseguests out of Dodge City. You even had to buy a hotel because you knew I'd never let them leave unless they had a decent place to live.''

"You *knew?*'' he asked in amazement.

"Let's say I wanted to believe in you,'' she demurred sweetly. ''Even when you were acting like a bastard, you thought you were acting in my best interests. How could I *not* love you?''

Chance sighed in wonder. ''I can think of a lot of reasons, but I have no intention of telling you what they are.''

"Good,'' she said, giving him a kiss. ''I'm tired of hearing what a bad man you are. I love you and you love me. We've both been foolish and silly and a little crazy, but those days are over now. No more lies and no more secrets. Agreed?''

"Agreed.'' His smile held relief and joy and more love than she had ever hoped to inspire. With a sigh of her own, she settled against his shoulder.

After a long minute, he said, "Now, what's this about not wanting to go back to Philadelphia?"

Elizabeth smiled against his warm skin. "Philadelphia has always been my home, but after living here, I'm afraid it would seem awfully dull."

"You want to stay in Dodge City?" he asked in disbelief.

"For a while," she said impishly. "After all, if you're going to run for mayor—"

"I am *not* going to run for mayor. That was Folger's idea of a joke."

"Then why are you meeting with him? I thought you despised him."

"I don't despise him. We merely disagree on the issue of prohibition. He asked me to organize a relief effort for the farmers because of the drought," he added offhandedly.

"My goodness! You really are becoming a respectable citizen, aren't you?"

An automatic denial rose to his lips but died there. Wasn't this what he'd wanted, Elizabeth's esteem? He gave her a self-mocking grin. "I suppose I am."

"So you see, your work with the farmers and my work with the prostitutes will keep us here for quite a while," she pointed out.

"You're not going to work with the prostitutes any more, Lizzie," he informed her. "It's too dangerous."

"Not for the mayor's wife."

"This is July, and the elections aren't until April."

"Then you really are thinking of running!"

"No, I'm not!" But she didn't look convinced. "Regardless, you are not opening up another refuge, not after what happened tonight."

Elizabeth had almost forgotten the horrors of the fire, and she shuddered at his reminder, but she could not let her own fears deter her. "Mike Loving isn't going to set any more fires," she argued. "And if you're worried about my personal safety, I wouldn't be living with the women. I'd be living with you.''

She knew that in time she could wear down his arguments. In the meantime, she was more interested in other things. She slid a leg provocatively over his in an attempt to distract him and splayed a hand across his chest, burying her fingers in the thick hair. ''Mmmm,'' she purred, pressing a kiss to his shoulder. ''I love you.''

Beneath her palm she could feel his heartbeat quicken, but he wasn't ready to give up just yet. ''Yes, you will be living with me, and we'll have to find a house very soon,'' he said in a valiant attempt to return to the subject at hand. ''I can't keep a wife in a room over a saloon.''

''You told the Folgers you had every intention of keeping me here in your bed and completely naked for quite a while.''

His breath caught in his chest, but he was resolute. ''You aren't going to take in any more whores, and we are going to have a proper home. Is that clear?''

''Of course, we'll need a larger place when we have a baby,'' she said, ignoring his ultimatum.

A baby? Chance froze, all other thoughts wiped completely from his mind. ''Lizzie, are you . . . ?''

He paused, hardly daring to speak the question aloud. For weeks the possibility had haunted him, but suddenly his dread had turned to hope. Gently, tenderly, he laid a loving hand upon the smooth plane of her abdomen. ''Are you with child?''

Elizabeth smiled mysteriously. ''I don't know.''

''What do you mean, you don't know?''

''I mean, I don't know. I wasn't a few days ago, but now . . .'' She shrugged meaningfully.

His grin was blatantly masculine. ''Would you like to be?''

Her expression turned innocent. ''Well, it's my duty, isn't it?'' she asked, mocking the many times he'd made the same claim.

''Yes, it is,'' he replied wickedly, letting his hand slide

lower. "This saloon may be the *Last* Chance, but I have no intention of enduring that same fate. Come here, Mrs. Fitzwilliam, and I'll see about giving you *another* Chance."

Epilogue

At the sound of the whistle announcing the arrival of the noon train in Dodge City, Elizabeth glanced up from her work. A tingle of anticipation raced over her. Chance might be on that train. His wire had not told her a specific date, promising only that he would return as soon as possible. Briefly, she debated the wisdom of making the trek down to the station just in case, but by the time she got on her coat and boots, Chance would have already walked over. Besides, she told herself as she listened to the howl of the winter winds outside the shuttered windows of the house, she couldn't afford to take foolish risks with her health.

Resolutely, she returned to her knitting. She was making a scarf, one of dozens she had produced for the needy farmers and their families this winter. She only wished she could do more for them.

A few minutes later, Elizabeth heard the sound of footsteps on the porch outside. She was halfway out of her chair, ready to race into Chance's arms, when the doorbell chimed. Disappointed, she sank down again. The door wasn't locked, and Chance would have come on inside, so she knew it couldn't be him.

Elizabeth would let one of the maids answer the bell. The house was swarming with maids, all children of starving farmers, as many as Elizabeth could find excuses to hire and then some. Outside the parlor doors Elizabeth could hear two of them squabbling over who should open the door. She smiled, wondering if they would let the person on the porch freeze to death before they came to terms. At last she heard the door open and then the delighted squeals of welcome that told her she had been wrong. Chance was, indeed, home.

Five months of marriage had not dulled the thrill she experienced every time she saw him, and she felt it now as she flung open the parlor door and found him shrugging out of his heavy overcoat. Heedless of their youthful audience, Elizabeth flew into his arms and delivered a resounding kiss.

"You're frozen!" she declared in the next breath, rubbing her hands over his icy cheeks.

"Then take me upstairs and warm me up."

"Mr. Fitzwilliam," she chided, as the girls giggled their appreciation. "I'll take you into the parlor by the stove. June, will you fetch Mr. Fitzwilliam some hot coffee?"

"Right away," the girl replied, hurrying off.

Elizabeth took his hand, but he held back. "Wait, I brought you something." He bent over to retrieve an enormous package, which he explained was the reason he had been unable to open the front door himself.

A few minutes later, when Chance had his feet propped on the stove, a mug of steaming hot coffee in hand, Elizabeth unwrapped her surprise, a silver tea service almost identical to the one he had bought her last spring.

"Wait until Barbara sees it," Elizabeth cried, setting the pieces in a semicircle around her. "Of all the things we lost in the fire, she regretted losing the tea service most of all."

"Is she managing to keep busy?" Chance asked, sipping his coffee. With no cowboys in town during the winter months, the prostitutes had left, too, so Elizabeth and Barbara's rescue operation had been temporarily suspended, and the new house Chance had provided for the effort now stood empty.

Elizabeth frowned. "She and I went out last week to visit a few of the outlying farms, and things were so bad that we brought some of the children back with us. Barbara is going to keep them in the house with her until the weather warms up.''

"Good idea. Did you get by to see the Dietzels?''

"Yes, and you'll be happy to know Helga gave birth to a healthy baby boy. Mother and son are doing fine.''

"That's good news, for a change.'' For a moment Elizabeth saw his tension ease. He'd been working so hard all winter, traveling all over the country trying to get aid for the farmers. She was glad to be able to tell him something happy for a change.

"Aren't you going to ask me what they named him?'' she asked innocently.

"Oh, no.'' Chance groaned. "I told you to talk them out of it.''

"I couldn't,'' Elizabeth lied, not having tried. "They named him Chauncey Fitzwilliam Dietzel.''

"Poor kid. He'll have to learn to fight before he learns to walk.''

"They'll call him Fitz. That should help some,'' Elizabeth explained, setting out the last of the tea service.

"Come here, Mrs. Fitzwilliam,'' Chance coaxed, holding out a hand. "I'm still feeling chilled, and I need a little human comfort.''

Elizabeth took the offered hand and allowed herself to be settled in his lap. She slipped her arms around him, under his suit coat, and snuggled into his shoulder.

"Mmm, you smell delicious,'' he murmured into her hair. His hand moved sensuously over her hip.

"Behave yourself,'' she warned. "It's broad daylight. What will the girls think?''

"They'll think we're old and decrepit and need a nap,'' Chance replied. His hand started a foray upward toward her breast, but she caught it and tucked it safely around her waist.

"Did you have a successful trip?'' she asked with wifely interest.

"Very. The good people of New York are just as generous as their neighbors in Pennsylvania. I brought back two carloads of clothing, and they've promised more."

"That's wonderful," she said, noticing his hand wasn't staying where she'd put it and recapturing it. Chance had made several trips to New England in the past few months to gather donations of food, clothing, and money for the farmers. He scorned the attitudes of those who would style him a do-gooder, insisting he was merely practicing sound economic principles. Sooner or later the drought would end, he argued, and we would need the farmers again. Helping them in their time of need was an investment in the future.

Elizabeth smiled inwardly, thinking how effective his arguments had been. "I've been wishing we could find some way to use the house on the South Side. Do you think we could get anyone to stay in it?"

A few days after his wedding, Chance had found himself the owner of a brothel with no madam when Summer Winters left town very suddenly. Her reasons for going became clear when Mike Loving explained who had inspired him to burn down Elizabeth's house. They'd heard Summer had set up shop farther west. *Much* farther west.

Chance had given the women in Summer's house the option of becoming respectable citizens or leaving. Elizabeth was surprised by how few chose respectability, but she put Barbara in charge of the ones who did the instant her friend returned from Chicago. Barbara had moved them out of Summer's house as soon as a new one on the North Side could be procured, and ever since then the building had sat empty.

"Maybe we could find some bachelor farmers who'd like to bunk down there," Chance theorized. "I doubt you'd get any families to live in a former brothel."

Elizabeth nodded, idly stroking the silky hair on the back of his neck. "I hate to see it sitting empty, especially when I know children are sleeping in dugouts on the prairie."

"The dugouts are usually warm," he reminded her

gently. He sighed. She worried so about the children. He suspected she was doubly concerned because she wanted one of her own so badly. Unfortunately, not even five months of his most devoted attention had given her one, and all the traveling he was doing now would not improve the situation. "Have you heard from Mavis?" he asked to change the subject.

"Yes," she said, sitting up straighter when she remembered some more good news. "Mr. Cooper has asked her to become the manager of the dormitory. And Molly's getting married!"

"Married? To whom?"

"One of the men who works in the shop. He knows all about her past, but he doesn't care. Isn't it wonderful?"

"Yes," Chance agreed, sharing her delight. "You must feel like the mother of the bride."

"I do, sort of," Elizabeth admitted. "I only wish all the stories could end so happily."

Chance touched her beloved face, wishing he had the power to chase away the unpleasant memories. No matter how much happiness came to the women Elizabeth had helped, she could not seem to forget the one dismal failure. "I brought back the headstone this trip, although I think you're making a big mistake trying to get the body moved. What did Amy ever do to deserve so much effort on your part?"

"Nothing," Elizabeth admitted sadly. "And don't bother reminding me how she tried to break us up and almost succeeded. She more than paid for her mistakes."

Amy's hopes of getting to New York had come to naught, in spite of her efforts to find a new protector after Mike Loving was sent to prison. She'd made the mistake of pitting two lovers against each other, only this time when tempers flared, she had been the victim. Another prostitute had found her lifeless body in her lonely, louse-ridden room behind the dance hall. Her lovers were long gone, and no one would even admit to having heard her screams.

"I just can't stand the thought of her lying up there on boot hill, the only woman with all those murdered men."

"We're going to move all the bodies when we put up the new schoolhouse," Chance reminded Elizabeth.

"I know, but I want her in the respectable cemetery, with a headstone with her name on it. I won't feel right until she is."

Chance sighed in resignation. "Women and their notions," he muttered.

"Yes," she said, snuggling back down against his shoulder, content in the knowledge he would humor her in this matter. "You're very patient to put up with my notions. I suspect I'll be having lots of them from now on. I hear women get them by the bushel basket when they're in a family way."

She held her breath as she waited for him to realize what she'd said. After what seemed an eternity, he whispered. "Lizzie?"

"What?" she asked, trying for innocence but knowing the joy of her secret showed on her face.

"Lizzie, are you . . . ?" His roving hand settled protectively over her abdomen. She nodded, blinking at the moisture forming in her eyes.

His smile was radiant, proud, triumphant, and awestruck all at once. "My God! You're sure? When? How long? When will it come?"

She laughed. "Late summer, I think."

"My God," he said again, and she could easily read the emotions playing across his face. Joy for the child they had made together tinged by pain for the child he had once lost. She knew this child would be more precious to him because of the one so long ago, and that was part of the reason she had wanted so badly to conceive.

His arms closed around her with tender fierceness, and he held her to the heart he had once thought incapable of love. "Now we'll have to go back to Philadelphia so you can have the best doctors," he said after a long time.

"Oh, please, not Philadelphia," she protested. "How

about Chicago? We can be there for Molly's wedding. And we can take Bill with us and introduce him to some beautiful heiress. It's the least we can do for him."

Chance rolled his eyes, but he said, "All right, Chicago it is. But we aren't going to name the baby Chauncey Fitzwilliam the fifth."

"Not if it's a girl," she replied sweetly.

"Not at all," he said, struggling to his feet while keeping her firmly in his arms.

"What are you doing?" she asked in surprise.

"I'm taking you upstairs. As an expectant mother, you need a nap, and I'm personally going to tuck you in."

"But I'm not sleepy."

His grin was deliciously wicked. "So much the better."

Author's Note

Whenever I read a historical novel set in a real place, the first question I ask is, "How much of this is true?" In this case, not much. As far as I have been able to learn, no one ever tried to rescue any of Dodge City's soiled doves. Chance and Elizabeth and most of their friends are completely fictional, although I have tried to depict the Dodge City of 1879 as accurately as possible.

I cheated a bit on Delmonico's Restaurant. The good folks at the Boot Hill Museum told me it didn't open until 1885, but it's such a well-known landmark of the town, I just had to include it. The Cowboy Band did not become known by that name until 1880, and Dodge City's famed fire company did not have any major fires to fight until 1885. The Good Shepherd Church did not exist, although it is loosely based on the Union Church, a nondenominational house of worship shared by worshipers of all the Christian denominations until they could afford to build their own churches.

The inspiration for the character of Reverend Folger was the Reverend O.W. Wright, a bold man of God who risked the disapproval of his respectable congregation by paying pastoral visits on dying prostitutes. Most of the politicians and merchants mentioned in the story were historical figures. Bat Masterson's and Wyatt Earp's views on women are not recorded, but I have credited them with opinions common to the time. The incident where Earp was fined for assaulting a prostitute actually took place. Jake Schaefer became a world-champion billiard player after practicing with gambler Charles Ronan in Beatty & Kelley's Alhambra Saloon.

The reformers worked long and hard to clean up Dodge City. They did run a candidate against Dog Kelley in the 1880 elections, Dr. McCarty, but he lost when Kelley's supporters brought in nonresident cowboys to vote illegally. By then the drought of 1879 had impoverished the farmers and made the cattle trade essential for the survival of Dodge, so the reformers didn't stand a chance. Although Kansas voted itself dry with a constitutional ammendment in 1880, Dodge City saloons continued to operate openly until the end of the cattle trade put them out of business in 1886.

On Saturday, April 5, 1879, a gambler called Cockeyed Frank Loving got into a gunfight with a freighter named Levi Richardson over an unidentified woman. They stood so close to each other in the Long Branch Saloon that at times their guns were almost touching. Richardson fired five shots and Loving fired six. Richardson was hit in the chest, side, and right arm and died within minutes. Loving received only a grazed hand. What became of him—and the woman—after the gunfight is unknown.

VICTORIA THOMPSON

VICTORIA THOMPSON lives in central Pennsylvania with her husband of 20 years, who proposed to her three weeks after their first date, and their two school-age daughters. A city girl born and bred, Victoria has been in love with the Old West ever since she lost her heart to Brett in the old "Maverick" TV series. She finally got tired of reading Western novels written by men in which the heroines were spineless ninnies and decided to write her own. When she isn't writing, she serves on the board of directors of Romance Writers of America and is active in her local RWA chapter.